Satan's Chamber

Also by Molly Best Tinsley:

Fiction
My Life with Darwin
Throwing Knives: Stories

Non-Fiction
The Creative Process

To Carol and John —
Thanks so much for all your support!

Satan's Chamber

MOLLY BEST TINSLEY
KARETTA HUBBARD

Enjoy

Karetta Hubbard
Molly Best Tinsley
Karetta Hubbard

FUZE PUBLISHING, LLC

FUZE
PUBLISHING LLC.

1350 Beverly Road, Suite 115-162
McLean, Virginia 22101

satanschamber@gmail.com

ISBN–10
0-9841412-0-0
ISBN–13
978-0-9841412-0-3

Library of Congress Control Number: 2009906951

Cover design by Chris Schmelter
Design and typesetting by Scribe Inc.

Prologue

2 April. Khartoum, Sudan. 1600 hours.

Blatantly American in pressed khakis, polo shirt, and loafers, he moved through the dark-skinned throng with the athletic stride of a man immune to doubt. Behind the silver lenses of his Predator Ray-Bans, his trained gaze swept the avenue from side to side.

A stately woman approached with a basket of flat bread on her close-cropped head. Her loose dress could have been hiding anything. So could the dingy rags on the toothless crone who squatted curbside hawking onions and bruised fruit. She grabbed at the cuff of his pants and wouldn't let go. He gave her a few dinars and kept moving, unperturbed.

A huddle of young males in long Muslim tunics blocked the way, forcing him out into the street. It didn't bother him that they turned and stared. It was the ones who didn't seem to register his passing that activated his sixth sense, his inner radar. They were the reason he'd strapped the holstered Walther TPH to his right calf. It was his just-in-case weapon, for social situations. Nothing he'd carry into an anticipated blow-up, but at close, courteous range, it served fine.

Hot winds had smothered the city with yellow dust, coating the two rows of stone lions on his right, which guarded the concrete approach to the National Museum. Remembering a secret meeting there the week before, he forgot his Agency cover—Dr. Peter Thornton, Economic Affairs Officer, U.S. Embassy—and for an instant, he was simply himself, Tyler Pierce, closet idealist, sucker for a crusade against injustice.

Plenty of that in this crazy African capital, where giant construction cranes were erecting a Disneyland of five-star hotels, corporate outposts, and foreign banks, while the crumbling side streets reeked of monoxide, animal dung, and death. On the city's fringes, disease-infested camps teemed with refugees who'd been driven out of their villages by the government-backed militias. They were hungry and desperate. They had nothing left to lose. The good news: given their huge numbers, even Mukharabat, the crack security police, couldn't keep tabs on them all.

On Pierce's left oozed the gelatinous brown Blue Nile. Up ahead, past a hazy bridge, it collided with the White Nile and became *The* Nile, natural wonder of ancient history, whose annual floods brought life to the desert plains.

At the heart of Khartoum two mighty rivers merged and flowed forward. If there was a message in that—*Unity in difference*—it wasn't something the President, a.k.a. Generalissimo, would ever hear, a man who wanted to be all things to his army and no one else. The man loved to hate. Dealing with him was like waving a cape in front of a bull. You got a lot of stamping and snorting. You stepped in a lot of shit.

Up ahead sat the convention center someone with a sick sense of humor had named Friendship Hall. The Chinese had built it twenty years ago, one of their earliest footholds in Africa. This week the sterile, brick and concrete structure hosted a car show, another routine opportunity for Peter Thornton to monitor economic affairs. So what if Tyler Pierce's knowledge of economics was strictly College 101? No one ever called on him to offer economic advice anyway.

Across the street a black Toyota Land Cruiser idled and sported a dusty film. On the plaza, a brand new C class Mercedes glimmered in the late afternoon sun. You didn't have to be a Ph. D. economist to figure the annual income of an entire Sudanese village wouldn't make the down payment on a machine like that. Admirers in skullcaps and flowing robes peered and prodded at its parts like it was a captured beast.

The secure mobile on Pierce's belt began to vibrate. He slowed his pace and clicked it open to a familiar voice: "Maud here, returning your call."

"Tell me how she's doing," he asked his closest friend, Deputy Director of Intelligence for the CIA.

"Top five percent of her class, off the chart in professional fitness, but chronic loner."

"Nothing wrong with that."

"Chip off the old block. Not great with authority."

"What's that supposed to mean?"

"Neither one of you ever listens to me."

"I want you to tell her I'm proud of her," Pierce said.

"I'm sure she knows."

"Tell her when this op is history, she and I are going to go biking in Vermont."

"What op?"

"And tell her I did it for her."

"What op, Tyler?" Maud's voice insists.

Pierce veered onto the plaza. "Something's about to give."

"What are you talking about?"

"Contrary to all the so-called *facts* about this place: I've targeted a moderate Muslim. He's pretty high up, or rather *was*. So expect a breakthrough for the good guys."

He squinted up at the entrance to the building, where he recognized the stout young man in a white tunic who stepped away from the masses loitering around the glass doors and touched his cap.

"I assume you've filed a full report."

"Don't give me that shit, Maud. I didn't choose this one. It chose me."

Pierce snapped the phone shut and moved in the direction of Ahmed, his most reliable asset. He stopped to feign interest in the Land Cruiser as Ahmed disappeared inside the Hall. After circling the automobile once, Pierce followed. The air conditioning was set on frigid. A low-slung Nissan Teana parked in the giant lobby was being overrun by fans.

Ahmed disappeared through an archway off the lobby. Pierce checked his Longine wristwatch, a gift from his wife before his daughter Victoria was born. Still that twinge of pain when he remembered the inscription, *Today is a gift . . . That's why it's called The Present.* She'd wanted him to know his child in real time–not photographic flashbacks. Young and healthy, neither of them had a glimmer twenty-four years ago how limited her own time would be.

After exactly three minutes he eased himself towards the opening. The sweat he'd cracked on his walk over made his clothes clammy. Casually he glanced into a long gallery. On one side a view of the river through floor-to-ceiling glass, on the other, Ahmed's mustached profile gazed at a wall hung with poster-sized photographs.

"I never could figure out how they get cars inside buildings like this," Pierce confessed in Arabic.

"There are hidden doors," Ahmed replied without turning his head, the signal that all was going as planned. The two men surveyed the enlarged photos: a schoolroom of grinning children raising their hands; a waving shopkeeper outside his spice stall in the oriental *souk;* a gorgeous, ebony-skinned woman draped in electric colors.

Two more men appeared. Ahmed introduced only the one in the turban: Mahjoub Elradi, former Speaker of Parliament, recently and unexpectedly released from prison, where he'd served twenty-two months of a five-year term for becoming too popular with the people. The other, who remained near the gallery exit, had the blank look and massive bulk of a bodyguard.

"I'm honored to meet you," Pierce said, offering a hand.

The former Speaker of Parliament kept his hands behind his back but lifted his flat, grey beard and peered at Pierce through owlish spectacles. "Men from your country all look the same to me," he concluded.

"I trust you're in good health," Pierce said.

The Speaker shrugged his narrow shoulders. His eyes were so close together they looked crossed, making for a puzzled expression. "Allah protects those who respect His name, Mr. Thornton," he said.

"In the name of Allah," Pierce said, "your country has been turned into Hell."

The former Speaker nodded. "However"—a smile split his dark face from his grey beard—"this Hell will burn itself out. We are prepared to build something new on its ashes."

They moved on to study a photo of a busy construction site: a crane lifting a concrete slab onto a wall in the sand. The caption read *The Future of Sudan*.

"Change will bring many rewards," the former Speaker continued. "Born of the marriage between democratic process and capital investment."

"I'd be pretty darned surprised if the United States of America wouldn't be willing to help pay for that wedding."

"You speak, of course, in an unofficial capacity," the former Speaker said.

"I think I can make it official, pending certain guarantees."

Decades of surveillance pulled Pierce's attention to the pair of men cloaked in white robes and head coverings who had stopped at the entrance to the gallery to confer. One was small and thin as a boy, the other resembled a draped mountain. Why were their backs to the windows with a river view like that? Why didn't they move on? An arsenal of listening devices could have been hidden underneath those robes. Another visitor looked in, scanned the posters, then left in search of big fuel tanks and mag wheels.

Elradi's beard bobbed up and down. "Such as what guarantees does your country require?"

"Religious tolerance, for starters," Pierce said.

"Of course," said Elradi.

The other end of the gallery was blocked by the bodyguard. Pierce had let that pass. Now his shoulders twitched. A vague uneasiness converted suddenly to certainty: *abort the meeting. Get out. Set up a face-to-face with Ahmed, arrange to meet this bigwig at a later time. Take the damned operation back to square one.*

But he overrode his instincts. He'd walked fine lines before, faced worse odds. There was a whole new world at stake, if only he and this guy could reach an understanding.

Elradi brought his right hand from behind his back and offered it to Pierce. Its fingers hung limp, grotesquely bent. "My jailers took a very large hammer to these small, but useful bones," he said in a flat voice.

Pierce gripped the man's cold, spongy flesh. Were Elradi's new politics too good to be true? You could never be sure what anyone was up to in this battered country, and this man had sung the tune of a hard-core extremist back when he was in power. Still the right things often get done for the wrong reasons. At the periphery of his vision, Pierce caught the pair of ghost-like robes drifting closer. *Shit*, he realized, fight reflex kicking in.

He could feel the two strangers gazing at *The Future of Sudan* over his shoulders. Idealism was a luxury he could no longer afford. He gave a backward jab with one elbow, then spun around and swung a fist up under the jaw of the smaller man, launching him into a back-dive to the floor. His head-piece went flying and his skull made a satisfying crack as it hit the marble tile.

No time to grab his weapon, Pierce heaved a shoulder into the thick tent of a man pressing against his flank. It was like trying to move a refrigerator.

Pierce lurched away and unleashed a kick to the general area of the man's groin. The bulky attacker staggered backward. Aware of an unpleasant sensation, Pierce checked the man's hands for a weapon, but the guy was doubled over them, clutching his mashed crotch. Pierce grabbed at his own lower spine, expecting to feel a knife, but there was nothing. *Disc ruptured? Who are these bozos, anyway? Where is Ahmed? How come no one's pulled a gun? Something's off—*

In three seconds everything changed. His brain was exploding. His arms and legs jerked in spasms. He grabbed at his throat as his jaw locked open, transforming his enraged protest into a string of feeble barks. Saliva dribbled from his mouth. His knees buckled. The last thing he saw was a blank, blurry face rushing toward him.

McLean, Virginia. 0600 hours.

The secure call beamed into the Office of the Deputy Director of Operations, Central Intelligence Agency, from the Embassy of the United States, Khartoum.

A cultivated, sardonic voice delivered its message: "It is my unpleasant duty to inform you people that they have taken out the so-called Peter Thornton."

"Circumstances?"

"Broad daylight. Trade exhibition."

"I guess one of his NIM crackpots turned against him."

"National Identity Movement? I couldn't say."

"All those rebel groups have their factions."

"By the time we got someone over there, the police were busy turning it into a riot and no one knew anything. We've checked out his quarters."

"Anything interesting?"

"A doll."

"Who?"

"Not a who. An artifact. As in hunk of carved stone? Shaped like a woman, you know, small waist, big—"

"I got it, I got it. Jesus Christ! I'm talking about his asset list, OK? Contact numbers?"

"Afraid not. He liked to brag that he kept everything he needed in his head. Look, my best guess is the President's security police—I mean who else—"

"Sounds good to me. Bag up the body."

"We have a slight problem in that department: there isn't one."

"There isn't one what?"

"Body. It was not recovered."

"For Christ sake, but you saw it?"

"Witnesses did."

"You're calling in to report a rumor?"

"From one-hundred-percent reliable sources."

"Well, how about you take a break from your tea party and locate a hundred percent of that fucking corpse?"

The Farm, Williamsburg, Virginia. 0900 hours.

A young woman threw open the French doors of the converted country house, stepped out onto the veranda, and spread her arms wide as if to embrace the view. Victoria Pierce wore nylon shorts, a ragged sweatshirt, and her burnt orange curls defied the rubber band tasked with clumping them on top of her head. She kicked one bare, well-toned leg up onto the stone wall and stretched over it. It was a perfect day for a run—sun shining, yet chilly—a pristine world of green leaf buds and new grass.

Three guys strolled out of the stone barracks after her, laughing and shoving each other. They tossed her a greeting, then took off running with flashy speed down a path through the grass. By the time she heard the hollow pounding of their shoes on the wooden bridge over the creek, she was ready to follow.

She'd have liked more of a challenge than a hokey obstacle course, like maybe to take off along the stream and then follow the river till it hit the ocean. On a day like this, anything seemed possible. She could run forever.

In a matter of minutes she'd thumped over the creek and caught up with her three classmates whose pace had slowed. Briefly she considered adjusting hers. They were talking baseball. Social chit-chat. She could do it if she had to, though never quite comfortably. She preferred solitude. Alone, she could be more herself. Melt into the morning. A surge of energy propelled her forward.

"Show off," called out one, not unkindly, as she took off towards the woods.

The dappled trail was so fragrant with new life she could taste it. She vaulted the fallen trees as if they were the hurdles she'd run in college, picked her way through the piles of rock, scrambled through a pipe tunnel. After seventeen minutes, barely winded, she sprinted into the sunny clearing toward the final challenge.

Fifty yards ahead was The Wall—*total piece of cake*. Suddenly the strength went out of her legs and she shuffled to a stop. A woman was standing in front of the eight-feet high, smooth concrete obstacle waving to her, a woman in a pale grey pantsuit, her platinum gray hair perfectly coiffed in a style that had gone out of style twenty years ago.

Maud Olson and Tory's dad went through CIA 101 together. Maud had been a "friend of the family" ever since, a status that she seemed to think entitled her to offer Tory unsolicited advice whenever she felt like it.

In an instant, Tory's surprise turned to dread. What could be so urgent that Maud would have risked her designer shoes tromping around in the wet grass?

Jebel Barkal, Sudan. 1700 hours.

The far-off horizon rippled between sand and inky sky. In the mid-distance stood pyramids, some crumbling, others intact and sharp. At their center, the ground seemed to have heaved up a tall, crooked ship of a mountain. At one end jutted a separate narrow pinnacle, like a figurehead, or a forearm capped with a stone fist. Or some would say, the flared head of a cobra poised to strike. The mountain was Jebel Barkal, the holy center of ancient Nubia, now an under-funded archaeological site north of Khartoum.

At the base of this mountain a canvas awning four meters square was strung on posts above the sand shading huge slabs of stone. Most were piled in disarray, but some had been set side by side like giant puzzle pieces. These were stained a startling blue, superimposed with either yellow stars or black vultures in flight.

A blue-clad African woman sat in the sand her head bowed over one slab as if in prayer. A golden cobra bracelet gleamed against the dark skin of her upper arm. Time and again she raised her face—her eyes rolled back to white, her cheeks streaked with tears.

Along the edge of the awning, three armed Sudanese in tattered Western clothes and flip-flops observed the woman's grief helplessly, while an older man with light brown skin had taken off his thick glasses and kept swabbing his eyes with a handkerchief. Time seemed altered; it was as if he could feel the earth turn and the world darkening minute by minute.

The older man was the first to notice the ominous bass notes competing with the woman's cries. Then her bodyguards picked it up, the thump-thump of hoof-beats. They raised their M-16's. The woman leaped to her feet.

What took four seconds seemed to last hours. Three men on camels appeared around the edge of the nearest pyramid, each aiming automatic rifles. A volley of gunshots blended into one. Two of the woman's guards collapsed into limp heaps on the sand. At the same time a scarlet stain bloomed on the chest of one camel rider before he floated in slow motion to the ground. The older man locked his arms around the woman, and they seemed frozen like that forever, him struggling to pull her back behind a pile of slabs, her resisting, until she wrenched free and time began to race again.

She gave three screams and the sky filled with feathered missiles plunging toward the attackers, large grey falcons, talons extended. They flew at the two remaining riders, clawing their faces. The firing stopped. The camels halted also, and trampled the sand in place as the woman shook her fist at the two remaining riders and ripped out curses they did not understand.

An instant later, the riders were digging their heels into the camels' flanks and bearing down on her, each thrashing at the raptors with one hand. One man hurled an elongated object at her with his free hand. Then came the second, gripping his rifle by the barrel. She saw it coming, wrong-side first, didn't understand. She raised her hands to her face and began to turn, an instant before he slammed the butt at her, catching her right eye.

It was over. Three camels and two riders vanished into the distance, leaving their comrade to bleed out along with the woman's slain guards. She herself lay flattened on her back, as the older man rushed over to help her. Her bare skin was pocked with grains of sand, the cobra bracelet bloodied but unbent. Blood gushed from her right socket, washing out its crushed remains. Yet she smiled grimly. She, Kendacke, queen of the mountain, was still very much alive.

She turned her head and her left eye came to rest on the oblong missile the attackers had left behind. It was the ugly purple-grey of necrotic flesh, slightly bent, an elegant wristwatch encircling its narrow end. Thus at the same moment she realized it was a human arm, she also realized whose.

Five years later . . .

1

25 August. CIA Headquarters, McLean, VA. 0830 hours.

The line at her turnstile crawls forward. She fights the urge to switch, figuring as soon as she does, the new line will slow to a halt. Tory Pierce has no time for downtime. It's too much like running in place when you could be out there, surmounting new challenges, forging new paths into the unknown.

She inhales deeply. She's always thought the air inside the Agency's cavernous main lobby had a special smell, the smell of courage. It's where she feels closest to her dad, as if his spirit still hovered around a certain star engraved on the marble wall behind her. That star and his name in the Book of Honor testify to the ultimate sacrifice he made for his country—the Agency's take on her father's disappearance, not exactly hers.

Finally. Her turn. She sticks her ID on the scanner. The metal arms open, ushering her into the real CIA.

High heels click on the marble floor, as the bureaucratic hordes flow past clutching briefcases. Tory falls in with the crowd heading toward the elevators. Inside, she swipes her badge across the number seven then fades to the back as the car fills. Six floors later she is the sole passenger. The doors part to reveal two large gentlemen in identical grey suits and striped ties stationed on either side of the corridor. They flash her mechanical smiles as she emerges. Very few people are allowed on the power floor for the Directorate of Intelligence. You either worked here, or you got here by invitation only. If you were crazy enough to show up otherwise, you were escorted back into the elevator by these two well-dressed bouncers, a notation appeared in your file, and you might as well resign from the Agency effective now.

Maud Olson is married to the Agency. Her first choice would have been Tory's father, but his choice was to console himself with dangerous special assignments instead of remarriage after her mother died. Tory wound up at her grandparents', then boarding school, then Princeton. All along she's been pretty much left to figure things out on her own. That's usually meant noting her weaknesses, and managing, if not to eliminate them, at least to hide them from public view.

Maud's "professional guidance" has always felt a little oppressive, like carrying a balance on your credit card. And Maud's promotion last year to the top slot in the DI has made the situation worse, straining mutual politeness to the limit.

The grey corridor is bleak: no art on the walls, no windows, only grey doors, numberless and nameless. The thudding rhythm of Tory's flat-heeled shoes helps steady her mind. She knows why she's been summoned, and she's determined to stay calm, professional. Outside Maud's office, she forces a deep breath. She is three minutes early. She brushes the sleeves of her jacket, straightens her skirt. Maud's elegance can make you feel like a rumpled incompetent.

She slips a hand into the outside compartment of her briefcase, pulls out a carved stone the size of her thumb, gives it a squeeze, and drops it into her jacket pocket. It's her only link to a lost time, to the one person whom she'd thought it safe to trust.

She once more presents the badge around her neck to a scanner on the wall. The door clicks open.

2

"Storm warning, Victoria," Maud's secretary says, peering up over the rainbow-striped frames of her glasses, which stand out like a protest against her nondescript dark suit. "Have a seat and brace yourself. I'll get you some coffee."

"I can do it, Isabelle." The woman is twice Tory's age, but first names are standard throughout the Agency, a practice that has nothing to do with relaxed intimacy, everything with anonymity. "So what's the issue?" Tory pours skim milk into the fragrant hazelnut brew and takes a sip.

"Have you seen today's *Post*?"

Tory shakes her head. "Don't tell anyone—I go right to the Sudoku."

"Let's just say the President's men are making very creative use of the facts again where China's concerned."

"See? Why bother reading the paper?"

"You've got a point," Isabelle says with a smile.

The door opens, and there is Maud, in her starched grey dress and silver neck scarf, filling the anteroom with the flowery fragrance of her expensive soap. She's only five feet two, to Tory's five five, but her ramrod slimness still makes Tory feel blobby and short. Her skin is pale and clear as porcelain, while Tory's is sprinkled with freckles. And Maud's hair has always shimmered like polished silver, swept up in a sleek French twist, whereas Tory's corkscrew-curly carrot-top has a will of its own.

Her eyes meet Maud's across twenty years shaded with loss. Today the older woman makes no move toward the usual awkward hug. For that, Tory is grateful, though a little unnerved. "You wanted to see me?" Tory asks.

Two computer terminals, one wall of floor to ceiling plasma screens, another of commendations and accolades from almost three decades of Directors and Presidents whom she has loyally served: everything in the inner office reads knowledge and power.

"Always a pleasure," Maud says, but her smile is forced as she waves the younger woman into one of the straight-backed chairs and takes a seat behind her enormous desk. Its top is blanketed with open newspapers. "China," says Maud, throwing up her hands, as if it were the name of a difficult child.

Tory knows better than to reply.

"They're set on undermining the global order, they're a threat to nations everywhere, and here's the punch-line, they're putting all their money—which by the way is the money *we* pay them to smother us in cheap consumer goods—so they're putting all *our* money into *weapons of mass destruction*, nuclear, nerve gas, you name it. Can you believe it? Oh, and they're testing missiles that can reach our west coast. They must want to wipe out all their family members in California." Maud gives the papers a slap. "Is that the China you saw?"

"I was a cog in a very big machine, Maud. A pretty limited perspective."

"Well, I've studied every bit of intel we've got on the country. And it doesn't come close to spelling this baloney." She gives the top newspaper a slap. "But of course, it's not your fault. You've done very well. Congratulations on the commendation."

"I could have handled a little more of a challenge. I always pictured Dad dashing around with high-level government officials, or at least underworld types. Me, I had to listen for hours to lonely misfits, hoping they'd spill one useful grain of intel."

"Your father dealt with his share of misfits."

"Like who?" Tory asks, expecting the usual curtain to descend: *I'm not at liberty to say.*

"They're everywhere," the older woman says instead. Her slate-blue gaze tightens. "Tell me about your next assignment."

"You know I'm not supposed to talk about that," Tory says.

"Not to some Joe Schmoe on the next barstool, you're not—"

"And you know I don't spend my free time hanging out in bars."

"I should hope not."

"OK," Tory says, ending the charade. "I'm leaving for Africa in three weeks. But you know that too, because you know everything."

Maud arched one perfectly plucked eyebrow. "I thought we laid that one to rest three years ago."

"How can I lay it to rest when my father—"

Maud cuts her off. "The situation's only gotten more dangerous over there. It's the rule of violence, Victoria, and it makes China look like a convent. The genocidal outrage in western Darfur is only the most recent layer. The government invokes Islamic law, which it distorts to selectively disregard human rights. It deputizes militias to attack aide workers as well as Sudanese villages. Meanwhile the factionalized rebels are fighting among themselves."

"I'm doing my homework."

"And I'm telling you no amount of homework can prepare you for this level of lawlessness. Anything goes in the name of oil." She swings back around to face Tory. "Besides which, recent intel coming out of Sudan has been unreliable. The striking thing about the country right now is the silence."

"If you mean the world's response to the violence."

"You know what I mean." Maud rises and begins to pace the maroon oriental carpet. "It's no post for a relative novice. I expressly asked you not to put in for it."

"So, I didn't."

"You didn't?" The eyebrow rises again, like a Nike symbol.

"Why bother, when I knew you'd veto it anyway? Or at least that's what I expected."

"You're right about that. If I'd been in the loop." Maud's voice trails off, her brow pinched in thought.

"I asked for Cairo or Nairobi."

"Fine. I'll get your assignment changed."

"Un unh, Maud. It's a done deal."

"No," Maud interrupts. "It's not in anyone's best interests for you to serve in your father's station."

"I can't believe you don't want to find out what happened."

Maud pauses before she answers. "He was the best and the brightest, Victoria, and I miss him to this day." The woman's eyes seem to be pleading for something. Tory looks away.

"You think *I* don't? He's all I've got, Maud." The older woman looks as if Tory has just slapped her. "The thing is, *Killed in the line of duty*, and we never know why, or in the name of what, and we never see the body? That just doesn't work for me."

"It's pointless to brood about details."

"These are not details! We don't even have proof that he's dead!"

Maud shakes her head and rotates her chair to face out the window.

"Besides I won't be brooding," Tory goes on. "I've been brooding for five years, if you mean thinking about it, every day, wondering what the hell happened. In Khartoum, I'll be *doing* something. And maybe I'll find something out."

Maud swivels back to face her. "The Agency specifically prohibits mixing professional duties with personal needs."

"Screw the party line. Besides, someone's got to monitor the Chinese interest in Sudanese oil, OK? I happen to have some expertise in China now, which happens to be the one country poised to challenge our global supremacy."

"Oh god, now you're bashing them too."

"You can't deny that China's all over Sudan."

"They want gas for their cars just like we do."

"So I'll be keeping an eye on them."

"What's wrong with Paris?"

"Who's Paris?"

"I'll get your assignment changed to Paris. Or Rome."

"I'm going to Khartoum. Someone has got to break the silence."

"God, you're just like your father, the star of your own, private, heroic saga."

Tory can't help smiling. "Thanks. So listen, I've been trying to research the National Identity Movement, and I'm having a hard time getting my hands on the file."

"The NIM," Maud says. "It's not exactly breaking news—you've got sufficient clearance. Just call it up."

"It's temporarily unavailable. So I requested hard copy. It showed up incomplete. You know, *sorry for the inconvenience.*"

Maud frowns.

"So I went over to Archives in person. Apparently the whole first section of the Sudan file isn't on the shelves."

Maud hardly skips a beat. "I appreciate your bringing this irregularity to my attention," she says through barely parted lips. "As soon as I locate the missing pages, I'll get them to you."

"Thank you," Tory says coolly.

The two sit in silence.

"In exchange for two requests."

Tory suppresses a groan. "OK."

"When you file your reports from Sudan, underline the *maybe*'s."

"I'm sorry?"

"I'm sick and tired of possibilities being presented as facts. Simply because something *appears* to have *potential*, it doesn't mean it *is*."

"Definitely. Got it."

"And once you're in country, call me *every evening* at 1800 hours your time."

"That's not exactly my chain of command."

"I don't need a lesson in chain of command, Victoria. I just need to hear you're alive and well."

"So you want to hear about every misfit who makes a lame pass at me."

"Every misfit," said Maud. "Deal?"

After a pause, Tory concedes. "Deal."

3

The minute the door closes behind Victoria, Maud's shoulders slump, and she shrinks into her enormous chair. The old Tyler-rumors flood back, ridiculous as the latest official spin on China.

You aren't supposed to get personally involved with your work, and the problem was, Tyler did, practically the instant his boots hit the ground in Sudan. It was right after the U.S. ordered the bombing of a pharmaceutical plant on the outskirts of Khartoum based on reports that Osama bin Laden was using it to manufacture chemical weapons. When the debris turned up no evidence of weapons manufacture—only a ruined stock of medicine—the Agency came under the gun for its flawed intelligence. Ty was sent in to provide damage control and totally overhaul counter-terrorist operations.

Bad choice. Who would have guessed? Ty always ran cool, detached, even cynical, but middle-age had brought out another side. He'd talk to Maud about his hopes for his daughter, and his concern about the world he was bequeathing her. While his success as a crack clandestine operative hinged on his ability to focus, stay on task, nail the details, Maud sensed he was starting to drift, think about "the big picture," as he put it. And Sudan blew his mind.

As the months went by, her phone chats with Ty were dominated by references to The Professor, who was supposedly putting Ty onto the *real* Africa. Soon the woman turned up in their conversations, and Maud stifled the surge of jealousy, as she'd stifled every other inconvenient feeling all her adult life.

"So you've recruited a couple of useful assets," Maud would say dryly, trying to bring Ty back to earth. "Congratulations on doing your job."

He began using his reports to promulgate opinions, weaving them so tightly into the facts that routine scrubbing couldn't remove them. Had he fallen for a "left-wing group committed to fomenting violence both within and beyond the borders of Sudan," which was the Agency and State's official position on the National Identity Movement, or had he identified Sudan's only hope? Either answer cut her off from him, so she settled for none.

Well, hindsight has proven the NIM to be just another fringe nuisance, a victim of violence not its perpetrator. Maud swivels to the computer on one wing of her desk and pulls up the section on Sudan. The onscreen overview informs her that indeed all file sections are on the shelf, except the earliest.

What surprises her is its closing date, 15 June 1998. Three months before Ty's tour in Khartoum even began. Why? What did those pages contain?

Then a logical explanation for the file's disappearance dawns on her. Maybe one of the analysts who mistakenly flagged that "pharmaceutical factory" permanently "misplaced" it years ago, hoping to consign his or her error to oblivion. The missing section probably has nothing to do with Maud's concern, which is plain and simple: keeping Victoria out of harm's way.

4

25 August. South Sudan. 0100 hours.

Around the oil fields north of Bentiu in southern Sudan, the nights are neither quiet nor dark. Like giant candles, skeleton towers shoot blasts of sulphurous flame non-stop, while the rigs thump their deafening rhythm, up, down, up, down. To Kendacke, her single eye surveying the toxic scene from a grove of scorched trees on a distant rise, the pumps look like huge, insatiable, steel birds, silhouetted against the hot orange sky.

It has been an exhausting journey, leading a squad of her most veteran soldiers from their desert headquarters outside Khartoum, across the unofficial, contested border between northern Sudan and the south, into this humid region where vegetation used to thrive. Traveling only at night, along the bank of the White Nile, they have come in search of the Chinese-made HC 120 helicopter, a small, light aircraft nicknamed The Hummingbird, whose body and tail rotor have been designed to reduce noise.

According to a well-placed informant, a pair of these choppers is hangared at the refinery. According to one of her visions, the National Identity Movement must take possession of them. Access to such aircraft will ease immensely Kendacke's mission, her continuous cycle of secret visits to the remote villages and refugee camps in all corners of her ravaged country. There was a time when she only preached her message of courage and unity. Now she also prepares the people to defend themselves and retaliate against government assaults.

The refinery itself sprawls behind a chain-link fence and coils of razor wire. A row of trailers, parked perpendicular to the fence just inside, ends at the single entrance to the compound, which is guarded by two armed Chinese in Petrol Beijing uniforms. On the roof of the squat, central building, two more guards sleepily rotate position with automatic rifles raised, clear as day in the light of the gas flares.

Concealed by an outcropping of rock, Lewis Kvol takes all this in through binoculars. A long, lean man with deep brown skin and high cheekbones, his forehead bears the diagonal welts of initiation into the Dinka tribe. Now he gestures to five others to join him. They carry a mix of weapons, American M-16's, as well as Kalashnikovs and grenades the government issues to its militias; their uniforms are midnight blue.

The two black helicopters sit outside on their pads, which means they'll be easier to steal. It also may mean they're intended for use at any moment. Impatient, the young commander gazes across at the hill. The sweat pours off him in the humid heat, and the acrid smoke from the oil flares burns his nose and throat. Finally he sees the falcon. At 200 kilometers an hour, it's a black blur against the hellish sky. In a flash it's on top of them, flapping its wings to brake, before it folds them into its body as it alights on Lewis' outstretched, leather-gloved wrist. After such speed, the picture of immobility.

Lewis removes the rolled message from the bird's foot and reads by the fiery light: *Eight men in main building. Three in front office with computers, five in back room taking time off. Ready, 0335, Go.*

Lewis releases the bird for its return flight, then he and his men begin creeping toward the cover offered by the trailers. Four minutes later, from their position on the hill, Kendacke's snipers attach their silencers, take aim. The first roof guard, then the second lurches backwards and falls. There is no sound above the din of machinery.

Lewis' team shoots off the lock on the gate and sprints for the Hummingbirds' asphalt pad. Suddenly a siren blares. A probability he couldn't cover—an electronic tripwire—and now the central building is spewing Chinese guards firing automatic pistols wildly.

Lewis and his men dive for cover behind two trailers, as Lewis lobs a grenade into the bunch of screaming, trigger-happy foreigners. Then hitting the survivors with a withering barrage, the six of them dash for the coveted aircraft, split into two teams, and take possession. Hordes of workers begin spilling from the trailers behind them. Most of them are unarmed, yet suddenly Lewis' side window shatters and the side of his head burns like a snakebite. His hand comes away sticky with blood.

He's got to block the pain, the head-splitting noise, the danger, everything but the control panel. He focuses on remembering the instruction and practice he got from an American advisor to the Liberation Army. To reinforce the lessons, he downloaded cockpit photos off the Internet and memorized them. He can't afford to wonder if his comrades will be capable also of getting the other bird started, and lifting off. He barely notices the blood soaking the shoulder and front of his shirt as he hurls another grenade through the busted-out window to buy time.

He turns on the battery power switch and fuel valve, then hits the button on the cyclic. The full-body vibration reassures him the engines are running. He takes off the rotor brake, slams the throttle forward, pulls back on the collective, and exhales with relief as the slow whine of the turbine revs up, and the chaos surrounding him starts dropping away.

He can't help letting out a shout of triumph when he sees the second Hummingbird rising below him. The operation is running smoothly. As the aircraft maintain their ascent, Lewis' two teammates pick off pursuers through the broken glass. Don't the Chinese have anything bigger to throw at them? Their shooting seems more angry than accurate.

Another glance down brings the answer: the Chinese weren't going to destroy their aircraft unless they had to. Now they have to.

At the edge of the crowd, one man shoulders the long, fat launching tube for a SAM—surface-to-air missile. On a rush of adrenalin, Lewis yanks back on the collective, accelerating his climb, his stomach sinking. At the same moment he hears a deafening blast. The Hummingbird below him teeters, and drops away. It crashes into the ground and bursts into flames.

Lewis shoves the cyclic forward, his head snaps back as the aircraft lurches ahead. His jaw clenched against pain and panic, he recalls the stories of American pilots, their hands twisting in the air to demonstrate *yanking and banking*. But this is no jet he's in. He dumps the collective, puts in full left rudder, and swings towards the man about to shoulder another SAM. Like an American cowboy, there's only one choice—go out in style. He heads towards the man, aiming right at him.

Pulling in more power, he noses the aircraft down, surprised at how quickly he's gaining speed. His whole body comes alive with the thrill of the dive, though it may be his last. Nearing the point of no return, Lewis can clearly see the man's horrified features. Then like a pillar that suddenly crumbles, the man's knees collapse, he drops the weapon and flops prone in the dirt.

Lewis pulls back on the cyclic, so close to the ground a dust cloud forms behind him. Then he is rising, eyes riveted on the crest of the hill. It's in front of him, then it's underneath him. He is safe.

With a heavy heart, he stabilizes the aircraft and turns his attention to the aching weight dragging at the side of his head—his left ear hangs by a thread of skin. He yanks it off and throws the bloody thing out the broken window into the trees. His other teammate ties a bandana over the wound while he pilots the bird towards a clearing near the village of El Obeid. By morning, Kendacke should be there to meet him for the return to the sacred mountain, Jebel Barkal.

5

Like a train zipping along a track, Maud's two-inch Ferragamos click a steady rhythm down the white marble corridor. Once home to the Directorate of Operations, this wing has been newly christened *National Clandestine Service*.

Maud has known its deputy director Gordon Gray since day one, when she, Ty, and he were raw recruits. The son of a wealthy Boston family, Gordon exudes the impeccable manners and unflappable amiability that Maud has always tried to imitate in an effort to overwrite her own child-hood on a soybean farm in Iowa. But while Ty became her pal, she's always felt more rivalry than friendship with Gordon, in spite of his persistent attempts to date her.

This late in the day, there is no one to stop her marching right into Gordon's office. She catches him tipped back in his gigantic executive chair talking on the phone. His finely-chiseled features tighten at the sight of her, before stretching into a genial smile. A slender man, almost too good-looking, his dark hair streaked with distinguished gray, he nods at one of the seats facing his desk, as he terminates his call. He levels his chair. "Maud, what a pleasant surprise. What can I do for you *this time?*" he asks, as if to imply that she is always demanding, never satisfied.

"Well, I've got a couple of questions," she says, ignoring his tone.

His pretends to flinch. "Fire away."

"What's the story exactly on Ty's daughter?"

"High performer. Smart, self-starter, good closer, hard worker, what do you want to hear?"

"What did you do, let her seduce you?"

"Maud! You flatter me."

"How could you post her to Khartoum?"

"I love it when you get angry."

"And I hate it when you act like a second-rate roué. Could you answer my question?"

"I would never have considered her for that station," Gordon says, his voice turning chilly.

"Well, someone did, and it's absolutely ridiculous. This is her second tour!"

"To be honest, I assumed you were behind it. And since you always know what you're doing—"

"I want you to put someone on her, Gordon. Your very best."

"We're not a baby-sitting agency."

"Then cancel her orders."

"Listen to yourself, Maud. Don't you think you're personalizing this a little?"

Maud glares at him.

"Relax," Gordon goes on, "she's not exactly the only one of us over there."

"You could have fooled me."

"There you go—time to tee off on NCS."

"Your guys aren't exactly coming up with any new and exciting intel from those parts."

"Maybe you should sign up with Netflix."

"I'd rather be able to access complete information on the Sudanese National Identity Movement," Maud says.

"I'm afraid I don't know what you're talking about."

"Well, that may be half the problem."

"What problem?"

"Someone in your office checked out Part One of the Sudan file, no name, no date."

"Files get misplaced."

"They shouldn't."

"I'll put out a memo."

"That would be good." Maud rises.

"Now can I interest you in the Symphony tomorrow night?" Gordon asks. "They're performing Schumann's Fourth."

She can't believe he is so tone-deaf to emotion.

"The first movement's amazing," he goes on. "It explodes with insane passion. I think you'd like it."

Maud does an about face and fists clenched with frustration, marches from the room.

By the time she's back in her office, her composure regained, she has planned her next move. She punches Line Two, her direct link to Admiral Johnny Falco, Chairman of the Joint Chiefs of Staff.

6

13 September. Khartoum Airport, Sudan. 0800 hours.

She's been dreaming this for five years: Pierce, the Invincible, radiant with energy and confidence, vaulting from the hatch of the EgyptAir turbo-jet, ready to take on the bad guys that took down her dad.

Instead she's got the weird sensation that she doesn't quite fit inside her body. She figures it's the shock of the heat, which sears her face, the inside of her nose and throat. Besides, she's been awake for almost twenty-four hours, and besides that, the day before she left Virginia, she'd marched into Total e-Clips and ordered them to chop off all her hair.

Scanning the crowd inside the muggy, sour-smelling terminal, her senses heighten. She could swear someone is watching her, tucked in among the dark, eager faces waiting for friends and family, someone who wishes her harm. The thought crosses her mind—how could she even begin to identify such a person? *If there were such a person. And why would there be? Thanks, Maud, for planting your seeds of paranoia.*

Then from the back of the jostling crowd a tall man waves an arm and steps forward. It's a gawky white guy in a khaki suit and crooked bowtie. Granny sun-glasses. Straight, light brown hair in need of a cut. He's flashing an oblong card like he's making a bid at an auction. Big letdown. The card is printed with her cover name—*Veronica Clark.*

On the State Department website she memorized, Bartholomew Wilkins is named as the supply officer at the Embassy. In other words, bottom of the ladder, a specialist in procuring toilet paper, cell phones, diet sodas, flashlight batteries.

"Good morning, mademoiselle," he says with a click of his heels and a bow, which causes his tiny, round sun-glasses to pop off his nose and dangle around his neck. His eyes are an unusual speckled blue, but they slide away from hers.

He shoulders her backpack before she can stop him, but in the process drops some papers he'd tucked under one arm. As he bends to retrieve them amid the bodies shoving past, her pack swings up and thumps him in the back of the head. Irritated beyond belief, she can feel the sweat dripping from her pores as she stoops and gathers up what turn out to be maps, annotated and modified in ink.

24

"Updated them myself. Accurate maps are hard to come by here, probably connected to the fact that the government prefers foreigners to get lost," Wilkins says as he wrestles her pack under control and straightens his jacket. "Which is why I'll be taking you everywhere you have to go."

"I don't think that'll be necessary," Tory says. "But thanks for these." She pats the papers she rescued.

Wilkins slips his dark glasses back on, and launches into a long story about his mother and how she brought him up to be a gentleman. "Hope you won't take it as sexual harassment," he goes on, as he clasps her by the arm and moves her past general customs, where the crowd seems to prefer forming wedges instead of lines. He guides her over to the last station, which is empty, then makes a big show of his ability to speak fluent Arabic to the heavily armed officials.

Though she's wearing a baggy linen sack of a dress, as advised, and a shirt with sleeves, she still feels exposed, as if someone in the crowd is focusing on her with cold eyes.

She insists on rolling her own bag out to the embassy's Jeep Wrangler, then as soon as he has the hatch open, she heaves it into the back and darts around in order to beat Wilkins to the passenger door. With a shrug, he turns back to the driver's side and lowers himself behind the wheel.

As they pull away from the terminal, she peers ahead through the haze towards the strange city that swallowed her father. She sucks in a deep breath—she is finally here. Then all of a sudden the reality of how much she doesn't know hits her like a giant wave. It seems to wash away three weeks of intense training and the determination that got her through it. Her hands begin to tremble, and she clamps them together in her lap. Then she has to clench her jaw to keep her teeth from chattering. *Just chilled,* she tells herself, *reaction to the air-conditioned car after the oven outside.* Three long conscious breaths and she has regained control.

Wilkins is lecturing her on the importance of PF-70 sunscreen. This guy is obviously a myopic detail person, and she tunes him out until he leans across to pull a tube from the glove compartment and almost drives off the edge of the highway into the sand. He slams on the brakes and skids to a stop. Behind them a battered black Hyundai Santa Fe slows and refuses to pass though the way is clear.

"Oh, my god. I should have been paying attention," she blurts.

"I know," Wilkins says. "We're about as close to the sun here as you're going to get."

"I meant that car. It's tailing us."

"What car?" Wilkins tips his gaze up to the rear view. "Oh, that car."

"You guys don't get any surveillance training for this post?"

"Nah. Why? Did you?" He tosses the sunscreen into her lap and pulls back onto the road. The Hyundai is right behind.

"Of course not," she lies. Tory looks back but her eyes can't penetrate the car's dusty windshield. "Typical, isn't it? They preach protocol up to the eyeballs, but when it's stuff that might come in handy—"

She's interrupted by an explosive backfire, and then the Hyundai pulls even with them. She hunches down in her seat, stunned at the obvious loophole in her prep. No one mentioned she might hit trouble before she got her hands on her military issue Glock 19.

"Hey, relax," Wilkins says.

Is he kidding? A dark male face, emaciated and scarred, half-squints at them through the Hyundai's window. Where the left ear should flare, there is ragged, scabbed flesh.

Wilkins waves. A long thin hand rises and waves back.

"What makes you think he isn't armed?"

"Half the people in this city are packing something. He just wants us to know he's following us."

"And that's OK?"

"We don't have a lot of choice."

Beyond the four-lane highway are scattered shacks patched together out of anything, mud dwellings, dark bodies squatting in clusters, naked, pot-bellied children, unidentifiable hunks of rusting metal, a few scrawny goats.

"There's always choice. Where's *your* weapon?" Tory demands. When he doesn't answer, Tory punches open the glove compartment, rummages around and pulls out a grubby 9mm Beretta. She's sure her father could handle this kind of situation in his sleep. She checks the chamber. No more practice sessions back at the Farm. This is real.

"Put it away," says Wilkins calmly. "We haven't been fired on."

She checks her side mirror. The Hyundai is sticking to them. "Well, you could help out here, you know," Tory says.

Wilkins hits the gas and the Wrangler hurtles forward. In the rearview, the Hyundai recedes for a minute but slowly crawls back into range.

The next thing she knows, her neck snaps to the left as their vehicle exits the highway on two wheels, skids to the end of the ramp and hangs a left, narrowly missing a donkey-cart piled with oranges.

The road is residential where houses are shielded by enclosures of white-washed mud. Wilkins swerves around a parked car and sends a rusted barrel of trash flying. A group of women shrink back against a wall. "Did I mention you should apply that stuff three times a day?" Wilkins asks. "If I had anything to say about it, I'd make that official policy."

Tory stares at him dumbfounded, then turns away to see the Hyundai pop into sight. In the next minute Wilkins has cornered right. They swerve down a street with higher walls and larger homes, shaded by an occasional tree. Before the jalopy can appear again, he lurches left into an alley, then another left, and dead end. "How's that?" he asks. The way is blocked by a high, blank wall crowned with a coil of razor wire.

Tory glares at his profile—set jaw, straight nose, those absurdly tiny lenses. She can't believe he's driven them right into a dead end. She throws open the door to a blast of heat. "I'll take care of this," she says, clutching the old Beretta. Wilkins grabs her wrist.

"There is nothing to take care of."

She yanks her arm up against his thumb and adrenalin surging, races back to the corner, then out into the empty, trash-strewn alley to its entrance. She peers along the narrow, dusty street in both directions, feeling indignant and silly, plus totally baffled: there's only one car in sight, idling at the far corner. It's almost like someone waved a wand over that Hyundai and transformed it into a shiny beige Toyota Land Cruiser, which wasn't there before.

7

13 September. Jebel Barkal, Sudan. 0800 hours.

Safe, for now. In a whirling cloud of sand, with a minimum of noise, and under a moonless sky, her mechanical bird has carried her home from another distant village. Once the churning dust settled and a guard helped her down, her pilot removed the aircraft to the concealment provided by a deep crease in the mountain, the same canyon that shelters her cages of trained falcons.

Now Kendacke has disappeared into the mountain too, darting into its cave-like entrance, then sliding into a crevice behind the far wall. Her quickening steps take her down a side tunnel, shored by rough wooden beams, into the bowels of the earth.

She must stoop to pass through the doorway into her apartment. As she crosses the threshold, her exhausted legs give out. She places the object she has been carrying in her shawl in the middle of the stone floor then sinks to her knees before one wall—etched with ancient hieroglyphics, punctuated with the repeated symbols for her name, *Kendacke.* She draws strength from the story they tell, of her lineage from the first female pharaoh to her prophesied return in present day. Images of primitive female bodies flank the prophecy, the globes of their breasts and bellies promising fertility and health.

For Kendacke life has become a desperate flight from village to village, trying to stay one step ahead of the militias, dishonorable crazy men armed by the government to eradicate all Sudanese who are not Muslim and many who are, if their homes cluster on identified oil fields.

When she and her forces can get to the villages first, they have a chance against the demon riders, who come thundering in expecting the population to flee before them. If the huts start disgorging lethal bullets and grenades instead of defenseless targets, the shock is often enough to send the mounted cowards into retreat.

As a fugitive from the government, Kendacke used to travel crude, barely visible roadways, always under cover of night, taking circuitous routes only she and a handful of loyal natives could navigate. Her forward progress was never predictable: too many obstacles, mechanical breakdowns, detours to avoid possibly hostile encounters. The new helicopter is supposed to ease these concerns, yet this expedition landed Kendacke in a village where patches of smoldering ash were all that remained of thatched huts, and flies swarmed over body parts already rotting in the sun. Somewhere there is a break in her information chain, causing her to arrive a day late.

A small boy, still alive, whimpered for his mother. Blood trickled from his open mouth and he cried red tears. As she gathered him to her breast, he made a gargling noise and went silent. In a clump of brush, Kendacke discovered a girl of four or five with a baby strapped to her back, reeking in its own waste. Neither child seemed able to make a sound. They stared at the bread Kendacke offered as if they had no idea what it was; as soon as they gulped her precious water, they vomited.

And then in the center of the village, *that*. That mound of bones concealed now by her blue shawl. More than an affront, or a wound, these bleached curves of a human rib cage were a personal message to her, a sign that she had been expected, a warning against future attempts to help her people.

She'd gathered the bones up with a bitter smile, knowing that she would use them to her enemies' regret. Then all she could do was transport the two surviving children to the next village and hope the women there might give them comfort. But in the next village, the people were digging shallow graves for more desecrated flesh.

Kendacke moves over to a small chest holding a basin and a pitcher. Although she can wash the sweat and dust from her face and arms, no one can erase the images burned into her aching brain.

She removes her blue cloth headdress and all but one of her sacred necklaces and places them on the chest, then sheds her blue wrapped skirt and top, puts on her night shift, and sinks onto the straw mat beside her cot. Far above, at the entrance into her temple, four guards with automatic rifles think they can protect their beloved leader's sleep. She pulls a machete from underneath the cot. Beside the weapon on the mat, she lays her last necklace, a carved stone pendant of female shape, along with a photo of an adolescent girl.

"I'm thankful you are not here to see," she says to the picture. "The ache in my heart and body is nothing compared to the suffering and despair of the people who have lost everything they love." Kendacke's tears begin to flow. "It is for the children I grieve most, my darling. There is coldness in the eyes of the survivors, the sign of soul-death, I'm afraid."

The sobs rack her body now. Always she must fight the numbness and force the sorrow to tear her heart. To avoid it is to join the living dead.

The photograph mutely smiles back at her as she stretches out on her cot. Kendacke closes her one eye and tries to imagine success for the celebration of the double cobra to take place in less than a month. It will be the first time in over five years that she has dared an appearance in daylight, presiding over a public ceremony for this annual event. Twenty-two mornings from now, sunlight will hit the Jebel at such an angle that a gold plate on its pinnacle will send the beams down a natural chimney into the mountain's core.

Earth and sky will be wed, and a state of blessedness, however fleeting, will descend all around.

This year Kendacke plans much more to share with her hungry people—a promise that this blessedness will last beyond a moment in the sun's course and permeate their future, a promise she will transmit through both words and flesh.

An hour later she is still wide awake. She cannot empty her mind of anxiety, but after years of practice, she can leave it. She soars back to the peaceful village of her childhood, then deeper into the past, to the ancient kingdom of Meroe in the fertile valley of the upper Nile. There is an amulet the Professor has shown her in the National Museum: the goddess Isis suckling a Nubian queen. Kendacke flees the day's horror to become that royal infant, her distant ancestor, cradled in the divine embrace.

For now she is safe.

8

---

12 September. McLean, Virginia. 2300 hours.

Maud's feet are sore, she's way behind in sleep, and she just struggled through a five-hour meeting of a joint task force on China policy, which managed to reach no agreement about anything. Still her pride flares at the number of vehicles dotting the lot outside the off-campus headquarters of the National Clandestine Service. Despite their contentiousness, her Agency colleagues are clearly dedicated 24/7 to serving their nation. Besides she loves always having a special parking slot for her thunder gray Cadillac CTS.

She fumbles in her Dolce e Gabbana platinum handbag for her keys, missing from the little pocket where they belong. *A place for everything and everything in its place*, she rebukes herself. *The more the distractions, the more you must rely on the rules to see you through.* She extracts her wallet and Blackberry and sets them on the silver hood. Next comes a small, zippered bag of cosmetics and a bottle of Tylenol. Finally she produces the keys, just as the belongings on the hood slide to the concrete. "Shit!" she mutters as she stoops down to pick them up.

The highly polished finish of her car reflects motion, a flash of color behind her. She springs upright, turning on a young Caucasian man in a button-down red plaid shirt and khaki pants towering over her. His body looks solid, his face nice-looking in an average sort of way. "Need some help?" he asks.

"I'm fine, thank you," she says with a polite smile.

He grins back. "Maybe you're working too hard."

"Part of my job description, I'm afraid. Have we met?"

"Not yet," the man says, then abruptly turns and heads for the main door of the building.

Very carefully now she organizes her purse, climbs into the car, buckles herself in, each movement deliberate, smoothing over the oddness, even the impertinence of the encounter.

It's a ten-minute drive to her high-rise, a gated complex on the periphery of Tyson's II, the mega mall of upscale stores that Maud chooses to ignore. People who shop there have more money than brains. She prefers Nordstrom's, where her methodical forays turn up quality merchandise on sale.

She taps the brake to warn the car behind her that he is tailgating. He gets the message and retreats. Then a red light ahead catches them both. She looks up to check her rear-view mirror. It bounces back the glare of sudden high beams. Then it goes dark altogether. Then high beams again. A signal? All at once the possibility that she is being followed turns her familiar route strange.

The traffic is light at this hour, and the emptiness of the four lanes feels vaguely threatening. Carjackers? She's been teased enough about the conspicuous luxury of her car to jump to that worst-case conclusion.

Her surveillance training is pretty rusty: when the light changes, she squeals out of the intersection like a teenager. The car behind her, headlights on again, does the same. She loops off Rte 123 onto a side road that runs parallel, through developments of townhouses, most of them dark. So does her tail. Choking on adrenalin, she runs a stop sign, turns left, then barges through a red light back onto 123.

No more headlights. She doesn't dare check the rear view, but grips the wheel tighter with her left hand and yanks her phone out of her purse with her right. She calibrates her speed to hit only green lights. She has to run one yellow, then realizes there *is* a car behind her, as it barrels through the red. Of course there isn't a police officer in sight.

Soon the brightly lit gate to her complex forces her to stop. She draws short breaths, trying in vain to fill her lungs. It takes forever for the entry code on her windshield sticker to be read electronically and the signal to raise the barrier. As her finger fumbles to tap 9-1-1, she takes one last look around. A sedan has pulled to the curb fifty feet away.

No one gets out. All at once recognition flashes and she snaps her phone shut: a Chrysler Concorde, standard issue for the Secret Service. She downshifts from anxious to puzzled. In daylight she can spot these cars anywhere, and anyone who would use one to follow her would know that.

She pulls into the complex, then turns to watch as the black sedan rolls past the descending gate. The driver, male, wears a red shirt. She notes the license number before it disappears into the dark.

9

Maud's condo on the tenth floor is sparsely furnished with blond Scandinavian pieces she bought years ago, intermixed with a few antiques her grandmother left her. The large living room opens onto a balcony, and on a clear night she can look out over thousands of lights almost all the way to Dulles airport. As if reading a twinkling map, it comforts her to be able to identify key buildings and roadways by their lights. A place for everything; everything in its place.

The view barely smoothes her ragged nerves tonight. She stands at the window peering down, breathing hard, until her twelve-year-old Siamese Lily lets out a hoarse complaint and slinks towards the kitchen. As if weightless, the creature leaps up onto her indoor "patio," a broad tray attached to the kitchen window sill, from which she keeps an eye on the local bird population while Maud is at work. "Sorry to keep you waiting, old girl," Maud says, as she opens a can of gourmet feline food.

The cat arches into a parabola and continues to chew Maud out.

"Oh stop it. It's very chic to eat late. All the best cats—"

Maud's hand stops midair as it reaches for Lily's empty bowl, which always sits on the right end of the tray. Tonight it is on the left. Her ears buzz with alarm: something out of place. Was she careless this morning when she set down Lily's breakfast? Out of the question. *This is ridiculous*, she tells herself, hoping to replace anxiety with indignation. She tries to take a deep breath, but her tight chest prevents it.

She picks the animal up, kisses her rough nose, and asks face to face, "What's the story, old girl?" More scratchy meows.

Maud plops down on the couch. The only light in the room comes from the screen of her laptop, where the reflection of Lily's feline eyes floats like a ghost's. "Wouldn't want to meet you in a dark alley," Maud says, ruffling the cat's ears before moving her aside. Lily stretches, rearranges herself, plops down on the pewter-grey leather sofa, and resumes purring.

Maud's first level clearance, password *silverdove*, gives her access to the data bank for Secret Service cars. She enters the tag number. The car is identified as residing on the Rosslyn station lot, exclusively owned by the Secret Service. It's also in for brake repairs, and not available for use.

Maud gazes off at the lights beyond her wall of glass. Lily squeezes onto her lap beside the computer, meowing to be petted. Maud ignores her. Ridiculous or not, she has to muster the energy to perform a sweep of her apartment before she can rest.

10

13 September. U.S. Embassy, Khartoum, Sudan. 1130 hours.

The broad residential street has shrunk and clogged with small, noisy cars and darting pedestrians. On either side, squat concrete structures, every third one an abandoned shell.

The silence since Tory got back in the car is getting awkward. OK, she over-reacted. She needs to get some sleep, get back on center. And she needs to bring up what just happened so this supply clerk won't think she's ashamed of it. "Who do you think those guys were working for?" she asks.

"Whom," says Wilkins.

"What!?"

"Correct grammar. It's one of the building blocks of civilization."

"Right. So besides sunburn issues, grammar lessons, and meaningless surveillance, what else should I expect?"

"The embassy's pretty much a bare bones operation at the moment, which is fine with me," Wilkins says in an even tone. "I'm a jack-of-all-trades myself."

"How do you tell who's who?" Tory asks.

"The Marines are in uniform, and the Sudanese employees have dark skin, and David Kimball's one of a kind—"

"Wilkins, I'm talking about out there. Friends from enemies?"

Wilkins throws her a glance. "Assume something in between."

After an eternity of stops and starts, they turn onto a broader avenue, and make steadier progress, ending abruptly at more concrete and coiled wire, plus a uniformed white man with a rifle.

The Marine waves them through an opening and up a slight rise. The road arcs around to the blockish embassy. It looks like one of those no-frills hotels that crop up at interstate exits back home. Except for the spiked iron fence in front and another armed Marine.

She follows Wilkins across the tile lobby, empty but for some potted palm trees and a dark-skinned man at a desk. Her body is beat, but her mind is on high alert—watching for something, a last trace, a clue. As she lets herself be led up a curved flight of stairs, light spills into the hall from an open door, and her hopes rise. The brass plate says David Kimball—Chargé d'Affaires: someone who actually worked with her father.

She'd been briefed before leaving Virginia on his puzzling career, successful tours in one hot spot after another, then a sudden downward spiral in Sudan. When her father was presumed killed and the embassy shut down, Kimball was bumped up to his current slot, but failed to shine. Things have gone from disorganized to chaotic. He's a place-holder, while the real decisions come out of Cairo.

He was probably handsome once, with his thin nose and lock of white hair flopping in an aristocratic wave across his forehead. But now his jowls sag, he has pouches under his eyes, his tie is loose, and sweat stains the armpits of his rumpled dress shirt.

"This must be Veronica," he says, coming around his huge desk, his voice smooth and cultivated, a touch bemused.

"Ronny's fine, sir" Tory says.

"Ronny, it is, and although I am your putative superior, I insist you call me Dave. Save the *sir* stuff for the knights on white chargers." He is shaking her hand and offering her a charming smile when the smell hits her, like stale hospital, or too ripe cheese. "When they warned me I was going to be spied on, I thought, *May she be a lovely spook with green eyes.*"

Tory laughs politely, as if he's told a joke, while her hopes of gleaning something meaningful from his memory of her father pop like bubbles. "I think my job description specifies collecting data on the local economy and quality of life, not fellow diplomats."

"What do you think *I* have been doing for the last eight years, reveling in cocktail parties?"

"Booze is taboo here," Wilkins explains.

"I do know that," Tory says, thinking, *Somebody should tell* this *guy*.

"If I had a dollar for every Note to File I've sent stateside . . . But *our* first-hand impressions aren't good enough," David Kimball says, raising his fist. "The desk officers just sit on everything they get from me. When construction starts on our new, improved, and impregnable embassy, I'll be replaced." Kimball's eyeballs bulge and redden. "The American corporatocracy is desperate for everyone over here to kiss and make up. Shower each other with sweets and flowers. They want to hear the Peace Accord is working, so they can get in on the oil money like everyone else. See, Darfur is only a minor nuisance, more than offset by our intelligence interface with Mukharabat." His voice surges in volume. "They're willing to blink at corruption that makes a sewer smell sweet."

"Sir," Wilkins says, gesturing to keep it down.

"I'll be working with numbers," Tory says. "They won't lie."

The man allows Wilkins to guide him back behind the desk. "No. I suppose not. But will they wring a few pertinent necks? It's our only hope, you know." Kimball calms suddenly. "This handsome young man here seems to think you might be wired?"

"Actually, I need to crash for a while," Tory says.

"Never mind," the Chargé d'Affaires mutters. "I don't care who's listening. This is hell-on-earth. The truth will set you free, my friends. I'm living proof. Better late than never."

Descending the staircase, she wonders exactly which necks her putative superior has his eye on—Muslim? Tribal? American? Other? And what in the hell does *putative* mean, anyway?

11

"Last stop, Hilton," crows Wilkins, after a halting but pleasant enough drive along the *Sharia el Nil*. There are trees, anyway, and other unfamiliar foliage, and through the haze of exhaustion Tory registered some impressive structures—the National Museum, places with promising names, like Friendship Hall and the Blue Nile Sailing Club, though the broad river on their right is more brown than blue.

"Reception at the President's Palace tonight at 1800," Wilkins says.

"Too bad I'll be asleep."

"You've been expressly invited."

"You've got to be kidding. I'm a drone, Wilkins, a glorified bean-counter."

"They want to make a good impression on the U.S. Or maybe they want to appear to want to make a good impression."

Tory fumbles in her backpack for her secure mobile and checks it for text. Nothing to let her know how to pick up her weapon.

"I'll be your escort," Wilkins says, as if that's supposed to make everything cool. "And you can call me Bart."

Tory just stares at his round dark lenses.

"I mean instead of Bartholomew." He parks the SUV in the shade of the overhang. "You know, Dave's right about your eyes."

"Did your mother teach you to say that, *Wilkins?*"

"Sorry." He opens his door. "The thing is, he's right about a lot of things. Too bad he's got no credibility."

She climbs out into the heat, but in her fatigue allows him to chug around to the hatchback for her luggage. She bends into her open door to retrieve the backpack. As she straightens and turns, she is startled by two boys with spidery legs and arms dancing in front of her. The taller one wears a baggy Nike T-shirt. Her eyes fix on the mouth of the smaller, which has been pulled off-center by a diagonal scar. Her insides cringe at the pain it speaks of.

She steps back, but caught between the car and its door, there is nowhere to go. She is overwhelmed by the metallic smell of poverty.

"Welcome to our city," they chant, holding out their palms. "Thanks," she says, trying to smile back through her dismay.

She scrounges in the pocket of her pack. "Want some gum?"

"Coca Cola?" says the taller boy. "Ten dollars?"

"All I've got is gum," Tory says, as Wilkins forces his right arm in front of the children to grab the car door.

"That's enough. Excuse us," he commands, as he drags Tory away from the kids.

"We friendly people," the taller boy says. Tory manages to dig out the package of gum and tosses it toward him. He catches it and commences a little victory dance. Her involuntary giggle stops short when her gaze falls again on the smaller boy's torn mouth. She pulls out a bag of smashed potato chips and a ballpoint pen. She holds them out to the child tentatively and is relieved when his eyes light up.

Meanwhile Wilkins works to propel her into motion. As she stumbles through the parting glass doors of the hotel, she puzzles over this supply clerk's torso, which briefly pressed against her. It felt solid as steel. She glances back at the lanky geek bobbling her suitcase and backpack. Something doesn't compute.

12

The exclusive Riyadh section of Khartoum is home to the Sudanese whom fortune has smiled on, who require privacy and protection from the vagaries of the city's masses. Having made their money in other parts of the world, they supplement it now with native oil currency and government favors. Adam Marshall, for whom privacy is as crucial as oxygen, has purchased his *pied à terre* here, a three-storey pink stucco residence concealed by a pink concrete wall topped with razor wire and broken glass.

Always loyal to the guy in the mirror, Marshall and his investment firm, Mephisto, have constructed a labyrinth of transnational activities that even *The Wall Street Journal* has never successfully mapped. With major holdings in weapons and oil, the life source of modern civilization, he once shored up the Shah of Iran and the President of the Philippines. He maintains ongoing ties with the Saudis.

Mephisto's current interest in Beijing Petrol is merely Marshall's latest excuse to keep a residence in Sudan. He discovered the country years ago as a ravenous market for small arms he had no trouble supplying. Since then he's always privately considered his visits more pleasure than business: amid the rampant corruption and lawlessness he feels more alive, exhilarated, at home.

His lush hidden garden is a personal paradise, sustained by expensive water and cheap local labor. At this time of day, near twilight, the oblong pool in its midst shimmers like 24 carat gold and the fronds of the palms that shade it rustle with the breeze.

Marshall relaxes in his shirtsleeves on the veranda beside its waters, sipping his favorite Armagnac, and puffing a Romeo and Julieta Escudos, limited edition 2005. His skin is startlingly pale, but his black hair and black goatee give drama and definition to his otherwise soft features.

His breathing deepens, nostrils flaring, as he contemplates the hours ahead. His eyelids slide closed. Behind him, on a stool against the house, a bald, broad-bellied Chinese man sits like Buddha in a business suit—Mr. Marshall's personal acupuncturist—utterly immobile despite the fly exploring his shiny skull.

A handsome, dark-skinned young man in a black suit steps out of the house, dispatches the fly temporarily with a flick of his hand, and approaches his boss. "Would you like a refresher, sir?" The accent is clearly American, with a trace of the Bronx.

Eyelids click open. "No thanks, Arthur, need to be sharp for the reception tonight. I've planned a private party afterwards."

"Yes, sir," says the young man, averting his gaze.

"Better check that there are fresh towels in the Gymnasium."

"Right away, sir," Arthur says.

What Mr. Marshall calls the Gymnasium, a windowless room on the third floor, contains special equipment manufactured out of black vinyl and steel. Arthur never looks at it long enough to figure out how things work. He also avoids catching himself in the floor-to-ceiling mirrors on the walls. At the far end of the room hangs a red velvet drape, which Arthur has been ordered never to touch. "For special people," Mr. Marshall has said, "on special occasions." Arthur has never questioned or disobeyed.

Now he removes several red towels from the closet in the adjoining bath, and places them on the warming bars above the Jacuzzi. He is heading back downstairs when the inside phone plays the opening of Beethoven's Fifth. Arthur has to return to the Gymnasium to pick up.

"What's going on up there? You playing with yourself?" Mr. Marshall's idea of a joke.

"No, sir," says Arthur.

"Well, I'm ready to go."

"Right away, sir."

Downstairs Chen is helping Mr. Marshall into the jacket of his sharkskin Canali suit. The Boss checks himself in the hall mirror, tightens his necktie, straightens the matching pocket handkerchief, and tugs at the starched cuffs of his shirt. He smiles at Arthur, and takes a couple of fake jabs at his face. The young man flinches back, and Mr. Marshall laughs. "You are a good man. Lucky to have you. And Chen, you take excellent care of my house."

Chen bends forward at the hips.

Arthur holds open the rear door of the Mercedes for the Boss then slides in behind the wheel. As he turns the ignition, he hears the Boss declare, "Let the games begin!"

13

Tory and Wilkins arrive at the Presidential Palace at 1800 sharp, leave their vehicle outside the gates, and pass through the metal detector. Next Tory is escorted into an upright coffin of a booth where a woman performs a further search. At least Tory thinks it's a woman, based on the timid eyes and pair of hairless hands patting her gently, the only evidence not concealed by yards of rough-woven cloth.

Afterward the woman gropes around in Tory's purse until she hits something. She pulls out the stone figurine with female curves and her eyes go round with fear.

"A gift from my father," Tory says in Arabic. "For good luck." The facts: someone found the object in her father's Khartoum quarters; the Agency passed it on to her.

The woman keeps turning the artifact over, as if looking for a trigger or fuse. Tory tries to act indifferent, but suddenly, that hunk of stone represents all she values in the world. She jams her hands into her own armpits so as not to deliver a chop to the poor woman's neck and grab the figure back. Finally the woman returns it to the bag and returns Tory to Wilkins.

A Kalashnikov-toting guard leads the two of them around one wing of the sprawling palace, its three-storey white façade a lacework of arched porticos. Compared to its glossy pictures, it looks faded, in need of paint. On its side lawn the guard halts at the entrance to a huge white tent. Off to the left, a fluorescent sun sinks into the river at the spot where the two Niles join, bleeding orange into the shimmering ripples. The majestic effect is broken by shouting servants running every which way carrying trays and boxes. There isn't another guest in sight.

"It's always like this," Wilkins says. "Their time versus ours."

"You could have let me nap longer."

"Absolutely not," he says with surprising passion. "Give in on one thing and you might as well hand over the store."

The tent begins to fill up with people of every skin shade, almost all male, many in western dress, many of them Chinese. They stand in clusters, sipping syrupy chai, the national drink, contributing French, German, Chinese, and Arabic to a moderate, unfocused din.

If Veronica Clark has been expressly invited to this function, no one acts like it. But thanks to the noise, the perfume of exotic spices mixed with sweat, the lure of the unknown, Tory's fatigue peels away like a shroud, leaving intense curiosity. She's just about to plunge into the crowd, circulate, connect with the Europeans, possible sources, get a feel for things when

Wilkins' hand clamps her arm like a manacle. He has his agenda. He begins easing her from one turbaned minister to another, introducing her to each with the same little bow and elaborate speech. "Your Honor, Bartholomew Wilkins of the Embassy of the United States of America. May I present Veronica Clark, our new officer of Economic Affairs?"

As her name is pronounced, Tory's inner voice whispers, *That man, the one who disappeared, remember, almost six years ago—which one of you knows about that?* But she bows to each minister with the formal greeting, "*As-salammu alaykum.*" Hello, peace be with you.

"As we informed your offices last week," Wilkins continues, "Ms. Clark will be soliciting your help in gathering data in order to update an economic report."

Then an awkward silence descends as the minister and his entourage wait for the American intruders to move on.

Tory is wondering if Wilkins is capable of anything *but* awkward moments when a man catches her glance and nods. He's dressed more colorfully than anyone else in the room, and his white hair caps his light brown face like a halo. His onyx eyes, magnified by thick glasses, look a little bewildered but intelligent. Her sensors hum *Potential asset.* She has to shed Wilkins long enough to introduce herself.

"Who's that," she asks her keeper.

"You don't need to meet him," Wilkins says.

"I think I can decide something like that."

"He's a local gadfly. Teaches at the University, and if he weren't an American citizen, he'd be in big—"

"The University?" Her nerves buzz. Her father mentioned friends at the University in his letters.

The man is in front of her now, extending a hand. "That's right," he says, taking hers. "James Crawford. I turned down the Metropolitan Museum of Art thirty-odd years ago during an episode of temporary insanity. Now I patch together a living teaching at the University of Khartoum, curating at the National Museum, directing the excavation of an ancient site northeast of the Capital, a little of everything."

Something in the man's voice, a mix of kindness and resignation, freezes Tory speechless.

"Well, Dr. Crawford, always glad to find you alive and well," Wilkins says, shaking hands.

"You and me both." The man pulls a card from the leather pouch hanging around his neck, and hands it to Tory. "We have unearthed discoveries of interest which I would be happy to share with you, in the unlikely event that you find yourself with an hour or two of leisure time. I'd better leave now while I still can, but my contact information is on the card." He melts back into the crowd.

14

13 September. McLean, Virginia. 0800 hours.

If Maud loves anyone, it's the people who work for her. Since taking over the Intelligence Directorate a year ago, she usually finds a reason to visit her domain downstairs at least once a day. At the sight of her team glued to computer screens, paging through thick reports, and keeping the in-house lines buzzing, she usually feels a surge of warmth and connection. Together they are going to resurrect the Directorate of Intelligence out of the ashes of all its failures—from misidentified bombing targets to the bungles of 9/11. It's time for the Agency to get it right, do it right, make it right.

Today the moment is tinged with doubt. Someone in one of those cubicles, in one of those offices, has opted off her team. Maybe more than one. Well, she's damned if some conspiracy of insecure male egos is going to sabotage her.

Because that's what it's about, the intelligence slowdown, the obvious surveillance last night, her condo entered, objects moved around, maybe a wire, though she failed to detect one. Someone is trying to scare her, nudge her into playing the hysterical woman. A tough label to shake—the more intensely you protest, the more you seem to confirm it.

As a woman, she's had to fight—without really appearing to fight—for every advancement. Her enemy: a secretive system which metes out the plum assignments, the "keys to the kingdom," in the men's room or on the golf course. She's determined to make her career proof that a little brilliance and a lot of relentless hard work will win in the end.

The mahogany table almost fills her private conference room. She sits on one of its long sides facing the door as two men file in—her hand-picked Chief Analysts on the Africa desk. Until recently Maud's been able to take the accuracy of their recommendations to the bank.

Tremaine Jackson, a Black Studies major from Harvard, is fluent in a dozen African dialects. Maud forgives his verbal aggressiveness because he's so damn smart. Tremaine's partner, Paul Livingston, a pale, nerdy mop-head with eczema, never speaks unless spoken to because he's profoundly shy.

"Looking good today," fires off Tremaine as he pulls a chair out across from Maud, places his pad and pen on the table, and sits down. "Big plans for the evening?"

Maud lifts an eyebrow. She is dressed in a pantsuit of her usual grey, a matching silk scarf wrapped around her shoulders. Her grey hair is, as usual, swept up in a twist.

"I didn't call you in here to speculate on my social life," she says, fingering the folder she's placed face down on the table in front of her. "I need the latest developments in Sudan. Who can start?"

"You've got your militia attacks on the increase in Darfur, thanks to the fact that it's sitting on more oil fields," Tremaine rattles off. "You've got the President doing his China dance: *I give you oil, you give me weapons, and while you're at it, build me a multi-million-dollar hotel and a golf course outside Khartoum.* He's screwing the South out of oil revenue, as usual. He can't stand the First Vice President because—"

Maud has lowered her head as if to listen. Now she shakes it slowly from side to side. "I said, *latest* developments. What's going on, guys? If I believed the intel coming across my desk, I'd conclude that apart from Darfur, Sudan's as uneventful as the Bahamas." *We've got people to protect over there*, she wants to add, *people who can't remember to pick up a phone and let me know they're safe.*

"I've got to turn on the BBC to find out a couple tons of surplus rice just left China for Port Sudan," she continues. "Think this humanitarian sop to the refugee situation will find its way into any starving mouths? And what about the NIM and that woman who fancies herself a religious leader? Why did I have to spend yesterday afternoon pounding the virtual pavements of cyberspace, trying to figure out what she's up to? She's running her own refugee camp or something. I hear a spike in visa applications from foreign journalists inspired a media blackout by the Mukharabat." She pauses for effect, then clucks her tongue at them. "And still no sign of the missing file. It must have dropped off the continent."

Paul reaches down into the briefcase next to him, pulls up an inch-thick folder, and waves it with a sheepish smile.

"Where did you find that?" Maud snatches it from his chapped hand and strains to keep her voice under control.

"I wish I could claim credit, ma'am," Paul says. "But actually, it found me. It was sitting in the top drawer of my desk this morning."

"And you have no idea who had it?" Maud asks.

Paul looks as if he will die of shame. "Maybe someone who *thought* they were acting for the good of all?"

"Since when is tampering with intelligence acting for the good?"

Both men look down between their knees.

"I'll pretend that incredibly stupid remark did not come out of your mouth, Paul. Meanwhile I'd suggest the two of you leave, go back to your offices, and start writing me up a situation report on Sudan, as of September 16, 0900."

"That's tomorrow," Tremaine says, while the red patch on Paul's forehead turns purple.

"You got it," says Maud.

Maud takes the folder back to her private office, settles in behind her desk, and opens it randomly. She scans an account of twenty Chinese tanks, supposedly bound from the Polish Army to Yemen, arriving in Port Sudan. Then one of the tabs catches her eye—KENDACKE. Her face gets hot. Her hands start trembling. Of course. It felt like snooping eight years ago, violating Ty's privacy. It still feels like snooping today.

But did she overlook something in this file back then, blinded by the mess of personal need? What Maud remembers: Kendacke had been a prostitute, or else a student, or else a thief. Maybe all three. The woman was a crafty survivor, with slippery beginnings, until Ty arrived in country, and tried to turn her into an African Joan of Arc.

Now as she flips to the KENDACKE tab to give the pages another read, her stomach sinks. They aren't there.

Maud sits for a long time staring at the wall, feeling empty. Someone's definitely trying to get to her. Time to brace up for another fight.

15

13 September. Khartoum, Sudan. 2000 hours.

Tory munches a rolled-up appetizer of unidentifiable flavor and shares her strategy at Sudoku with two sweaty men claiming to be engineering students from Russia. When they happen to mention that the purpose of the reception is to honor the chief engineer and the firm that will be building a state-of-the-art sewage system for Khartoum, she turns and glares at Wilkins, who is directly behind her, of course. He's chatting up an attractive Sudanese woman dressed for success in a western suit despite the muggy heat inside the tent. Her lips are like ripe plums, and she tilts her head flirtatiously.

"When the project is completed," she tells Wilkins, "there will be ten sewage lift stations in strategic locations around the city. The main pumping station will have twin 600 mm force mains and be 8 km in length."

"That's a lot of force," Tory says, breaking in with a fake smile.

Wilkins introduces Veronica Clark and explains her function at the Embassy.

The woman, the assistant Chief Engineer, doesn't bother to smile back. "The mark of a civilized society is how it manages its waste removal."

"Also grammar, I'm told," Tory says, pulling Wilkins away. "You couldn't let me catch up on sleep," she blurts in his ear.

"I only told you what they told me," Wilkins answers.

"Who's *they?*"

Just then the noise in the tent rises noticeably. A dark man in white robes and headpiece eases through the opening, flanked by five Chinese men in suits.

"The President?" Tory whispers.

"Minister of Oil. The President never attends his receptions."

Tory has to hand it to Wilkins for tenacity. Within minutes he has pushed his way into the circle surrounding the minister and launched into his spiel about Veronica Clark's special mission while the oil minister looks down on her like she's a flaw in the carpet and the smiling Chinese squint right through her.

"We hope to learn of the positive impact of the Peace Accord on the Sudanese economy," Tory says in Arabic. A young Chinese with a round baby face and lips like pink worms, translates into Mandarin. "As military expenditures decrease, we expect oil profits to be redirected to the betterment of social programs." A heavy silence is filled by the surrounding babble. Tory inhales deeply then adds, "I am also very curious about the National Identity Movement."

The Minister jerks as if she'd pinched him. "No such movement is in existence," he says.

"I didn't realize," Tory says. "When did it die?"

Grabbing Tory's arm again, Wilkins tells everyone, "*Ila liqaa*," Arabic for till our paths cross again, and drags her off into the crowd.

"Jesus, Ronny, what got into you to mention that?" he demands when they're out of earshot. His tone is furious, but he smiles down at her for the benefit of anyone watching. "The NIM are considered insurgents. You want to get yourself killed?"

"No," she says, "just noticed."

"Why in the world?"

"Never mind."

"Jet lag," Wilkins decides. "Let's get you back to the hotel."

Just then the Oil Minister calls out, "American lady, come here."

Yes! Tory weaves her way back through the guests, Wilkins following her, along with countless curious eyes. As soon as they are in the Minister's presence, Wilkins begins explaining their early departure. The minister cuts him off.

"First Vice President," he says to Tory. "You are invited to speak with him. Tomorrow. Thanks to him, the unlawful movement you mention is no more."

"I am indebted to your honor," Tory says. "What time tomorrow?"

"Anytime." The Oil Minister is above such details.

Just then the cluster of Chinese separates to reveal a stocky man with grey-white skin beside the Oil Minister. He wears a dark suit, red silk tie, and his starched white shirt looks like he just put it on.

"I'm sure the Minister will excuse the interruption," he says in perfect American English, acknowledging Tory's surprise with a small bow. His receding black hair leaves him with a dagger of a widow's peak, echoed by a short goatee.

"Mr. Marshall, of course," answers the Minister. "And tell me, what is the matter with the servants when our honored guest lacks refreshment?"

"I'm fine, I'm fine. Never mix food with pleasure," the man says offering a soft white hand to Tory. "Adam Marshall."

Adam Marshall! She tries not to show surprise. She knew of him—*who didn't?*—but purely as an abstraction, a name inscribed at the very top of the organizational tree of Mephisto, a multi-billion dollar conglomerate. His concrete existence has always eluded the public eye. "Veronica Clark," Tory says, gripping his hand firmly.

The man looks amused, and gives hers a slight squeeze before he lets it go.

"Bartholomew Wilkins." Wilkins sticks out his hand so aggressively that it bumps the glass of tea in the hand of one of the Chinese guests, sending a brown splash down his own pants leg. The composure of the Chinese explodes in raucous laughter.

"Your first time in Sudan, Miss Clark," asks Adam Marshall, his acid-green eyes burning into hers. It's like he's trying to tell her something, something far more important than the tea party humming around them.

Tory nods. "And yourself?"

"As the honorable minister can tell you, I turn up here from time to time. Like a bad penny."

"No, no, Mr. Marshall always is welcome," protests the Minister. "Here is his true home."

"In what connection do you turn up?" Tory asks.

Mr. Marshall pulls at his shirt cuffs. "I'm an optimist. I believe in happy endings."

The Minister nods and the Chinese muster a chorus of blank but beaming smiles.

Adam Marshall's soft white hand clasps her elbow, trying to peel her away from the group. "I couldn't help overhearing your question about the NIM," he says into her ear. "I think I can be of some use."

Tory resists the pressure. "Great. Tell me how I can reach you."

"Why not right now?" His other arm circles her back.

She throws a glance in Wilkins's direction. He is dabbing at the stripe of tea on his pants with a napkin.

"I knew your father," Adam Marshall whispers.

Her heart stops then races. "My father?"

"He was quite a man."

"Then you're from Wisconsin?"

"Why, are you?"

"Born and raised in Madison. Cheered for the Green Bay Packers before I could talk."

"I'm a football fan myself," Adam Marshall says. "I think the game's a great metaphor for life."

"The First Vice President," the Oil Minister calls out in English as the young lady and Mr. Marshall move off. "In the afternoon."

Wilkins stops fussing over his clothes and jerks upright. Tory ignores him.

"I have a car outside," Adam Marshall says.

That's when Tory remembers she forgot to call Maud. Oh well, Maud probably didn't mean for her to start on the day she arrived. What could happen in only six hours anyway?

16

13 September. Jebel Barkal, Sudan. 2130 hours.

A sand-blasted Hyundai Santa Fe hisses along a crude road north of Khartoum. Though its headlights are off, and there is only the faintest light from a quarter-moon, the driver's night goggles allow him to navigate unerringly the narrow strip.

Less than a mile from the site, his senses click into higher alert. On this windless night, something is moving. He peers ahead but sees nothing. He can't risk another brush with the security police—his worn-out excuse for an automobile would never be able to elude one of their Land Rovers twice in one day. No choice now but to put on the brakes.

He pulls a Norinco M-77B within reach, a weapon he collected last week from a sentry outside a militia camp, after surprising him from behind and dragging his dagger across the man's throat. One less threat to some innocent village.

Two hundred meters in the distance a large patch of scrub brush at the side of the road shifts again.

He runs possibilities at lightning speed. Worst case: an ambush attempt, he trades fire, the noise lures Kendacke's guards away from the mountain into the fray. He is just deciding he'll pull a 180 and draw the would-be attackers in the other direction when the unmistakable bulk of a hyena slouches from the bush across the road and is swallowed by the dark.

He watches and waits, but now everything is still. He presses the accelerator, his heart pumping and brain cheering with relief.

Soon shadowy pyramids and ruins of pyramids loom ahead. Hundreds of white tents surround them like scraps of litter. The fragile village is alive with activity. Its occupants have arrived on foot, in carts dragged by donkeys, in the beds of rusty pick-ups. Each has a story to share of an arduous journey, hiding by day and moving along secret routes by night, of avoiding attack and grieving over the makeshift graves of those not so fortunate.

There are the tired, hungry pilgrims, many of their jeeps and trucks pirated from the Sudanese Army and the Chinese oil fields, and the others, their protectors, with guns. A detachment from the People's Liberation Army has flown in from the southern city of Juba in two aging Chinook helicopters. Kendacke's ever-swelling personal guard has begun to establish a makeshift perimeter of salvaged metal and a stolen spool of razor wire around the enclave of tents and ruins, with dogs to help patrol it.

A bonfire of camel dung burns just outside the large courtyard formed by the temple footings. Guards and pilgrims encircle its light and warmth, partaking of mashed beans, or *fuul*, flatbread, and fellowship. The middle of the courtyard harbors a sheet of white canvas anchored with rocks, which hides The Professor's ancient stone tablets. His team of volunteers has finished reassembling them in time for the ceremony, only to find the central row of three tablets missing. Further excavations have uncovered nothing, and the scene they portray remains incomplete.

The new arrival slides his car among the other vehicles at the mountain's base and retrieves a knapsack containing four more handguns and half a dozen grenades from the back seat. He drags a small rocket launcher from the trunk and straps it to his back.

Gliding along the stone face, away from the encampment, he approaches the temple entrance. Two guards stand at attention just inside it, and further inside, two more are sleeping. All are armed.

Crouching on the right side of the entrance, he pulls his double-edged push dagger from his boot and unsheathes its ¼-inch steel blade. He sets it in his right palm and picks up a rock with his left. He tosses the rock toward the entrance.

Instantly both guards step away from the opening, rifles raised and aimed in the direction of the tossed stone. From behind, the man jumps the closest one, a female, and holds the dagger point to her neck. "Make a sound either of you, and I open this girl's throat," he warns in a hoarse whisper.

The other guard whips around, flashing a light on the attacker's face. "Lewis!" The guard tries to grab him, but Lewis steps back pulling his captive with him. "Come on, Lewis. You looking for trouble?"

"If I can get the drop on you, anyone can."

"We got back-up. Inside."

The two dozing guards are leaning against the sides of the entrance now. "Sure you do," says Lewis shaking his head with disgust. "Is she here?"

"She sleeps."

"I am going to have to disturb her."

He slips the knife back into his boot, then strides into the antechamber, and slides around the slab at its end, pulling the sack of guns and the launcher after himself. He makes the twisting descent to the supply chamber, which also serves as an armory for the assortment of weapons the NIM manages to beg or steal. After depositing the latest, he goes down one level more to the room. The door squeaks slightly as he stoops to enter then closes it. He is six and a half feet tall, dark as a panther, gauntly handsome in his midnight blue jumpsuit, despite his missing ear.

He unties his boots, steps out of them, and eases across the room to the sleeping woman. Settling himself onto the mat, he gently strokes her short, rough hair.

She doesn't move. "Kendacke, Kendacke . . . There is no time for sleep."

She pulls a sheet over her head, hungry for a few more minutes of oblivion. "Is it daylight already?"

"Not for a long time, but I have much to tell."

17

13 September. Khartoum, Sudan. 2130 hours.

The driver holds open the rear door of a black Mercedes 500 SEL. Impeccable in a well-tailored suit instead of a uniform, he is tall and strong, an African prince.

Tory gives him an appreciative smile as she slides onto the leather seat. *Now we're getting somewhere*, she thinks, as Adam Marshall climbs in on the other side and closes the door. Her head fills with the spicy fragrance of his cologne.

"So what is a lovely young woman like you doing in a hellhole like this?" Mr. Marshall's grimace asks her to pardon the cliché.

"So how do you know my dad?" Tory asks back, trying for casual.

Mr. Marshall laughs. "That, my dear, is a very long story. Where have they put you up?"

"The Hilton?"

"Lucky girl, to have avoided the American compound."

"They'll probably move me there eventually. But right now I can't complain. My room looks out on the Nile."

"You know, you can call me Adam."

"And where are *you* staying, Adam?"

"I have my own little place."

"Then you're not in the compound either."

"No, but *I'm* not official."

"Then why are *you* in a hellhole like this?"

"Why is anyone anywhere? Investments."

"What about U.S. sanctions?"

"My investments are indirect."

"Just out of curiosity, are the Sudanese people getting any benefits from your indirect investments?"

"I've always had a weakness for idealists," Adam says with a stiff smile.

"It's my job to ask," Tory says.

"I find it charming," Adam says.

"When bands of starving Sudanese start attacking Chinese oil workers, doesn't it sort of put a crimp in investments?" Tory asks.

"Your point is well taken," Adam says, and there's something about his dead, even tone that signals the subject is finished. Still she perseveres. "So were you here in 2001?"

"2001?" Adam sits back and laces his fingers behind his head. "I don't recall. Arthur?"

"Yes, Mr. Marshall," says the chauffeur, to Tory's surprise. Scratch African prince—his accent whispers New York.

"Was I here in 2001?"

"One week, March 14 to March 21, Mr. Marshall. On your way back to the States from Israel."

"Amazing, isn't he? Driver, palm pilot, electronic notebook, all rolled into one, aren't you, Arthur?"

"Whatever you say, Mr. Marshall," Arthur says.

"What were you doing back then?" Tory asks, off-hand.

Adam shrugs. "Meetings with the Ministers, dawn to dusk, as I recall. We were trying to get construction going on the oil pipeline, wasn't it, Arthur, the one those crazy rebels keep sabotaging?"

"Yes, Mr. Marshall. Always big problems with security in the south." Arthur pulls the car to a stop under the Hilton overhang. He opens her door, and extends a hand.

Her hand in Arthur's, Tory searches his inscrutable brown eyes. "What I'd give to have your memory," she says with a smile, thinking, *You and I need to talk.*

He gives her a solemn nod. Like he might be thinking the same thing, but that is impossible. Mr. Marshall is calling to her across the car roof. "Can I interest you in something to drink?"

"Sounds good," she says, nowhere ready to give up the campaign. *Why not see what he serves with it?*

18

13 September. Jebel Barkal, Sudan. 2200 hours.

"You are late," Kendacke says yawning. "I could not remain awake." She flips over on her mat and again pulls the covers over her head.

"A brush with the security police required a retreat to one of our safe houses until dark."

Kendacke snaps upright. "What do you mean, brush?"

"I will explain after I prepare the smoked meat I have brought for you to eat."

"I need information, not food."

"What you need is to make some changes in your guard. These inexperienced boys and girls are an accident waiting to happen."

"Their hearts are loyal."

"You need more than hearts. Call in a few *men* who know what they're doing."

"The *men* who know what they are doing, such as yourself, have more important things to do than take care of a powerless woman."

"More bad news this trip?"

"The village of Bol is a ring of ashes."

Lewis grits his teeth. "He gave no word."

"It may be that he didn't know."

"He knew. There was a big meeting with the ministers a couple days ago. He sent me a note afterwards—the idiot. My father entrusted a message to some kid on the street, and gave the boy an address! A wonder I have not been picked up by now."

"What did the note say, Lewis?"

"The Chinese are sending a shipment of rice to our people in the settlement camps."

"This is good news."

"Right, and the bad news, which he decided not to mention, is that innocent villagers must continue to be punished for that helicopter we made away with. He plays both sides, Kendacke. That's what cowards do."

"I would like to meet with him."

"Don't be ridiculous."

"I would like to thank him. For all the times he chooses our side instead of theirs."

"Well, they are watching him very closely now, pressuring him to prove his loyalty to the government. And he is a weak man, out of his depth among those animals. As readily as he passed us information, he will betray us to save his own life. You think he would pass up an opportunity to betray you? Oh, Kendacke, everyday I worry that something terrible will happen to you."

"Everyday something terrible does happen to me."

"You know what I mean. Too many have too much to gain by your death."

"Ah, my death. It glimmers before me like the sun's beams hitting gold. Always before me. Never within reach."

"Do not speak that way. Your people need you. I need you."

"And all your bodies need to be fed. When will the rice arrive?"

"We will never see it."

"No, I suppose not." Kendacke reaches up and draws Lewis down in an embrace. "But let us pretend for a moment that it appears like a miracle during the celebration of the Cobra. A fountain of rice rushing up from the sand like a geyser of oil. Let us dream together about that!"

Lewis fights the urge to surrender to her warm flesh. "There is more news, which may be turned to our use. The man who called himself Peter Thornton? His daughter has arrived in Khartoum."

Kendacke snaps upright again, rolling Lewis off onto the floor. "Does James know this?"

"He is the one who told me. Following in her father's footsteps, he said. Piol and I were at the airport when she arrived. A young woman with speckled skin was picked up by the tall, pale Wilkins fellow from the Embassy."

"Their television and newspapers are finally giving a few lines to our government's atrocities, and their government sends us a *girl*. Someone they can control, who will tell them exactly what they want to hear."

"Remember that you were practically a girl when you took on our mission," Lewis says.

As if a new thought suddenly changed her mind, Kendacke rises up from the mat to her full height and presses a hand to her breast. "Oh, Lewis. Suddenly I see what it means. The man called Thornton's daughter! This news does lift my heart."

19

13 September. Khartoum, Sudan. 2200 hours.

The Hilton's dimly lit café could be anywhere in the First World. The female server leads them to a booth, and Tory slides onto the curved leather seat encircling its marble table. Palm trees multiply in the mirrored walls, and an unexpected bottle of expensive brandy materializes from Adam Marshall's attaché case.

The alcohol doesn't seem to surprise the server as much as the server surprises Tory: above a starched white bib and black Western dress, her face is distinctly Chinese, yet it's crowned by a helmet of platinum blond hair. With a demure smile, she unscrews the bottle and plunks down two crystal tumblers.

"But I thought—" Tory says, when the woman leaves.

"Rules are made to be broken," says Marshall as he pours. "I'll tell you, that diplomatic babble gets old fast when you're cold sober." He passes her a glass. "And frankly the Chinese get on my nerves."

Tory checks over her shoulder. No point in offending the server, who has enough on the two of them right now to put them both behind bars. "They are a mass of contradictions," Tory says softly, taking a polite sip.

"I don't know about that."

"I meant the common people."

"Them again," Marshall says with a groan and a wink.

"Torn between village and city, traditional culture and pop culture, agrarian communism and industrial globalization—"

"You sound like a textbook."

"It's not just textbook."

"Oh? What is it then?"

"I did public relations for Syntech in Beijing for three years. Before I took the Foreign Service Exam. What are you smiling at?"

"When was that? When you were fifteen?" He gives her chin a fatherly pinch.

To keep from saying something she'll regret, she takes a gulp of her brandy. She isn't much of a drinker, preferring to get high on extreme exercise, and for a full minute, she can't suck in a breath, while her eyes water profusely.

Smiling, Adam picks up her glass and moves it away from the table's edge. When she has recovered, he says, "You must have noticed that the Chinese government monitors every time you blow your nose."

"Actually," she says in a thin, burned voice, "what I noticed was that Chinese businessmen began as patronizing sexists and ended up coming to me for advice."

"And you enjoyed that?" Marshall asks.

"Having their respect? Of course."

"Of course. But allow me to offer you a tip based on years of experience: the Chinese leadership is never going to change. They're out for world domination. A puppet government in Khartoum and control of Sudanese oil are preliminary steps along the way."

The bleached blond server polishes glasses across the room, her face expressionless. Tory tries another tiny sip of her drink. "That's one viewpoint."

"I'm sure I don't need to tell you who's providing the government here with the helicopters it uses to gun down its own people," Marshall goes on.

"That's right, you don't."

"And? You still think free trade and empathy will bring out their inner Boy Scouts?"

"I thought you were going to convince me that you know my father."

"Knew him. And I mourned his untimely passing as did hundreds of others."

Tory's heart flip-flops but she raises her eyebrows in mock surprise. "Well, I regret to inform you that my father's alive and well."

Marshall tips the bottle to replenish her glass. The other hand snakes along the top of the leather seat too near her shoulder.

"You realize," he says, "there were some who thought he was a loose cannon."

She shifts her position away from the encroaching white hand. "I don't know what you're talking about," she says, convincingly, because her head is swimming from the brandy, and besides, *loose cannon* doesn't fit the upstanding, straight-arrow parent who came across in his bi-weekly letters.

"But then headquarters has that old textbook problem, doesn't it? They don't want you thinking outside the box."

Tory takes another small taste of brandy to avoid having to answer. *There's always a missing piece to the puzzle,* her father used to say. It feels like she's driving uphill on gravel trying to reach it: no traction.

"Your father made the mistake here of trying to take out the President," Marshall says, his goatee bobbing up and down like a furry tongue.

"That's quite a stretch." She remembers her dad's advice: *Picture all possible outcomes. Plan for everything, even your accidents.* He'd never have conceived a high-risk op like that.

"Security police picked up the would-be assassin he hired, one of those loony refugees from the south, they convinced the guy to name names, then they came after your dad."

Tory's ears buzz. The crazy story, the brandy, maybe both? The shaky disorientation of that morning threatens to swamp her again: that feeling, so unfamiliar, that she is out of her depth. All those scripted rendez-vous in dark corners of restaurants back in Virginia, those verbal duels with flabby, retired case officers getting paid to masquerade as important targets—they were nothing like this. Adam Marshall's absolute self-assurance, his claims to have known her father, his wandering hands, the heavy smell she inhales with every breath—it takes her whole concentration just to fight through all that.

"Is this some kind of absurd joke?" she asks.

"How do you mean?"

"That story. I don't know where you got it."

Marshall laughs and puts his hand over hers.

She jerks hers into her lap. "It has nothing to do with my father."

"You're right. He was too smart a guy. But basically that's the gist of what his own people tried to put out there." He traces her nose with his finger and pronounces it, "Perfect."

She snaps her head away and pushes aside her glass. The stuff was going down too easy. "Sorry. My dad's still alive and well in Wisconsin." She has a little difficulty controlling her tongue. *No more brandy*, she decides. "He owns a chain of hardware stores and repairs antique clocks in his spare time." She makes a move to slide off the bench but her spine gives up. Her brain fights off the possibility that there is more than just brandy in that glass, that she's fallen for the oldest trick in the book.

"You're as creative as you are beautiful," Marshall says.

"I didn't make that up," she says, which is certainly true. She didn't write her own cover story.

Marshall leans toward her. "Pretty clearly, your old man was selling something the Agency didn't want to buy." She can feel his breath on her eyelids. "You *are* beautiful, you know. In a Wisconsin sort of way, of course."

She straightens her posture, and musters every ounce of will to turn on the seat to face him. In the dim light his eyes seem to glow.

"Pretty clearly your old man had enemies," Marshall goes on.

She shivers. "My old man was president of Kiwanis."

"Inside the Agency." His hands clasp her shoulders, he is pulling her closer—too close to that cologne—it's making her faint.

"No." She whips free and scoots backwards on the seat.

"Think about it. The guys with hammers, who don't want to hear about anything that isn't a nail? They make up their minds an innocent pharmaceutical factory's producing nerve gas so they can bomb the hell out of it."

Nothing is making sense. "You clearly . . . do not know . . . my father," she slurs.

"How long have you been with the Agency?" he asks.

She wrenches away. The palm trees are spinning.

Marshall keeps talking. "Long enough to know how it works, right? Tyler Pierce was not toeing the party line."

It feels like she's wearing a mask and the eye-holes are shrinking. She thinks she hears Maud, whose face is looming right into hers. *Personal needs*, Maud says, shaking a finger. *I told you so.*

20

13 September. Fairfax, Virginia. 1230 hours.

Admiral Johnny Falco, his wife Francesca, and their old friend Maud Olson sip iced tea on the wide deck overlooking the garden, where pink crepe myrtle blossoms droop like graceful hands. It's a perfect Indian summer day.

Slim and elegant in jeans, Francesca has the high cheekbones, flawless skin, and dark, expressive eyes of a fashion model. Her trademark red fingernails flash as she pours Maud more tea. "God, I can't believe how long it's been since we all went to the Vienna Inn to celebrate my premature retirement from the Agency," she says. "Remember, Maud? You and me, Tyler and Gordon."

"*You* celebrated, *we* mourned," says the monochromatic Maud in her safe grey linen shirt and slacks. "We all had a lot to learn."

"Damn straight," says Johnny, the guy who'd turned Francesca way back when—from junior operative to old-fashioned wife and mother. "Just because Frannie could take down a guy twice her size in hand-to-hand, she thought she was invulnerable."

"Reminds me of Ty," Maud says. "And Victoria's the same way. Now she's finagled this tour in Sudan."

The bug-zappers planted at the outside corners of the deck hiss with another victim.

"I can't figure that one." Johnny takes off his cap marked GRANDAD #1 and scratches his white crew cut. "And Gordon still has nothing to say?"

"Unless you count *mind your own business*. Since he doesn't try to sec-ond-guess Intelligence, he suggests I should keep my nose out of Clandestine Service."

In white slacks and perfectly tucked button-down, Johnny stares beyond his swimming pool into the woods that edge his safe, meticulously groomed half-acre. "This administration plays everything so damn close to the vest. Wheels within wheels, need-to-know lists, until you don't have a clue who you can trust or what's really going on."

"And Victoria's assignment is the least of it."

"Maud, what's wrong?" Francesca asks. Her friend's stiff upper lip is quivering. "You know you can trust us."

A private and self-sufficient soul, Maud can't bring herself to blurt her encounter with the Secret Service the night before or this morning's confrontation with Paul—not until she's figured out how these incidents fit into the messy picture her life has become. "Let's just call it a major slow-down in the feeds from Sudan. Particularly frustrating, because of Victoria's assignment, naturally, and my wish to keep close tabs on her. On top of that, someone over on Gordon's side of the house seems to be playing games with an important file on the country. On top of that there's China. You've seen the B.S. in the press lately."

"Now, Maud, no two people are going to see eye to eye on China," Johnny says.

"Well, I'm not getting all the intel coming in. A couple of times last week when I asked for some original docs, they were forwarded with certain sections blacked out. As if I were a junior analyst!" Maud stops. "I'm sorry, I'm whining. It's nothing. Bureaucratic inefficiency. It gets to you sometimes."

The three sit in a silence broken by the sizzle of hapless insects against the bug zapper.

"That doesn't sound like inefficiency," Johnny says finally.

"The guys still can't accept that you're a powerful woman," Francesca says with disgust.

"That's the truth, certainly, and for twenty-four hours, I've been seething inside, snapping at everyone, digging in for another battle. Then this morning it dawned on me: what if that's what I'm supposed to do, get all wrapped up in my own difficulties?" says Maud.

Francesca and Johnny exchange a glance. "We're not following," Francesca says.

"I mean, why all these systems breakdowns now? Maybe they have nothing to do with an assault on *my* career. Maybe I *am* personalizing—Gordon called it that. I hate to even say it, but now I've got this sinking feeling that all the random glitches are connected to the fact that Tyler's daughter is wandering around on her own in one of the most lawless spots on the planet."

"And someone wants your potential for intervention effectively neutralized," says Johnny.

Maud nods with a shrug. "Intervention, *prevention*, basically out of the picture. Here's another one. The missing file I just mentioned? Today it flew back home to roost, minus one section."

"Which file exactly?" asks Johnny.

"Which section?" Francesca asks at the same time.

"It's the earliest intel we picked up on the Sudanese National Identity Movement. Back when we were slipping military equipment and A-team support to the South. It was mostly about how the NIM purported to seek a peaceful way for the country's many divisions to come together and share in its wealth. Their concept was hatched in Khartoum at the University, so you can imagine—all idealistic theory, no concrete plan."

"How do you know there's a section missing?" Francesca asks.

Maud hesitates.

"That's all right, I can leave," offers Francesca.

"Don't be silly," Maud says. "It's lowest level clearance. The missing section concerned that woman."

"What woman?" Francesca asks, then immediately adds, "Oh, that woman."

"When she began to . . . appear in Ty's reports, naturally I thought it wise to check her out, see what he was dealing with."

"And?" asks Francesca.

"The pages I read eight years ago are no longer in the file."

"They must have been juicy," Francesca says.

"What I remember was all over the place: she'd been a slave in the household of the Finance Minister, not to mention the Amazon who brought the NIM down to earth and built its private army. Then there was evidence that she was sleeping with Americans, a la Mata Hari, and the mother of an illegitimate child she mysteriously did away with."

"Sleeping with Americans? But that was all *before* Tyler, wasn't it?" asks Francesca.

"Please," Maud says. "The chronology *is* muddled, but we don't *know* that about Ty."

"Of course not," Francesca says.

"The point is, complete file or not, *she* is quite a customer. No thanks to my Africa team, but I'm currently picking up chatter about some sort of rally she's organizing outside Khartoum. That's got to be like waving a red flag in front of the powers that be."

Johnny seems to wake from a reverie. "No ID on any of her American . . . connections?"

"Rumor. Everything from mercenaries to vagabonds, take your pick. It took a while for her to start registering on our radar."

"Wheels within wheels," Johnny says. "But I want you to relax about Victoria. I told you there's someone very good in place who can look out for her."

"You mean John Doe?" Maud asks.

"You know I can't say who he is," Johnny says. "But we hit the jackpot in that regard: a topnotch kid I met when I was Commandant at the Naval Academy. He's on undercover assignment now with the Counterterrorism Group."

"A kid?"

"Well, we older-but-wiser types are in short supply."

21

13 September. Khartoum, Sudan. 2230 hours.

The man who calls himself Bartholomew Wilkins ditches the Jeep a block from the Hilton, tucks his old Beretta into his waistband, and approaches on foot. It pisses him off that a guy like Marshall can work so fast—it must be the smell of money he gives off, the aura of power or something. Why are women suckered by that crap?

Damned if the Mercedes isn't parked right on top of the hotel entrance with the chauffeur inside. Wilkins considers striding right past him and through the well-lit doorway like a hotel guest, but the prospect of being caught in the middle between two unknown entities holds him back.

Figuring there must be a service door somewhere, he heads around the side parking lot toward the back of the building. The delivery doors are locked. He bangs on one until his knuckles sting. The sound is feeble, the darkness huge. He sprints around the rest of the building, arriving back where he started, sweaty, heart pounding more with anger than anything else. Drag women into the picture and things get too damn complicated.

He decides to approach the chauffeur and play it straight. *I know who you are, here's who I am, now where's that woman I escorted to the President's reception?*

He's thirty feet from the car when the front door opens and the chauffeur unfolds out of the front seat. He is body-guard big. Wilkins ducks behind the skinny trunk of a palm. Lucky for him the guy is double-timing it into the hotel and doesn't look around.

Wilkins takes a couple deep breaths then eases in after him. Too much light in the lobby relative to the adjacent café. Not good. Step into that doorway and he's a framed target. From his angle he can't see what's going on, but he's in the sight line of the server standing behind the bar: someone he's never seen there before, surprisingly an Asian woman, with an even more surprising head of platinum-blond hair. He waves his arms like semaphores until she looks up. She gets the idea and drifts out to him.

"I could use some help." He pantomimes the request as best he can.

Her almond eyes take him in unblinking. "I speak good English."

"OK." He pulls out his wallet and produces 8000 dinars, about $20.00. She shakes her head and pushes it away. "*She* could use some help."

Wilkins gives the server a quick appraising look then pulls a transmitter the size of a book of matches from another pocket. "Think you can put this in your apron and go back to your job?"

"Slice of cake," she says.

"Um, right. I'll be here. If you can stand close to those guests, it's better."

She moves closer and turns a coy gaze up to his. "Like this?"

"Do what you can."

"Sure thing," she says with a shrug.

He fits in the earbud and retreats to a shadowy corner of the lobby, beside a palm tree in a planter. The fronds hang in his face.

A minute later he hears the server's lilting voice. "Is the lady unwell?"

A thin voice replies, "The lady got herself a little overextended, that's all."

"Then you will need assistance?"

"Thanks, but we'll take care of it." Silence, then the same voice hisses, "So what took you so long? Never mind. Give me a hand."

Then the server makes a suggestion. "Perhaps the lady would benefit from strong coffee?" It's followed by a dainty scream, then a roar that jangles Wilkins' eardrum.

"What the hell do you think you're doing?" screams Marshall.

The micro-receiver picks up the server weeping apologies. Marshall's tone changes from enraged to soothing. "No use crying over spilled coffee, young lady. I have plenty of shirts. Now, why don't you tell me where you're staying, and I'll have a little something sent over to prove no hard feelings. Quite the contrary."

"Mr. Marshall, with all due respect, I suggest we call it a night." Must be the bodyguard.

"What are you talking about?" Marshall's voice strains with the effort of not-yelling.

"Given the circumstances, sir."

"I *make* circumstances."

"Not entirely, sir."

"Who are you all of a sudden, Mr. Moral Minority?"

"I don't mean it like that, Mr. Marshall. You've got important work to do and limited time to do it." The chauffeur pauses. "To be sensible, we should just help this lady up to her bed."

"My friend here is such a Puritan. Do you know what that word means, Puritan?" asks Marshall's silky voice. "Well, that's good news. I'll have to look you up the next time I'm in town. It really has been an unexpected pleasure." Marshall's voice gets low and clipped. "I'll thank you, Arthur, to let me decide when the night is over. I really don't need a lot of melodramatic garbage right now."

"That was exactly my point, Mr. Marshall."

A long pause. "I *am* a little tired myself."

"You've had a very long day, Mr. Marshall."

"I'd appreciate it if you would discretely dispose of poor Miss Clark here. I'll wait in the car."

"Sounds like a plan, sir."

Marshall must be rifling through Ronnie's stuff because there's a long silence before he says, "It's got to be in here somewhere. Christ, their handbags are as muddled as their brains." More silence, then, "What do you know—an honest-to-god, old-fashioned *key*!"

Wilkins has vaulted from the sofa, and disappeared into the EXIT-marked stairwell. He tears up four flights, three steps at a time. He cracks the door onto the hallway and waits for Veronica Clark to appear, draped over the chauffeur's shoulder like a duffel bag, while the server from the café fiddles with the key to her room. The server pushes the door open and the man and his burden disappear inside.

Soon the man comes out again. He hands the server a folded wad of dinars as they step into the elevator, and are gone.

22

13 September. McLean, Virginia. 1330 hours.

Maud and her secretary are exactly the same age, but Isabelle has three grown children who have flown the nest, so her habit of mothering has shifted to taking care of Maud. The downside: although Isabelle complains that her husband snores, has the social skills of a twelve-year-old, and spends his free time on the golf course, she's convinced Maud needs a man in her life, and never tires of trying to introduce her boss to *friends of the hubby's*. The upside: Isabelle can be counted on to do anything to safeguard Maud's welfare and promote the Directorate of Intelligence.

"How would you like to go for a little walk?" Maud asks her now.

Isabelle knows what that means. Audio surveillance is impossible in the public corridors, which makes them the best place for Maud to tap into the juicy Agency grapevine via Isabelle.

"So what do you want to know?" Isabelle asks, as the two women click toward the main lobby, eyes focused forward.

"I'm not exactly sure yet."

Isabelle winks. "Time for me to pull out the cloak and dagger."

"This assignment is off the record, off the clock, and if you get caught, I have to disavow any knowledge of your activity."

"You're telling me the mission's impossible?"

"I hope not," Maud says, suddenly serious. "Lives may depend on it."

Isabelle squares her shoulders. "It's Tremaine, isn't it?"

"I don't know."

"Well, he *is* pretty full of himself. You know, with my kids, I always believed in structure, setting limits, even if it meant—"

"I think we have more than a management problem."

"He's very ambitious," Isabelle offers.

"I like ambition," Maud says. "As long as it's rooted in loyalty."

Isabelle nods. They are standing now in front of Memorial Wall. Maud knows exactly which tiny star represents the rise and fall of Tyler Pierce. "Why don't you have a chat with the secretary in his section, get a sense of his telephone activity, any appointments or meetings outside the DI, see what this guy's been up to. Because he sure as hell hasn't been feeding information to me."

23

14 September. Khartoum, Sudan. 0100 hours.

When Wilkins hits the lobby, the server is waiting for him.

"Will you be searching for something?" She extracts his transmitter from the breast pocket of her jacket and waves it in his face.

"You mean besides a stiff drink?"

"Gin or scotch whiskey?"

"Scotch would be fantastic."

She thrusts a shoulder in his direction. "And do you care for something to chase your scotch whiskey?" Her lower lip protrudes in a pout.

Wilkins runs a hand through his damp hair and shrugs. "Don't tempt me."

"My grandmother always said to strike while the fire is hot. She was tough lady. Saved my life when I was just born. My parents wanted boy." She plunks a glass on the counter, but when he tries to pay her she waves it away.

"Here's to your grandmother, then."

"How about this wild and crazy 'do? If they even notice there is person underneath it, they assume she is bimbo." She presses his transmitter into his palm. "I like you."

"That is the impression I'm getting," he says. "You're new in the Capital?"

"I arrive one week ago. However, I quickly jump into hot pots—is that how you say it?"

"Why not?"

"Yes, I have been about."

"I think you mean *around*. You have experience."

"I have much experience."

"Interesting."

"You want to party on down?"

The young man shakes his head. "Strictly business, for now."

"Just checking. I too am strictly business. Now this guy with pointed beard, he want to mix business—"

"What do you know about him?"

"Some in my government care for him. I do not."

"How do you know that, about your government?"

"I figure things out."

"Well, you don't have to waste any brain power on me. I'm Bart Wilkins, supply officer, U.S. Embassy."

"I am called Meiying, surname Liu. Meiying means beautiful flower. My grandmother pick out according to Zodiac."

"Very nice. Meiying. I have several good friends among your countrymen here."

"I finish my job in two hours."

"You know, I better catch some sleep if I'm going play chauffeur tomorrow for that one." He jerks his head upward to indicate Ronnie.

"How about I give you a rain chip?"

"Uh. Sounds good."

"I return in the morning. For the whole day."

"I look forward to seeing you then."

If, in the last two hours he'd looked backward at the right moment, the man who calls himself Wilkins might have glimpsed a small wiry figure in a long, striped robe and skullcap shadowing his every move.

24

---

14 September. Khartoum, Sudan. 0800 hours.

Sunlight slices her eyes. Her head feels like a cracked melon, and a foul taste coats her mouth. She doesn't know where she is, then she does. She remembers a goatee, skin like putty, a suffocating odor of spice. *Adam Marshall, the bastard.* She let herself be tricked. Maybe drugged. All that talk about knowing her father disarmed her. She tries to pick her way back through the fog of the night before. Did the man mention her father by name? How could he have? If he knew her father, then he knew her!

It all screams failure: she's ruined everything. Twenty-four hours in-country and her cover already blown. Her whole life she's driven herself to live up to her father's legend, and now in one night she has blown it in the worst way! Feeling hollow and worthless, she heaves herself over to face the wall. As she does, she hears the sound of ripping cloth. The skirt she wore to the reception is twisted around her legs. She still has on her microfiber panties.

A quick inner scan of her fully-clothed body deflects the torrent of self-condemnation. She's OK. Untouched. Then how did she get up to her room and into her bed? She tries to review the whole evening from the café on, but keeps getting bogged down in vague half-memories. Could she chalk it all up to her own stupidity, drinking more than she could handle in her jet-lagged state, and passing out? Could Adam Marshall even have taken care of her?

She knows what she should do: contact her branch chief in Cairo, inform him that her identity may have been compromised. But then what? Even if it hasn't, she gets yanked home to Headquarters like a naughty kid. Stuck in a box for at least one tour, and all the information this parched country hides will be lost to her forever. Not an option.

She needs to get back on the horse that threw her, get in touch with Marshall. He might be a good guy. In fact he may be the reliable, higher-level person her training's taught her to identify as a source for the big picture.

She staggers up from the bed, digs her satellite phone out of her purse, and calls the number Wilkins punched into its memory the day before.

"Now what?" he says when he answers.

"Good morning to you too!"

"The way you dropped out of the proceedings last night, it could only mean trouble."

"Nothing happened, OK?" She makes herself pace back and forth, thinking the cool tile floor on bare feet might clear her head.

"Then why are you calling me?"

"Do you *know* the man who drove me back here?"

"Wouldn't that be your department?"

"Chill out. I want to contact Adam Marshall."

"Sorry. Can't help you."

"I don't believe there isn't someone over there who knows where he's staying."

"He's got a mini-mansion in Riyadh. That doesn't mean he's ever in it. You must know he's CEO of the Mephisto Group? One of the richest men on the planet. Maybe *the* most secretive."

Her attention is caught by a small white card on the bureau, anchored by the handle of her brush. "Yeah?"

"He's in and out of a lot of places," Wilkins goes on. "On the lookout for investment opportunities. Read, chances to feed on third-world blood and sweat. Ever heard of vulture funds? Marshall's take: You buy up the debt of a distressed country at a big discount. Then you go after the full amount yourself. Picture repo tactics on a giant scale. And that's just one twig on his money tree."

The card is blank except for twelve embossed numbers. "Well, personal opinions aside, I've got a job to do," Tory says, clicking off. It irritates her to have to keep prying stuff out of Wilkins. And with all the homework she did on this place, why didn't she come across anything that flagged Adam Marshall? The man knows how to cover his tracks.

She makes a mental note to ask Maud about that, calls down for some coffee, then wrestles off her dress and heads for the bathroom. She would have liked a hot, bracing shower before she tries the number on the card, but the water that trickles over her in the black marble stall is just as lukewarm and rust-tinged as it was the afternoon before, smelling faintly like blood.

She yanks a blouse and blue cord skirt out of her open suitcase. When she reaches into her pack for the city maps Wilkins gave her, a hardback guidebook to north Africa tumbles out. She pries open the back cover to find something she's been waiting for—her Glock 19. *How in the world did it get in her room?* she wonders, enjoying for a moment the heft of it against her palm, then checking the clip. It's loaded. She hears a tap-tap and a soft voice singing, "Room service."

She shoves the gun back into the book, the book into her suitcase, throws on the skirt and blouse, then opens the door to find a white linen suit encasing Bart Wilkins.

25

"May I enter?" Wilkins asks, balancing a small tray on the long fingers of one hand, a tiny cup and saucer upon it.

"Give me a break," Tory groans, taking a step back.

"Your shirt," he says, taking a step forward.

She has matched the buttons to the wrong holes. She turns away from him to fix the problem. "How did you get here so fast?"

"I was in the area anyway."

She turns back to find him so close that the tray is right next to her hand. She picks up the little cup, pinky and ring finger curved ridiculously, and takes a slug of the bitter, grainy drink. It goes down all wrong and triggers a coughing fit.

While she tries to get a grip, Wilkins decides to move furniture. He drags a rattan chair under the ceiling light and removes his wingtips. Then he climbs onto the cushion and teeters there, all skinny six feet of him, as he fiddles with the fixture.

"What's the matter," Tory half-gasps.

He explores the fixture he's removed. "Eureka!" he exclaims, then loses his balance, one leg flying out, arms swimming to regain it. "Bug," he says, holding up something the size of a pebble between thumb and finger. He reattaches the fixture and steps down. "May I?" he cocks his head toward the bathroom.

"Whatever," says Tory. She hears the departing micro-transmitter plunk into the toilet, followed by a flush and Wilkins' reappearance.

"So whom do you think planted it?" she asks.

"Actually, I think the nominative case is correct in this instance."

"What?"

"Who. Who planted it?"

She glares at him.

"It could have been anyone. I could have done it myself."

"Did you?"

"Come on, Ronnie. Whose side do you think I'm on?"

"I'm beginning to wonder. I don't like being stalked."

Wilkins shrugs. "The bug does explain, maybe, why you're billeted here instead of in the compound. Well, not explain, per se, but there is a certain consistency."

"What are you talking about?"

"Your special treatment."

"Are you envious?"

"Not really. Just intrigued. And you have a meeting already, this afternoon. With the First Vice President. Yes?"

"Look, I don't need a handler. You said call if I wanted something, right? Well, I did, want something, and I called. But now I don't, so you can go."

"How about a ride to the Ministry of State?"

"How about I walk and you leave me alone?"

"It's over a mile."

"I ran the Marine Corps marathon last year."

"If you insist. But on one condition," Wilkins says.

"Are you kidding? Who are you to be laying down—"

"Promise me you'll stay away from Adam Marshall."

She stares out the window. From her vantage, a wide island blocks the spot where the Blue and White Niles join. "What are you, being a jealous male or something?"

"Don't flatter yourself."

The rough edge to his voice snaps her gaze back to him.

"Sorry to be so blunt," he says more amiably, adding a bow. "A reflex stemming directly from the fact that if Veronica Clark gets herself in trouble, the accountability buck stops right here." He points at the knot in his silly tie.

"If all we worried about was getting into trouble, we might never get at the truth of this sad country."

"Exactly what truth do you think you're going to learn from this Marshall guy?"

"How about something we don't already know?"

"Well, that really narrows it."

"I'm not going to be one of those people with a hammer who can only see nails." *Where in the world did that come from?*

"Meaning?"

"For one thing, he's got a pretty informed take on the Chinese."

"He ought to. He's in bed with them."

That surprises her after the way Marshall bad-mouthed them last night. "What do you mean?"

"The Mephisto Group owns Beijing Petrol."

"I'm sorry, but the Chinese government owns Beijing Petrol."

"That's what you already know. I'm trying to tell you something you obviously don't."

She stares at this man in his socks and freshly pressed suit, this supply clerk acting like he's higher up on the learning curve. Is he bluffing? She hands him his shoes. "I'm sure the Mephisto Group invests in a lot of different things."

"And that makes Marshall god."

"I didn't say anything about god."

"Vice god? Hey, I like th—"

"He's an all right guy, OK? Look, Wilkins, I was very stupid last night. I had a little too much to drink. Adam could have taken advantage of me, but he didn't."

"First name basis, huh?"

"Don't go there. He found my room key then got me up here to my bed, tucked in the covers, everything."

"How do you know? You were out cold!"

"Who told you that?"

"An educated guess," Wilkins says.

26

A gust of wind uncoils along the street. The churned up sand scratches Arthur's eyes. Sheltered by an abandoned kiosk, he curses to himself and puts the cap back on his telephoto lens. A coating of dust turns his dark arms the tan of his loose fitting shirt and khaki pants. He pulls out a pack of playing cards and puts his nervous energy into shuffling them, keeping his eyes on two figures waiting out the storm in a doorway across the street: a teen-aged girl and her older escort. A bump near the waist of the escort's loose dashiki suggests a weapon.

What the hell does the Boss want with these photos anyway? Arthur squints to make sure his subjects are staying put. *No*, he decides. *I don't want to know.* The stuff he can't help remembering is bad enough.

The worst was a while back—it feels like last week, the way it still haunts him. He delivered the Boss to the penthouse with his latest. Sharp lady, they always are, and smart—this one was a law student at Columbia.

Arthur never knows how the Boss meets these ladies—as chauffeur, he's usually not in on the kick-off. By the time his services are called for, the goal line's in range. But it was enough to make you disrespect the whole sex, that even the smart ones fall all over themselves to hook up with a super-rich, Central Park sleazebag.

Arthur dropped this one off under the awning of the apartment house, and the next time he saw her, she was dead.

He'd been marking time in the Mercedes shuffling cards, waiting to take her back uptown, when the call surprised him. The memory makes his stomach clench still: all that white furniture trimmed with gold, a white tufted headboard, white satin spread—the enormous bed unopened, barely wrinkled—in the middle of it, the woman lying face up, nothing on, the eyes and mouth horrified open, no mark of violence on the pale flesh, which was already turning grey.

Above the bed, a big oil painting, almost like a photograph, showed another woman stretched out naked on one of those old-fashioned beds. She had healthy pink skin and a very different expression on her smiling face.

Marshall was sitting on the edge of the bed in a white silk robe, staring across the room like he was looking at someone, but no one was there.

"We have a problem, Arthur."

He wanted to shake that white man until his head snapped, yelling, *What do you mean* we? *I had nothing to do with this.* Instead he closed the woman's eyes and forced the mouth shut. "What do you wish for me to do, Mr. Marshall?"

"Get rid of her. Wrap her in the sheet, take her away." The bastard had no common sense.

Pretending it was one of those plastic dummies they have in stores, Arthur lifted the body and set it on a small carpet with flowers all over. He rolled the rug around it, then, as if the whole thing weighed nothing, lifted it onto his shoulder, and left.

Maybe he was unlucky that night. If he'd run into someone in the service elevator or the underground garage, if he'd been caught, made to come clean, tell the truth, maybe he'd be a free man today.

But no, he'd pulled it off—driven around Manhattan with a fucking corpse in his trunk, till common sense told him to take her out to the country, across the Tappan Zee to Route 624, due north into Connecticut for a half hour, where he found a lonely two-lane road that ran through some woods. There above a ravine that sloped down to a creek, he let the carpet unroll and deposit its stiffened cargo.

When he thinks back to that night, though, something doesn't make sense. The body sank into the piled leaves and branches, but it wasn't exactly buried. Arthur figured someone was going to find it, someone would report the woman missing, there would be a search, and didn't police searches always check ravines? There'd be some sort of media noise, the other shoe would have to drop. But it never did.

In Khartoum, now, the wind is letting up, and the girl resumes her walking.

Through his lens Arthur picks up her face. Her skin is lighter than his, a milky shade of brown. The air is still murky, but her large eyes, gold like a cat's, look wise, even when she is laughing at something her escort says. When Arthur zooms in more, the haze melts and he catches a super-white mark on her front tooth. The Boss complained the last time the close-ups weren't close enough. Arthur zooms in even further. *Take that*, he thinks, *and that*, as he snaps six shots of her smiling mouth, centered on that tooth, with its spot, beckoning like a star.

27

The President, a.k.a. Generalissimo would rather stare down an enemy than meet the eyes of a neutral acquaintance or friend. When he spends the night with his wife, he orders her to turn her face to one side before he heaves his bulk onto her, then fixes his gaze on her jangling earring until he is done. And in the chamber where he receives visitors, the two massive, white brocade chairs are usually arranged side by side. Unless the visitor is Adam Marshall.

While the President disdains the subtleties of politics and mistrusts politicians, Adam Marshall is a businessman, and the gap between ruthless businessman and cold-blooded warrior is not very wide. Even among his peers, Marshall is different. He speaks fluent Arabic, for one thing, and when he came to Sudan sixteen years ago, it wasn't to get his hands on oil, but to offer first-rate arms and encouragement to the President's fledgling regime. Thus for this meeting with Marshall, the two chairs have been turned at an angle, to facilitate the exchange of a glance now and then, while still leaving it easy enough to look away.

They are alone except for the guards flanking the doorway. Marshall has raised his glass of tea to propose a toast. "As ever, to the future of Sudan," he says, pale and compact in his well-pressed dark suit. "And may the success of our partnership continue."

The burly President raises his glass in response. His brown uniform has grown tight in the armpits, and the huge epaulettes look like slabs of decorated gingerbread. Wielding absolute power over an oil-rich country, he has narrowed his repertory of expressions to two—arrogance and boredom. "To success," he says, combining them.

Both men set down their glasses without drinking.

"So, friend Adam," the President says. "I hear the Americans have added a new person to their Embassy to spy on me. A girl, and pretty."

"Would you like to be introduced?" Marshall's grin displays bleached white teeth.

"Should I?"

"Not worth your time."

"Why do they do this now?"

"Why not?"

"Who is she?" the President barks.

"A nobody," says Marshall. "A novice, full of ignorant enthusiasm."

"Sometimes innocent eyes are seeing things the sleepy veterans miss."

"More often innocent eyes don't know what to make of anything. They must turn to others to be told what it is they see."

"Innocence makes big messes."

"Trust me," Marshall says. "She'll be fine."

"She must be watched," growls the President. "As you all must be."

Marshall pulls a leather case from his breast pocket and removes one of his embossed cards, stamped with the simple black shape of a bird, wings spread, crested head showing the beak of a raptor. "We've got more important things to discuss right now," he says, handing it over. "This is it: the container your men should watch for. This bird has been clearly stamped on each end."

"Very good. This is *saqr-et-tair*."

"Whatever you say."

"I say it is our Hunter-bird. From the Sudanese coat-of-arms."

"Our Chinese friends are very clever then. Now the container should have been loaded in the middle of the bottom layer, to discourage spot checks. So it'll be among the last coming off."

"The trucks are conveyed to Port Sudan one week ago," the President says, all at once respectful. "Twelve of them to transport the rice to the army base here. Where it will be dispensed to those who deserve it." He glances at his friend out of the corner of his eye, to see if he gets the joke. The President's old army buddies have expensive tastes they could never satisfy without supplementing their soldier's pay when chances present.

"Your hunter-bird is going to be considerably heavier," Marshall continues, all business. "You don't want anyone handling it except your men."

"Adam," chides the President, his black eyes twinkling, "are they not all my men?"

"You know what I mean."

"For that, there is a flat-bed. My men transport the considerable heavy container to a military garrison in the desert outside Port Sudan. There we have airport and hangar where two aircraft are waiting, more courtesy of our clever Chinese friends."

Marshall sits back in his chair and lets his gaze brush the President's. "Why two?"

The President makes a fist the size of a small ham and pounds his other hand with it. "Two will remind stupid, crazy people who is in charge."

"Fine." Marshall's lower jaw slides forward as he processes the information. "Sounds like everything's on track," he says, breaking the lengthening pause. "There'll be a lot of hand-wringing and wrist-slapping, but who's going to mount any serious retaliation? The African Union's got no balls. Neither does the U.N. And the U.S. is stuck up to the crotch in the Middle East and Afghanistan." He has almost convinced himself. "Two planes: why not? Two chances to have the Arab world bow down at your Honor's feet are better than—"

"The first plane is for what you call a test-run."

"A test-run would not be wise, Mr. President. The element of surprise is absolutely crucial to the operation. As it is, getting one pilot past anti-aircraft is not one hundred per cent guaranteed."

"Then this test-run becomes the real thing. It will show the world what we can do. Much power comes from the future threat."

"Where do you have in mind?"

"Right here."

"I really don't think it would be wise to deploy chemical agent in your own city," Marshall advises the President, barely able to keep the conde-scension out of his tone. This President was an orphan. He spent his boy-hood begging on the streets of the Capital until he joined the army.

"We will deploy it 125 kilometers north of here, near Karima," announces the President.

"What's near Karima?"

"A mountain of stone and endless sand. And someone you will never see long enough to get your hands on," says the President.

"With all due respect, my friend, what are you talking about?"

"That woman."

"What woman?" Marshall asks automatically, but as soon as he's asked, he knows. Spots of pink rise along his pallid cheekbones. "Oh, for god's sake. I thought that one was, I don't know . . . hasn't she been out of the picture for some time now?"

"She is very good at being out of the picture and in the picture both at once."

"But surely she's no threat to Your Honor."

"She gives the people hope. She teaches them to attack my militias. We raid her gatherings, we take the traitors into custody, men, women, we use knives, and other things, to make great discomfort for their bodies, and still they don't talk. The other prisoners see this, but they keep silent as well."

"With all due respect, she seems like very small potatoes," Marshall says.

"What does it mean, small potatoes?"

"It means she and her followers aren't worth the changing of an otherwise brilliant plan, my friend." He sounds condescending again. "It's a waste. I mean you've got a shot at making a big statement with this stuff. Why whisper when you can shout loud and clear?"

"She has more followers than you know. They are on the move from every corner of this land to the mountain called Jebel Barkal."

"So put up road blocks."

"Road blocks where there are no roads? That is not funny, friend Adam. We cannot track all of them, and the size of her camp continues to grow.

We have conventional bombs, of course, thanks to the Chinese, but the destruction of a religious site of such prominence is deemed unwise."

Adam Marshall frowns in obvious displeasure.

The President's hand stabs for emphasis. "I tell you, she is planning something, that woman, a demonstration against our government, some stupid, crazy trick for publicity, we don't know exactly. It will happen soon. And we will be ready."

Marshall clears his throat. "Your honor, my friend, please believe me: the greatest Muslim will be the one who takes on the proudest, most greedy infidels, not he who gets distracted by a half-crazed bitch. Send an army detachment to the mountain, but save the good stuff—"

The President interrupts. "The army is spread thin between the South and Darfur and the militia are slow and inefficient, when compared to your agent, your magic bird of prey."

"This is not good," Marshall mutters.

"You trust me, friend Adam, everything will go very smooth. Because this time there will be no refugees, no women wailing, no children with big, hungry eyes, and no journalists to wire their propaganda all over the world. They will all be silenced." The President ends with a jabbing nod of the head. Then he notices that Marshall's gaze has gone wide. "What are you thinking, friend Adam?"

"Nothing."

"Very good. Then we are moving forward, with the Hunter-bird."

"You know, that thing looks like a vulture to me. Not exactly a symbol of good luck."

The President smiles. "Soon my friend Adam will see different. It will take care of the woman who betrayed us both."

28

The walk to the Ministry of State takes fifteen minutes. The sand-dusted sidewalks are mostly shaded and whatever sweat Tory cracks evaporates instantly into the dry air. She left her weapon behind, locked in her suitcase along with the box of cartridges she discovered in one of her sport socks. But there turns out to be no metal detector at the building, nothing to stop her shuffling up the concrete steps and through the clouded-glass door.

Inside a faint smell of must replaces the monoxide of the street, and it's almost as hot. She has to wake the guard dozing at an old wooden desk. She tells him in English that she has an appointment with First Vice President Kvol. He shrugs. She repeats the statement in Arabic. The man brightens, displaying a number of missing teeth.

"Ah," he lisps in English. "His Honor is not here."

"I believe he is. Could you buzz him or something?" she asks, though she notes the absence on his desk of anything to buzz.

"Buzz?" asks the man.

Tory pulls out her phone. "Do you have a number for him? Telephone, number?"

"Aha!" he says, hopping up from his desk and disappearing down the hall to the left.

On the wall above hangs a giant portrait of the President, frown creases between the bushy brows and mouth flexed in an expression of disdain. It's flanked on one side by the Sudanese flag, on the other, by the Republic's coat of arms, which sports a bird that looks like a cross between the American eagle and a stork.

The guard is back. With a bow and an extended hand, he gets her to follow him down the empty corridor. He opens a door at the end, and she steps into a large, dim office. A mahogany desk sits askew in the center. On one wall, a single mahogany bookcase holds a set of leather-bound volumes and a boom-box. Underfoot, a thick, Chinese carpet with a moss-green field; in the far corner, three chairs covered in moss-green velvet. A small rotating fan barely stirs the smoke-filled air.

Beside an expanse of moss-green draperies that conceal the window, a towering man puffs on a cigarette. His long face is made longer by a grizzled beard. He wears a loose, printed dashiki and trousers, sandals, and a white baseball cap, the visor of which he flips up as he offers her one of the seats. His eyes droop like a bloodhound's.

Taking shallow breaths of the toxic air, Tory perches on one chair, fumbles open her leather case, and extracts her clipboard. Every sixty seconds or so, the fan swings her way, teasing her with a flutter of relief. She has almost gone through the water in her bottle, and her mouth is dry as styrofoam, but she thanks him for being willing to speak to her so soon after his return from the south.

"I have been in the city for many days now, I believe."

"Oh, I was under the impression that you—"

"Under the impression, yes," he interrupts. "An interesting phrase. In my country one finds it wiser to create many different impressions in the conduct of ones business. This requires frequent changes of plans." He looks down his long, flat nose at her and offers a bemused smile. "I believe there is another American expression, something about steering under the radar?"

"Close," Tory says. "And why exactly is that important?"

"I see you are ready to be my student, with your pen held so eagerly."

"It's important that I do justice to your point of view, Mr. Vice President."

"Is it?" Again the wry look.

"If it bothers you, I mean if you'd rather speak off the record—that's an American expression meaning . . . Why are you laughing at me?" she asks, because he is making no attempt to suppress his mirth.

"I beg your pardon, but I am not laughing at you but at them."

"Them?"

"My friends in the Ministry of Intelligence—can you not feel their conscientious presence in the room? Sucking every one of our words, off the record or on, into their hungry little machines. They are truly the best in the world."

"Well, I don't know about that," Tory says.

"Come, come. They haven't anyone to answer to. Except our venerable leader." Vice President Kvol lifts the drapery away from the window, and cocks his head to look out. "You are here at his indulgence."

"Actually, I am here because my country ordered me. To gather information about your country's economic—"

"Tell your country to check the Internet."

"Of course we have other more sophisticated tools, Mr. Vice President," Tory says. "My perspective is only one of many to be compiled into the official report which is necessary if we are to properly evaluate the readiness of your country to enter the free world community without sanctions."

The Vice President slaps the drape back against the wall and begins pacing the carpet. "After which your country can join with a clear conscience every other country that has descended on Sudan greedy for our oil. Tell me, how do you plan to eject the Chinese?"

Her cover role, which seemed so logical on paper, is careening around the office like a deflating balloon. "Your country is comfortable then with its current level of dependence on China?"

The Vice President shrugs. "We have no choice but to be extremely dependent on someone."

"Allow me to point out that if my country were to *descend* on Sudan, as you put it, we would encourage your government to use oil revenues to improve quality of life at the grass roots—"

"Hah! Grass is very difficult to grow in the desert."

"I am planning to make a trip to Juba, if you—"

"It is a mistake to plan," the Vice President says, shaking a finger.

"Well, at some point my job will require me to visit the south, and if you could kindly recommend a friend of yours whom I might contact—"

"Most of my friends are dead."

"I'm sorry."

"Why? Your country does not care."

"But I do." The words surprise her and bring the Vice President's pacing to a halt. She isn't even sure they are true. "I suspect there's something special in your country, something the Internet has missed." More words rising without forethought from who knows where? "Can you tell me anything about the National Identity Movement?"

There is a long silence. The Vice President lights another cigarette.

She plunges ahead. "Does it still exist?"

"Why are you asking me?"

"Every piece of data is important for an accurate picture, of course. A friend of mine passed through your country in the late nineties. I believe he had some dealings with that group, whatever it was."

"Why don't you arrange to interview him then?"

"He is forever unavailable." Uttered in this stuffy office to this stubborn man, the fact feels devastating. "But he did tell me that the NIM held great hope for your country."

The Vice President studies her for a long moment, then his voice becomes barely audible. "In my country to the south, the oil wells have turned the water to poison. Villagers and livestock drink the water and die. It is hopeless."

"No, it's not." Her emotion surprises her. As if a door opened, marked *Private.* She backs off, refocuses on the public picture. "What I mean is, the United States would like to see Sudan develop economically and grow." That was safe to say. "It is in everyone's interest—stability in Sudan would help stabilize the whole—"

"Stability is not in *everyone*'s interest."

"It's difficult for me to proceed if you keep interrupting."

"Then you wish to fire me from the job of teacher?"

"My personal wishes are not on the table, Mr. Vice President. My country must determine, number one, that you are no longer friendly with terrorists."

Bemusement returns to his face. "I assume you are referring to *foreign* terrorists?"

"*Foreign* terrorists. And, number two, that the Peace Accord will be honored. The civil war will be checked."

"Ah yes, civil war, our national dance. One part is performed by the armed militias on camels, or the airplanes with bombs. The other part, by the villagers, fleeing on foot."

"Then in your perception, hostilities are not winding down?" Tory goes on.

"They are winding down in the south because there are fewer and fewer villages to attack."

"Is stability in *your* interest, Mr. Vice President?"

"My interest is not on the table, as you say."

"Is it in *your* interest to be so evasive?"

A soft buzz sends the Vice President's hand into his pants pocket to produce a mobile phone. He checks the number. "It would hardly be evasive for me to tell you, Miss Clark, that whatever you find out about the National Identity Movement, it will make no difference." The buzzing continues. "And if I were to say that to you, I would doubtless be telling you too much."

"I can wait outside," Tory offers.

The Vice President shakes his head. "I have no secrets." He flips open the phone and says, "Yes?"

Tory caps her pen and returns her clipboard to her case, all the while keeping her eyes on the dark face as it utters a few syllables in an unfamiliar tongue. His down-turned eyes veiled by long, straight lashes, the Vice President's smile stiffens into almost a grimace as he absorbs the message: "Yes," he says after a silence, oddly shifting to English. "I had guessed as much. But I am afraid now is not the most opportune . . . Of course, but it may be asking too much . . . very well." He hangs up but still stands gazing at the carpet.

He's as unreadable as the language she didn't recognize. "I want to thank you very much for your time," she says.

"Think nothing of it," says the Vice President. He waits for her to rise, then escorts her to the door. As he opens it, his other hand locks onto her upper arm and she makes a startled noise. He shakes his head sternly. "I hope our paths will cross again." Holding her in place, he closes the door.

She stands stock still, breath held, against the wall. Humming to himself, he strolls back to the desk, pulls a CD from a drawer, and inserts it into the boom box on the bookcase. The notes of a piano fill the room—like something fresh cascading through the smoky air. The Vice President moves back in her direction, entering her space. She shrinks into the corner.

He pats the air with one hand to calm her. "It seems I must extend an invitation to you," he says softly.

"An invitation? From you?"

"Off the record, yes. To visit Port Sudan."

"You are offering to take me there?"

"Only in spirit."

"And when do you suggest I should go?"

"When it is time. I will send word to you."

"And who in Port Sudan am I—"

He interrupts her. "The NIM is everywhere," he whispers. "And nowhere as well." Then with a sad smile, the Vice President soundlessly opens the door and eases her out, piano chords rippling behind her.

29

14 September. Washington, DC. 0300 hours.

Roger Booth, Vice President of the United States, is having another sleepless night. A large, colorless man with heavy-lidded eyes and bushy eyebrows, he plays bad cop to the dull-witted President's good cop, and is convinced everyone is out to get him: the Taliban, al Quaeda, radical Shiites and Sunnis, not to mention the experts in their horn-rimmed glasses, who spin their intellectual bullshit about the different belief systems and motives that separate one bunch of Islamic maniacs from another. As far as Booth is concerned, they all look alike and think alike.

They're hiding in every village, from the mountains of Afghanistan, to the marketplaces of the Middle East, and they're determined to hit American power with every cheap, sneaky trick they can think of. You go after them on the ground and you get ambushed by snipers, improvised explosive devices. *Improvised! Shit.* You hit them from the air, and before you know it, a pack of murderous fanatics morphs into a pile of dead women and children.

He shoves himself upright, rolls out of bed, dons robe and slippers, and pads down the dimly lit hallway to his study. Amid the six telephones on the desk, his Blackberry bears a new message: *Policy updates. Urgent. Noon, Metro Club, private room. AM.*

Booth's schedule for the day is packed. No time is worse than another, but he ignores the *urgent*, and writes back: *Noon won't work. Try cocktails. Be there when can.*

He sinks into his chair and picks a large paper-clip out of the bowl on his desk. He pries it open then begins twisting it, immersed in a waking dream: this "war" against the unshaven hordes won't last forever. All it's going to take is one brilliant operation to shift the conditions of contest into a more heroic gear, to assert America's unassailable power once and for all. It will go down in history: Booth's legacy to his country.

The stage is almost set. The audience hasn't a clue.

The paper-clip snaps.

---

30

14 September. Khartoum, Sudan. 1800 hours.

The sight that greets her in the Hilton café sends Tory's appetite south. Balanced on a stool at the marble bar, with his back to the entrance and knees splayed like a long, skinny frog, sits the inevitable Wilkins. Facing Tory, her honey-colored skin and almond eyes crowned by a bleached-blond bouffant, is last night's server. Luckily, the woman isn't about to notice Tory. For some incomprehensible reason, she is so into Wilkins that she seems to glow.

Double trouble, Tory thinks. *Hassle and potential embarrassment.* She'd rather starve than run that gauntlet, particularly now, when she needs time to collect herself and try to put together the puzzle of the First Vice President. It was like trying to communicate with a whole different planet. The interview had conveyed a mood rather than useful facts. She couldn't call it a success.

Wilkins catches sight of her in the mirror over the bar. He swivels on his stool, tall drink in hand. "*Bon soir, mademoiselle!* Pull up a chair," he calls. "Meiying here mixes a wicked lemonade."

"I'll try the courtyard," Tory says.

"It's hot out there," Wilkins observes.

"I'll try the courtyard," Tory says, remembering that she'd better call Maud.

"She's tough as nails," Wilkins remarks to Meiying.

The server smiles at him as if she knows different.

Tory strides past the two of them and out the French doors. In the distance the sun's final rays bounce off the Nile. Cool currents rustle the palm leaves and spread the fragrance of hibiscus blossoms closing for the night.

She takes a seat on the half-wall at the edge of the veranda, looking out over the water, where she figures it will be safe to talk. She's just opened her secure sat phone when Wilkins appears, a white napkin draped over his arm. "Would the mademoiselle care for an appetizer?" he asks with a bow.

"I didn't realize you worked here," she says.

"Jack of all trades," he replies.

"Of course." He gives an irritating click to his heels. "I guess it's pretty obvious why you were in the area last night and first thing this morning."

He shrugs.

"I'd like some time alone, OK?"

"You haven't let me regale you with the special for today."

"*What* about time alone don't you understand?"

"Maybe how you can think there is such a thing." He executes an about-face and goes back inside.

31

14 September. McLean, Virginia. 0710 hours.

After a night of insomnia, Maud has been at her desk for an hour. She'd waited all yesterday for Line Five to buzz, working to convince herself that its silence meant nothing. But today is different. Victoria has had time to get settled. Maud keeps reminding herself that she has placed the girl's welfare in Johnny's capable hands, but really if she hears nothing from her today, she's going to have to do something rash and impolitic, like strangle Gordon Gray with his own power tie.

Eight minutes later the call comes through. Maud punches a button, and there Victoria is, frozen on one of the screens on the wall. Though larger than life, to Maud she looks small and defenseless. Her damp, chopped-off hair sticks out in points like one of those punk rockers, her valentine of a face is flushed, maybe sun-burned already, and her green eyes are so bright they look almost feverish.

"Are you feeling all right?" Maud asks.

"I'm fine, Maud. Busy. I got pushed into attending a reception the minute we landed, and just plain forgot to make contact. I apologize—"

"How did it go?" Maud asks.

"Like schmoozing in a sauna. A lot of sweaty Chinese in suits."

"Were they wearing their horns and cloven hooves?"

"Well, they weren't exactly friendly," says the young woman. "But then females don't register on their radar."

"I'll take indifference any day over a lame pass from a misfit." Maud's attempt at lightness meets with strained silence. "So any other people of interest?"

"Not at the moment," Victoria says.

"Well, I just wanted to let you know that someone is watching out for you," Maud says.

"I appreciate your concern."

"I'm not talking about myself. I lined up someone there, in-country."

The young woman's jaw drops. "Is that like a warning?"

"Actually, it was intended to be reassuring."

Victoria takes a deep, audible breath. "It's not very reassuring to think you're being second-guessed."

"No one's trying to second guess you," Maud can't help snapping. "As hard as the concept of teamwork may be for you, Victoria, the reality is you may need back-up at some point in time."

"Well," Victoria says after a silence, "it better not be one of the losers I met from the Embassy, or I'm in big trouble. The Chargé d'Affaires is a lush, and his assistant's a geeky lech, if you can picture that combination."

"This guy's counter-terrorism."

"God, they're the worst. What's his cover?" Tory asks.

"Obviously that was not divulged to me."

"Exactly how am I going to call on him for back-up then?"

"You'll know."

"I can't believe you couldn't leave well enough alone, Maud."

"You sound exhausted."

"Hungry."

"Get something to eat right now. We can talk more tomorrow."

The young woman nods good-bye and logs off.

As the screen goes dark, Maud feels a twinge of fear. Her intuition, tuned to tone and body language, whispers that Victoria is already stretched to the limit, and like her father, too proud to admit it.

32

The possibility of hostile surveillance is one thing—part of her training. Someone watching out for her is something else—a concept that unnerves her. But then going one-on-one with Maud has often left her feeling sort of off-balance. Even when the conversation has nothing to do with him, it's like Maud is dangling The Key to Tyler Pierce, which she refuses to hand over.

OK, prospective back-up. Tory's mental scan lands right on Adam Marshall, and she allows herself a cheap thrill at the possibility that someone so important might be concerned for her welfare. No matter what Wilkins tried to imply about Adam's intentions last night, didn't actions speak louder? Didn't she wind up getting safely put to bed? Wasn't Adam the one with the easiest opportunity to drop off her weapon? And all that talk about her father—it was hard not to think the man did know who she was. But in a corner of her mind she hears her father caution: *beware of wishing—it can dull your edge.* How many men with inscrutable, unlimited wealth work for the CTG? Such men don't serve their country, they serve themselves.

Still, she thinks, she is going to call him. She'll be more on her guard this time. She pulls out the all-white embossed card. She will laugh, apologize nonchalantly, suggest they stay in touch. She straightens her posture, draws a deep breath, and punches the number into her phone.

A male voice comes on after one ring. It sounds like Arthur's. *Due to urgent business, Adam Marshall has departed the Democratic Republic of Sudan,* the recording advises. *He is scheduled to return at a later date.*

OK. Could you be a little more vague? She is tucking the card back into her handbag, when she notices the other: *James Crawford, Ph. D. Curator, National Museum of Sudan.*

How could she have let him slip her mind? *Discoveries of interest he would be happy to share with her?* He is way too old to be her "protector," but he has totally opened the door to contact, and she'd better march through. She sidelines Adam Marshall in her thoughts. She has a job to do. She begins punching the new digits, then has to stop and fold up her phone.

Wilkins is approaching with a tray. "I brought you some peanut soup and flat bread," he says, setting it down on the wall. "You need to keep up your strength."

Her mouth waters at the aroma. She thanks him. He stands there. "Don't let me take you away from more important things."

"Whom were you calling?" Wilkins asks.

"Wrong numbers," she snaps.

"I was merely curious as to whether you were having any luck," he says huffily. "The cell service in Khartoum is pretty hit or miss."

She takes a spoonful of soup. "Not bad," she says. That's an understatement. It's delicious. "Well, as I said, thanks so much for bringing it out."

Wilkins nods and backs towards the door. "Anytime." His clumsy heel catches the leg of a chair, causing him to stagger, then rubbing his calf, he turns and exits.

She practically inhales the rich, spicy soup, and when she's slurped the last spoonful, she punches a call to James Crawford and makes a date to meet at his house tomorrow afternoon. She refuses to be annoyed at Bartholomew Wilkins' face appearing and disappearing behind a pane in the French door.

33

15 September. Jebel Barkal, Sudan. 0400 hours.

Seven hawks circle in the haze, dropping white seeds from their beaks. The people shout with joy, reaching toward the sky. In the next moment, they fall to the sand spilling the seeds from their open mouths.

A silver balloon descends from a cloud and lands among the temple ruins. Men climb out of the basket dressed in silver. Silver masks cover their faces. The cloud follows the men as they approach the people lying still on the ground, with smiles on their faces and eyes wide open. The sun rises in the east. The holy site seems at peace.

Kendacke awakens shivering and sweat-soaked. She reaches for Lewis, slumbering beside her, so oblivious. She presses her body against his.

The same dream tonight as last, and again the same end. What does it mean? It predicts happiness for her people. Then why does her heart race with terror?

34

14 September. Washington, DC. 1700 hours.

Two Secret Service agents throw open the door to a private cherry-paneled room in the Metropolitan Club, a stately marble structure that spans an entire city block in the heart of Washington, DC. Its members, drawn from the upper echelons of government, military, and business, bask in privilege and proximity to the ultimate seat of power, the White House.

Inside the room, Adam Marshall holds a young Chinese woman on his lap. They appear to be kissing, behind the long black veil of her hair. The gas fire dances in the fireplace, two brandy snifters twinkle on the table in front of them, and his hand is up her skirt. Unsure how to react, the agents await instructions from the man at the door.

"They're OK," Roger Booth says, shaking his head. The rich wood, damask, and leather of the chamber are light years from the fourth-floor walk-up on Chicago's South Side where as a kid, Booth slept on a pull-out cot in the living room, amid the rotten smell of the meat-packing plants and the thuds of his mother's body "bumping into things" in his parents' bedroom. Adam Marshall lived in the same building. The two of them played it back to back in the neighborhood, and dreamed up strategies for getting out.

"Yeah, don't worry, I already frisked her," Adam says, then gives the young woman's bottom a swat. "To be continued."

"When?" she protests, leaping to her feet and straightening her emerald green silk suit. The agents make a quick circuit of the room as Booth enters, with Arthur close behind him.

"Arthur will take good care of you until it's time to leave for the opera," says Marshall to the woman.

When she has been removed and the Secret Service have completed their sweep, Marshall picks up the Armagnac, swirls the liquid, and enjoys a sip.

Booth takes the wing chair across from him, while a waiter places his scotch on the table along with the separate glass of ice he always asks for, removes the second brandy, and disappears, the secret service behind him. The whole well-choreographed change of scene takes under two minutes.

"What is it they say about insanity?" Booth asks, tipping a chunk of ice into his mouth and giving it a couple of crunches. "You do the same thing over and over but expect different results?"

"You're jealous."

"The Chinese Trade Ambassador's *daughter*? For Christ sake, Adam." Roger stares at this friend he grew up with, disgusted that he works so hard on his looks: he's had a nose job and god knows what else. And it's one thing to dye your hair, but your beard too? And that cologne? It all betrays a vanity that isn't manly, to Booth's mind. Booth's mind contains a lot of thoughts he keeps to himself.

"A well-timed fling isn't going to jeopardize the game, Rodge. If anything, it removes me from suspicion."

Booth attacks another cube of ice. "The Ambassador could have you rendered to Mongolia and beheaded just for the hell of it, and no one would ever find your body."

"They're not the monsters you want to think they are."

"They just announced an 18% increase in military spending."

"And what was our increase?"

"Look, I didn't come here to debate China. We've got a more important issue to address."

"I believe *I* called this meeting," Marshall says.

"I'm bringing J. F. on board," says Booth, ignoring him.

"What?" Marshall can't hide his shock. "He's a fucking boy scout!"

"I'm not saying give him the whole itinerary. But the Chairman of the Joint Chiefs ought to be able to guarantee the Chinese ship's safe passage through the Gulf of Aden and the Red Sea if anyone can."

"He's so clean he shits soapsuds!"

"You could never forgive him for walking off with Francesca."

"I can forgive him fine. I'd like to yank out those red talons of hers, though, claw by claw."

"Beside the point. I don't want to be worrying about pirates blowing the whole shipment into fish food."

"But it's fine if Mephisto goes down the tubes."

Booth tips some more ice into his mouth, and while he chomps on it, says, "You always land on your feet, Adam. Worst case: you wind up working for me instead of the Chinese."

"I don't work for the Chinese," Marshall mutters. The Italian loafer he's propped on his knee begins to twitch.

Booth tucks his chin and scowls at his friend over the tops of his wire-rims. "I'm not the one whose lack of impulse control gets him into messes he can't clean up."

Marshall's foot stops twitching.

Booth checks his watch. "So why was it you wanted to see me?"

"In case you're interested, the operation seems to have acquired an added layer." Marshall can barely hide his relish at taking his old friend down a notch.

"What are you talking about, layer?"

"Oh, the Generalissimo has thrown a little kink into the plan. He wants to deploy the agent against a rebel group within Sudan."

Booth leaps to his feet, spitting bits of ice. "Shit. Nobody's going to add any *layers*. You'll have to talk him out of that one."

"Believe me, I tried."

"Try harder."

Marshall shrugs.

"God dammit, we're running out of time." Booth's eyebrows bounce as he pounds one fist into the other hand, lunges towards the door, has his hand on the knob, then turns around, and marches back. "Look. This isn't going to work. Another massacre of a Sudanese tribe made possible by China? The international community isn't going to skip a beat."

"Hey, pal, settle down. The Generalissimo's not trashing the original plan. He just wants instant gratification first, like a kid in a candy store. You show him a bunch of lollipops, he's got to eat one of them now."

"While he's having his premature fun, we're losing the element of surprise on the primary target. No."

"*No* isn't on the table, Rodge. Look, even if our friends get shot down over the primary target, the international community *will be* suitably pissed. God knows what your little scenario's going to do to the world economy, but who asked me? You just better know what you're going to say to all those red-blooded American consumers when there's no more cheap stuff to stock their Wal-Marts."

---

35

15 September. Khartoum, Sudan. 0900 hours.

Thirty-five years ago, Professor James Crawford flew into Sudan from Atlanta, Georgia, to help save the treasures of ancient Nubia before the new Aswan High Dam flooded the plains of the Upper Nile. He stayed on to save his soul. By the time four Nubian temples had been reconstructed on the grounds of the National Museum thanks to his diligence, he'd become a public figure in a quiet way. He was awarded a medal by the Sudanese government, appointed professor at the University of Khartoum, and curator of the Museum itself.

It was a rare decade of peace in Sudan, and Crawford spent it excavating traces of the ancient kingdom of Meroe, a civilization that rivaled the Egyptian in material and cultural wealth. Thus in the sands of the Sudanese desert, he discovered an infinitely more nourishing source for his roots than plantation slavery in Georgia.

Then came the coup that decreed Islam the religion of Sudan and *Sharia*, the law. Civil war exploded. It has been the constant ever since. The only thing that has varied is the stakes. For when the current regime took power, the layers of shale underlying the Sudan desert were found to contain vast deposits of oil.

Today Professor James Crawford lives on borrowed time. Like someone with cancer, he's passed through the denial stage and the angry stage. At the Museum everything's broken, the air-conditioning, lights, plumbing, windows and glass cases. At the University, he's been relieved of teaching duties, and his more outspoken students are being detained and brutally tortured.

There is little he can do but continue to fight for the preservation of their ancient culture, evidence of black Africa's major contribution to the birth of civilization. For years, his efforts have focused on the temples and tunnels of Jebel Barkal, where several years ago the desert yielded an unexpected treasure: a slab of etched stone, preserved under the sand for thousands of years. His team unburied its twin, and then another after that, until there were twenty-five of them piled around the foot of the mountain like pieces of an ancient jigsaw puzzle. Some bore the outlines of stars set against a sky painted with traces of black. Others showed crowned birds, flying into a blue distance.

James Crawford has been driven ever since by the insane hope that in fitting the pieces together, he will reconnect the Sudanese people to the power of ancient Nubia. At the same time, he feels the end of his own life approaching like an adamant wall. As the current regime takes increasing pride in its isolation from the world community, his international reputation offers only dwindling protection. On good days, he's resigned. On bad ones, he feels strangled by a sense of futility.

That is, until two weeks ago.

He hadn't expected anything unusual to come from his meeting with Bart Wilkins, the personable, well-spoken young diplomat who'd sought him out when he first arrived at the U.S. Embassy. Wilkins seemed determined then to learn everything he could about the lay of the land.

Of course, Crawford didn't tell him *everything*. He still doesn't, having learned what a dangerous commodity information is in Sudan: greed for it does almost as much damage as the greed for oil. But Crawford has been getting together regularly and publicly with the young man to share a morning tea—he figures the connection can't put him in any more peril than he already is, and it may put him in less.

Two weeks ago Wilkins asked him as usual about the National Identity Movement. As usual Crawford backpedaled, emphasized its humanitarian mission rather than its politics, offered nothing about Kendacke. Though she's been underground for over five years, many people remember her, those in power with hatred. Crawford has serious doubts about her decision to emerge for the Feast of the Double Cobra, for it puts her at great risk.

"Anything new at the Embassy?" Crawford asked as soon as he could change the subject.

"Actually we're looking at a 25% increase in staff," Wilkins said. "In other words, one more warm body coming in on permanent assignment."

"In what capacity?" Crawford asked, thinking only to keep the conversation away from the NIM. When Wilkins replied, "New Economic Affairs Officer," it was like being kicked in the chest.

"What's the matter?" Wilkins asked.

"Nothing," said Crawford.

"It doesn't look like nothing."

"Oh, the title brings back sad memories. I was good friends with his predecessor."

"Is that right?"

"You may be aware that he seems to have met an untimely end."

Wilkins nodded. "Heard something of that nature. It's *her* predecessor, by the way."

"I beg your pardon?"

"The replacement's female, and a super-jock to boot."

"What exactly is a super-jock?" Crawford asked.

"Let's just say that when I offered to answer any advance questions she had about this place, she didn't write back asking about opportunities for shopping."

"About what did she inquire?"

"She likes to run. She wondered if there were public tracks and whether she'd have to wear long pants and sleeves to use one."

"She would probably not feel out of place using the facilities at the University. Though they're in terrible disrepair."

"I probably shouldn't be telling you this, but want to know what she lists on her resume? That she holds the Ivy League women's record for high hurdles. Now I think that's a little over the top, if you'll pardon the pun."

Crawford was gripping the table as though he expected an earthquake.

"All right, what did I say this time?" Wilkins asked.

Crawford didn't hear the question. It was drowned out by the memory of another voice, a glimpse of a self-deprecating grin. *Pardon my shameless parental pride, but you've got to take a look at these pictures.*

Some years ago, Crawford had taken that look and seen a young woman in shorts and a tank top, one leg bent, the other thrust forward, clearing a hurdle as if it were a crack in the pavement.

Yesterday, braving an appearance at one of the President's receptions, Crawford recognized her instantly.

And now in a matter of hours, she will be knocking on his door.

36

Tory turns back to the cab driver to tell him there's been a mistake, but with a hiss of tires on loose sand, he spurts away. The house in front of her is a shambles—broken windows, crumbling walls, and a front door swinging free. Chickens peck in the littered yard; from the shadows inside, dark faces peer out at her. The wind whips a plastic bag up the pot-holed street.

Then she notices on the other side of the street the long, whitewashed wall. As she crosses towards it, a wrought-iron gate becomes visible in its forbidding expanse. Beyond the filigree, masses of gorgeous pink flowers hug a whitewashed house.

The gate is locked. She tries rattling it, then notices a button. Before she can push it, Professor James Crawford is there, flinging open the wrought iron and ushering her towards a carved mahogany door.

"Sorry to startle you," the Professor says. His eyes seem shrunk by his coke-bottle lenses. He wears a loose, dark blue shirt. "I've been waiting since breakfast."

"I thought we agreed on eleven," Tory says.

"Of course we did." He beckons her into the cool interior. "I'm just an old man with a weakness for hope. Which leads to impatience. Then you had no trouble finding us?"

Us? Tory inventories the room: mix of European period pieces and African carvings, packed bookshelves lining one wall, baby grand piano in the opposite corner. No *us*. "The main challenge was getting away without my embassy escort."

The Professor gives a deep laugh. "If you're referring to Mr. Wilkins, he would be warmly welcome here."

"I didn't realize the two of you socialized."

The Professor grows solemn. "Socializing is not an activity that applies to my life," the Professor says. "Mr. Wilkins is simply a fine young man."

Tory offers a non-committal smile, but her attention has been snagged by the outdoor courtyard with a table and a tiny fountain, bedecked with more of the pink blossoms, and the tall, thin young woman in a plain, pale blue shift who has risen to enter the house.

Her skin, the shade of milky tea, seems faded compared to the Professor's robust brown. Her hair is pulled away from her perfect, oval face in corn-rows, leaving nothing to compete with her eyes—a shade of amber that would be unusual anywhere, but in Africa, a genetic miracle.

"This is my godchild, Amanirenas," Professor Crawford explains.

Sure, she is, Tory thinks, stunned into cynicism by the young girl's beauty.

"Please call me Mani, mum," the girl says.

In all her own striving to project competence and confidence, Tory senses she'll never come close to this girl's effortless poise.

"And this is Ms. Veronica Clark," Professor Crawford goes on. "A very special envoy from the United States."

What's that supposed to mean, Tory wonders as the younger woman stretches a graceful hand for her to grasp.

"Welcome to our home, mum," Amanirenas says in a resonant voice. Her lips part in a smile that reveals a pure white star on the off-white of one front tooth.

"Thank you both for inviting me," Tory replies. But her heart sinks when Mani follows them out to the table in the shaded courtyard. How is she going to pursue any agenda, professional or otherwise, with a third party present? She might as well write off the whole visit as a waste of time.

"Now," says the Professor, once Tory has taken her seat, "you two keep each other company while I go assemble lunch. I had to give up my house-keeper some time back, after it became clear that there was no one in this city I could trust." He turns slowly and moves back inside. From behind, his shoulders are noticeably stooped.

"I cut up the fruit, mum, for the salad," Mani announces.

Tory nods a polite smile, then feels the awkward silence rise like flood waters around them. "Are you from Khartoum?" she asks.

"I am from nowhere, Mum. And everywhere. My blood flows from the bright beginning until eternity."

"I see," says Tory.

"Amanirenas can be a shade dramatic sometimes," the Professor calls from the kitchen.

Mani hangs her head, then rolls her gaze up to Tory. "Have you ever visited the Central Intelligence Agency, mum?"

Tory hides her shock. "I can't say that I have, but I'm curious, why do you ask?"

"It's for my homework, mum."

"Homework? How old are you?"

"Almost fifteen, mum."

The Professor reappears carrying a tray. "Mani attends the American School, and she's chosen the Central Intelligence Agency for her current affairs report."

Tory is surprised to feel so relieved. This beautiful girl really *is* Crawford's godchild, and not some under-age live-in. "Well, you seem much more mature than fourteen," she says.

"Thank you, mum."

The Professor is arranging plates of food around a slab of thin bread the size of a large pizza. "*Fuul,* the national dish," he says pointing to a mound of pale paste. "In case you haven't yet encountered it. The proper way to eat it is with an assortment of salad, tomatoes, onions, salt, and *shotta*—a fiery chili powder. We flake bits of strong *jibna* cheese into it." The Professor demonstrates. "Then drown it a bit in oil and scoop it up in the bread."

"And afterwards, there is my fruit," Mani reminds them.

"Correct. Now I assume you're ensconced in reasonably comfortable digs?"

"The Hilton," Tory says.

"Really? Nothing available in the compound?"

"I'm perfectly comfortable."

"I'm sure you are, yes, but, well, a bit remote from reality."

"I realize that. It's one of the reasons why I called you. You must teach me the reality here. But tell me, first of all, what is it *you're* hoping for?"

"I beg your pardon."

"The weakness you mentioned when you greeted me?"

"Ah yes, I should have known you wouldn't miss a single detail."

The Professor's smile makes Tory slightly uncomfortable. "Listening carefully is part of my job," she says. "So exactly what are your impatient hopes focused on?"

"Well, I hope for the preservation of Sudan's rich history, even though the artifacts that proclaim it are being destroyed in the name of economic progress. And in the face of so much violence and chaos, on all sides, I continue to hope for peace."

"The whole world cries for it," offers Mani, "the way a child cries for her mother's embrace."

Tory, taken aback, can't think how to respond.

"Does it seem too much to ask?" says the Professor.

"Those goals are so, I don't know, noble," Tory stammers. "I'm not sure what I can, if I can—"

"We must each resist barbarism in our own way, Miss Clark."

"You can call me Ronnie," Tory says.

The Professor gives her an odd look, then turns to his ward. After munching small mouthfuls of the bread and *fuul*, she has pushed her chair back from the table and folded her hands in her lap. "Perhaps you would entertain us for a bit on the piano?"

With a silent bow, the girl rises and reenters the house. In a moment the strains of her playing waft outside to mingle with the burbling fountain. At first the soothing sound lulls Tory, but very soon her muscles tense and her mind shifts into alert. Classical music may not be her thing, but she can recognize the piece she heard only the day before.

"What can you tell me about the First Vice President?" she asks.

The Professor pauses, then suggests, "You should probably speak with him."

"I already have. But it isn't clear to me what he stands for. Is he anything more than the government's token non-Muslim?"

"Maybe time will tell." After a pause, the Professor lowers his voice and leans forward. "Here is a good man who has placed himself between the proverbial rock and hard place."

"A good man who's building a large bank account in Nairobi," Tory points out.

"Ah, yes, . . . Ronnie, that is indeed the rumor."

"Not rumor," Tory says. "Substantiated fact."

The Professor nods sadly. "It is so easy to lose ones courage in this country."

"And gain millions."

"People acquire large sums of money when they decide they are not worth anything better."

"So much for noble goals. What's your opinion of Adam Marshall?"

"I have no personal knowledge of Adam Marshall, though I was introduced to him on one occasion, which I am sure he promptly forgot."

"Do you think he has lost his courage?"

"My guess is he never possessed courage to begin with. Was he one of your reasons?" the Professor asks.

"I'm sorry?"

"You mentioned other reasons for getting in touch with me."

"Did I?" It's as if the jet lag she has been fighting all of a sudden overcomes her. *My father. What did you think of my father?* She hears Maud's voice chiding, *Personal need.* "I'm not sure what I had in mind. A slip of the tongue, maybe."

The piano eases into a minor key, a theme that exudes loss and yearning, and to her horror, Tory feels the sting of tears in her eyes.

"Samuel Barber's *Adagio for Strings*," says the Professor. "Mani's own piano adaptation."

"Amazing," Tory says, thinking, *Got to get out of here.* "Listen, I want to thank you for your time, and for the wonderful meal, not to mention the lovely music."

"Must you leave so soon?"

"For now, I think it would be better . . . " She rises. "Would you mind calling me a cab?"

"I wouldn't mind," the Professor says, "except that one might show up around midnight, if you were lucky. I, on the other hand, am perfectly happy to drive you back to the embassy."

"There's no need for you to go to the trouble," Tory says.

"It's no trouble. I'll take the opportunity to say hello to Mr. Wilkins. We haven't spoken in over a week."

"What about Mani?" Tory remembers the wretched squatters in the abandoned house across the street.

"The wall is high, and we always lock the gate. She will be fine."

37

The conversation in the car is stilted. It isn't until they have turned onto Abdel Latif Avenue that the Professor clears his throat and says, "I once had a very good friend on the staff at the Embassy here. He held your same title, in fact—Economic Affairs Officer."

Tory stiffens. "I never told you my title."

"Ah, well, I also have ways to substantiate facts," the Professor replies.

"And where is this friend stationed now?"

"I think you know."

"Somewhere nice, I hope," Tory says.

"Believe me, so do I."

"After this, I think Paris or Rome would be only fair."

"I'm afraid this country treated him very unfairly," the Professor says.

Her nerves on high alert, she blurts, "What happened?"

"There is a woman I think you should meet. It would be, how do you people put it, of mutual benefit to you both?" He reaches under his loose shirt and produces a small, cotton sack, which he hands to her.

Inside, Tory discovers an elegant wristwatch. She turns the face over and reads: *Today is a gift . . . That's why it's called The Present. Your Susannah.*

It's like a kick in the solar plexus. She can't speak.

"The woman I mentioned?" the Professor goes on tactfully. "The watch comes from her. She told me to tell you things aren't what they appear in this country. Expect the unexpected. One of these days the sun may even come up late."

"Tell me where this woman is," Tory says, "and how I can get in touch."

38

15 September. McLean, Virginia. 1300 hours.

Just as Isabelle's repertory of gaudy eye-glasses seems to mock her inter-changeable dark, tailored suits, her dainty body language contradicts her solid, matronly bulk. Today she tiptoes into Maud's office, drops a folded note on her boss's desk, then minces a few steps back, where she waits, hands folded demurely, her smile radiating success.

Just had lunch with Tremaine's admin asst. Surprise! Maud looks up. Isabelle cocks her head toward the door.

A few minutes later Maud has locked her office, Isabelle has slipped the note into the shredder, and the two are heading toward the lobby.

"Don't ask me who's fraternizing with whom in the storage room," Isabelle says, "because I promised Margot I wouldn't tell."

"I suspect it'll be brought to my attention soon enough," Maud says. "What about Tremaine?"

Isabelle's voice lowers. "All tests turned out negative, boss."

"You know, I'm actually relieved to hear that. But I guess it's back to the drawing boards."

"Not exactly. Margot says that Jenny says Paul is up for promotion. Jenny's his A.A."

"That's certainly news to me."

"Jenny says he's circumventing channels."

Maud stops in her tracks. "Not Paul." How could he come out of his shell long enough to get into trouble?

"Margot says Jenny's going around bragging. The woman should have her head examined," Isabelle continues. "So I went out for coffee with Jenny, and told her even though her boss is the smartest analyst in the division, I hoped she wasn't going around telling a lot of people what I'd heard through the grapevine because it would increase the level of inter-office jealousy. That's when she leaned over and whispered, *OK, something big is going down,* and told me Paul's got a direct channel to the Deputy Director, NCS."

39

The offices on the seventh floor are all but deserted, where Gordon Gray stands at a half-open door, studying Maud studying her computer screen. His tie is loose and the jacket of his Brooks Brothers suit slung over one shoulder.

Thirty years ago he was just out of Yale, basking in his mother's disapproval of his career choice. She'd thought the Agency was socially dubious and wanted him to follow his father and grandfather into banking. Maud was Midwestern wide-eyed, determined to be sophisticated. The Agency was a step up.

After the first week of intense training at the Farm, Gordon knew: Maud would be the one to make it to the top. It's what his own mother used to scold him for: he lacked drive. He always let down in the final lap. Besides Maud could turn being a woman to an advantage. She was attractive enough that you liked having her around, but not so attractive that your hormones went haywire. Unless you were Gordon Gray, a cut above the Agency's typical macho knuckle-draggers.

He is utterly charming when he wants to be, he makes large donations to the Opera and the Symphony, and he can still do seventy-five sit-ups and fifty push-ups every morning without breathing hard. But he is a man drawn to the unavailable, the chaste, perhaps repressed female, like a moth to flame.

He clears his throat.

Maud looks up with a start. "My god, you scared me."

"Everyone else seems to have had the sense to call it a day."

"So you just walked on in."

"You're awfully jumpy."

Yes, she thinks, *given the probability that you've turned one of my own guys, I'm jumpy*. The question is, *Why?* She's back to thinking *personal vendetta*, and frankly, it doesn't surprise her about Gordon. He has a narrow, petty streak—she's always felt that. She takes off her glasses, places them on top of the smallest pile, and rubs her eyes. "What can I do you for, Gordon?"

"Thought I'd check in on Pierce's daughter."

"I just spoke to her." Maud checks her stainless steel bracelet watch. "My god, it was fourteen hours ago."

"And?"

"She's off and running. No details."

"Good. She has an excellent record, Maud."

Maud begins straightening her desk.

"I sent a personal note to the Chargé d'Affaires, asking him to keep an eye on the girl."

"That would be David Kimball, the alcoholic?"

"If we terminated every alcoholic over at State, we wouldn't have a department left." He pauses. It is more than annoying that as his superior, she can keep him standing there. "May I sit down?" he finally asks.

"Sorry. I'm awfully busy."

"So am I."

"Of course." She smiles and nods toward a chair.

That irresistible smile. How many times has he played to her vanity so he could watch the prim mouth relax, the blue-gray eyes unfocus and begin to twinkle? "So tell me, does it get a little lonely at the top?"

"I think you can answer that question as well as I can."

"I've got a few more guys over my head than you do."

Maud goes back to desk-straightening.

"Let me take you away from all that."

She freezes, but doesn't look up.

"I don't mean forever. For what's left of the evening. How about the veal Oscar at the Ritz Carlton, with a nice bottle of wine?"

"Tonight's not a good night."

"That's it? I don't even get a rain check?"

Maud is silent.

"Don't tell me you finally realized how many rain checks I have. I could paper a wall with them. I'd have to live to a hundred to cash them all in."

"I'm sorry, Gordon."

Gordon jerks upright. "Sorry? For Christ sake, Maud. What do you think I am?" A feverish ruddiness floods his usually pale face.

"I don't know. I mean this is a particularly difficult time."

"You think I'm a fool. That's what you think, isn't it? How many times have you come to me to help you out—in exchange for a rain check. I've always thought maybe, eventually, you'd be ready to come down off your high horse and join the human race. But I was wrong. You'll always think you're perfect. Too good for anyone. So you're on your own now." He shoves himself out of the chair and heads for her door. On the threshold, he turns, both hands raised in exasperation. "He's dead, Maud. Get it? Tyler Pierce is dead. Life goes on." He turns and storms out.

40

16 September. Jebel Barkal, Sudan. 0730 hours.

Inside the rattling red Explorer, the pancakes Tory scarfed down for breakfast keep threatening to heave. Off in the distance, 360 degrees around, the lumpy sand blurs into hazy sky.

"You're sure this is a road?" she asks.

The Professor talks through the white cloth swathed around his whole head. "If we're moving more than fifteen kilometers an hour, it's a road."

"And you're sure that thing works?" She nodded at the GPS attached to the dash.

"One has to trust something," he says.

Tory isn't sure about that one. Closing her eyes to fight the nausea, she hangs onto her door and tries to roll with the SUV as it bounces along over scattered rocks, spraying sand in its wake. When she opens them again, she almost yelps with relief. Through her dark lenses, a black-water lake shimmers off to the left dotted with palm trees and wading cranes. Maybe the Professor will agree to stop long enough for her stomach to settle. She is about to suggest it when the lake and trees evaporate and the cranes become the scattered parts of a car. Heat mirage. And beyond it, another: a crooked table-top of a mountain rising from the flat.

Minutes pass and the mountain doesn't disappear. Tory sits up straighter. From the rubble around its base, plumes of smoke swirl skyward. Soon she catches the faint smell of roasted meat, hears goats bleating, and sees scurrying movement among patches of white. The rubble becomes tents propped on poles, the movement, hundreds of human beings spread out across the sand. Here and there loom pyramids in different stages of ruin.

"Many more people are on their way," says the Professor, "to attend the upcoming Feast of the Double Cobra. It used to happen twice a year, around the equinoxes. This one will be the first in quite some time."

"Why were the feasts suspended?" Tory asks.

"You must ask that question of Kendacke, the woman I have brought you to meet."

The Professor pulls the Explorer between two beater trucks, thus closing one gap in the circle of assorted vehicles around the perimeter of the camp. "Welcome to Jebel Barkal," he says, "center of the universe, and birthplace of the divine. I speak from the Nubian point of view, of course. You'd better drink more water, by the way."

The night before when she checked in with Maud, the older woman's normally controlled voice had slid up the scale to shrill when Tory mentioned the plans for today's trip. "No," Maud said. "I want you to stay in Khartoum. There's something going on at that mountain place."

"And what would that be?" Tory asked.

"I'm sorry. I've been squeezing blood from a stone, trying to upgrade the intel. It's all level one and two rumor, at the moment."

"Tell me what you've got."

"Give me another day, Victoria."

"I can't. The invitation's tomorrow. From a potential asset. A guy who knows everything."

"OK. Does he know that there's a demonstration taking shape at that mountain, which is highly likely to bring out the government militias in full force?"

"*You* give me *two* days, and I'll either shoot your rumors down or substantiate them. That's my job."

The Professor scoots around now behind the SUV and comes back with some ice cubes in a paper cup. They're already beginning to melt. Their cold wetness helps her stomach a little. She rewraps her headscarf, reapplies Wilkins' sun-block, then crunches across the expanse of coarse sand and pottery shards behind the Professor.

A bunch of round-bellied kids with skinny legs spot the newcomers and come running over to bounce along in their wake. She smiles at them and they scramble to hide behind each other. Their dark skin is coated with a chalky film, and their eyes, though friendly, look old and clouded. *A militia attack here? These kids?*

The Professor waves her gaze to a natural stone column at the prow of the mountain. "Tell me what you see at the top of the pinnacle."

She shields her raised eyes with one hand. "Nothing. A big lump of rock? I don't know."

The Professor utters a few syllables to the children and they melt away. "Imagine a rearing cobra, its body poised to strike."

"I'd rather not."

"You may recall seeing this protective snake in pictures of pharaohs, at the center of their crowns? A phallic symbol, expressive of Amun's power to generate life."

"What's Amun?" Tory's attention is on the children sand-skiing down the lower slope of the mountain, tumbling over each other.

"The ancient Egyptians' god-in-chief. His name became the standard way to end a prayer."

"Amen," Tory says with a laugh.

"When Egyptian imperialists moved in on Jebel Barkal around 1500 BC, they took one look at that pinnacle and decided it must have been Amun's birthplace. Of course, it had been a sacred place to the Nubians for centuries. They had no problem assimilating the Egyptian gods to their own culture, then rising up against the Egyptian colonizers and crushing them, even installing themselves as pharaohs over Egypt for a while! Eventually Amun was displaced by Osiris and his queen-sister, Isis."

"Isis? Hey, I've heard of her," Tory says.

"Ah yes, it's quite a story, isn't it, her brother's murder and dismemberment, and her quest to find all his pieces and put them back together?"

"I'm sorry. I guess I was talking about a super-hero in a TV show I used to watch."

"So that's what good old lowbrow American culture makes of the Egyptian goddess of rebirth," the Professor says.

"So tell me the real story."

"I'm afraid it goes on and on," the Professor says. "Isis and Osiris, brother and sister, husband and wife, were originally Amun's emissaries to humankind. They brought many gifts, from agriculture to a social structure. But a third sibling, Seth, envied their power and goodness and plotted to kill Osiris through trickery. He chopped up Osiris's body and scattered the parts. Then Isis made it her mission not to rest until she had found the pieces and resurrected her brother. At the two equinoxes now, when the sun rises at just the right angle to reflect off the gold disc inlaid there at the top, some believe that these divine spirits still abide and give certain Nubians special powers."

Tory shivers in spite of the heat. It's like someone struck a tuning fork with perfect pitch. Or like a channel has opened to a different realm, and she can sense the spirit of her father. Three days in country, and she is definitely where she ought to be.

They have now circled the mountain so that it rises between them and the camp. "Here we have the fruits of my archaeological labors for the last six years." The Professor points to a huge square of white canvas stretched across the sand inside a ring of ruins.

Tory stoops to lift the cloth. "Sounds interesting."

The Professor places a hand on her shoulder. "They're a surprise, actually."

She backs away. "For whom?"

"I'd like to think, the world. I'll explain later. Let's go inside."

"Inside what?"

"Keep hydrating," he says, and guides her to a spot in the mountain where two stout pillars, connected by a stone lintel, mark an entrance. A boy and girl in their late teens loiter on either side clothed in navy blue jumpsuits and berets in spite of the heat. They greet the Professor with youthful enthusiasm. Their arms cradle M-16's.

41

Tory steps into the gloom of a round ante-chamber. The stale air hints at vast expanses of time. She shuffles along behind the Professor and his flashlight beam into a hall lined with crumbling statuary, which dead-ends at a wide stone panel. The Professor runs his circle of light over the etched and painted human figures, finding the edge. The next thing she knows, he has disappeared, leaving her alone in the dark.

"Remember that Bible story about passing through the eye of a needle?" asks his disembodied voice. She inches closer to the wall of stone where it seems to come from. "This is the Nubian equivalent."

Suddenly a hand grips her upper arm, forces her back to the wall, then eases her gently behind the stone. The space is so narrow that she must turn her head and point her feet sideways to keep her nose and toes from scraping. *I look just like one of the people in that picture outside*, she realizes, but then the slit widens to a corridor which pulls them downhill in the dark. Several minutes later space opens: she is in a second round chamber illuminated by two carbide lamps and decorated with bas-reliefs carved in the walls.

"This room was a birthing place," the Professor tells her.

"You're kidding," Tory says. "How could a pregnant women squeeze through that crack?"

The Professor laughs as he unwinds his turban. "There are other ways in. Other channels to the outside."

"It smells different in here, more modern."

The Professor nods toward the low opening on the opposite wall. It must be the source of the slight breeze.

"Would you care for a little refreshment?" He removes another bottle of water from his leather bag along with dates, flat bread, goat cheese, and three plates.

The sight of the food inspires nausea. "No thanks."

From a corner, he drags out three folded rugs and opens them on the ground. "Make yourself comfortable, then."

Tory takes a seat, and unhooks her Teva's to clean the sand out of them. The cool floor soothes her hot, bare feet, while her eyes sweep the shelves along one of the walls, and try to penetrate the dark corners. Feed sacks, more lanterns, wooden boxes: something flopping out of one of the boxes catches her gaze. An ammunition belt. Then an upright row of rifles.

"Hello, James," comes a melodic voice.

Tory jumps up and turns towards the hole in the wall. There in the shadows stands one of the tallest women she has ever seen, a dark figure draped with cloth so blue it seems to glow even in the murky light. A huge knot of the same fabric crowns her high, round forehead. She towers over the Professor as they embrace. Then she takes a step towards Tory, fingers outstretched.

"I am Kendacke," the woman says, with a British accent, "heir to the throne of the Nubian people."

Her hand in the woman's firm grasp, Tory silently revises the introduction: *meet the NIM.*

"Veronica Clark," Tory says, retracting her hand. "Would it be rude to ask how you got in here?"

The woman's lips curve in a smile. She tilts her head a notch, and the lamplight falls on her eye. The right one is sunken, without an iris, crumpled white. "Let us hope I will not have to show you today. But welcome to my temple, and my hiding place, I regret to say, for five years." Her greeting seems more song than speech.

"I guess I don't need to ask who you're hiding from."

"The government men with machine guns and machetes spare no one, children, women, elders. Unborn babies are ripped from the wombs of their mothers, then kicked around for sport. Since I was a girl, there has been this violence. I have resolved to make it stop."

"May I ask how you propose to do this?"

"Will you help?"

"Me?" Tory blurts, then collects herself. "My assignment is to report on your economy, I'm afraid—"

"Your government has plenty of reports. The entire world has reports, still my children drown in their own blood."

"I don't know what to say," she admits, thinking, *What happened to my father?*

A strong hand comes to rest on Tory's shoulder. "Good," the strange woman says, her tone changed from imperious to kindly. "Shall we sit here together and enjoy the wonderful food from James?"

In one continuous motion, she sinks onto a rug. Less gracefully, Tory and the Professor join her.

Kendacke raises a date in one hand, a piece of cheese in the other. "Three thousand years ago, my ancestor led the Nubians into battle against their Egyptian oppressors and rose to rule over them," she declares. "We shall do the same with these butchers who rule us today."

"How?" Tory asks. "They've got the money, power, weapons."

"Do not confuse brute force with power," Kendacke says. "Our movement offers the power of spirit, the power to fill the empty heart and turn despair to hope. And the spirit works not through money or guns but through symbols."

Tory gnaws on a crust of bread. How can she possibly help this woman? Does she even want to? Can the power of spirit rescue Kendacke from the attacks Maud warned of? "Have you heard anything about the government invading your camp here?" she asks.

"They have done such a thing before. We are always expecting it. We fortify a perimeter against the militias as best we can," Kendacke says. "The holy mountain itself has protected us from bombs. So far."

Tory imagines the breeze in the room blowing up from an abyss on the other side of that hole in the wall. The flared head of a cobra rises in her mind's eye. Should she simply blurt her question: *what happened to my father?* Her thoughts are interrupted by the sound of her name. The wrong one.

"Victoria?"

Before she can stop herself, Tory answers. "Yes—I mean, I beg your pardon."

"We know who you are, Victoria." Kendacke offers her an odd smile, a blend of sadness and warmth. "Please do not look so worried. We would never wish you harm."

42

16 September. En route to Jebel Barkal, Sudan. 0830 hours.

A beige Toyota Land Cruiser veers off the paved road onto the barely visible track through the sand, its driver and passenger swaddled from head to sandals in dingy cloth. Swerving to avoid rocks, they cross the barren landscape, monotonous clumps of thorny scrub, an unidentifiable carcass under a clump of buzzards, the abandoned chassis of some old vehicle.

Riding shotgun, Umar Hassan holds a mobile phone pasted to one ear. Suddenly his whole body clenches and he lets out a groan of disgust. "The satellite shows a moving vehicle," he announces in Arabic. "About five kilometers behind us. I do not like complications."

"Maybe tourists," the driver says. "They are like sheep. They all must visit the boring mountain so afterward they can make a little check mark on their list."

"I think not. I smell another American, one who will interfere."

"Maybe you should ask for back-up."

Umar snaps shut his phone. He adjusts the shoulder holster under his robe. "Not necessary. Drive faster. We are twenty minutes ahead of this intruder. Make it more, and we can accomplish plenty."

The car lurches forward. "You are stubborn man, Umar."

"If I start something, I'm the one who finishes it."

43

16 September. En route to Jebel Barkal, Sudan. 0830 hours.

"Don't let me down now, you hack," the pith-helmeted Wilkins mutters as he steers the Jeep Wrangler onto the packed sand and tries to accelerate. The fresh car tracks spell urgency, but his own worn tires keep skidding, and he has to slow to a frustrating crawl.

His phone buzzes. He flips it open to hear the voice of the server in the Hilton café. It confirms his fear.

"You will have company," she says.

"Who is it?"

"A thousand Sudanese pilgrims, for starting."

"Fine. I like pilgrims. My ancestors were pilgrims. Who else?"

"Don't ask me to name names."

"Oh yeah? Where are they?"

"Hey, you big technology man. I am simple Chinese girl with open ears."

"All right, all right. When did they leave?"

"They should arrive at Jebel Barkal in perhaps one half hour."

"OK, so they've got a jump on me. At least they confirm that I'm on the right track. You'd think out of basic politeness she would have let me know her plans, but oh no, she's got to—Shit." His eyes sting from the sweat dripping from his helmet into them, mixed with a liberal infusion of sun block. He yanks a handkerchief from the breast pocket of his jacket and swabs it across his face.

"Dear Bart," the woman says, "do you not have back-up you can call for help?"

"Dear Meiying, I am overheated, underpowered, half-blind, and eternally grateful for your tip-off on the wandering Ms. Clark, but I do not need back-up."

44

16 September. Jebel Barkal, Sudan. 0900 hours.

Kendacke's words melt what is left of Tory's reserve.

"I shall never forget meeting your father," the woman says, her one eye glazing in the dim light. "He was the first white man who understood our struggle."

Tory knows she should be denying the connection, but in her hunger for answers, she says instead, "Thank you for returning his watch to me. I'd like to know how you found it?"

"All must be experienced," Kendacke says. "Not explained."

Is that a rebuke or a challenge?

"Your father's official focus, of course, was terrorist activity," the Professor explains. "That's what led him to investigate us."

"The National Identity Movement has been accused of many things," Kendacke says. "Because we believe the disparate tribes of Sudan can discover their common ground."

"By common ground, I assume you don't mean marketing oil," says Tory.

Kendacke smiles. "Oil is only one reason for the fighting. There is also the powerful symbol of blood. As it unifies one group, it divides that group from all others. We hope to offer new, more compelling symbols, to lift us above divisions—symbols such as an unspoiled child, for example, or the eternal heavens, or a martyr's bones.

"Through them, we hope to rededicate our common ground, which is right here, Jebel Barkal, the birthplace of African civilization. The missing link between God and humankind. We believe it holds the secret of peace."

"I'm sorry," Tory says. "I'm not following."

"Neither did your father," Kendacke says, "until he felt in his heart what it means when that secret is utterly lost. Back then it was less clear to the rest of the world what our President's intentions were. To swell the ranks of his army, he opened the jails and deputized the prisoners, giving them permission to . . . do anything. Steal, kill—"

"It was the first time your father attended one of our sunrise celebrations," the Professor interrupts. "Thousands of men, women and children had gathered here. I remember Kendacke was standing at the entrance to the mountain, leading the chant, when the drone of low-flying helicopters became suddenly deafening. Weaving among the ruins, with guns firing from their open doors, the aircraft pursued the fleeing worshipers who couldn't hear Kendacke's cries to take cover in the mountain. In minutes the helicopters were gone," James concludes. "And the sand was covered with the dead and dying, the air filled with moaning and wails of grief."

"That is how your father understood that we were not terrorists—but their opponents, and their victims," Kendacke went on. "There was one girl child lying in a black pool of blood near the temple entrance, whimpering for help. Your father raced to her from his cover, but . . . it was hopeless. That morning he pledged to help the National Identity Movement in any way necessary."

"He never mentioned anything like that in his letters."

"If he had, would they have been permitted to reach you?"

"The diplomatic pouch has complete immunity."

"From Sudanese inspection, yes," Kendacke says. "But what about your own government—the Central Intelligence Agency?"

Tory can't bring herself to object.

"We always called him Peter," Kendacke says, "though it was obvious that wasn't his real name. But when he bragged about his daughter, he called her Victoria, or Tory."

"Great," Tory says.

"I assure you, your identity is safe with us."

Tory drops her eyes from the woman's asymmetrical gaze. Adjusted now to the dim light, they blink at the sight of a stone figurine threaded on a leather strip around the woman's neck. "What is that?" she asks.

"The divine mother who watches over me."

Tory digs into a pocket of her backpack and produces a nearly identical shape. "Her sister," she says. Then she has the uncanny sensation of someone else speaking through her. "How can I help?"

"Accept our invitation to attend the Feast of the Double Cobra, which will happen in three days."

Become another target in the shooting gallery when the militia attacks? An answer sticks in Tory's throat.

Reading her mind, Kendacke says, "We tell the entire world that you will be attending, an American observer. The government will not dare to make an assault. And there are other reasons why you ought to be present," Kendacke goes on. "Why you belong here, with us."

Belong? Sorry, I don't do belonging. "Tell me what caused you to suspend these celebrations, and when," she says. "I have to know."

"It was your father's murder that sent me underground."

The chamber is dead silent. Tory sits absolutely still and lets the words circulate through her body like ice water. There it is—the answer, everyone else's answer, which she has never been able to accept. Yet here in this dim, underground chamber, there is something about this mysterious woman that challenges Tory's resistance, whispers that it is time.

"Do you have proof that my father was murdered?"

"Yes," Kendacke says quietly. "I have given you his watch."

"But how did you happen to have it?"

"It is not a simple story, and it is important for you to hear the whole of it," Kendacke says.

Just then a muffled stuttering burst, soft as a string of hiccups, launches the Professor to his feet. "What was that?"

Kendacke looks up at him with irritation. "Rifle. Probably Peter. He is a new recruit. I will have to speak to him."

"I think I hear shouts inside the temple. It's time to break this up, Kendacke."

"Why is it that you men cannot carry a weapon without pulling the trigger occasionally, *just to see how it feels?*"

"Maybe that's not why he fired," the Professor says.

"We are not finished here," Kendacke says.

That's right, Tory thinks.

"Kendacke, come on!" the Professor insists. He's already packed up the remains of the food and tossed the rugs into the shadows. "You retreat to your room. Tory and I will head for the south entrance. We can get a couple of the men to check out the situation from that vantage."

With a sigh as if she is humoring him, Kendacke folds herself almost in half and disappears through the hole she must have entered by. The Professor gives Tory a gentle push in the same direction.

"Wait a minute," Tory says. This is all happening too fast. Why couldn't this woman just tell her how she came by her father's watch? You know, the quick, *true* version? It's like this Kendacke is hiding something. It's possible, anyway, and the passage in front of Tory is way too form-fitting, the path ahead utterly dark.

"The sooner we see what we're up against—"the Professor says.

Tory interrupts him. "I think I'd rather take my chances the way I came in."

From the passage comes Kendacke's disembodied voice. "The fear will go away as soon as you take your first step."

"I'm not afraid, I am just going to—"

"Follow me," commands the voice. "Now."

At the same moment, behind Tory, the Professor places his hands on her shoulders and forces her to bend and move forward. Telling herself not to think about the constriction of the passage, or the possibility of a chasm ahead, one of those bottomless cracks in the earth, she hunches into dank-smelling darkness.

Her back scrapes the ceiling, and soon she cannot see anything. She can hardly breathe. She shakes off the idea of being buried alive, clenches her teeth against a scream, and concentrates on blindly shoving one foot in front of the other. This can't be a trick. Or can it? Is this what happened to her father? One step. Then another. Her lower back starts to protest the crouching position.

The Professor bumps up against her. "Excuse me," he says, and his voice in that space doesn't sound human. It's all she can do not to explode with pent-up anxiety. She opens her mouth to say, *That's OK,* and instead a moan comes out.

She clamps her mouth shut on it, for she realizes the tunnel has just expanded. It is still pitch dark, but several more steps and she can stand and walk upright. She can breathe.

Something rubs against her cheek. It's Kendacke's bare upper arm. The woman had stopped. What for? Just to rest against the wall? Tory's nerves flip on high alert, ready for anything. All at once the wall gives way. It's a door, opening to a blast of much cooler air and enough surrounding light to make out a flight of crude stone steps leading down.

45

They could be two more migrants in dust-stained robes and turbans, except for the late-model Land Cruiser, which they leave parked behind a pyramid. They make their way from tomb to tomb unnoticed by the hordes of pilgrims getting through another day in their slum of tents.

Umar gives his driver a shove in the direction of the mountain. His nerves are buzzing. "Faster, you lazy animal," he mutters, and shoves him again. He keeps one hand grasped on the government-issue Norinco M-77 pistol holstered under his clothes.

When they reach the boulders strewn around the base of the mountain, Umar grabs the driver by the neck of his tunic and pulls him up short. "Not so fast, stupid boy. Not so fast." He creeps out in front and approaches the entrance to the so-called temple occupied by the traitors.

Umar has tailed suspected insurgents more than once to this site only to exchange pointless fire, neither side willing to venture beyond cover of its protected position. He has hit the temple threshold with rocket-propelled grenades, reducing it to rubble. Days later, the rubble has been cleared away, and targets continue to disappear into the bowels of the mountain. When he proposes a more devastating attack on the mountain itself, someone up the chain of command wavers, gives in to world opinion, or maybe superstition, and denies the request.

But for this latest trip to the mountain, his official mission is secondary. For the past five years he has reaped the profits of a lucrative private contract— *moonlighting*, the Americans would call it: today he calls it being paid double not to let the American girl out of his sight. He'll try anything, even the obvious.

Thirty meters from the temple opening, he picks up a rock the size of a melon, heaves it toward the double pillars, then jumps back out of sight. It raises a cloud of dust as it thumps into the sand halfway there. Nothing. He steps away from his boulder and hurls another rock. Another thump, another cloud.

But then to Umar's utter surprise, he hears a yell.

"Lewis?"

Silence.

Then, "Hey, Lewis. Why do you always fool with us?"

A head appears under a blue beret, and then another, and then right in Umar's sights, a young man and woman, more like kids, in dark blue uniforms. They emerge from the opening, rifles raised to their hips. Umar fits a sound suppressor onto his gun.

The two foolish ones call again, but except for the noise of the awakening camp on the other side of the mountain, the silence continues. They start to back toward the opening, eyes darting nervously. *Hardly a challenge*, Umar thinks, as he fires. The man yelps, clutching his thigh as he buckles and goes down. The woman pivots and fires a burst in the general direction of Umar, in the same instant that he nails her in the leg.

Umar and the driver lie low for a minute to make sure there won't be back-up, before they scramble over to their victims. They find small puddles of blood draining into the sand around the guards' hips and retching sounds coming from the mouth of the woman. The black eyes of the man stare right at the sun.

Cursing under his breath, Umar throws himself down beside the woman. "Tell where she is," he hisses, shaking her by the shoulders. "Talk to me. How do I find her?" But it's futile—before his voice runs down, she is dead from a self-administered dose of poison. He drops the body and rises. "Come on," he says to the driver. "I don't give up this time."

Marching into the temple's anteroom, pistol ready, Umar confronts only emptiness. He leads the way into the hall of statues, pulls a flashlight from under his robe, and shines it over their contours, one by one. Aware that his driver is watching him, expecting something, he makes a show of grabbing the barrel of his gun and tapping different spots along the walls with the handle.

He reaches the painted slab at the end. His tapping hand feels the space between it and the wall. He runs his flashlight beam along the space. His heart beats a little faster. He replaces his gun in its holster, then inserts one whole arm into the space with room to spare.

"*Allahu Akbar*!" Allah is the Greatest, he shouts to his driver, who dutifully repeats the phrase. "Watch." Umar turns his back to the wall and inches himself into the space.

Half his body is behind the slab and he is just turning his head to fit it into the narrow space when a blast of light blinds him. His stupid driver seems to forget he is holding a gun and freezes.

"Kindly drop your weapons to the ground and place your hands on your heads," comes a voice, Arabic with an American accent.

46

"If it isn't my old buddy, Umar," says Bart Wilkins, as the smaller man emerges from the passage squinting into the light. The forged steel of his pistol clanks on the stone floor. "How about you and your friend step toward the exit. There you go. Let's get out of this cramped little mausoleum." He backs into the antechamber, his Beretta trained on the two men following him. "That's better, a little elbow room. Now we can have a chat." He flicks off his krypton flashlight. "What brings you to Jebel Barkal?"

"Cut it out, Wilkins," Umar grumbles from behind his shaggy moustache.

"Wish I could. Believe me, it's no fun trying to break in a green lady diplomat who's determined to acquaint herself with the culture of ancient Sudan."

"We are tourists and come in to get out of the heat," the driver mutters.

"Shut up," Umar says, giving him an elbow in the ribs.

"What about those two folks out there in the sand? The heat really get to them, did it?"

"Where is she then, this *diplomat* you say you are pursuing?" Umar asks.

"I wish to hell I knew," Wilkins says. "Because if she gets into trouble, the whole Embassy takes the blame. And she has no idea what she's doing. So I'd really appreciate you guys laying off, OK?"

"I follow orders," Umar says.

"OK, I'll give you a choice. You want to stay here so badly, fine: I take your weapon, your shoes, and the valve stems in your tires and you stay. If you want to go, go. Now."

The driver looks over at Umar like an obedient dog to his master. Umar is trying to decide if either option allows him to save face. Finally he adjusts his posture and strides toward the opening, grabbing his driver by the sleeve and yanking him along. The pair exits into the glaring sun.

After making sure the two men trudge toward their Toyota, and steer it up to the road, Wilkins drags the two stiffening bodies into the antechamber and collects the discarded Mukharabat guns. *Cheap Chinese junk*, he thinks as he clicks the safeties and shoves one each into the side pockets of his lightweight vest. *Where in the hell is Ronnie?*

Beaming his flashlight, he moves the length of the smaller room, and stretches a hand behind the stone panel. He sets the light down, and back to the wall, wedges himself a little way into the space. It's pretty tight.

Giving up on that, he picks up the flashlight and heads back outside. He gets a half-gallon bottle of water from his Jeep and folds his vest onto the rear seat. Underneath his shirt is sopping with sweat.

Head down he angles back toward Jebel Barkal. A shapeless fear gnaws at him. He tells himself to calm down, he is going to find her, people don't disappear into thin air. He should be pissed, not anxious: this whole escapade is a pain in the ass, he didn't need a run-in with Mukharabat. They're an unpredictable bunch and he'd just as soon stay off their radar. Then he hears, "Mr. Wilkins! Bart Wilkins!"

He looks up to see Ronnie and Professor Crawford wading across the sand.

47

"Are you all right?" Wilkins asks when she and the Professor have reached the temple entrance.

Tory shrugs. The question doesn't compute.

Wilkins turns to the Professor. "She looks, I don't know, gray."

"I'm fine," Tory says.

"It's been a difficult day," the Professor says, noncommittal. "Glad to see it's business as usual out here. We heard—"

"Not exactly," Wilkins says, beckoning them back inside the temple anteroom.

As her eyes accustom to the dim light again, Tory recoils at the sight of two bodies on the stone floor. Their blue uniforms are crusted with blood. "Jesus, Wilkins, what have you done?" she asks, turning away with a shudder as the Professor kneels over one of the corpses. She remembers being lifted to kiss her mother good-bye, how cold and waxy that cheek felt to her child's lips. Now she's lost her father too, without even a final glimpse. Was it like this?

"Actually," Wilkins is saying, "the leg wounds were courtesy of a couple visitors, but these two delivered the coup de grace themselves."

"I don't see any visitors," Tory says.

"I told them to get lost."

She stares at him, her brain in turmoil. "Right. They shoot two guards then take off when you tell them." Should she be believing anyone around here? To compound her dismay, the high-noon furnace seems to have baked her vocal chords, which squeak.

"Don't give me that look," Wilkins says. "It's a good thing I guessed to come out this way."

"Oh? It really helped these two, didn't it?"

"These assault rifles they're carrying don't exactly read innocent bystander," Wilkins says.

The Professor raises himself from the floor with a groan and brushes at his trousers. "The NIM does not go looking for trouble."

"But it sure finds its share," Wilkins says.

"You seem to be doing pretty well in that department yourself," Tory says.

48

16 September. Khartoum, Sudan. 1300 hours.

Amanirenas shuttles between angry and bored. How many times has she been told that the sacred mountain is her destiny? Yet today her Uncle James has gone there without her, taking instead the young American woman, who is short and has spotted skin.

The sound of the front bell brings a surge of hope. She peeks through the foyer window and can hardly believe what she sees: a big, handsome man standing outside the iron bars of the gate. Her heart flutters. She opens the door and slips out onto the stone slab of a stoop.

The man offers her a smile, both friendly and surprised, as if he expected someone else to respond to his ring. His skin is a warm shade of brown, and he wears a pretty shirt printed with a bright blue design. He has slung a black leather bag over his shoulder, as if he is looking for a place to spend the night. "I have come a very long way to speak with you," he says.

"It is over 5000 miles from the United States to Khartoum," Mani says.

"How did you know that's where I'm from?" The man looks amazed.

"Your accent. My guardian is an American expatriate," Mani explains solemnly.

"How fortunate that you speak English—from the sound of it, better than I do!"

Mani grins.

"I work for an American magazine called *Mademoiselle*. You might have heard of it," the man goes on.

She shakes her head. "My guardian tries to shield me from all American influences."

"Not a bad idea," the man says, "but every once in a while my boss takes a break from recycling the same old, same old fashion garbage and sends me out on a really interesting, important shoot."

Mani's jaw drops and in an instant she has darted back inside the house.

"Hey, that's just an expression, *shoot*. For taking pictures. See?" He starts to unzip his black bag.

Mani pushes the door almost shut. She peeks through the crack.

The man pulls out a black and silver camera. His voice is don't-be-afraid soothing. "I've come to Khartoum to take pictures for an article on teenagers around the world. Here, let me show you a copy of our magazine." The man extracts a folded copy from the bag, and spreads the cover open in front of her. Then he refolds it and wiggles it through the bars of the gate.

Slowly Mani opens the door. She meets the man's gaze and it holds her. She steps out again onto the stoop, a little farther, and then shifts her eyes to the magazine cover. They get wider. She folds her hands, and wrings them a little. "I am embarrassed for her," she says, of the flirty, revealing photograph.

"I know," the man says, "I am too. But I'm hoping that you, and maybe some of your friends, can give me a little information about yourselves, and maybe let me shoot—"

Mani can't help flinching.

"What is wrong with me! I mean *snap* some serious, informative pictures so the rest of the world will know what it's like where you live."

The comment hangs in the air like a question. Mani frowns as she tries to decide how to answer. She hears her Uncle James's stern instructions, never to open the gate for anyone. She knows that rule applies to people like the squatters next door. But this man? His eyes tell her he could do her no harm. They are deep, even sorrowful. Besides, he is handsome, and American. And she is bored. Because Uncle has gone off with a white American woman. Maybe the spirits have sent this American friend for her. Finally Mani shrugs and smiles, then unlocks the gate.

Inside the compound, Mani leads the man into the house. As she closes the door behind them, he hands her the magazine, slips the strap of his bag off his shoulder, and squatting, sets it down on the floor. Then he pulls something else from the bag, a piece of white cloth. He stands and gives her a sad smile. He reaches his empty hand towards her and cups it around the back of her head. For a minute she assumes he is going to hug her, and she is not afraid.

But then the cloth covers her nose and mouth, heavy and strange-smelling. She is too surprised to struggle. She feels a surge of panic because she can't pull in a breath, then everything goes dark.

49

16 September. Jebel Barkal, Sudan. 1300 hours.

Her chest is tight, her stomach queasy again. She clutches the watch in her pocket. She could go for a time-out right about now—crawl into bed, pull the covers over her head, and process some of this stuff. Five years of emotion press to get out. She blinks rapidly. *You asked for this,* she reminds herself as the Professor's Explorer rocks away from the site, the Jeep churning behind. *The real thing. No coffee breaks. Set aside personal need. Focus on this Wilkins guy.* Her father's advice pops into her mind. *Picture all possibilities, the worst-case scenario.* For a supply officer and part-time chauffeur, he's a little too nosy, way too involved with a Chinese barmaid, and now this pair of corpses? How does he stay a step ahead of her? *Guesswork? No way. Got to find out which side is pulling his strings?*

Now that her cover is blown with the Professor, it occurs to her that she could make a stab at officially turning him. His value as an asset probably spikes out of sight. He might have information about Wilkins. And what about this Feast of the Double Cobra? *Plan for everything, even your accidents. How?* The midday heat has taken over, and she sits there, pitched about like a bottle on the sea.

Finally the SUV hits pavement, making for a smoother ride. She begins the fishing ritual she's been taught. She doesn't get far in her spiel about being in a position, as a representative of the government of the United States, to help the Professor out in exchange for information—

"I have heard that one before," he interrupts.

Tory shrugs. She had to try.

"I'll tell you what I told your father: you are welcome to all the information you want about our Movement. The more our vision is shared with the world, the more the world will have to support us, and the more we will lead Sudan to become a model of unity despite differences. The National Identity Movement has had nothing to hide except Kendacke. And at this point in time, she is planning to end that situation. Your father was the last, and now you are the first. She has revealed herself to you."

"I don't know what she's revealed," Tory says. "She seems to know a lot more about me than I know about her."

"Her personal past is a closed book," the Professor concedes, squinting through his thick, dark lenses. "Some unspeakable experience at the hands of the militias, I assume. Before I knew her. She was abducted from her town along the Nile and imprisoned by the Government. They claimed she was defacing portraits of the President. She says she was only taking them down because their ugliness offended her."

"So, what about her *im*personal past?"

"Its tentacles stretch back to the centuries before Christ, when Isis-worship granted women their power. Elevated them to the status of warrior queens, consorts to the divine. Isis as in protective mother of everything, not a TV superhero."

"OK," Tory says with polite skepticism.

"Kendacke is the descendant of pharaohs. Royal blood flows in her veins."

"Come on, blood is blood," Tory says. "A or B or O."

"Well, then, let's just say a royal energy, a charismatic spirit, permeates everything she undertakes."

"What did my father say?" she asks.

"I beg your pardon?"

"After you gave him your pitch about the NIM. Did he stop there? Take the information and run? Or did he get involved?"

"I thought Kendacke made that clear."

"What Kendacke made clear was that he's dead."

The Professor presses his lips together as if remembering something he regrets. "It's all very complicated," the Professor says after a pause. "And still painful."

"You don't have to tell *me* that," Tory says, then the Professor's earlier words tug on her attention. "You said my father was the *last*?"

"The last to join her crusade. Losing him broke something inside her. Not courage, no, but a kind of innocence."

"And I am the first?" *What, sucker, guinea pig, bleeding heart?*

"We hope that you will become part of Kendacke's return to life, as it were."

"How far was my father willing to go?"

"We are almost to my house now," the Professor counters. "I invite you to dinner, and afterwards I will concentrate on assembling what details I can."

Why do they keep postponing the truth? "Do you know who did it?" Tory asks, impatience creeping into her voice.

"I beg your pardon."

"Do you have any idea who killed my father?"

"I have many ideas," the Professor says. "I'm sure I myself had a hand."

Tory stiffens. "You?"

"For allowing him to believe in the impossible," the Professor goes on. "And to step into the flames of hatred that consume this place."

"OK, were there any witnesses?"

The Professor pauses. "I know only that he was to meet with a politician, Mahmoud Elradi, who'd been in and out of favor with the regime. The man had just been released from prison when he got in touch with us, with the

NIM. Your father thought he could talk to him. Afterwards, Elradi himself dropped out of sight."

Numbly, Tory flips open her phone and calls Wilkins. "Change of plans," she says. Her mouth feels like cardboard. "I'm going to Professor Crawford's for dinner." When Wilkins says he'd like to accompany her, she replies, "Sorry, you're not really invited," and clicks off.

The Professor turns into the road that leads to his neighborhood and the embassy Jeep Wrangler recedes in his rear view.

Tory studies the Professor's blunt profile. *What details?* "Exactly how much did Kendacke reveal herself to my father?" she asks.

"As much as Kendacke's enemies wish her ill, her friends love her more. Your father was no exception."

"And she loved him back?"

He rolls into the alley behind his house, where he unlocks another gate, wide enough to allow him to pull his Jeep into the security of the walled compound. "They had an extraordinary bond," the Professor says finally. "The word love doesn't really do it justice." Then he guides Tory through the back door into the house. Once inside, the Professor calls for Mani.

When no answer comes, he gives Tory a shrug, as if to say, *Kids!* More sharply, he calls the girl's name again. As the silence lengthens, his eyes widen. He rushes from the kitchen, past the living room, and stumbles up the stairs, shouting the name. Burdened as she feels with her own unwelcome truth, Tory has to will herself to check out the garden, then the foyer. There the dark, licorice smell of chloroform hits her. Her throat constricts with dread. Adrenalin floods her veins, and the present emergency usurps the past.

She opens the front door and finds the unlatched gate. Behind her in the hall, the Professor has collapsed against the wall speechless with shock. She helps him into the living room and seats him on the sofa. "Has she ever gone to visit friends?" she asks him.

"She would always contact me in that event."

Tory flips open her mobile. "Then she has her own phone?"

The Professor recites the number and Tory punches it in. A faint ringing from above spurs the Professor back up the stairs. Then the ringing stops. Her own phone pressed to her ear, Tory hears Mani's lilting voice inviting her to leave a message and have a lovely day.

"I don't have to ask whether you have any enemies," Tory says.

The Professor nods. "And this is how the cowards get to me."

Tory stares at her directory of contacts, considers her three options, then punches one.

50

17 September. McLean, Virginia. 0730 hours.

Maud Olson doesn't look like a woman running on anger instead of sleep. Her grey designer suit is crisp, her French twist smooth, and her Lancome make-up artfully applied. Her two-inch heels click like a metronome as she heads in the direction of Human Resources and the personnel archives. She has just attempted to access them from the computer in her office, only to find the server down for system upgrades.

She is only half surprised when Ann-Marie, archive librarian, doesn't know anything about the updating. Now she paces the reception area while Ann-Marie cards the locked door and disappears into the stacks. Maud is not authorized to examine her own file, but she is determined to do something she should have had the guts to do five years ago. Marie returns and offers Maud the still-classified file of Tyler Pierce.

Alone in her office and braced for the sorrow, Maud places the document at the center of her desk and opens it. At the least this will keep her from brooding on Paul's betrayal and Victoria's daily phone call, which has yet to come. The first page hits her with the dark date and the announcement: *Senior Case Officer Tyler Pierce, missing, presumed deceased.*

The following pages present a terse, official account of his life, from date of birth through high school excellence in athletics, to his early acceptance by Williams College, and his recruitment by the Agency. He married Susannah, a junior officer in the Science and Technology Directorate, who subsequently gave birth to their first child, Victoria. Following Tyler's solo assignment to Rabat, Morocco, the family was posted to Riyadh, Saudi Arabia, where Susannah died of an infection following a miscarriage.

How little the facts have to do with the truth, Maud thinks. *They had both been so radiantly alive. She'd been quietly brilliant, and he was dashing, that's the word. Dashing and unpretentious and unflappably cool.*

Nowhere does the file register his struggle to be both parents to his small daughter, or his decision to put in for Reports Officer, a desk job, so she could live with him, and how he then almost lost his mind. It wasn't the fatherhood part—if he could have spent all his time with Victoria, he said, he was sure he would have been more than challenged and entertained. It was the desk jockey part. The bureaucracy part. The pattern of rewarded mediocrity part. When he gave the child up to the care of his in-laws, he said, it was like losing Susannah twice.

One of the best analysts in the world, Maud never could analyze her feelings for Tyler—they just *were*. Something less than romantic but more than sisterly. She's always been emotionally cautious, thus where men are concerned, completely inexperienced. Well, it hadn't taken a lot of experience to intuit that getting close to Gordon could open a chamber she didn't want to enter. The blast of hatred he released last night proved she'd been right all along to deflect his overtures. Still it had certainly unnerved her.

Maud pages through the summary of Tyler's considerable talents and his cluster of weaknesses—*loner, disrespectful of authority if he thinks the situation calls for another strategy, cowboy*. Copies of twice yearly fitness reports echo the same dichotomy. Nothing new there.

The very last document in the file snags her attention. It is dated two days before Tyler's death, and begins by criticizing his over-engagement with the NIM, the compromise of his objectivity.

Further indication of unusual behavior, even for Pierce: he has violated the prime directive and become intimately involved with the native woman Kendacke, who professes to be a priestess and the savior of the Sudanese people. Recent information confirms rumors that she has a child, hidden from the public, and that child is Pierce's. It also confirms that Kendacke's goal is the overthrow by the NIM of the current regime. Pierce is heavily implicated in this project. His unprofessional activity not only puts him in increased danger; it also delivers a set-back to relations between the United States and the Sudanese government, which has heretofore complied with our request to oust Osama Bin Laden and ban known terrorists in the future. We strongly advise that Pierce be reprimanded and recalled to Headquarters at once. Signed, David Kimball, Deputy Chief of Mission, Khartoum, Sudan.

Maud slams the file shut. She sits for a moment, eyes closed against this web of unsubstantiated rumor. Then she presses the button on her intercom. "Isabelle," she says, "Put a call in to the embassy in Khartoum."

51

17 September. Khartoum, Sudan. 1700 hours.

"How was your expedition?" David Kimball asks. As Tory feared his speech is already slurry. "Have you satisfied your curiosity *vis a vis* the noble savage?"

"I'm at Professor James Crawford's residence, David. You know who that is?"

"Ah yes, the international authority on something."

"The young woman he lives with has disappeared."

"Younger women have a way of doing that."

"He's her guardian. I should have said *girl*, she's a child."

"Why do the kids put beans in their ears?"

"David, please!"

"What am *I* supposed to do, call in the cavalry?"

"I'm sure there are people you could contact. Apply pressure, get answers, make threats, I don't know."

"You overestimate me," David says. "I'm not the good guy. I gave all that up. Sold out. If you know what's good for you, you'll steer clear of me. Leave me and my vodka supply outside the loop."

"David, listen. Whatever needs to be done, I'll do it. But you'll have to tell me where to start."

"I'm at the Solitaire Café watching the sun go down in more ways than one."

"Where is that?"

"This side of hell. I don't know. Amarat, actually. Somewhere on Fifteenth Street."

"I'll be there," Tory says and hangs up.

The Professor's shoulders are heaving with grief. She puts her arm around them and bends to whisper in his ear, "We'll find her, James. I promise."

Before she leaves, she goes through the house one more time. In the library, a drape across its one small window keeps it dark and cool. Books are stacked on the table and floor, papers blanket the desktop, but it's a clutter that looks organized—no sign of struggle, no sign of theft. Then the faintest scent registers in her brain. Something familiar, yet the more she sniffs, the more it fades. A red box anchors a pile of papers. The top one looks like a photograph of Jebel Barkal, centered on one part, the cobra pinnacle, crowned with a halo by the rays of the rising sun.

She refrains from touching anything. David will have to tell her how she can get the place dusted for prints, she thinks, then wanting one last hit of the smell, she goes back into the kitchen, opens the tiny refrigerator, takes a deep whiff of its insides, then races back to the library, as if to catch the odor by surprise.

"What in the world are you doing?" the Professor asks, but she is miles away.

Fortunately she hasn't had a minute in the last seventy-two hours to brood about her screw-up with Adam Marshall, but now she is thrust back into the still-vivid memory of a Mercedes interior, thick with the same smell.

52

Thomas Kvol, First Vice President of the Republic of Sudan, gives one of the two glass hemispheres on his desk a shake, and a miniature Eiffel Tower disappears in a swirl of white flakes. The fake snow brings back youthful memories of paradise.

For two years at the Sorbonne in Paris he studied political science, forgot about civil war and death, and let the pure cold of winter heal his spirit, that wonderful icy cold that preserves against decay.

Then he returned to his home in south Sudan, Bahr el-Ghazal Province, to the heat and hunger, to a ruined landscape dotted with grave-mounds crowned with thorns, to the pervasive odor of starving bodies, rotting corpses, and grief. Nothing had changed. It still hasn't, even though he inhabits a house in the Capital with enough space for a whole tribe, fifteen rooms, all but one furnished in the style of European royalty. He sits in meetings now with Sudan's Muslim rulers, but the meetings are meaningless, and the rulers continue to hold his own people, the noble Dinka, in complete contempt and to encourage their slaughter. Although he eats now from the table of his enemies, they do not consult with him. They give him no real power.

He has snatched it nevertheless.

He holds the second globe up in the air—a ski slope in the Swiss Alps—and watches the tiny particles lift and swirl. "You spread the word, then?" he asks the young man standing across from him in a loose western shirt and khakis. There in the Vice President's Safe Room, decorated sparingly with African teak and tribal masks, they choose the clipped syllables of their common Dinka tongue.

"The American Mr. Wilkins is most interested," Lewis says. "And you have alerted the new American woman?"

The Vice President nods.

"I wish the whole world could be watching what happens to this rice."

The Vice President lights an unfiltered cigarette and takes a deep drag of smoke as he gazes at his son, handsome in spite of the scarred flesh that replaces one ear. He has his mother's long, lean limbs, her thoughtful eyes, her shrewd sense of right and wrong. If only she had been spared in the massacre at Aweil, to see the fine man he has grown into. "As always, I beg you to mind your own safety."

"There are things more important than personal safety, father. You were a soldier once. In the past you were unafraid of risk."

"Perhaps in the present you confuse common sense with fear."

"Our current situation is far beyond the reach of common sense."

"All right, my son. What more would you have me do?"

"You eat very well."

Frustration launches the Vice President to his feet, stabbing out his cigarette, but he never raises his voice. "Lewis, whatever I learn, I pass on to you. If I learn nothing, if the President's men are being silent when they see me, if his servants turn their backs on me, then I have nothing to tell."

"Apologies, father. Your advance information has saved many lives and I thank you for it. When the government hyenas do not expect us, it doubles our striking power. And now these rice trucks you speak of—the minute they hit open road outside the port, my best men will be there to take what we can."

"Then for once perhaps a relief shipment will reach the mouths of the hungry instead of the bellies of the fat generals." The Vice President finds the prospect comforting. "Please tell the lovely one with one eye that I wish her celebration well."

Lewis nods.

"Perhaps it is impossible for the father to truly please the son," the Vice President says. "But I want you to know, the opposite is not the case."

"We are very grateful to you," Lewis says, ready to be gone.

The Vice President lights another cigarette. "I do not belong here, in this giant tomb of a house, in this nightmare city. My thoughts turn always to our proud heritage, Lewis."

"Yes, father."

"I am still a Dinka chief. My power flows from my personal dignity. I see your impatience, my son, but it is time that I remind you of the burial custom for Dinka leaders."

"Father, please. We don't have the luxury right now to indulge morbid thoughts."

"Our custom is not morbid. The Dinka chief asks to be buried alive in order to assert his power and dignity until the end. He converts death from enemy to helpful subordinate."

"Fine. And now I really have to—"

"You must go now, but I want you to take this with you," the Vice President continues, handing his son the alpine snow globe. "It will serve you and the Movement, when something happens to me."

Lewis doesn't ask how a piece of European junk can possibly serve him, but accepts the gift with a long-suffering look and stiffly endures his father's long embrace. "Nothing will happen to you, father," he says, before he slips out a French door into the dusky courtyard and is gone.

53

The Professor's red Explorer is covered with dust. Tory turns the ignition, starts the wipers, and as they scratch half-circles of clear glass, she punches another call. "Where's Amarat?" she asks Wilkins.

"What happened to the maps I gave you?" he asks.

"Obviously, I didn't bring them with me."

"I'm feeling a little under-valued here."

"Wilkins, please!"

"Where are you going in Amarat?"

"I don't have time for twenty questions. I'm meeting David."

He gives her directions from the Professor's. As she commits them to memory, he adds, "Don't expect much this late in the day."

She finds the Chargé d'Affaires sitting alone at a courtyard table holding forth to a pretty server. As Tory pulls out the chair next to him, he makes a slurred attempt to introduce her to "Ami, from the Philippines," then with obvious relief on her face, Ami-from-the-Philippines slips away.

Beyond the concrete half-wall, a beige Toyota Land Cruiser with tinted windows pulls up behind her Explorer. Standard transportation for Mukharabat: that little piece of information may be the only thing she can thank Wilkins for. She picks her backpack off the ground and settles it in her lap. Inside, in a flowered makeup kit, rests her Glock.

She leans in close to David. "We have got to do something," she says. "This kidnapping is unacceptable."

David meets her gaze with bloodshot eyes. "We're talking about a Sudanese national, right?"

"Her guardian's got dual citizenship."

"You know that means *nada*. How much cash are you carrying?"

"On me? Not much."

"If you want police action around here, you have to pay." He rubs the fingers of one hand with his thumb, then reaches into his back pocket and removes a silver flask and takes a swig.

"I can get you money. Please put that away."

"Haven't been caught yet." He rubs his fingers and thumb again, by way of explaining.

Sure enough, an olive-skinned man in western shirt and pants, probably the proprietor, stands in the doorway to the café, studiously avoiding looking at David. A young, blond couple is absorbed with arguing in German at one of the other outdoor tables. The Land Cruiser spews monoxide into the hot, still air.

"Besides, we don't know this wasn't a police job in the first place. That professor gives everyone the creeps," David continues, putting the flask back in his pocket. "Beady little eyes peering through those coke-bottle glasses. And living with a girl young enough to be his granddaughter. Well, used to live, anyway. Talk about dirty old man. There's a lot of that going around, by the way. Sweet young things like you have got to be extremely vigilant."

"What's that supposed to mean?"

"Oh, Ronni-o, Ronni-o, wherefore art thou Ronni-o? A rose by any other name would smell as sweet."

"With all due respect," Tory says, "I wish you'd stay on topic."

"Don't underestimate me, my dear. I've been around a long time. I am as guilty as the next guy."

"Jesus, this isn't about you, David, OK? It's about an innocent girl who's in danger of god knows what and us needing to take immediate action."

"Go ahead, rage at me. You have every right to. But you see, I don't do action anymore. The last time I got roped into action, someone died."

He pulls out the flask again and takes a long dose. Tory stares at his bobbing adam's apple as her brain juggles his innuendos. Slowly they coalesce—*he is talking about her father.*

"Which someone?" she asks sharply.

David stares at the lump of meat on his plate and slowly shakes his head.

"What did you do?" Tory demands.

"Precious little," David says. "Nothing. Which paved the way."

A commotion at the entry to the courtyard saves David from elaborating. Two skinny boys are tussling with the proprietor. Probably hungry, begging for food, while the American flaunts a full meal he's barely tasted, opting for his liquid diet instead. As Tory figures how to get the information she craves out of David, one of the boys breaks away and plunges over to their table, the proprietor on his heels.

"You are Mr. David, Mr. David. I have important message to you," the child blurts, just as the proprietor grabs him by the back of his Nike T-shirt.

"I will take care of this," he growls. "Come on you, out of here."

He yanks the gagging boy away by the neck. The boy's thin arm reaches toward Tory. His eyes plead. She recognizes him as one of the beggars outside the Hilton. "Let him go," she says. "He's a child."

"That kind of child is thief," the man insists but backs away.

The boy opens his fist under David's glassy stare. It contains a folded, sweaty note. David reaches for it uncertainly, takes forever to uncrumple it, then his ruddy face turns ashen. "My apologies, dear Ronnie," he says. "Something important. Must be taken care of immediately." As he pushes himself to his feet, he knocks over his chair and staggers out to the street.

Tory stares after him in disbelief. The life of an innocent girl, not to mention the wrongful death of her father—those things weren't important? David looks to the right and left as if he's lost. A horn honks, the driver's window of the Land Cruiser drops a couple inches, then David stumbles across the street and disappears into the back seat.

"Who gave you that piece of paper?" Tory asks the boy. He can't take his eyes off David's abandoned steak. She can't take hers off the departing Toyota. "I will give you food, when you tell me. Now. Who asked you to carry that letter?"

"No can tell anybody," the boy says emphatically.

"Was it someone you know? Or a stranger?" The car has vanished in the distance.

"I know it was stranger."

"What color was his skin?" Tory waves the proprietor over.

The child looks around desperately. "No color, I don't know."

"Would you mind putting the gentleman's meal in a bag, please?" she asks the proprietor. She notices that the second, smaller boy, the one with the terribly scarred mouth, has been inching his way closer to her table.

"It is a mistake, you know, to treat a thief kindly," the proprietor says, taking the full plate back inside.

Suddenly the smaller boy is on top of Tory, clasping her neck in his thin hands. For an instant, she thinks he's trying to strangle her, but he only wants to pull her ear closer so he can whisper, "Angry man with happy eyes. Nothing under the nose." The boy scratches at his own torn upper lip with a finger.

"Where did he find you? Where do you guys live?"

The boys look at each other then make vague gestures with their arms. Then just as the proprietor extends the sack to Tory, the older boy snatches it. The pair scoots out of the courtyard and race down the street in the same direction as the car containing David.

She's unlocking the Professor's Explorer when an all-too-familiar vehicle pulls so close beside her she has to shrink against the side of hers. The Jeep's window slides down, and Wilkins leans over his elbow to ask, "You OK?"

She stifles her relief. *Can't get sloppy. Don't need any help.* "Are you following me?"

"Don't flatter yourself. I have to eat too."

"And I have work to do, if you don't mind."

"Look, David's my job."

"Notice I can't open my door."

"Without those maps, you haven't got a prayer of finding him. How about getting in?" He cocks his head toward the passenger side.

No way. "No thanks."

Wilkins throws her a pained look. "Come on, Ronnie."

"I'm waiting for you to move."

"Jesus," he says, hangs a U-turn and spurts off down the street.

54

Arthur can't get enough of looking at her. He wouldn't call it attraction exactly—she's pretty and all, with those high cheekbones and uptilted eyes, but she's half his age, and it's just not about that.

As he lights one cigarette off the butt of another, he realizes she reminds him of Denetta, the kid sister he couldn't protect. Is it the vibes this girl gives off, even as she dozes, stuff like innocence, courage, honesty—what Denetta started with, the way her soul was on the day she was born, before the poison of the Projects began to eat it away.

His sister flashes across his mind as a kid, full of sass; as a teenager, decked out like a hooker and running with the wrong crowd. Denetta stoned. Denetta cutting school. Him coming home to find her crashed in her room glassy-eyed, the needle marks all over her arms.

And the final nightmare, going down to the police station where they were holding his sister on manslaughter charges. A drug deal had gone wrong and two people died. Mr. Marshall's attorney made it go away. Mr. Marshall paid for rehab, got her life on track. Even hired her as a secretary in one of his companies.

And Arthur has been licking the Boss's boots ever since. He smashes his cigarette out against his bare palm.

The girl's dark head looks like sculpted stone against the white pillow. She doesn't belong in this mirrored chamber, the Boss's so-called Gymnasium, his temple of self-love. She should not be lying here dosed with Valium, her hands bound with duct tape under the white sheet. As Arthur watches, her eyes open and blink to focus their golden gaze on him.

"Want something to eat?" Arthur asks.

Her head flops from side to side.

"I know you must be scared, girl. But I won't hurt you. I promise you that." He shoves to the back of his mind the thought that he can't speak for anyone else.

"Who are you?"

"Sorry. I can't tell you yet."

"You do not look ruthless," the girl says.

He can't help smiling. "Thanks. I appreciate that."

"My mother and my uncle, they have always warned me," the girl begins in a slow slur. "They are always telling me about ruthless powers in the world which will try to . . . my hands. . . . " Her long lashes flutter then close, as she drifts back to sleep.

55

From the spot he'd staked out behind a kiosk at the corner, Bart Wilkins watched two street kids laugh and rough-house in the vicinity of the beige Land Cruiser across from the café. When the taller pushed the shorter to the sandy ground, and the shorter took an extra second to bounce back to his feet, Wilkins clenched a fist and hissed, "Yes." For a few dinars, the kids had stuck a magnetic transponder under the rear fender of the idling government vehicle.

With Ronnie working on David, Wilkins figured he could relax for a minute—he had both his subjects temporarily in one place. But then those two skinny mercenaries darted across the street and into the cafe courtyard. Minutes later David disappeared into the Land Cruiser before it sped off.

In the long run, what could happen to the U.S. Chargé d'Affaires, besides a little aggravation, which David is too pickled even to remember? So Wilkins decided to let him go and stick with the girl. Wrong choice. That bird has flown the coop. On to Plan B.

The Land Cruiser is long gone, and Wilkins is mumbling things about Ronnie that would have launched his mother into one of her "spells." One hand on the wheel, the other snaps off the airbag panel to expose a computer screen. A quick click and a signal from the transponder starts inching the cursor along a satellite map.

Wilkins hasn't gone half a mile in pursuit when he has to slam on the brakes. Ahead in the middle of his lane, a cart of melons lies on its side, fruit rolling every which way. People are running around in emergency mode, some scooping the fruit up and making off with it into the twilight, others waiting with loaded arms while two men struggle to right the cart. Everyone is yelling, and a man is lurching up the street after two boys in flapping white T-shirts. One of them clutches some stolen booty in one hand; both fly like the wind.

Wilkins checks the cursor, shifts into reverse, hairpin turns, finds an alley where he can cut over several blocks, and moving as fast as he can, given the narrower, darker road, the potholes and pedestrians, takes off again in the general direction of the Land Cruiser.

He can't believe it when he spots those same damned kids on the next corner and they aren't running. Bent over, hands on knees, catching their breath, they are eyeing the front of his Jeep.

The next minute, his ride turns bumpy, then bumpier. He twists and squints out the rear window. In his brake lights he catches telltale red glints in the road behind him. Glass? Nails? He turns forward again and the boys' spot is empty. The Jeep's forward motion shudders to a crawl, then halts.

Halfway up the next block sits a three-wheeled *tuk-tuk*. Wilkins groans at the memory of a near-death experience in one of these souped-up tin cans that pretend to be taxis. He studies the moving cursor on his screen one last time. "What?" he exclaims, shaking his head. "No way!" He replaces the airbag panel, and lopes over to the blue-and-white deathtrap.

"Where you want to go?" asks the bored young man behind the wheel.

"The airport," Wilkins says.

The driver perks up. "Airport? You crazy? That's major trip."

"I can pay," Wilkins says, folding himself onto the ragged seat. "And the faster the better."

The driver's eyes brighten. "*Inshallah*!: God be with us," he shouts, and Wilkins clutches the puny metal frame as the *tuk-tuk* sputters into gear and prepares to defy the laws of physics, heading directly at any other car or person that gets in its way.

After a lot of swerving and honking, the road ahead gets clearer, and the *tuk-tuk* at full speed rattles like a beer can full of coins, churning up a cloud of dust that billows into the windows. Suddenly the driver hits the brakes, slamming Wilkins's knees against the metal barrier to the front seat. A herd of goats has ambled into their path. As the *tuk-tuk* lurches up to speed again, the animals leap to either side, bleating objections.

There remains the challenge of crossing four lanes of heavy highway traffic, which is traveling at three times *tuk-tuk* speed. Tires screech, cars swerve, and then in the farthest lane, a full-sized taxi, horn blaring, grows huge as it barrels at the *tuk-tuk*'s right side. Wilkins can see the whites of the driver's eyes before the vehicle just manages to veer to the left, and then the *tuk-tuk* is finally safe on the airport access road, approaching the loop in front of the terminal's tall arches.

It's dark now, and the Land Cruiser could be anywhere in the parking lot, invisible. Wilkins leaps out, throws 4000 dinars at the driver, and sprints through the door into the smell of stale sweat, cigarettes, and inadequate plumbing that is the Khartoum International Airport waiting room.

His phone vibrates. He flips it open. "OK, where are you?" is all Ronnie says.

"Where are you?"

"Airport access road. Front of the building."

"Hey, good instincts," Wilkins concedes. "So am I. Ditch the car and meet me at the main entrance."

"Is David with you?"

"I'm looking for him."

"What's going on, Wilkins? I mean does this happen often, with David?"

"This is not the time to chat," Wilkins says. "Just get over here." He clicks the phone shut and looks up to see her sprinting towards him. The two of them plunge through the doors and are stopped in their tracks.

The crowd is at rush hour density at this airport where most flights depart during the night. Everywhere passengers are standing in lines, patiently enduring a convoluted bureaucratic process to get out of the country that makes security at Dulles International back in Virginia look like a cakewalk.

Wilkins scans the cavernous, fluorescent-lit space for David's blue cord suit. Then he and Ronnie begin combing the expanse of orange plastic seats row by row. A fuzzy PA system announces the last call for Egypt Air flight 692. Two women wrapped in brilliant print dresses weep and cling to a young man fortunate enough to be escaping the country.

Then Wilkins catches sight of two armed men in uniform shoving their way through the crowd along the far wall toward the corner. He grabs Ronnie's arm and tries to ease in their general direction just as everyone else in the waiting room also seems to realize something's going down and begins pushing to see what it is. Swimming through the churning sea of bodies, the two Americans make out a patch of pale blue, a head of silver hair, finally a seated man, and a clutch of onlookers hovering around him.

With one ruthless shove, Wilkins clears a space for himself and drops to his knees in front of the twitching body sprawled on one of the seats. "David," he yells over the din, "tell me what happened. It's OK. We're going to take care of you. David?"

A couple of meaningless syllables come out of David's frothing mouth before it locks in a hideous grimace, and the twitching stops.

56

Professor James Crawford forces himself to rally, but he keeps falling back into a dark maw of guilt and dread, reliving the memory of a morning years ago. It was right after daybreak, before the heat, and he had only recently begun work on the excavation at Jebel Barkal that would become the center of his life. Back then he actually had an archaeological team, sponsored by the University, and they had just unburied the first extraordinary stone slab. After building a steel frame and setting up a block and tackle, the team managed to attach chains to its corners and flip it over. They dusted it off and found it was painted an azure blue that matched the glorious morning sky.

Some premonition made him look up from the pit at that moment and scan the blank horizon. He thought at first what he saw was a mirage, the tall column of blue cloth surrounded by a golden haze. But as the column moved closer, it took human shape. Soon it became a woman, and his team stopped working to gawk. In the midst of her slow progress, she stumbled and caught herself, which broke whatever spell had come over James Crawford, and he hurried out to meet her. When they were close enough, she locked her eyes on his and smiled. Nearer, and he saw her cheeks were streaked with salt.

She was a young woman, although she seemed ageless to him. She tossed aside the drape of blue cloth covering her left shoulder to reveal a sling across the front of her body, a sling that bulged with a dozing child. In one fluid motion, the woman slipped the sling over her head and placed the child in his arms, which extended seemingly without his willing them to receive it.

"You must help me take care of her," she said. "I see much difficult work ahead."

Now as he remembers Kendacke's words, a sob shudders through him. Mother and daughter had trudged all night across the chilly desert, in flight, she said, from the home of a highly-placed government official, where she had been a slave. She was more fortunate than most because the official's sickly wife had found her a comfort and her little girl amusing. "Though she was Muslim, she accepted my heritage. She treated us well and came to trust me," Kendacke said. "But no one was put on this earth to live in slavery. I knew I had to seek freedom for my daughter, and fulfill our destiny by coming home to Jebel Barkal." Three nights before, they had managed to escape.

And now he has failed them both. Anticipating Kendacke's distress compounds his own. In Mani's younger years he'd hired a wonderful nurse to care for the child, and once a week Kendacke managed to arrive at the back door during the night before the nurse's day off and leave the following night.

But when Mani started school, the nurse decided to marry and have a family of her own. James replaced her with a housekeeper who turned out to be much less than wonderful. Indeed, James had reason to believe that she reported to the government on Kendacke's visits, which became less frequent as the months went by.

One night, as he swung shut the wide back gate behind Kendacke's departing vehicle, a newly-acquired Hyundai Santa Fe, shots rang out, and he heard glass shatter. He ducked inside and ran upstairs to Mani's room. There the girl slept, undisturbed. For the rest of the night, he sat at his desk in the library, braced for bad news.

That time it never came. Instead when his phone rang, he heard an almost giddy Kendacke on the line. "Saved by the burned-out streetlights of Khartoum," she said, "and my new driver, an amazing man from the south named Lewis Kvol. The fools who dared follow me will not likely do so again. From now on, though, I think for safety's sake, dear James, you and Mani should visit me only at the holy mountain." After an incident like that, how could he ever have let the teen-aged Mani convince him she could be left home alone?

James is settling into another resigned vigil in the library when he notices the red box. Where did it come from? Cautiously he unlatches and lifts the lid. The box brims with what look like white stones of assorted sizes. He slams his fist on the desktop and lets out a shout of agonized protest, then composes himself, pulls out a folder from a drawer, and makes some notations. Any professor of archaeology knows the bones of the human hand and foot when he sees them.

57

The corroded tin hangar and stretch of sandy concrete go back to the time before Osama bin Laden funded the construction of the Khartoum International Airport, whose lights blink on and off now in the distance. A yellow taxicab sits at one end of the crumbling runway, high beams opening up the dark. Inside it, Wilkins is congratulating himself on talking fast enough to keep the corpse of David Kimball out of the hands of the Khartoum police. The driver is congratulating himself on the wad of cash Wilkins shoved at him to open the trunk.

Wilkins's satellite phone begins to vibrate. He sees the familiar number and flips it open.

"You beat me to the punch, Admiral!" Wilkins says, hopping out of the cab. "I was just about to contact you."

"Where are you?" Johnny Falco asks.

"Standing on an abandoned airstrip, waiting for a buddy in a Cessna. I'm afraid I've got to send our Chargé d'Affaires to Cairo. In a body bag."

"Jesus, tell me it was a heart attack."

"That's what I told the Khartoum cops, but I don't think so, sir. Trouble is, nothing's that clear."

"Circumstances?"

"Well, your *Parakeet* was right in the middle of it," Wilkins says.

"You've got her with you," the Admiral states.

"No sir. She had to return a car. But she should be locked up safe in her cage by now. I had an asset of mine, a good man, take her by the embassy then back to her hotel."

"You're sure he's reliable?"

"He went to jail for us, sir. They cut off his tongue among other things."

"Jesus Christ."

Wilkins recounts what he's been through beginning with Tory's phone call requesting directions. "I figure," he concludes, "get the body autopsied at a decent hospital, and we'll have a lot more to work with. Meanwhile one of our prodigies back at headquarters is hacking into a couple of airline computers. It might be handy to know if anyone on EgyptAir's flight 692, which left Khartoum around Kimball's time of death two and a half hours ago, is also ticketed through to Beijing on AirChina's flight 33. That's a popular itinerary around here."

"I'm not surprised."

"Kimball did tend to be a little outspoken with regards to his China opinions. He thought the Chinese were just as guilty of thuggery as the Generalissimo here and ought to be sanctioned too."

"Well, speaking of the devils, have you heard anything about a rice shipment coming into Port Sudan from Shanghai?"

"Is this some kind of set-up?"

"What do you mean?"

"Yesterday afternoon some locals approached me about keeping an eye on it for them."

"What kind of locals?"

"Guess you could call it a grass roots organization here, committed to feeding refugees instead of government fat cats."

"Well, I just promised Roger Booth a Navy escort once it exits the Indian Ocean."

"Vice President Booth? I don't get it."

"Neither do I, which is why I want you to find out what else the ship's carrying, besides a couple tons of humanitarian relief."

"Will do, sir." The droning overhead grows rapidly louder. "Just to alert you, sir, the Cessna is currently circling to land."

"Listen, you take the bird with you to Port Sudan."

"With all due respect, she's pretty green."

"Why do you think I called her Parakeet?"

"Roger. She and I depart for Port Sudan first thing in the A.M."

58

"Say what you have to say," orders Maud, cutting off Tory's elaborate explanation for why she's late reporting in.

"Hey, are you all right?" Tory asks. What happened to Maud's usual calm, controlled self?

"I'm in the car, on my way to a lunch meeting, after slaving in the office until midnight last night then back at the crack of dawn, trying to put together the full picture in Khartoum. There seem to be some mysterious detours in the information highway, but what I'm getting isn't pretty. Having to worry about what happened to you doesn't improve matters."

"Well, I've got something for you," Tory says, "unpretty and straight from the horse's mouth. David Kimball's been killed."

"I was afraid of that."

"You were?"

"I had no luck trying to reach him at the Embassy."

"I was with him before it happened."

"When?"

"Maybe three hours ago now. We found his body at the airport."

"Goddamn it to hell! I should have known *that*. You did write this up?"

"Right away. My stuff goes through Cairo though, remember."

"I don't care if it goes through Siberia. Major intelligence like that should have been screaming out of my Urgent basket by now."

God, the woman's never satisfied, Tory thinks.

"Well, are you going to tell me what happened?" Maud asks. "Last I heard you were going to play tourist for the day."

"That's right. We drove out to this mountain, Jebel Barkal, in the early morning. It's an amazing place, Maud. Sort of spiritual. All these pyramids around."

"David Kimball, please."

"I'll get to him. But first there's this woman who actually lives there, inside the mountain. She's the descendant of the ancient Nubian pharaohs."

"Oh, for crying out loud."

"Now, what's the matter?"

"Her again."

"You know Kendacke?"

"I know of her. Where are you right now?"

"At the Hilton. On the verandah."

"I think you should go on up to your room."

"Why?"

"Call me back from your room."

"I don't get it."

"She's dangerous."

"What do you mean?"

"Your boss is dead, isn't he?"

"And you think she had something to do with that?" Tory says.

"Kimball had no illusions about her. Unlike your father."

"Maud, I've talked to her. And let's just say it's pretty unlikely that she—"

A sound cuts her off: like someone clapping cupped hands. A split-second later a bullet pings off the wall under the cement balustrade where she is sitting. She snaps shut her phone and drops to the marble terrace. She grabs her gun from her backpack and peers through one of the gaps in the molded concrete.

The stars littering the sky shed meager light. Then a double flash, below her, along the riverbank, precedes two more muffled thuds and pings. She gives up on trying to answer the shooter, who is beyond her range. As long as she stays low, geometry will protect her.

She rolls across the terrace toward the French doors back into the dining room. She crawls over the threshold and pulls herself up, keeping her back to the wall, her hand behind her, trying to look dignified. When she lifts her eyes, there is that Meiying woman staring at her from under her stupid wig, with a guilty expression on her face.

"I am concerned I hear something out there," the server says.

I bet you are, Tory thinks, *setting me up to get killed*? "Don't look at *me*," Tory says. Misunderstanding the expression, the server politely averts her eyes. Tory quickly shoves her gun back into her pack.

"I'm sorry if you are frightened," the server says, face still turned away.

"I'm not frightened. I just dropped my phone."

As Tory heads for her room, she realizes that's the truth. She feels energized, not scared. She opts for the stairs, taking them on the run, by threes, fours, hurdling the adrenalin flood.

As she eases out into her corridor, her satellite phone begins to buzz. She flips it open to silence it, then back to the wall, gun in her other hand, creeps toward her room.

Once inside, she pops the gun back in her bag and calls Maud again.

"What was that?" squawks the woman's voice. She sounds like she has just run a four-forty, while Tory is hardly winded.

"What?"

"Why did you hang up?"

"You said I should get inside."

"Something just went wrong, didn't it?"

"I'm inside now."

"I want you to promise me that you won't associate with that woman, or the Professor."

"I'm trying to get useful *information*, Maud, which is more than my briefings at Headquarters had to offer." She's not going to mention the missing girl if she doesn't have to.

There is a silence on Maud's end, then she says, "Those two were almost certainly involved in your father's death."

"And that doesn't make them potentially valuable assets?" Tory asks.

"It makes them potentially dangerous."

"Come on, Maud, I have a job to do. Besides I thought you wanted to hear about Kimball?"

"You met him at a restaurant. He was drunk as usual. A kid brought him a note that caused him to leave the restaurant abruptly and get into a government car. You tried to pursue, got lost, finally found him at the airport, where he was gasping his last breath."

"Wow, you are good," Tory concedes.

"Well, thank you, Victoria," Maud says, her voice thawing a little. "I took a few minutes after you hung up on me to do a little research."

"In your car?"

"Actually I'm at the Army-Navy Club now."

"But how did you—"

"I've got my extra-mural sources."

"Did your extra-mural source tell you that the Embassy supply officer was already at the airport when I got there, not acting at all surprised by what was going on? I mean it's like he'd rehearsed the whole thing—took possession of the body, said he was going to make arrangements to have Kimball's body flown to Cairo for an autopsy. Then he pulled this baggage handler out of the crowd, a guy he just happened to know, who just happened to have his own wheels—"

"What if I told you I knew all that too?"

"I'd be impressed," Tory says, then her tone shifts. "But I'm telling you, I wouldn't be surprised if Kimball's body never gets to Cairo. There is something fishy about Wilkins. You should check him out."

"Thanks for the tip," Maud says.

"But I think I might have got something going with that guy he foisted me off on, Ahmed," Tory rattles on. "He's Muslim, seemed friendly, forthcoming—the kind of person who might want to help us out. Except he has a terrible speech impediment. Given my novice Arabic, I could hardly understand anything he said."

After she ends the call, she stands inside her door wondering how Maud could get that much information that fast, and what it means that she must not have heard about Mani's disappearance, because she never brought it up. Her thoughts are interrupted when a man steps out of her bathroom and begins to introduce himself, very politely, as if he were not pointing at her heart with a sound-suppressed gun.

59

"I don't like this," Maud says, as she closes her phone. "Unforeseen situation and she walks right into it."

"She'll be fine." Larger than life in his gold-trimmed uniform, Johnny pulls Maud's tiny hand through his arm and escorts her into the Army-Navy Club.

"This guy of yours doesn't call himself Wilkins, does he?"

Johnny ignores the question. "Remember, the deceased *was* a barely functional drunk." When they are seated, at one of the best tables overlooking the golf course, Johnny produces a manila envelope from his briefcase and tries to get her to smile. "Come on, Maud, don't I get a drum roll, at least?"

Maud sighs. "Of course. But I've got something I want you to read first." She plucks a folded document from her handbag. "From Ty's personnel file."

Johnny scans the page. "How much is true?"

"Well, he did have a hero complex, and it didn't take much to trigger it. So maybe he did create some bumps in the road for the diplomats. But it's not as if he went around proclaiming regime overthrow. This account is basically conjecture, opinion."

"So this Kimball guy just had it in for him. Some people are like that—they see someone who's confident, dedicated, good-natured, and they've got to bring him down."

"That tendency certainly explains the stories that made the rounds after Ty was gone," Maud says. "But if Kimball's been murdered, I'm not so sure it explains why he wrote this."

"How about two chicken caesar salads and two iced teas?" Johnny says, to get rid of the hovering waiter. Then to Maud, "So tell me what you're thinking."

"Timing," Maud says.

"Could you be a little more vague?"

"He was called away in the middle of a conversation with Victoria. Was he about to tell her something? See, what doesn't compute about Kimball's negative eval is, Ty was on *friendly* terms with the man. He told me more than once that Kimball never pulled rank, never unrolled the red tape, and seemed to have some sympathy for the plight of the Sudanese people."

"You know, I'd have to second that," Johnny says. "When I contacted my CTG guy about Victoria—all right, Wilkins—I asked him about the lay of the land over there. He mentioned that the Chargé d'Affaires took self-deprecation to the point of self-destruction, but it was hard not to like him. Yes, the guy was choosing to poison himself with booze, he said, but then you find out the wife he loved dumped him on grounds of desertion when he was assigned to Khartoum, and you begin to understand where he's coming from: stuck in the lowest circle of hell and paying half his salary in alimony to boot."

"So Mr. Good Guy turns nasty *two days before Ty disappears?*" continues Maud. "Is it just a cruel irony that Kimball's censure concludes with a recommendation to yank Tyler? I mean if that had come any sooner, it might have saved Ty's life. We'd have brought him home, or maybe at least been alerted to the fact that he was in jeopardy. Instead, Tyler suddenly vanishes, right after Kimball has slipped an explanation into the record that everyone can buy off on: Ty was working for the rebels and the government took him down. Timing."

The waiter sets down two plates of greens with chicken and the glasses of tea, then leaves.

"And before the damned personnel bureaucracy can get around to doing its job. You're pretty good at this, you know that?" Johnny says.

"Not good enough," Maud says. "The whole business is starting to feel like déjà vu. First Ty and now Kimball—why aren't we seeing these things coming? I'm beginning to think our whole operation in Sudan is compromised, and may have been for quite a while."

"That's not all that's compromised," Johnny says, pushing the sealed envelope in Maud's direction. "Here is your personnel file."

Maud raises an eyebrow. "I take it I haven't won an Oscar?" She slides a manicured fingernail under the flap. She begins scanning the pages.

"Try favoritism, unprofessional relationship with Tyler Pierce, disloyalty to Agency, you name it."

"The bastards."

"And I thought the Pentagon was bad for Byzantine intrigue. I'm beginning to understand why you think Tyler might have been an inside job. Listen, I ran this by Francesca last night, not in so many words, of course, but you know Frannie, she has a knack for putting her finger on the right button. First words out of her mouth were *Gordon Gray.* Think he could go off the rails?"

Maud pauses. "How far off? He's a detail guy, Johnny. His world doesn't extend much beyond Agency politics. I've pretty much decided he's trying to zap me for personal reasons, because he's basically petty and more interested in building a power base than fulfilling the Agency mission. But farther than that? I just can't picture Gordon going farther than that. Besides, it's still possible, isn't it, that we're just looking at a lot of troublesome but discrete events?"

"Well, I've got one more event to toss in the hopper. It involves Roger Booth."

"I barely know that man."

"Wish I could say the same."

"That's right. You two go back, don't you?"

"All the way to the mean streets of southside Chicago. We were blood brothers, had each other's backs, all that macho stuff. Which is why he thinks he can ask a favor, which he hasn't got the guts to put out there as an order." Johnny pauses to chew a mouthful of salad.

"And that is?"

"He wants the U.S. Navy, i.e. yours truly, to protect a rice shipment from China heading to Port Sudan. Sure, there are pirates in those waters, and possibly terrorists. But it's not like the Navy's got extra destroyers to throw around. Besides when it's Roger Booth who's spouting the humanitarian motives, I start smelling dead fish."

"But you agreed?" Maud asks.

"I'm going to. We might be glad to have a little back-up in the region. In case events over there get more troublesome and less discrete."

60

---

17 September. Khartoum, Sudan. 2140 hours.

"Who are you?" Tory asks, visualizing the hook punch to the jaw followed by the roundhouse kick that would drop the small, thin man in skull cap and striped *jellaba* standing in front of her—that is, if he weren't aiming a gun at her with both hands. It and his mustache seem too big for the rest of him.

"A friend," he says.

"Friends knock on each other's doors," Tory says. "Friends don't point weapons at—"

"It was necessary to get your attention," he explains, in heavily accented English. "Without getting the attention of anyone else."

The odd look on the server's face flashes across Tory's memory. "What about the person who let you into my room? You must have gotten *her* attention."

"A Hilton master key is a simple purchase in this city. But why don't you sit down? It will also be necessary for you to leave your bag here, against the wall. Friends do not confiscate each other's weapons, but they may ask that they remain out of reach during a friendly discussion."

Tory tosses her pack onto the desk, shoves the rattan chair against the wall, and flops into it. "OK, what do you want?"

The man slides his weapon into a holster under his tunic and seats himself gingerly on the edge of the desk chair, as if acknowledging he doesn't belong in her room. "Perhaps there is something *you* want also. I understand you are a collector of data."

"I'd sure like to know who took a couple of shots at me from the riverbank."

"They were not aimed at yourself, I assure you." He chews on the lower edge of his mustache.

"OK. So your buddy out there creates the distraction while you're busy breaking into my room."

The stranger shakes his head. "Perhaps we are merely impatient for you to hurry upstairs to meet with me. For I am making this special effort to mention to you a wonderful opportunity. A tip, you Americans call it. Something of interest will take place in the city of Port Sudan which you must not miss."

"Well, that was quick," Tory blurts.

"What was quick?"

Tory clamps her big mouth shut. "Nothing."

"You were expecting this invitation?" the man asks, visibly surprised.

Tory catches herself before answering this time. "Maybe, maybe not."

"Someone else has mentioned Port Sudan to you. Who is it?"

"I've talked to a lot of people in the last couple days."

The intruder nods thoughtfully, as if scanning a list in his mind.

"OK," Tory goes on, "what if every one of them told me I just had to see the hustle and bustle of Port Sudan?"

"Then I must chime in like a monotonous echo. But they are probably not serious," the man says. "And I am."

"Who are you working for?" Tory asks.

"That is not important."

"I'm just supposed to follow instructions from a total stranger?"

"Yes. Without discussing them with anyone." He cocks his head at Tory as if that were a question.

"Fine," she says.

"Without the utmost secrecy, there could be grave consequences. Now you will be here, downstairs, in the lobby, at 1800 hours tomorrow. I will accompany you to the airport. The flight is not long. Two hours approximately."

"And what exactly am I not going to miss in Port Sudan?" *Could this be about Mani?*

"I do not exactly know."

"So you're expecting me to find out and tell you?"

The man rests one hand on the gun he has sheathed under his tunic. "That won't be necessary."

61

The click of the lock pops Arthur alert. The Boss is back, giving himself a once over in the mirrored wall as he enters the Gymnasium.

Does he notice the slight pause before Arthur jumps to his feet? Because the disgust Arthur's been stuffing for months, years, is starting to weigh him down, gum up the works.

Mr. Marshall's gaze moves from his own reflection to the sleeping girl.

What's the bastard thinking? Arthur doesn't even want to go there. "You look tired, sir," he says, which is the truth—tired and messed up, like he's had on his suit for a couple of days. "May I suggest a good night's sleep? You must be jetlagged."

"What has she had to eat?" Mr. Marshall asks.

"She's too scared to take much."

"I want her to eat, Arthur."

"I've been trying," Arthur says.

"Anything she wants, she gets? Understand?"

And anything you want, you take. "Understood, sir."

The Boss moves to within two feet of the bed.

Don't touch her, Arthur thinks, *don't you dare lay a clammy hand on her, or I'm going to take the knife in my pocket and gut you like the jackal you are.*

Another step by Mr. Marshall and Arthur's breathing stops. *Can I do it? Cross the line into your fucked-up world? Hell, I'm already there. If you ask me to leave the room . . . When you ask me to leave the room . . . You are gone. And no one will miss you.*

The Boss is next to the bed now, looking down. Every muscle in Arthur's body tenses. The sedated girl sleeps on.

"She's beautiful," Mr. Marshall says.

Arthur swallows bile.

"This may be the best thing I'll ever do," Mr. Marshall goes on.

"I'm not in a position to judge, sir. But if you don't mind me commenting, you've had a long, hot day—you don't look yourself right now, sir—and this . . . *affair,* well, there's always tomorrow."

Mr. Marshall doesn't take his eyes off the girl. "I don't know, Arthur. I haven't made up my mind yet."

What is that supposed to mean? Arthur's stomach knots along with his fists.

62

Tory can't sleep. She's pushed the desk over to block the easily breached door to her room and set her Glock on the nightstand. She stares at the ceiling with wide-open eyes. Where is Wilkins getting his information? How does he stay one step ahead? He's a supply officer. He and she should not be on equal footing. She mutters the things she could have said to him when he insisted she get into that guy's car at the airport—all the indignation has to come bubbling up and out of her system.

Underneath it, there is the giant emptiness of her father's death. She knows she can't go there. Her brain gropes instead for knowledge, answers to fill in the blanks caused first by those gunshots outside the mountain, then Mani's disappearance, then David Kimball's lurching departure from the café. That man was implicating himself in some capacity, and now he's dead.

At the edge of her mind hovers a possibility she doesn't like. Suppose Kendacke and James aren't the only ones who know she's undercover. Maybe those gunshots were *not* meant to get Ronnie Clark, well-meaning Economic Affairs Officer, off the verandah and up to her room. Maybe they were aimed to strike the daughter of Tyler Pierce.

Beware an angry man with happy eyes and no mustache, she thinks. What about the man who's flying her to Port Sudan? Does his ample facial hair make him safe? How badly did she blow it when she just assumed the guy had been sent by the First Vice President? How stupid of her: the First Vice President is from the non-Muslim south. If she'd only stopped and thought that the intruder's clothing marked him as Muslim, she would have been more careful.

She keeps turning the pieces around in her mind, looking for matching contours, a way to fit them together. The remembered scent she picked up in the Professor's library settles over everything like a fog. How could Adam Marshall have kidnapped Mani? Wasn't he "out of the country until a later date"? Besides why would he bother?

She realizes she'd rather avoid the piece that includes him. She wants him to have known her father, yet doesn't. She doesn't care if her cover's blown with him, yet does. She still harbors a faint hope that he's the one watching out for her, but resents the whole concept. Couldn't someone else besides Adam Marshall use that same heavy cologne?

What about the Professor and Kendacke? Had they really cared about her father or simply used him? If this situation with Mani hadn't interrupted everything, wouldn't they have divulged the puzzle of his death by now? Tory isn't used to trusting people; she isn't even sure what trust means. But there *was* something clear and authentic about Kendacke, her solemn statement that, yes, she had proof of Tyler Pierce's death. That was more than anyone else had been able, or willing, to offer Tory. If anyone deserved to be trusted, shouldn't it be this woman? She had taken away Tory's last shred of irrational hope that her father had somehow survived his disappearance, but in exchange, hadn't Kendacke given her that one sentence of truth?

Maud's suspicions don't faze Tory. They probably spring from some personal, spinsterish resentment that Tory would rather not speculate about.

A predawn glow begins to lighten the room. Better get started early, she figures. All she's got to do today is find a missing Sudanese teen-ager before flying over to Port Sudan.

Right!

63

18 September. Khartoum, Sudan. 0700 hours.

The First Vice President sits at his desk, sipping grainy coffee, smoking a cigarette, and gazing at a photo framed in silver filigree: a striking woman flanked by two small girls with wide, delighted smiles. The portrait is all that remains of them.

Years ago he and Lewis were deployed with the People's Liberation Army around Bentiu when an Arab militia attacked their home, sparing no one, treating the occupants the same way they treated the furnishings and crockery, the surrounding acacia trees. What they didn't steal, they smashed, or chopped down.

He picks up the snow globe from Paris and gives it a shake, watches the snow settle, then shakes it again. When he hears the knock on the door, he sets the magic sphere aside, stubs out his cigarette, and turns his hands to better use.

"I have been expecting you," the First Vice President says, when two men enter, the one in white pants and shirt-sleeves, the other in army uniform, clenching a Kalashnikov.

"Then you are ready to admit the truth," says the civilian. "You are a traitor to your country."

"No. Not to *my* country. I am loyal to my country, a beautiful place, peaceful, rich in resources."

"You are a stupid man to talk so much," says the civilian.

"If I am so stupid, then why does my heart break?"

The soldier gestures with his gun. "You will come with us."

"Why should I come with you?" asks the First Vice President, rising, wrapping one hand around a different sort of globe, in the side pocket of his safari vest.

"To answer questions," says the civilian.

"But you already know everything."

"There are still questions."

"Aha. I must become a toy for the sadistic pleasure of Mukharabat," says the Vice President.

"You are traitor," spits the soldier.

"You will please place both your hands where we can see them," says the man in white.

"Certainly." The First Vice President offers them, palms up.

But the man in white has momentarily turned to the soldier, who has shifted his weapon and his attention to unclasp the handcuffs from his belt. For a precious instant they are unaware of the olive-drab fragmentation grenade on their prisoner's left palm, his index finger already through the pull ring and, quick as a magician, lifting the pin away. Now the faces of his two unwelcome visitors gape in disbelief.

An instant later the soldier has braced his rifle and begun firing in wild bursts. The bullets rip into the flesh of the First Vice President, splinter his desk, shatter the family portrait and the snow globe from Paris, as the four-second fuse on the grenade burns down. The deadly stuttering of the rifle swells to a thunderous roar.

64

Tory pulls on light cotton drawstring pants and a loose overshirt, and to be ahead of the game, her backpack is already loaded with toothbrush, toothpaste, handgun, ammunition, and change of underwear. There's a tapping on her door.

It's Wilkins with a tray. Fruit salad, sweet roll, a cup of that grainy coffee. "Rise and shine," he says.

"Oh god," she replies. "What are you doing here?"

"We've got places to go, people to meet."

"What did you do, sleep with the server again?"

"That sort of remark doesn't say much for your powers of analysis. We've got a job to do."

"What do you mean, we? I've got my own agenda for the day, and I really don't have time—"

"That's right, you don't. We have to be on the road before nine, if we're going to get to Port Sudan by dark."

"Is this a joke?"

"How about you get your shoes on while you're laughing?"

"Wilkins, a young girl who lives with Professor Crawford went missing yesterday. I need to find her."

"The lives of a thousand girls may depend on our getting to Port Sudan."

"I'm sorry, there is only one girl like her," Tory says—another gut feeling. "You know, you are the third person in thirty-six hours who thinks I should visit Port Sudan."

"I am?" Wilkins looks surprised. "Who are the other two?"

Tory shrugs, enjoying the fact that she seems finally to have gotten one up on him.

"Come on, Ronnie."

"Thanks for breakfast."

"Hey, was this desk always in the middle of the room?"

"I've got to find that girl."

"I don't know whom else you've been talking to, but if you would just stop and think for a minute, you might realize you have got to hang with me on this one—Port Sudan and right now."

She replays the paranoid ramblings of the First Vice President, the veiled threats of the intruder, and avoids meeting Wilkins' blue eyes. If there was something fishy about this guy, here was the chance to find out what it was. "All right," she says finally, "you win. But not by a landslide."

65

She doesn't like his questions. She gives the shortest answers she can, and still he nods knowingly, as if Milwaukee and retail hardware were really interesting subjects, then he asks something else.

"OK, your turn." She turns to face him. "Where are *you* from? What's it like? What do *your* parents do? Where did *you* go to school? And what did *you* do right after you graduated?"

Wilkins stares straight ahead. "I was only trying to make the time pass."

"I didn't get a lot of sleep last night. I think I'll catch some Z's. Wake me when you want me to spell you." She cranks her seat back and closes her eyes. Instead of falling asleep, she finds herself wondering what Wilkins' answers would be to those questions. Maybe she shouldn't be letting him off the hook, but she figures whether he's for real, or whether he's not for real, she'd just have to listen to some sort of cover story as boring as her own. And that's the last thing she needs.

They make a stop in the town of Atbara, a main drag of squat storefronts, sand-blasted jalopies, stray livestock and skeletal dogs. Wilkins fills up the Jeep, which he had equipped overnight with four brand new tires, after slipping an extra 20,000 dinars to the owner of a gas station near the Embassy.

At a food stand, he buys bottles of juice and another sweet, sticky pastry apiece. Then it's good-bye to civilization such as it was—the shabby buildings give way to round huts with thatched roofs, vehicles to scrawny donkeys, an occasional camel, after which the world narrows to a sandy asphalt strip across desert monotony.

The tires hiss along. Tory polishes off the pastry and tries to lick her fingers with cool dignity. She's probably consumed more sugar in the last seventy-two hours than she would in a month back in the States.

"Poor David, may he rest in peace," Wilkins says finally. "They never should have kept him in this inferno, not after it burned him out."

A sort of world-weariness in Wilkins' tone causes Tory to realize: having a boss like David probably loaded an awful lot of responsibility onto a lowly supply officer. In fact Wilkins has probably been running the Embassy show. Of course that's also given him enormous freedom. Which means he could have been getting away with anything. She sneaks a look in his direction only to catch him glancing at her. Embarrassed by the coincidence, each turns away.

I take it David wasn't much help with the girl?" Wilkins angles his gaze away, as if intrigued by the scenery—strangled vegetation, more grey than green, and weird tumors of rock breaking the horizon. "I might have been, you know, if you'd told me about it right away."

"Pulling you in just seemed too complicated, OK? Besides, maybe I assumed you knew everything. You usually do." *Thanks to your dubious sources, like the server at the Hilton café. God, you put a blond wig on a fire hydrant, and the guys line up to ask it out.* She makes a mental note to initiate a discussion with Ms. Wig at her next opportunity. "But if you've got any suggestions as to how to locate this girl—her name is Mani—I would appreciate—"

"Mani. The Professor's ward? That ups the stakes for me. As soon as we get back to Khartoum, I've got contacts I could share—"

"What about official channels?" she asks.

"She's a drop in the bucket," Wilkins says, shaking his head. "Nope. We'll be on our own in this one."

"*I'll* handle it then," Tory says.

"Let me know if you need anything."

Their eyes meet and dart away again. Tory stares out the passenger window. Her memory flashes to the bodies of Kendacke's two young guards.

Wilkins checks the rear view. "Holy shit! That's impossible!"

"What?"

"Those cars are so new and so hot, they aren't even in production yet for this part of the world. I've only seen pictures."

Tory swings around to look at Wilkins new love, which appears to be a speck of a vehicle in the distance speeding toward them.

"That car is perfect for this place. *The* Mercedes-Benz GL 420 CDI 4.0 SUV goes anywhere—mud, sand, rocky creek beds."

Tory frowns at him with puzzled disapproval.

"Hey, that car's got a two-speed transfer case and automatic locking center and rear differentials."

"Well, it looks like your life is complete," Tory says, swiveling again to see a Silver Mercedes growing larger by the minute.

Wilkins takes his foot off the accelerator and allows the Jeep to slow to 40 KM. As the GL looms closer, he pulls to the right, lowers his window and waves it past.

The large tank-like vehicle swings into the left lane, and eases abreast of them. She glances over, then freezes. Framed in its passenger window is Adam Marshall, raising the back of his hand to her. She can't tell whether it is a threat or a salute.

66

Suddenly the Mercedes accelerates and breezes past. It lodges fifty meters ahead on the diagonal, blocking the right lane.

Wilkins brakes to a stop. The GL driver is already out and moving toward them. It's her unexpected visitor from last night in the same striped jellaba and kufi, his shaggy mustache half hiding a smile.

"Great," Wilkins says.

"You know this guy?"

"Oh, yeah, he's an old *friend*," Wilkins says, lifting the armrest and pulling out a .44 Magnum Desert Eagle."

"Where did you get that?"

"Personal collection."

"What happened to the Beretta?"

"It's around somewhere." Wilkins lowers his window. "Who's your new boss, Umar?" He points the Magnum at the man's face.

"Good morning, Miss Clark," the man says, looking right past the weapon in Wilkins' grasp. "You are awake quite early."

"Your friend, here, gave me no choice," Tory says.

"It would have been more comfortable to travel by air to Port Sudan," Umar says, finding the ends of his mustache very tasty. "We must make him understand this fact."

"All right, then, what's the big deal in Port Sudan these days?" Wilkins says.

"You should not expect to know everything, Mr. Wilkins. You and I have learned by now that perfect intelligence is an illusion, to be found only in Paradise. And if I may make another suggestion: one of my passengers is covering this conversation with a Kalashnikov. Yes, yes, a quick glance at the rear window will confirm this minor bit of intelligence, Mr. Wilkins, after which you must conclude that there is no room in the picture for that over-sized toy of yours."

Staring straight ahead, Wilkins gives up his weapon.

"And Miss Clark, your pack, if you don't mind."

"What do you need with a lady's bag?" Wilkins asks.

"These are temporary measures, I assure you," Umar says, as Tory hands over her backpack. "Small formalities to ensure that you will follow us as far as a secondary road ahead, where we turn right and proceed for one kilometer."

They watch Umar jog back to his monster vehicle, then Wilkins starts the Jeep and rolls forward in the GL's wake. "If you ask me, Lover Boy Marshall has a strange way of dealing with his fellow Americans," he says.

Tory doesn't rise to the bait. She's feeling a little sorry for Wilkins, who's obviously in over his head. At the same time she feels confident for the first time since she arrived in country that she will be able to navigate whatever complex course lies ahead. "How do you know this Umar guy?" she asks.

"We've crossed paths a couple times. Over David's drinking and his big mouth. He's low-level Mukharabat." He swings the Jeep onto the so-called secondary road, its packed sand lumpy from disuse. "OK, open the glove box," he says, "and get out a small black case."

Tory does so, unzips it, and pulls out a metal disk.

"You need to secure it somewhere with a piece of that tape."

"Where did you get a Body Transponder?"

"Never mind that. But I'd suggest you think of a spot they won't pick up if they frisk you."

"Nobody's going to frisk me."

"Just in case, Ronnie. For once would you take me seriously? It's not as if you've got all the time in the world."

"Well," she says, "these boobs of mine aren't going to hide anything."

"You said it, I didn't."

She considers the sole of one foot, an armpit. "Don't look."

"I'm watching the road."

She tears off a square of tape, presses the device in its center, then slips it down the back of her pants and underwear, between her buttocks. It is definitely uncomfortable. "This is silly," she grumbles.

"We can only hope."

The Mercedes stops in the middle of nowhere. Wilkins pulls up behind it. Umar bounces out of the driver's seat and motions to Wilkins and Tory to join him on the sand. When they don't appear fast enough, he waves his hand and the SUV's rear window slips down a notch. The tip of a gun-barrel pokes out.

"Hope you remembered your sunblock," Wilkins says when they are standing side by side, as if that would have kept the heat from searing her eyeballs and nostrils.

Umar opens the passenger door to the GL, and Adam Marshall emerges in an immaculate pale grey suit. He raises a white umbrella to protect his pallor as he places his Italian shoes carefully on the uneven ground.

Tory throws Marshall a friendly smile, which he acknowledges with a stern twitch of his head.

Shit, she thinks and instinctively moves a step closer to Wilkins.

"Miss Clark," Marshall says, emphasizing the name as if to mock it, "I have business tomorrow in Port Sudan, and thought you might like to accompany me the easy way, by private jet. Since you seem to prefer a more time-consuming journey, I would appreciate your joining me for the remainder of it, following a security check, of course, by my friend here."

Umar slips a metal-detecting wand from under his tunic. Tory looks over at Wilkins, surprised as much by the wand's appearance as by the fact that he seemed to know it was coming.

"I don't think your granting my request requires permission from anyone," Marshall goes on. "And the fact is, it will be very much in your interest to do so. So if you don't mind . . . Umar?"

Tory plants her feet, toes out, and contracts every muscle in her lower body from the buttocks down. She stares ahead and tries to forget she's female. Umar takes his time, stroking the backs of her knees, her throat, her armpits. She tries mentally to remove all sensation from her body. She focuses on reciting the Pledge of Allegiance to herself. Meanwhile she can hear Wilkins' breathing getting louder.

"I'm fine," she tells him when Umar takes a step back.

"Of course you are," Marshall says, finally giving her half a smile. "The young lady and I have plenty to chat about. For example, the young lady and I differ on the subject of China's position in global politics, do we not, Miss Clark? In the next twenty-four hours, I predict her opinions will change."

"Sounds interesting," Tory says, perking up a little. "Any idea how and when we're getting back to Khartoum?"

"I've taken care of everything." Marshall places his right hand under Tory's elbow, then guides her into his vehicle. As the familiar spiced fragrance assaults her, her spirits sink. "What about him?" she asks, cocking her head in Wilkins's direction.

"He is free to go," Marshall says.

"See you later," she tells Wilkins, from the chilled space of the Mercedes. She glances into the dim rear section and exchanges a nod with the thick-set, convincingly-armed Chinese man sitting there. He hasn't a hair on his head. Or his upper lip.

"I don't think you've met Chen," Marshall says. "My acupuncturist. Never leave home without him."

Tory watches through the closed door as Marshall and Wilkins share some apparently unfriendly words.

Then Umar raises a hand, Chen's Kalashnikov delivers an ear-splitting barrage through the cracked window, and the left rear tire of the Jeep shrinks into the sand. A second blast to the left front tire accomplishes the same thing. Wilkins reaches into his inside jacket pocket for his phone, Umar cocks his head away from the vehicles, and Wilkins lobs the phone in that direction. A third report from the Kalashnikov kills it in midair.

"I wouldn't call that *free to go*," Tory says, after Marshall has settled into the seat in front of her.

"We didn't blow out his feet, did we?" Marshall replies.

67

The billows of dust from the departing dream-car fade from sight. Wilkins slides behind the wheel of his defunct Jeep, removes the airbag cover, and for a while watches the cursor that represents Tory's responder inch east along the computer screen. Then he puts the airbag cover back in place, gives it a fond pat, and climbs out of the vehicle.

A click on the stem on his oversized watch switches the face to a compass. He lifts the back seat of the Jeep and yanks out a leather sack, unpacking sun block, bottled water, and dates in order to get to his hand-held computer complete with GPS, a back-up sat phone, and a map he drafted himself of the Sudanese railroad system.

This is his payback for letting Umar off yesterday at Jebel Barkal: Ronnie kidnapped, the confiscation of his weapon, the macho massacre of one of his mobile phones, not to mention one more god-damned pair of tires. Otherwise the rest of his equipment, everything he needs to find his way out of the middle of nowhere, including the Beretta holstered on his right calf, has been left intact.

From the space under the seat he also pulls out the vest from the day before, a Norinco pistol in each inside pocket. He sticks one and the clip from the other into his sack, then tosses the empty gun back into the Jeep. He puts on the vest. Hardly a fair trade, but such is the predictably unpredictable course of this game called Spy.

Still he is worried, more about Ronnie than himself, even though the infernal heat has already brought his blood to a boil. It pounds inside his pith helmet, and he can feel his skin burning through the thin fabric of his short-sleeved shirt. With a resigned snort, he slops lotion on his arms and neck, then pops a date into his mouth.

He flips open his phone, presses speed dial, then waits for the beep. "Admiral? I've got the damnedest thing to report. Parakeet and I are on the road to Port Sudan as per your orders when we're intercepted by Adam Marshall. That's right—one of the richest guys in the world, and he's chasing Ronnie and *me* across the Sudanese desert? And we're all trying to get to Port Sudan? Come on, Admiral. You obviously know more than you're letting on. Sir.

"Anyway, one of Marshall's thugs—who also happens to be Mukharabat, by the way—anyway, the jerk grabbed Ronnie, shot my wheels out, and took off into the sunrise. I did get her to attach a GPS transponder—go into the CTG website—code name Parakeet, of course. If you could track her and keep me posted, I'll follow up when I get to the port. I'm on Sat2. Over and out. Sir."

Wilkins studies the map of train tracks. The GPS route pegs Atbara at twenty-five kilometers back. His best guess is that the railroad track is several kilometers to the north. He takes a slug of water. No way of knowing when the next train will pass through. The published schedules are more decorative than real, designed to attract potential investors to Sudan.

Wilkins repacks his bag and starts trekking.

68

18 September. Jebel Barkal, Sudan. 1130 hours.

When the Professor comes upon them amid the crumbling statuary in the temple anteroom, wrapped in a farewell embrace, he cannot bring himself to speak. As much as he wants to share the burden of pain, he dreads witnessing its destructive impact.

"James," she says cheerfully, when she notices him. "It is a happy surprise to see you back so soon. Tell him the news, Lewis. We have such good news."

"It concerns possibility, not certainty," Lewis cautions.

"But I am certain. The Feast of the Double Cobra will indeed be a feast. Food for hungry bodies as well as hungry souls. For Lewis has a plan to obtain plentiful rice, and I know it will succeed." She peers at the older man more closely. The vivacity in her lovely smile fades. "What is it? Your eyes. Something is terribly wrong."

The Professor opens his mouth but words fail.

"It's Mani," Kendacke says, her voice dead calm.

The Professor nods.

"Something has happened to Mani," Kendacke continues, mercifully speaking for him. "Our enemies. She has fallen into their hands. Oh, no, no." Her voice slides up into a scream, which she abruptly stifles.

"Tell us," Lewis orders, his arms cradling the woman.

The Professor summarizes what he knows.

"Enemies," Kendacke declares. "They are all frightened men. Cowards. Afraid that a mere girl may possess more true power than they do. Merciful Isis!" Her anger melts and she slides to the earth where she rocks back and forth, a low moan emanating from her lips.

The thin veneer of hope has cracked, and for a long moment, all three struggle in silence against the welling up of despair. Then Lewis kneels beside his lover. "We must find your daughter. The ceremony cannot take place without her. I'll search the desert with the Hummingbird, and then the city—we have so many people there. I promise you—"

"No," Kendacke interrupts, suddenly still. "You must pursue the rice. It is just as crucial for our survival. James will help me. He will contact the American Embassy. Maybe they can give assistance."

"I'm not hopeful. The Americans will be in a state of turmoil. The Chargé d'Affaires, David Kimball, was found dead last night at the airport. Foul play is suspected."

Kendacke slumps, head in hands.

Lewis tries in vain to raise her face to his. "I must return to the Capital to gather a second squad for this rice operation. You must not leave the mountain while I'm gone, Kendacke. It is clearly too dangerous."

The woman shrugs off his hands and rises to her full height. "Two days from now, the divine energy of the sun will penetrate our temple. Neither danger nor foul play can prevent that. James, you must maintain contact with Victoria. Even in turmoil, she will rise to our aid."

69

---

18 September. Nubian Desert, Sudan. 1130 hours.

Each time Tory tries to steal a glance through the slit of the rear window, she meets Chen's heavy-lidded eyes. The fact that his upper lip lacks a mustache is never lost on her.

"Where's Arthur today?" she asks Marshall. This silent gunman can't be his permanent replacement.

"Arthur is handling some very important business for me," Marshall replies.

As the Mercedes climbs up onto the paved road, she takes one last look back: distance and the desert heat have transformed poor Wilkins and his Jeep into a stunted tree and a shimmering rock. A cold dread invades her chest. Wilkins has survived three years in this country, he's got all those precious maps, his hoard of sun block, he will survive this, she tells herself. Then her mind flashes to David gasping his last, and she's less sure. Meanwhile the irritating pressure of the metal transponder she is sitting on reminds her that Wilkins has given up being traced in order that she can be.

"You are going to thank me for this," Marshall says.

"Being coerced at gunpoint?" Tory asks the back of his head.

"I'm talking about landing a piece of top-rated intelligence about our false friends, the Chinese."

"Syntech is just a paragraph on my resume, Adam," Tory says. "I haven't kept up with China since I left."

Marshall shifts in his seat so he can look her in the eye. "Do you really believe that I believe that gathering economic data on this pathetic flop of a nation is going to strengthen the national security of the U.S.?"

"I believe in doing my job."

"And I believe you take after your father: you'd never pass up a chance to save the world."

"My father sells hardware."

"Fine. If by that you mean diverting U.S. weapons from the Sudanese Liberation Army to his own pet mob of crazy insurgents. Once upon a time."

Tory clamps her jaws shut. Her mind races.

"Sorry. I see you have a selective approach to the truth. How very American." Marshall turns back around in his seat.

"Well, you've managed to insult the nationality of everyone in this vehicle."

"These guys pledge allegiance to *me*," Marshall says. "If you knew any better, you would too."

"So why did you have to completely disable Wilkins."

"Never trust a man who wears bow ties."

"What kind of approach to truth is that?"

"Look, he hasn't particularly distinguished himself in his tour here, has he, Umar?"

The driver shrugs, then shakes his head. "Nah. He has beginner's luck sometimes. That's all."

"So he's more than just a supply officer."

"Less. He's a bungler," Marshall says. "You want to wander around Port Sudan with a bungler for a guide?"

Tory doesn't answer. The inescapable smell of Marshall's cologne nags at her memory: the foyer of the Professor's house, the missing girl, she herself as much as abducted. She doesn't like the conclusion staring her in the face.

Just then she hears the tinny opening bars of "God Bless America," the ringtone of her sat phone. Her backpack is in the rear with Chen where Umar stashed it.

Marshall ignores the sound. "You're safe with me. We have a date tomorrow to see some sights you are not going to forget."

The ringing stops.

---

70

18 September. Jebel Barkal, Sudan. Noon.

"That was very odd," the Professor reports, when he reappears in Kendacke's room underground after making the call. He finds her kneeling before the wall etched with the rounded shapes of female deities. "Her phone rang to its limit, and I was preparing to leave a message, then decided to hang up, wait a few minutes, and try again. It rang again at least ten times, and this time she answered. She says she is traveling to Port Sudan with an important American businessman, someone her Embassy *boss* ordered her to accompany. She apologizes for leaving Khartoum suddenly and promises to help us when she returns."

"Her Embassy boss?" Kendacke asks. "Didn't you say that man is dead?"

"Exactly. And it was Victoria who informed me of that fact last night."

"You didn't ask her what she meant?"

"There was something in her voice that urged against it. She was under strain, not herself."

"What about the important American businessman?"

"I didn't have to ask about him. I'm afraid that would be one Adam Marshall, the man you have ordered me never to mention in your—Kendacke, what are you doing?"

She has bent low over her knees, until her face rests on the sandy floor.

"I'm sorry, Kendacke, but you wanted to know."

After a long moment, she swings herself upright. "Someone must be notified," she says in a flat voice. "She is in grave danger."

"I tried the number of Bartholomew Wilkins. I couldn't even make a connection."

"He will destroy her."

"Wilkins?"

"Adam Marshall. He will destroy her as he tried to destroy me."

71

"I have not been completely honest with you about my life," Kendacke begins, "but it is not my own past I thought to protect. The first part is all true: my parents lived near here, in Karima. They kept orchards, and their harvests were plentiful—mangoes, dates, figs. When my mother felt the first birth pangs, she hiked to this mountain in order to deliver me to the goddess Isis inside the temple.

"My parents respected the depth of our history and taught me to read the ancient language, to understand the call of falcons, and to revere and defend the power of the sacred mountain above any worldly regime in control of Khartoum. Which is of course why I was picked up in the streets for speaking against the President and thrown into that jail cell, where it was so crowded we had to sleep standing on our feet.

"Over the years of our friendship, James, I have often thought that it was foolish of me, unnecessary to have altered the facts of my story from that point on. As if the divine Isis might be threatened and rendered powerless by the worst in human nature, when instead the challenge of evil and impurity simply makes her stronger. Indeed, my daughter is living proof.

"It has always seemed too difficult to go back and correct the untruths, but I must do so now. For you see, dear James, the man who picked me out of a group of prisoners, to whom I was sold as a slave, was not a Sudanese government official but his American neighbor. He was a wealthy businessman who traveled often to Khartoum but never stayed long. And so the couple next door, the government official and his wife, agreed to take care of me in his absence—in other words, become his assistant jailers."

"The American neighbor—was that Adam Marshall?"

Kendacke ignores the question. "Not a day went by that I didn't think of ways to escape. But the house was protected by security guards and an alarm system." She raises her fists in the air, as if against phantom aggressors. "When my daughter was born, I couldn't bear the idea of slavery for her. Still I watched and listened. Preparing food at official gatherings, I heard men bragging about the atrocities inflicted on the provincial tribes of Sudan. There was no doubt. I had to escape. My ancestors were calling me to a higher cause."

"How *did* you escape?"

"The official and his wife were childless, and they came to think of Mani as their daughter. They hired a nurse to take care of her while I did house-keeping, a Muslim woman from the nomadic Beja tribe, seeking a better life in Khartoum. As she grew to love Mani, I grew to trust her. And indeed, she unlocked the house and gate for us to leave in the middle of one night. I will never know at what sacrifice to herself."

Kendacke's words leave behind a cold, damp silence. Finally the Professor asks again, "Adam Marshall is Amanirenas' father?"

Kendacke nods. "When he returned to Khartoum, which was several times a year, I was taken to his home. He used me, as his consort." The Professor removes his glasses and rubs his eyes. "I tell you this, for in the following days something may happen to me. She must know everything, if she is to come into her full power. The horrible parts of her past will only strengthen her special gift, the eye at the center of her heart."

"Kendacke," Crawford says sadly, "I'm afraid there's not much chance of my outliving you. When Mani is found, you will tell her yourself."

Kendacke presses herself against the stone wall, her arms stretched wide. "Ancient mother, my namesake, who also lost an eye in battle, who led the Nubians to victory against Egypt, I pray on behalf of my daughter, whose first words were in the ancient Nubian tongue. Spare her to accomplish the impossible, and become a warrior for peace."

72

18 September. Nubian Desert, Sudan. 1300 hours.

He has run out of water and dates. His trail shoes are full of sand, his clothes, stiff with dried sweat. But Wilkins has found the tracks and is moving east along them, fighting the heat-induced delusion that it would be wonderful to lie down in the sand and roast to oblivion. Why bother to keep going? The train was due to pass his spot twenty-seven minutes ago. Obviously it isn't running anymore.

Cut it out! he orders himself. *Twenty-seven minutes is nothing, not even an eye blink.* The numbers on his watch shift. Twenty-eight minutes. He trudges on.

At thirty-three minutes, he stops. Thinks he hears something in the distance. The dull roar of an engine? Aural hallucination?

He plants himself squarely in the middle of the track and peers down it. He thinks maybe he can just make out a plume of smoke. Then he is certain he is seeing smoke, and an engine takes shape from a smudge of blue. The blue brightens as the engine gets bigger. He hasn't the strength to jump and cheer. His arms flop around as he tries to wave them.

The train slows, whistle shrieking. Now he can see the conductor furiously motioning him off the tracks. He can see the man's white-rimmed, incredulous eyes. Wilkins can't will himself to move. The engine grows larger. It's huge. Blindingly blue and loud.

At the last possible moment, he falls to one side. The train slows a little more as it passes him by.

He picks himself up and stumbles along beside the string of faded yellow cars. Passengers shouting encouragement from open windows and from the roof boost his energy. A man on a platform between cars extends an arm to him. Wilkins reaches for it with all the will he can muster, stretching every muscle out to his fingertips. But the two hands can only brush as the train passes, and Wilkins can't get enough traction in the sand to catch up.

The passengers begin yelling for the train to stop. It keeps on moving. The man between the cars jumps off, another man comes vaulting out of an open window, several others drop from the roof, tumbling into the sand. Finally, as they scramble to their feet and join the chase after the train, the screech of the wheels signals its halt.

One man is beside Wilkins, helping him hobble toward a platform between cars. Another extends a hand and drags him up onto it.

Inside each car is packed. Every seat contains at least one body while others perch on suitcases in the aisle. The unbreathable heat, the fetid humidity, the screaming children—the torture continues—more than Wilkins ever had to face in training.

Just as he thinks his knees will melt and send him sprawling across this lumpy carpet of humanity, he spots a man beckoning him cheerily from the end of the car. Wilkins climbs over a half-dozen passengers in order to grasp his outstretched hand.

Tall and burly, the man introduces himself as Arop Deng. A graceful twirl of his wrist presents his wife and four beautiful teen-aged daughters, in drapes of bright cloth tied at the shoulder.

Arop explains that he owns a small stand in the *souk* in Omdurman. He travels to Port Sudan four times a year to buy cheap merchandise from the Chinese ships to carry back to the city to sell there. His whole family is involved in transporting the packages of watches, handbags, transistor radios, ballpoint pens.

He is lugging five bags of the red onions his family grows in their courtyard. He intends to sell them in Port Sudan to increase the funds he will use to buy merchandise from the ship. Still he offers one bag as a gift to Wilkins, who thanks him profusely but refuses.

A tall man wearing a long grey *toube* and skullcap offers Wilkins a bottle of juice, which his parched lips and tongue won't let him turn down. The man introduces himself as Sharif, a lifelong resident of Sudan's port city. He makes a spot so Wilkins can place his briefcase on the filthy floor and sit on it. Sharif can't say enough about the glories of his birthplace. Between his detailed descriptions and the continuous clickety clack of the wheels on the track Wilkins is lulled to sleep.

73

18 September. Arlington, Virginia. 0630 hours.

Maud's silver Cadillac pulls into the near-empty parking lot of the Army-Navy Country Club and rolls to a stop alongside a navy blue Buick LeSabre, front to rear. Both drivers' windows slide down. "Your car or mine?" Maud asks.

"I'll be right over," Johnny replies, grabbing his mug of coffee and his attaché case. Resplendent as always in his gold-encrusted dress blues, he interrupts the process of lowering himself into Maud's passenger seat to watch a Verizon step-van enter the lot, swing past the mainmast flagpole with its fluttering pennants, and around the side of the brick building. It stops in partial view.

"See what I mean?" Maud says, when he has closed himself in next to her.

Johnny shakes his head. "Asinine charade. They've got to know we know."

"Right," she whispers. "But who are *they?*"

"There's only one way to find out." He starts to get out of the car. Maud grabs his arm.

"I don't think confronting that guy is going to tell us anything. He may even work for Verizon! Let's listen to the radio." She flips it on, and the wailing of some country-western singer fills the car.

Johnny folds himself back into the passenger side. He pulls a yellow pad and clipboard from his attaché case and a pen from an inside pocket. He writes, *Just in case they really have some equipment on board.* Then he says aloud, "So, Maud, how's that nasty cold you've been complaining about?" On the pad, he writes, *Some tough news.*

"Actually," Maud says, throwing him an inquiring look, "it was a stomach virus—one of those deals where everything around you makes you want to throw up." Then she really thinks she might, because Johnny's tidy, upright script has written, *My man lost V. but we know where she is.*

"Oh no," Maud gasps, gripping the clipboard.

Johnny reaches across to write the question, *Do u guys have anything interesting on A. Marshall?*

Very low profile, Maud scrawls, then thinks for a minute. *Big China investor, long-time friend of Sudan.* She covers her mouth with one hand, her face full of alarm.

"Yeah," Johnny says, knitting his shaggy white eyebrows. "And I've had enough of this garbage." He opens his door. "With all due respect, I think it's time to reach out and touch someone, with this." He raises a clenched fist.

"Oh, Johnny, don't waste your energy," Maud says. "We can go somewhere else." But he has already vaulted onto the pavement and now strides across the parking lot aiming for the service road at one side of the red-brick, white-trimmed clubhouse.

As he passes a bed of blood-red chrysanthemums, Maud hears a squeal of tires, then sees the Verizon truck begin to close its distance from him. She gives a useless scream as he jumps into the flowers, barely avoiding contact with the vehicle, which now barrels head-on at her Cadillac. It swerves at the last minute, but she takes a sharp jolt as it clips her front fender.

Johnny limps back to the car dripping fury, and drops himself onto the seat. Maud has fumbled out her phone and, with shaking hands, tries to press 9-1-1.

"Don't waste your energy," Johnny says, taking the phone from her. "You were right."

"But my car."

"We can't afford the distraction right now. It's what they want."

"Who are *they*?" Maud asks again.

"Let's go over to the golf course. We'll walk this thing off."

"If only *they* were the old boys out to get *me*," Maud says as they move along the path for golf carts. "I could take care of that in a coffee break, but it's . . . Oh god, what is going on? You're sure Victoria is with Adam Marshall?"

"She's got a transponder on her, so we've got their precise location."

Maud takes a deep breath. "OK. Back to square zero."

"Don't I wish?"

"What's that supposed to mean?"

Johnny shakes his head.

"Wait a minute, are you holding something back?"

"I've always downplayed my connection to Booth, right? And why not? Since I left Chicago for the Naval Academy, we've lived on two different moral planets, and now with him in the White House and me where I am, well, I'd hate for anyone to assume a cause-effect thing, you know what I mean?"

"Johnny, you are where you are on sheer merit. No one would ever believe otherwise."

"Thanks. The thing is if I soft-pedaled Booth, I buried Adam Marshall."

"Buried? Are you trying to tell me he's an old chum too?"

"*Chum* was not an operative word on the south side of Chicago."

"OK, *blood brother*, then."

Warning shouts waft towards them from a party of four golfers with a seven A.M. tee time. Johnny takes Maud's arm and turns her around toward the parking lot.

"Marshall was a varsity boxer at Cornell," he says. "He was a good guy to have on your side . . . what's the matter?"

"When you and Booth . . . discussed the boatload of rice, did Pierce's daughter ever come up?"

"Why would it? With all due respect for her importance to you, she's not going to register on their radar."

"I'm not so sure. Marshall showed up at Ty's in-house memorial on the arm of then-Director Hanson. Turned a lot of heads, as you can imagine—a rare bird like that. He said he'd known Ty and wanted to pay his respects. That was news to me. Have you stayed in touch with those two?"

"Yeah, we get together for drinks a couple times a year. But I've always been the odd man out."

"Well, let's say Marshall knows Victoria's a novice. Could he have somehow influenced her assignment to that god-forsaken country, figuring her lack of experience would enable some operation he's planned? Marshall asks Booth for a favor; Booth asks you. The operation probably involves that rice, but how, I don't know, since they're also managing somehow, maybe through Gordon Gray, to systematically frustrate my ability to pick up the leads."

They reach the cars and stand looking at the Cadillac's scraped fender. Johnny shakes his head. "My gut tells me you're on the right track, Maud," he admits. "But where are the specifics?"

"Well, there's one known quantity. Almost. Gordon's planted his own pathetic snitch right under my nose. I've been watching his communications."

"I've got another former student over in Naval Intelligence."

"Thanks, but I ought to be able to handle this myself." Still feeling that jolt, she lowers herself gingerly into the driver's seat.

"This guy's an IT genius."

"The Agency has its geniuses too."

"But are you absolutely sure now which ones you can trust?"

Maud's perfect posture sags as she realizes the truth.

"You'll need email logs, telephone contacts."

"I know, I know."

"We can tie my guy into your personal computer."

"How can I repay you?"

"I've taken a lot of verbal abuse over the years from those *chums* of mine. Nailing them would be its own reward."

74

18 September. Port Sudan, Sudan. 1700 hours.

Sheltering this Hilton's entrance is a stucco overhang braced by two arches. To Tory's relief, Marshall has reserved three rooms, hers in the middle.

The elevator isn't working so the four of them climb the stairs to the second floor, Chen carrying two suitcases and Tory's backpack in one beefy fist like a bunch of bananas. In front of her door, Marshall hands Tory her own key with a deep, sarcastic bow. She looks at him with determined neutrality— her brain is full of questions that can't be asked. Not now. Top priority is to be left alone for the night. "Trust me," Marshall says. "Tomorrow we'll get at the truth."

With a blank face, she closes her door.

The room is twin to the one she left in Khartoum, marble tile, double bed, desk, rattan chair, armoire instead of closet. Is there a bug, a videocam? She is too fatigued to care. And thirsty. After the unexplained fiasco with that brandy, she was taking no chances in the car. For eight hours she staunchly refused bottled water from the Mercedes' built-in refrigerator. Now she up-ends the bottle of water in the Hilton bathroom and guzzles it.

She uses the toilet, smoothly removing and palming the transponder in the process. Relief to both bladder and bottom. Then as she pulls up her baggy pants, she slips the transponder into one of the pockets, defying a hidden lens to catch that.

She has just stretched out on the bed when a soft tap, tap sounds on the metal door. Her heart sinks.

She drags herself to the peephole. To her surprise, it frames an unfamiliar dark face. She opens to find a young man carrying a large round tray, dotted like an artist's palette with mounds of food, a circle of flat bread folded into quarters in its midst. He sets it down on the desk then backs out, thanking her.

It all looks absolutely delectable. Her stomach cramps with longing. How could you drug bread? She pulls off a piece, scrapes it around the edge of the bean paste, then practically swallows it whole. She waits, mouth watering, for a numbness to begin taking over her brain. When it doesn't, she pulls off another piece of bread and attacks the edge of a different mound. This one contains meat! Savory meat. In a flash, she has gobbled the whole platter.

She can't believe it. Her mind feels more focused not less. Her mood surges, then plummets at the interruption of another knock. *Shit. Here it comes*, she thinks. She takes a deep breath and braces herself to talk fast, resort to hand to hand if necessary.

She cracks the door. There is Umar, holding out her backpack. "You forgot this," he has the nerve to say.

"Why, I don't know what's happened to my memory these days," she says, snatching it and closing the door. She rummages through it, knowing what she won't find. But fortified by food, she decides that the lack of a weapon and a phone are not going to stop her.

She flicks off the overhead light, moves over to the draped window and peeks out, thinking surely she can manage to scramble down a single storey. What luck! Her room opens onto a sort of fake decorative balcony, which is right above the stucco overhang that shelters the entrance to the hotel. She cranks wide her window. From it she should be able to lower herself to the patch of roof, then shinny down the steep slope of one of the arches—

Something white moves in her peripheral vision. A bulky figure in loose, white tunic and pants is waving his arms and kicking his feet in a slow dance. She cranes her neck to see where he could have come from, and sees that his room, next to hers, has French doors that open on a fake balcony. All he had to do was climb over the railing.

His face is shadowy, but his mouth is stretched open in a grin as fake and luminous as the Cheshire cat's. He is looking right at her. "I teach you *tai chi*," he says. "Very good for health."

"No thanks," she tells him, cranks her window shut, and yanks the drapery back in place.

She flops into the chair, head in hands. The pillow beckons. So tempting to get horizontal, rest, but she cannot give in to this captivity. She heists herself up again and crosses to the door. Eye to peephole, she finds the bulging corridor empty. She opens the door a crack, pokes her head out, and checks in both directions. Nothing but blue doors cut into peach-colored walls.

She straightens her shoulders then steps outside. She tells herself she is simply going to find the ice machine, and strides down the hall to the exit. She pulls open the fire door and slips into the stairwell. The door clanks shut behind her, and she starts down the short flight of steps. On the half-landing, she glimpses something white moving below, then the stairwell goes dark.

She freezes. Her ears pick up the rhythm of slightly labored breathing. She turns slowly, grips the rail, and begins inching her way back up the steps. Two, three, four. The breathing gets louder, more rapid, the darkness feels electrically charged. Six, seven, she reaches the second floor landing and fumbles to open the door. A hand clamps her arm, a manacle grip. She thrashes to get free, hears the sounds of her own panting struggle magnified by its futility.

Then there is light. Beside her Mount Acupuncturist has his other hand on the switch and shakes with silent laughter, though his grin looks more like a grimace.

Angry mouth, happy eyes, and not a hair on him. "I was looking for ice," Tory says. "I'll need some for the bruise you're going to leave on my arm."

"Ah yes," he says, tightening his grip and leading her back to her room. "I bring you."

Only minutes later, he taps on the door and hands her a second water bottle and a plastic bucket of ice.

What are there, two of those guys? She takes another peek out the window, fully expecting to see that fake Cheshire grin, but the space is empty now.

She calms her nerves by brushing her teeth for a long time. Then she bends over the bathtub and attacks her hair with a comb. Sand rains onto the porcelain. If only she could also comb away the idea that Chen is behind Kimball's murder. And where that puts Marshall.

She yanks off her running shoes and socks and lies down again on the bed, one hand over the tiny receiver in her pocket. As she drops off to sleep, she sees her father standing on a stage, with a box the size of a coffin by his side. It's like a graduation—folks waiting to file past him. She and Wilkins, of all people, occupy the last places in line. Then the music of whatever you call that wedding march begins, and the line moves forward onto the stage, but what her father pulls out of the box and hands to each graduate one by one is not a diploma, but a sub-machine gun.

75

18 September. Vienna, Virginia. Noon.

To be less conspicuous, Johnny has changed out of his uniform into the blazer and slacks he keeps at the office, but as he and Maud select a booth in a back corner of the Vienna Inn, they stand out nevertheless. With their perfect grooming and natural elegance, not to mention the laptop Maud opens onto the table, they are clearly something other than two silver-haired retirees out for the lunch specials.

"Your guy's fast," Maud says. "Tell him if he ever wants a job at the Agency, he's hired."

"What have you got?"

"Gordon's official phone log, for starters," Maud says, as soon as they have given their coffee orders. "First the bad news. No evidence of communication with my African analyst."

"Sorry to hear that."

"Not a big deal. Gordon would know better, and he can always meet Paul face to face. Now the good news: six calls in two months to this number." She turns the screen to face him. "It's a satellite job registered to RedCape, Limited, which is a subsidiary of Mephisto Group, which as we all know is owned by blood brother Adam Marshall!"

The ruddy color deepens in Johnny's face. "Shit."

"Second that." She pulls the computer back and taps in some instructions. Then she returns the screen to Johnny. "Here's Gordon's email log. Multiple messages from *Genesis@mephisto.com*, which turns out to be the oh-so clever moniker of *Adam* Marshall."

"What's he got to say?"

"It's trivial chatter, Johnny. Weather forecasts, health updates, travelogue. They've obviously agreed on a simple code. But so much for my 'little picture slash personal rivalry' theory of Gordon Gray. Yes, he's always had a chip on his shoulder towards me—after all, the world is out to keep him down because he's a wealthy white male—but this link to Marshall—it makes him a goddamn traitor. Something is going down, and I bet it's no accident it's happening on Tory's inexperienced watch."

"I'd be glad to take this to Director Terrell along with you, if you'd like some support."

"You're on. Just as soon as we cast a little bread on the water and see where it turns up."

"Want to be a little more vague?"

"Where does Booth fit in? We need to get some connections spelled out in black and white, cause and effect. Did I ever tell you the Agency's unofficial motto? When at first you don't succeed, try disinformation."

"Keep going."

"Even Gordon couldn't block the horrid news from Sudan this morning—the First Vice President was blown to bits in his residence. It made the second page of the *Times*."

"I'm not tracking."

"The First Vice President represents the non-Muslim South, and everyone is writing this off as assassination by Islamics backed by the President. But we're going to promulgate a different story: five-level intel from Victoria Pierce. We'll say she found a suicide note in Kimball's pocket litter, confessing that he abetted a black op run by the NCS to take the guy out."

"OK. But why would the NCS—"

"It doesn't matter. The International Court keeps threatening to indict the President. Our theory will be maybe this was supposed to get them moving. Or make them give it up. It doesn't really matter which. Wheels within wheels, right? The guys love it. But Kimball couldn't live with himself." Maud drags a finger across her throat. "I'll be meeting with my Africa analyst shortly, or rather Gordon's Africa analyst, to pass along the news. Then we track its journey through the system."

76

September 18. McLean, Virginia. 1400 hours.

"Mind if I borrow this?" Maud asks, picking up the mug Isabelle has just washed out for the day. *At my age, there's only one good reason to take up aerobics*, it declares on the front side. And the backside elaborates—*to hear heavy breathing again.*

"Anytime, boss," Isabelle says. "Want me to make a fresh pot?"

Maud shakes her head. "I'll be up all night as it is. But you could keep Paul waiting five minutes, before you buzz him in."

Isabelle winks her approval.

Maud places the mug at the center of her cleared desk, then takes a position by her window to wait.

A buzz and the door opens.

"You wanted to see me?" asks Paul as he pokes his pale head in.

"I asked you to show up five minutes ago."

His usual timid expression goes blank.

"Have a seat." Maud waves him to the chair facing the desk. She crosses her arms and paces away from the window and back while he shifts position, crossing first one leg, then the other. "It's about David Kimball's death," she says finally. "Apparently job pressures were getting to him more than we realized."

"We always knew he drank his lunch, which made him a little short on realism when it came to—"

"He committed suicide, Paul. We've got the note."

"Interesting. My sources haven't referenced any note."

"Your sources are forty-eight hours behind the curve. I'm dealing with someone in real time."

"I see. You're sure it wasn't planted?"

Staring at him as though he insulted her, she says, "Are you questioning my contact?" She notes with satisfaction that his averted eyes have come to rest on the mug. "Here's the problem. According to Kimball, the First Vice President was the target of one of our black ops." She rotates the cup in Paul's face. It catches his eyes, then they dart away. He begins scratching at a chapped place on his neck.

Maud hides a smile at his discomfort. "Kimball's note indicates he felt implicated in the death because he had prior knowledge of the op but was powerless to stop it. Kimball also requested that his effects be shipped to his sister in Oregon."

A pause. Her analyst clears his throat. "OK. What would you like me to do with this?"

"Get it into Kimball's file, of course. Otherwise, nothing. And I mean that. Not a word to anyone. I hate dealing with this deniable covert stuff. You never know whose toes you're going to step on, or who's on your side, do you know what I mean?"

Paul jerks his head forward, pops from his seat, and practically runs out of the room.

Maud lifts the empty mug as if in a toast. "Round and round the wheel goes, and where it stops, nobody knows."

Ten minutes later, Isabelle has her orders, and Maud has left the building and moved her car from its premium parking place to a remote corner of the Agency lot. With one part of her mind, she is finishing the *Washington Post* spread across the Cadillac's steering wheel. The other part keeps drifting to her laptop, open on the passenger seat. The Agency prohibits personal computers and phones from entering the premises, but this is her lifeline to the truth.

She flips to an inside page of the paper and finds herself staring at a photograph of an elegant, young Chinese woman. Beside her, a man is making every effort to turn his head away from the flash. The caption: *Chinese Trade Ambassador Zhang Hui and his daughter attend a Kennedy Center performance of* The Barber of Seville *with Adam Marshall of the Mephisto Group, a conglomerate with ties to Chinese industry.*

She's halfway down the first column of the article when a tiny light and a faint hum alert her to activity on her computer, upstaging Adam Marshall. *Bless you, Isabelle!* She pictures the matronly bulk of her secretary right that minute diligently schmoozing with the secretaries in the Africa section, keeping her eye on Paul and making sure he's aware of her surveillance. And realizes he better stay where he is.

One small step for womankind, Maud thinks, as the list of Sent Mail from Paul Livingston pops up on her screen, and the last message to appear is addressed to GGrayNCS.

77

19 September. Port Sudan, Sudan. 1000 hours.

Port Sudan: Bart Wilkins' travel buddy, Sharif, touted its beauty and majesty, its beaches and beautiful weather.

It turns out to be dingy, dusty, and steamy hot at high noon, a grid of littered streets lined with square, colorless buildings. Wilkins' body, clothed now in grey *toube* and headscarf, aches from spending nine hours folded tight on the floor of the train. He can't help smiling, though, at the memory of Sharif decked out in pith helmet and American khakis with their cuffs rolled up.

Thanks to the friendly Muslim's directions, he has no trouble finding "the finest shop in the city," that happens to belong to Sharif's best friend, and sells animal feed and car parts as well as shoes. He buys himself a pair of sandals. He hates to leave his almost-new Merrill hiking boots, but the shopkeeper seems happy with the exchange. Wilkins heads for the harbor.

The approach is a concrete promenade along the beach, featuring a couple of cafes. The sand itself seems to double as a rubbish dump, discouraging swimming or sunbathing.

He takes a seat at a table under a faded umbrella and orders himself beans and bread and half a dozen bottles of a nauseatingly blue sports drink made in China, which he forces down to replenish all the vital stuff his body has lost through its pores. Then he passes under the arch that marks the official boundary of the harbor. He is taking it slow along the main pier, looking for the Chinese freighter, when his phone begins to vibrate.

"So parakeet flew the coop," the Admiral says in a calm, flat voice. "I thought I put the best on this assignment."

"Admiral, your confidence is not misplaced. But first of all, she's as stubborn as a jay, and second, you know more than you're telling me, so I am at a distinct disadvantage when it comes to anticipating glitches, if you don't mind my saying so. Sir."

"All right, all right, simmer down. You're up against a master here."

"If you mean master thug."

"So you actually saw Adam?"

"Great. *You're* on first name basis with him too."

"Believe it or not, he and I grew up together in Chicago. We never had a thing in common except the desire to make something of ourselves. I did it my way. He did it his. And all I can tell you right now is that his way's starting to smell to high heaven."

"With all due respect, that can't come as a surprise to you, sir. Nobody gets that rich on arms and oil—"

"I know, I know. What am I supposed to do, gun him down in his New York headquarters?"

"Sorry, sir. It feels like crap that I let her slip through my fingers."

"Well, thank the lord your tracker is working. It's reading at East 37.21 longitude and North 19.57 latitude, which from here looks pretty close to the water. Think you can get to her before someone decides to toss her in the brink?"

"I'm on it," says Wilkins, punching the coordinates into his GPS. "Literally," he adds, because the red dot showing her location pops up on his screen practically under the arrow that marks his.

78

The Mercedes' idling engine oozes diesel fumes into the steamy heat, but inside the fragrant interior remains cool, and the tinted windows dim the sun's glare. It's a good thing too, wasted fuel or not, because Tory is stifling, shrouded in a dark brown, itchy *jilbaab* and a headpiece that covers everything except a narrow slit for her eyes.

"The problem is those freckles," Marshall told her this morning, as if that explained why disguise was necessary in the first place. "You might be interested to know your new cover: you are the widow of one of my oldest friends."

"What happened to Umar?" she asks, because now Chen is behind the wheel.

Amidst the sweaty chaos of the harbor, Marshall's manicured finger indicates an agile figure, like a swimmer, emerging from the sea of workers then diving back into it. "Umar's got his own job to do," Marshall says. "Ours is to keep an eye on that, over there." He cocks his head in the direction of the long, low-riding ship tied up in the right hand berth. It is marked with Chinese characters and stacked with brightly painted containers.

Up on deck, the Chinese crew members in blue flapping shirt-sleeves strap containers to the crane that maneuvers them over to the edge. They lift the gate at one end, and sack after sack tips into a portable elevator which lowers them to dock level then flips them onto a conveyor angling up onto the back of an army truck spewing black exhaust. There dark-skinned men in cammie pants and T-shirts push and tug them into tight-packed layers. Then with a throaty roar, the truck pulls out and rumbles right past the Mercedes. A minute later an empty one rattles in to take its place.

"Operation Rice for Refugees," Marshall says.

"Did you just make that up?"

"What, your boss never told Ms. Economic Advisor about Rice for Refugees?"

"Not in so many words," Tory says, staring out the window. The phone call she fielded from the Professor, and now this, the second time David Kimball's come up, without anyone mentioning his death. Is Marshall playing innocent? Chen's got to be the killer. Each time she goes there, adrenalin shoots into her veins.

"That's odd. Why do you suppose David would want to keep an important operation like this from an important player like you?"

"The ongoing relief efforts here are not exactly a secret," Tory says.

"But a charitable donation from the *Evil Empire*?" He turns around with a wink. "Ah, I can see you're savvy enough not to buy the charity part. It's a tactical investment, to guarantee a future of plentiful oil. That seemed like a reasonable trade-off to me."

"To *you*?"

"I brokered the deal."

"You did?"

"I did. Sucker that I am."

"Why sucker?"

"If any of this stuff ever makes it to the refugee camps, it'll be because someone got lost on the way to Army headquarters in Khartoum, and I knew that going in. But I thought it was a smart move anyway."

"But you don't anymore."

"Good guess."

"Why not?" Outside the endless, boring cycle of unloading continues. Her gaze snags on a tall figure in a long, grey *toube* and grey headscarf. Half-blocked by a pile of broken pipes, he's leaning against the wall of a low building opposite the ship, a mobile phone tucked up to his ear. Her heart leaps. Wishful thinking? Sunglasses and afternoon shadows hide the man's face.

"If I told you, you wouldn't believe me. Particularly not you, in your dream world, where everyone's supposed to get along because they're all just like you."

"I don't think that."

"Neither did your father really."

"I wish you'd stop that," Tory says.

"No, he was driven by the oldest ulterior motive in the book."

"What would that be?"

"X-rated."

Tory snorts a laugh. "You do not know my dad."

Marshall ignores the remark. "Right now there's something you have to see with your own eyes."

She glances out the window to check on the man. He is gone.

"I'm going to do you a favor," Marshall is saying. "I'm going to wake you up."

"Since when did you do favors?"

"Sometimes they're inevitable. Like collateral damage."

"What's in this little operation for you?"

"More money."

"Don't you get tired of that?"

"Do you ever get tired of breathing?" Marshall asks, in a tone that screams, *I'm in control.*

"Believe me, it's not that easy under all this crap you're making me wear." Beneath the outer feed sack, she's got on her shirt, under that her bra, and tucked into one of its A cups, only slightly uncomfortable this time, is the transponder disk.

"Trust me," Marshall says.

Hah!

79

19 September. Jebel Barkal, Sudan. 1630 hours.

"The room was at the center of the house," Lewis says. "The explosion gutted it. Nothing left except some exterior walls, surrounding a pile of rubble."

Kendacke and James receive the news in silence. Then Kendacke opens her arms and Lewis staggers into them. "I always hoped to meet your father," she says.

"I know. You were right, I was wrong, I have been unfair, ungrateful, unworthy—"

"No. War hardens the heart, Lewis, and the Capital is a battleground. There is no need to scold yourself."

"He warned me of this. He knew the government planned his death. I refused to listen. I might have saved him."

"A battleground, and enemies everywhere," James reminds him. "Your father was a brave man."

"You don't know how brave, Professor. When I met with him yesterday, he wanted to talk about the traditional burial rites of our tribe. I couldn't believe the irrelevance. Or so I thought."

"Ah," Kendacke says. "He was confiding his last wishes. Tell us. We will do everything we can to honor his remains."

"Not necessary. Like a true Dinka chief, he has done it for us."

"What do you mean?" Kendacke asks.

"Immediate reports are calling the explosion criminal activity by anti-government rebels, of course. The politically astute will assume Mukharabat. But it was neither; it was my father himself, practicing our tribal custom of live burial."

"We know of the Dinka tradition," the Professor says, "but I don't understand how—"

"He could never allow them to arrest him. I am positive of that. It is the one true thing I hang onto in this. He was in control at the end. He figured out a way to blow himself up."

"Then that pile of rubble was his burial mound!" the Professor says.

Lewis nods. "And I am positive also that he took a couple of the President's police with him. So. I have nothing left but this"—he pulls the small, glass

hemisphere out of a leather pouch hanging from the belt around his hips—
"and, let us hope, a ton of rice." He hands Kendacke the snow globe. "I
leave this with you. Yesterday I silently ridiculed it; today I pray it has the
power to convey every grain of that rice into our hands."

---

80

19 September. Port Sudan, Sudan. 1800 hours.

Skin, Tory thinks, as sailors and soldiers become a blur. *Why make such a big deal out of the way light happens to bounce off our bodies? So some read honey, others chocolate. In China they thought my freckles were a deformity. David Kimball's skin looked like raw meat. The man he disappeared with was no color. An angry man with happy eyes. No mustache. Chen.*

Marshall breaks her reverie. "OK," he says. "Here we go."

His skin is the color of the sliced chicken in the sandwich he invited her to choose from the mini-fridge. She's getting crumbs all over her brown smock as she wolfs it down, but she couldn't care less. "Don't you ever eat?" she asks him.

"Eating causes loss of concentration. You're a case in point. Notice anything different out there?"

"It's getting dark."

"I was referring to the subject of your so-called surveillance?"

She takes a closer look at the ship where a container has been maneuvered to the edge of the floodlit deck. Its blood-red color stands out despite the dusk, as does the bird, with wings spread and the hooked beak of a predator, stenciled in black on its end.

Beside it, two men nod and gesticulate in animated conversation. The one in uniform must be the Chinese captain. The other looks like Umar again. Aboard ship and on the dock, sailors and soldiers stand dangling limp hands, looking down the pier.

A shrill beeping penetrates the Mercedes interior and gets louder. Chen checks the side mirror then pulls his vehicle over to the left. As a half-loaded truck rolls forward, away from the side of the ship, a long flatbed fills the space, its cab backing it in.

The sailors scramble to attach the hooks to the container. Steadily the crane lifts it off the deck, then with a lurch, moves it out over the pier. The sudden shift in direction causes it to rotate.

"Idiots," Marshall mutters, as the huge red block turns slowly above the positioned flatbed.

As if to substantiate Marshall's judgment, one of the soldiers hops onto the bed, arms over his head, and as the container descends, tries to stop it from twisting. It swats him to the ground like a fly.

Finally the crane simply slams the container onto the bed with a crash that probably reverberates through the whole city. Marshall has looked away, one hand shielding his eyes. Luckily, the container is almost lined up with the bed. It takes only three more lifts and crashes to maneuver it into place.

81

Like watching toenails grow. Elephants gestate. Bart Wilkins keeps shifting his spot on the pier, always keeping the Mercedes and the freighter in his line of sight. The former never moves, while the unloading of the latter is taking forever.

At one point he strolls over to a cart near the entrance to the harbor where a man is selling skewers of roasted meat.

"What is it, chicken?" Wilkins asks in Arabic.

The man doesn't understand the question.

"From the goat?" Wilkins asks in English, making horns with his fingers and giving a little bleat.

"No problem," the man says, with a palms-up shrug. "*Hawaja*: foreigner eat?"

Ravenous for some solid protein, Wilkins hands over the 2000 dinars, and is devouring the first stringy chunk when a rat scrambles from behind a stack of crates and runs right over Wilkins' foot. The man's eyes meet Wilkins'.

"Don't tell me," Wilkins says, and takes a second bite. He heads back to resume his surveillance. "I always wanted to get the plague."

A continuing nothing: one sack of rice after another, tossed from freighter to truck, freighter to truck. Full trucks depart, empty ones replace them. *There's got to be a less labor-intensive way to unload this sucker*, Wilkins is thinking. As if in response, the pattern of activity breaks.

A rice-laden truck pulls away from the ship, and instead of an identical replacement, a loud siren begins bleating, warning of a vehicle in reverse.

Wilkins's phone begins to vibrate. It's Danny Banuelos, his counterpart in Cairo.

"Just got a preliminary report on David Kimball. Thought you might want to know."

"Shoot," Wilkins orders.

"Well, your guy appears to have died of heart failure. No signs of foul play or struggle. Only poison showing up in his system is alcohol, but given the levels, and a necrotic, enlarged liver, you probably could have guessed that."

"Yeah, David was a gentleman and a drunk."

"The only other thing of any possible interest was a fat lip."

"Well, he always was asking for one."

"Usually when someone gets punched out there's damage to teeth and nasal cartilage, but he shows none of that—just a swollen upper lip. Like an insect bite. You didn't notice it when you bagged him up?"

"Can't say I did."

"Well, it's there in the report. Maybe he had one too many and walked into a post or a doorframe or something, except again, you'd think there'd be some associated injury. It's kind of hard to whack yourself in that one spot, without hitting—"

"Holy shit!" Wilkins interrupts. With an explosive crash, the crane has dropped a container onto a flatbed.

"You OK?" Banuelos asks.

"Yup. Well, Kimball was a man of many talents. May he rest in peace. Thanks, Danny." Wilkins snaps his phone shut. He ducks into a doorway of a squat office building as the flatbed rumbles past, then follows it out of the harbor and watches it disappear down a road lined with waiting *tuk-tuks*. Several drivers beckon to him and call out prices. *No way.* Tuk-tuk's are permanently off his to-do list. With rapid strides he retraces his route to the shop of Sharif's friend, hoping the man will know of a place to rent a car.

82

19 September. Marafit Garrison, Eastern Sudan. 1900 hours.

"You can't just tell me what's going on?" Tory asks. They have left the city far behind, and their headlights illuminate one more bad road, edged on one side by a warped barbed-wire barrier. They are presumably following the flatbed, though it vanished long ago into the twilight.

"I'm not sure myself," Marshall says.

"Right." This guy's a piece of work. Through the folds of her *jilbaab*, she fingers the transponder. It better be functioning.

"What if I told you that in spite of China's claims, their offensive chemical weapons program is alive and well?" Marshall asks.

"I'd say they're putting their trade status at grave risk and they wouldn't do that."

"And that's why I won't bother to tell you."

"Wait a minute."

"Just remember, though, trapped in every legal pesticide is an illegal nerve agent waiting to escape."

"If you seriously suspect that, you should be informing the State Department."

"What do you think I just tried to do? Chen, how much longer?"

Chen reaches into a compartment beside his seat and pulls out a set of night binoculars. When Tory takes her turn with them, the darkness far to the left lightens and looks much more interesting.

She can make out two hangars, and parked in front of them, a pair of small biplanes and a giant transport that probably hasn't been off the ground in twenty years.

"That's a runway," Marshall says, of a flat stretch in the mid-distance behind the barbed wire.

Tory tightens the focus on the aircraft under the lights, bright white—symbols of hope. "The U. N.!" she notes with relief. "What are they doing here?"

"Don't be so gullible, for Christ sake," Marshall says. "White paint is cheap. Hide the binoculars now."

Chen turns left at a break in the wire fence and stops. He slides the window down, the humid heat floods in, and an armed man in fatigues emerges from the dark interior of a cinderblock sentry station. The only light is that cast by the GL's high beams. The guard rests his arms where the window was and leans into the vehicle. His body odor collides with Marshall's cologne. His head turns toward Tory, and he emits some undecipherable grunting noises. She has already lowered her eyes.

Marshall explains in Arabic that she is a widow of an old friend and hands the man a folded letter and his card. The man retracts his head and barks more noise into a walkie-talkie. After a burst of responding static, he waves the Mercedes through.

After five minutes, a haze of light is visible ahead, which turns out to emanate from a long low building with electricity. The flag of Sudan still flaps on its pole in front.

"If you could call this a military base," Marshall says, "then this is Headquarters. I'm paying the Commander an official visit. All off-duty personnel have been ordered to meet and greet me. You see, they love me. I'm their China connection. Meanwhile you are welcome to stretch your legs. Got it?"

"I'm supposed to wander around unarmed?"

"Chen will go with you."

Chen turns in his seat as far as his jowly neck will allow and gives her a thumbs-up.

Another jolt of adrenalin. It all reads like a strangely constructed trap.

"Be careful," Marshall advises. "Wherever you find the rice, there'll be trigger-happy dimwits running around."

I bet, she thinks. "What's the big deal about rice?" she asks.

Just then a senior officer of the Sudan National Army marches down the steps of the building in epaulets and beret, with his retinue of aides, one of whom opens Marshall's door. Marshall climbs out and confers for a minute with the Commander, who then has to insert his head into the off-road SUV and check out the latest of Adam Marshall's widows. Again Tory drops her head and retracts her pale hands into her sleeves.

"As always it is an act of charity for your Honor to bestow your company on these helpless ones," the Commander tells Marshall in Arabic, then slams the door.

83

"Chen see how far this go," her chauffeur says. Having parked for all of three minutes beside a row of trucks, they are hanging a left off the main strip of road, resuming a snail's speed in the direction of that other sphere of haze brightening the night sky. Soon Tory can make out the source of the light—the floods mounted on the backside of one of the hangars. At a distance of half a kilometer, the flatbed with its red container of cargo comes into focus. Chen brakes the GL.

"Get out now," he orders, holding open her door.

Then what? This can't be it, Marshall going to all this trouble to stage her death?

There is no cover between her and the hangars except for a crumbling mud bunker. Chen marches down the sloping sand, then waves his arm for her to follow him. *He's not acting like a captor*, she thinks, skidding clumsily after him. *But then where could I go?* He trots toward the bunker.

By the time she reaches it, she is drenched in sweat under her tunic and her running shoes are crunchy with sand. Chen invites her to take a seat on the broad stoop across the front, then waits patiently as she empties her shoes. He hands her the binoculars again. The scene at the hangar has become clearer: brand-new asphalt, two steel cranes, a pair of trucks dragging long wagons, swarms of dark men in T-shirts and fatigue pants.

The men fumble around on top of the container, apparently hooking its lid to the chains dangling from a crane. As soon as they jump down, the chains lift one end of the lid and flip it onto the tarmac with a deafening crunch. The men scramble back into the container and two to a sack, begin heaving them onto the ground.

Someone gets the idea to produce a knife and slash at a sack, dig his hands into the rice, and throw it in the air. Soon other bags are slashed and the men are pelting each other with handfuls of rice. Three armed guards stand aside, indifferent, while the second crane, its chain equipped with a large claw, rolls alongside the container. Suddenly the claw drops into the container. The party's over. The men retreat to safer perches along the corners to wait while the claw tears its way down through the rice.

It lifts out sack after sack, ripped and disgorging grain. Finally the crane operator calls for help and the men shove themselves off the sides of the near-empty container and disappear into it. A few minutes later, the chain begins pulling up until the claw appears, above the container, and Tory can see what it holds in its grip, rice streaming off it: a long, steel canister, tapered at one end like a bomb.

84

The mother of the man who calls himself Wilkins swore on her Limoges china that she'd disinherit him if he ever developed an interest in motorcycles. Such poor excuses for vehicles were beneath her family's dignity. Tonight a sputtering Honda rental scooter, with its barely functioning headlight, offers a faint taste of what he gave up in order to maintain the public image of his ancestors, who built their estate on Philadelphia's Main Line before anyone started calling it that.

With the breeze in his face, he lets himself imagine speeding along the beach, a gorgeous woman behind him, her arms wrapped around his waist—he comes back to earth with a jolt when he realizes he is picturing Ronnie, with her green eyes and helmet of fiery curls.

When did this gnarled barbed wire begin on his left? He can't make out anything on the other side of it but more flat sand. He stops the scooter to check in again with the Admiral on Ronnie's coordinates. But once his noisy vehicle is silenced, his ears pick up echoes from somewhere beyond the fence. The clamor of alarmed voices? Suddenly a resounding thunk, like an automobile collision.

Cursing his lack of night goggles, he lays the scooter down in the sand on the opposite side of the road then follows the fence, shining the concentrated beam of his pen-flashlight, looking in vain for a low spot he might be able to vault. He removes the Norinco from where he has tied it to his waist and the Beretta from its holster, and holding the weapons above the sand, snakes under the wire on his back at a place where the lower strand has rusted out.

After shaking out his clothing, he ties his headscarf to the fence, re-stashes the guns, and sets out in a crouch following the sound. An aura in the sky ahead promises some version of civilization. About a half-mile on, the noise level has increased, and he discerns an expanse of tarmac and two large aluminum hangars flooded with light.

He looks around for some cover that will allow him to move closer and notices an abandoned mud bunker. Coming around one side of it, he hears an unmistakable voice.

"Oh my god, what is that?"

Wilkins flattens himself against the crumbling wall as a second voice replies. "Weapon mass destruction. Good. We go now."

"Not yet. I've got to see what they do with it."

"Mr. Marshall say time to go," Chen insists.

The name is all Wilkins needs to hear. Norinco drawn and cocked, he slides along the wall, until he reaches the corner. Easing around the edge, he raises the gun with both hands, takes aim at the center of Chen's back, and fires.

The massive body staggers then topples onto the sand.

Parakeet suppresses a startled scream, and before Wilkins can identify himself, she takes off around the other side of the bunker, running. He can't risk shouting to stop her.

Heart pumping, Tory leaps off the stoop, hitches her heavy tunic up to her thighs, and heads across the sand toward the old road where Chen left the car, every cell in her body primed for speed.

The pounding in her ears taunts her with voices, spurring her determination. She reaches the empty vehicle and blows past it in the direction away from Headquarters. She has never lost a race.

But she has never tried to compete in Muslim attire, which has the same crippling effect on female mobility as a tight skirt and high heels. Its folds slip down and catch between her knees; she has to use her arms to keep scooping them back up. She halts on the old roadbed to yank it over her head. It seems forever that her face is stuck inside its utter darkness, and as she finally gets it peeled off, she hears her name. Or is it the pounding in her head? Flooded with adrenalin, she whirls around, sees no one, then takes off past the back of the second hangar, where nothing is going on, into the moonless dark.

If she has to die, she thinks, she wants to die running, hitting her stride.

But no gunshots follow her.

She cuts over toward the fence when she has left the hangars well behind. She will find a spot where she can vault the barbed wire, and retrace the route back to Port Sudan. Then what?

She needs to get to a phone, get online, reach Maud.

She needs to find Wilkins. Her mind flashes to the pathetic figure standing beside his crippled SUV under the desert sun. Poor Wilkins.

The next thing she knows, her foot catches on a protruding stone. She flies forward and lands face down in the sand.

Adam Marshall is outside his comfort zone, his sacred private space profoundly violated by the crush of shouting, sweating bodies packed into the central hall of the headquarters. Sweets are shoved in his face, hands slap his shoulders, grip his arms. He detests the body's fluids, odors, appetites. They are all evidence of its weakness, its failure to be controlled. Even his own has begun to betray him here in the unventilated room. His shirt collar and armpits are damp. He struggles to breathe.

Everyone is toasting the gift from China. It will raise them to first place among African nations. They will be revered and feared by the whole world. And it will end the civil war once and for all, so that Sudan can enjoy the prosperity Allah intended when He placed the vast reserves of oil under its land. They can't raise their glasses of tea high enough.

Smiling stiffly, Marshall sneaks glances at his watch. Though he enjoys subterfuge for his own pleasure, he detests having to play-act for someone else's ends. These cat-and-mouse maneuvers with Pierce's daughter might have made for a very amusing seduction if they'd been on his terms. As tools of Roger Booth's paranoia, they're getting pretty tiresome. But that's power politics for you, as opposed to power business. The first is a game of charades, the second, a boxing match.

After almost an hour, Marshall cocks his head in the direction of a small, thin man in civilian robes, who weaves his way over through the crowd. "Time to round up our widow," Marshall mutters between clenched teeth.

"You are gathering yourself quite a collection," Umar says.

"Always temporary, Umar," Marshall says. "This too shall pass."

19 September. Nubian Desert, Sudan. 2200 hours.

There will be no second chances. The timing must be exact. Following a single flashlight beam, the four men slip like shadows into a ring of boulders twenty meters off the desert road.

Silent and methodical, they set down the heavy cages they are carrying, check their watches, remove the safeties from their weapons. Francis Magok, Lewis Kvol's second in command, puts on their one set of night goggles and fastens a sound suppresser to the end of his M40A3 sniper rifle. The others pull on leather gloves, then reach into the cages and extricate the sleek falcons, which they leash to their wrists.

Lewis is sure they'll have surprise on their side. He knows now that his father's safe room was definitely wired, so the Army will be expecting this ambush to be launched according to his original plan, right outside Port Sudan, not here, 200 kilometers to the west. The soldiers driving the trucks will have relaxed into a sense of security. Meanwhile the Nubian village a mere kilometer to the east should slow the convoy's momentum.

To the southwest, the sandy asphalt disappears into darkness toward Atbara, and a fork in the road. Continue straight and you reach Khartoum. The road to the right leads to Jebel Barkal.

The birds emit low *kak-kak*'s. They stretch and retract their wings, impatient to play their part. The men wait in silence. They will have one shot at getting this right.

Francis' sat phone begins to buzz. Lewis' fuzzy voice tells them he has spotted the caravan, five kilometers to the east. It consists of nine trucks. "Traveling fast," he warns them. "Maybe forty kilometers per hour. Let us hope the village slows them down."

As if killing that hope, a hoarse rumble soon becomes audible in the distance. Within minutes, the first headlights prick the dark.

When the first truck rolls even with their position, Francis makes out two guards riding on top of the capacity load. The second truck, following closely, is similarly full and manned. The gap is longer between the second and third, longer still between the third and fourth. A piece of good luck.

Five minutes have passed when the sixth truck thunders by. Francis raises his falcon. "For the future unity of our land," he says, as he springs its leash. The others do the same and the birds' crescent wings fan and lift their bodies into the air, their eager, triumphant squawks debating the noise of the diesel engines.

They swirl around the eighth truck, but then the headlights of number nine appear, and a high-pitched whistle from the ground redirects them to plunge toward it. They swoop at its windshield, causing the driver to hit the brakes and almost topple the soldiers straddling the bags of rice. Off-balance, the two exposed men fire their weapons in wild bursts as the birds begin to attack their faces.

Hearing the shots, the driver tries to pick up speed again, but as the truck pulls past the rock outcropping, Francis raises his M-40, it disgorges two muffled bolts, and the soldiers on top crumple onto the load, like puppets whose strings have been cut.

Another inaudible signal from the ground calls the birds to desist, to give over the mission to the larger bird humming into sight. It hovers over the isolated truck, calibrating its speed to match the vehicle's. A young man in blue swings down a ladder from its open door.

One of the guards on the truck sprawls face down, his mortal wound staining the rice below. The other, bleeding near the shoulder, aims a wobbling weapon at the man on the ladder, who leaps onto him as his wild shot glances off the chopper's belly. A young woman emerges, also uniformed in blue. She descends the ladder and drops onto the load.

The truck driver remains oblivious. He keeps gunning his engine, but the truck is slow to accelerate, and the woman has already slashed a hole in one of the forward bags. Heaving it onto the roof of the cab, she rolls it back and forth, releasing a slow stream of rice to cascade down the windshield. The puzzled driver is forced to pump the brakes and stop.

88

19 September. Marafit Garrison, Eastern Sudan. 2230 hours.

"Oh my God," Tory says, reflexively brushing away the hand Wilkins offers to pull her back to her feet. "I *thought* that was you, this afternoon, on the pier. Where did you get those clothes—"

"You all right?" Wilkins asks shining his flashlight right in her face.

"Would you chill out?" She parries the flashlight with her arm. "It's me."

"I'm glad to see you too."

"Yes, well someone just took out Chen," she says.

"Chen? Another new friend of yours?"

"He's one of Adam Marshall's men."

"I'd say he got what he deserved. Come on."

"You don't know anything, Wilkins."

"I know who left me to broil in the desert. And I'm not interested in finding out what they do for an encore." Wilkins has her by the arm and is trying to drag her over to the barbed wire.

"Wait a minute. *You* shot him!"

"Ronnie, we need to get out of here."

"Me with you? I don't think so."

"Shit."

"You're the one who preached to me about not shooting unless fired on. Then you take out a guy who was helping me!"

"Look, we can discuss all this later."

"Plus there are those two dead guards at the mountain."

"Let's get somewhere safe."

"Our safety isn't exactly a priority right now. Did you see what's going on over there?"

"Neither one of us can inform the world that Sudan is importing weaponized nerve gas if we are both dead."

Her shoulders sag. "That's what that is, isn't it?"

"My best guess," Wilkins says.

"I knew it couldn't be good."

"I don't know what the hold is that Marshall and his goons have on you, but I would suggest—"

"I'm just trying to do my job, Wilkins."

"Well, maybe don't try so hard."

"What?!"

"It's as if you've always got to prove something. When what you and I really have to do, asap, is get this intelligence to the right people. Agreed?"

Tory hesitates. The logic of this thing keeps pulling her in opposite directions.

"I don't know what there is to think about," Wilkins says. "For Christ sake, we're on the same side."

That's what they all say, she thinks. Then a throaty rumble and headlights announce the approach of a military truck on the garrison road. When it halts behind the Mercedes, Tory can see she and Wilkins have managed to put only 300 meters at most between themselves and it. She grabs Wilkins' arm and says, "Let's get out of here."

Ducking down, Wilkins pulls her along the fence to the spot marked by the piece of cloth. He drops to the sand, and clumsily limbos under the rusted-out wire. Briefly she considers hurdling the fence, but the footing's bad, and the prospect of a rusty barb catching skin deters her. She flops down and wriggles the hard way after him.

89

Wilkins pushes the scooter along the road until he makes out an outcropping of sandstone some distance off the road. "We'll wait out the excitement over there," he says, then steers the thing onto the loose sand where it bogs down.

He switches to pulling as Tory shoves it from behind. "You know, neither one of us has the whole story on these CW," Wilkins says. "But I'll bet my life Marshall's in it up to his eyeballs."

"OK, then why did he bring me all the way out here, risking his own life, not to mention his poor bodyguard's, in order to tip me off?"

"I don't know, but there's someone who's going to want to know all about it." Finally Wilkins can wedge the scooter between two rocks. He fishes under his tunic for his sat phone and punches a number. "The parakeet has landed, Admiral, sir," he declares, "and so has the rice. Seems it comes with a bonus. As soon as a little dust settles here, we'll be heading back to Port Sudan, probably on foot. Full report then."

Admiral? Wilkins is talking to an Admiral? Tory screws up her face at the obviousness of it—how could she not have realized? "So that's who you are," she says. "The one who's supposed to keep me out of trouble."

"Didn't I tell you that?"

"I'm not talking about your Embassy detail. I mean who do you really work for, Wilkins?"

"Whom."

"Did that give your ego a little rush?"

"You first."

"What?"

"Whom *you* work for."

"You're impossible." Tory would like to stomp away, but there's nowhere to go.

"Still, hanging with me is your best bet of getting back safely to civilization."

"Debatable. How do you know Maud Olson?"

"I don't. Apart from that she's Director of Intelligence, CIA."

Tory stares up into his face, but the expression is masked by darkness.

"*Whom* were you talking to?"

"Very good. And you *do* know Maud Olson?"

"Damn it, *you* first." This is like arm wrestling, equal opponents straining themselves into paralysis.

"I am a Naval officer," Wilkins says, "attached to the Embassy in Khartoum. Honest."

"And you just happen to be on chatting terms with an Admiral?"

"Admiral Falco was Commandant when I was at the Naval Academy. I played football, he's a fan, my first class year we beat Army by 13."

"So?"

"He took me under his wing. Sometimes he asks me to do special favors. Like look out for greenhorns."

"I don't believe it."

"My turn. And you are?" Wilkins asks.

"No way," Tory says blankly. "You probably know anyway." Maybe she should be impressed with the strings Maud can pull. Instead she feels snared in their web.

"So I'll continue to call you Ronnie?"

"I think we've got a huge operation on our hands here, regardless of what we call each other."

"Unless you'd prefer Parakeet."

"What?"

"Your code name. The Admiral came up with it."

"Would it kill you to leave me one shred of professional dignity?"

"Hey, parakeets are pretty savvy birds. I used to have a pair of them when I was—"

"Put a cork in it, Commander, OK?"

---

90

19 September. Port Sudan, Sudan. 2330 hours.

"This is too easy," says Wilkins. He has scouted the perimeter of the Hilton and its mostly empty parking lot. No sign of an Army vehicle or the Mercedes GL that roared past them hours ago, its headlights pointing blindly ahead.

"I don't like this either," Tory says. As if they're preferred travelers, the sleepy desk clerk has just offered Tory her backpack from a side office, then just as readily handed over the key to the hotel's Business Center, and pointed them down a marble hallway.

"Thirty-six hours ago the guy kidnaps you and holds you at gunpoint. Now he's virtually telling you God Bless and sending you on your way? I don't get it."

"Could you be wrong about him?"

"You're getting sucked in again."

"But why did he set it up for me to check out that army base? He may be toast now, for all we know." Tory unlocks the glassed-in cubby-hole that contains two hotel computers.

"I could have died out there," Wilkins says.

"But you didn't. Thanks to him, I saw first-hand what they've got going at that base right down to those biplanes painted United Nations white! The bastards." She turns on the computer.

"Hey, you can't put the information out there for anyone to pick up," Wilkins says.

"Of course not." She reaches into her backpack, pulls out a small black encrypter, and plugs it into one of the computer's ports. "Thanks to Marshall again, for taking such good care of my stuff." She signs onto the Net.

"Beware of wealthy maniacs bearing gifts," Wilkins mutters.

"Would you cool it?" Tory says, already launched into a full account of her day for her Branch Chief in Cairo. As she cc's the office of the Director, National Clandestine Service, her mind flashes to Maud, whose directorate should receive the intel, scrubbed of any sign of its author, in what, forty-eight hours? A lot can happen in two days. Briefly Tory considers breaking protocol and copying her report to a separate message, direct to Maud. But what could Maud do that the NCS wouldn't? As soon as she logs off, she'll give Maud an off-the-record call—she owes her one for today anyway.

"So," she asks Wilkins, shutting the computer down, "when are you going to call in the Marines, preferably with magic carpet?"

"Shit," Wilkins says. "It's Mr. Wonder Bread himself. He's not toast yet."

Tory rises and turns.

Beyond the Business Center window, a smiling Adam Marshall, looking slightly less impeccable, raises his right hand in an ironic salute.

91

19 September. Jebel Barkal, Sudan. 2330 hours.

"You are a mere boy," Lewis says as he removes the prisoner's blindfold. "How many years, fourteen, fifteen?" Lewis opens the wooden box against one wall and pulls out a bottle of alcohol, a tube of ointment, and strips of white cloth. "Where are your brains?" He yanks off the kid's makeshift bandage.

He slips his dagger out of his boot, spills alcohol onto it, then probes at the bloody hole in the boy's shoulder. The kid chokes on his own groans. Finally Lewis wiggles the slug free. He spills alcohol on the oozing wound.

"They wave dinars in your face, dinars and a big gun, and you give them your loyalty. You think it's a game." Lewis begins winding the strips up over the boy's shoulder and under his arm.

The boy stares at him with dazed eyes. "What is happen to me?"

"It's you who must answer the questions, boy." Lewis uses more cloth strips to secure the kid's ankles and wrists. "You wait in this room until your other two stupid playmates get here by car, and while you wait, you can think about how a boy could bleed to death from a hole in his shoulder."

"Where is this room?"

"I have told you: I ask the questions." Lewis wipes off his dagger and resheathes it.

"My feet say, it is downhill. We are underneath the earth." The boy's eyes bulge like falcon's eggs and he is panting as if out of breath.

"I'll be back when the others get here," Lewis says. "Then we'll all have a little talk." He heads up the corridor to the camp outside, to wait for the truckload of rice.

Behind him, the boy begins to scream. "This is Jebel Barkal. The mountain. You bring me to Jebel Barkal. Take me away from here. I beg you. Take me away."

92

19 September. Port Sudan, Sudan. 2330 hours.

"There's one way to solve this thing," Parakeet mutters to Wilkins, then she flies out of the cubicle. "Hey, I don't believe it!" she chirps. "I was afraid you'd been compromised—"

"The Sudanese honchos were a little pissed off. They can sympathize with my weakness for widows, but not when I can't keep them under control." Marshall's gaze swivels to Wilkins, and his smile tightens.

Jaws clenched, Wilkins glares back at him. He can read nothing in his yellow-green eyes, nothing but arrogance, self-assertion.

"You obviously fared better getting to Port Sudan than I did," Wilkins says. He slaps the sides of his robe releasing clouds of dust. "Care to share your travel secrets?"

"It's no secret," Marshall says, his lips barely moving, "that everyone and everything has a price."

"Then you're an exception to your own rule," pipes up Parakeet. She rests her hand on Marshall's sleeve. "Nobody paid you to go out on a limb like that. I'm really sorry about Chen."

Marshall shrugs.

Parakeet blabs on: "Thanks to you, we've exposed an atrocity waiting to happen—"

"I assume that by now you've transmitted the information through appropriate channels?" Marshall asks.

"I just filed a complete report. Tagged it Priority One, Extreme Urgency."

"Excellent. You're as resourceful as you are pretty."

She gives him a concerned look. "You understand, there are sure to be repercussions, immediate actions which may impact—"

"Of course, of course. Don't worry about it. I'll be out of here for the States tomorrow"—he checks his watch—"well, it's already tomorrow, isn't it? So this afternoon. But no one's going to make the connection between another one of Mr. Marshall's women and a case officer of the CIA."

The truth of Ronnie Clark's identity hangs in the air like a challenge. "You have some pretty weird ideas, Mr. Marshall," Parakeet says after hardly a pause. "But I appreciate the assistance you've provided us in the State Department to better accomplish our mission. Hopefully, your negative blowback will be minimal."

"Thanks," Marshall says, then as if the thought has just crossed his mind, asks, "Have you made any phone calls?"

To Wilkins' complete surprise, Parakeet shakes her head and says, "Where was I going to get a phone?"

Marshall gives a twitchy smile. "What about this guy?"

She shrugs. "I just bumped into him a few minutes ago."

"Why don't you ask him?" Wilkins says.

"Well?"

"Don't you remember? Your friend Umar blew my phone to bits."

"I suspect it wasn't your only one."

"Suspicion correct." Wilkins pats his side pocket. "Thanks to my old back-up, I've been able to stay in touch with the Admiral."

"What are you talking about?"

"John Falco, Chairman of the Joint Chiefs? I've heard rumors he's an old friend of yours?"

"You're bluffing."

Wilkins pulls out the phone and flips it open. "Want to try any of the outgoing numbers?"

As if the question were magic, Marshall's posture relaxes, his expression softens, and his eyes seem even to acquire a twinkle. "No, no," he chuckles. "I believe you. It just took me a minute. I mean it's a helluva a coincidence. So you're in the Navy?"

"More or less. Attached to the Embassy."

Marshall's goatee bobs up and down as he processes the information. "So what did old Johnny have to say? I'll bet he was surprised to hear I was caught, or almost caught, doing something for the greater good instead of personal profit."

"I suspect nothing you do ever surprises him."

"Ah well, he wouldn't admit it if it did. Look, I was about to suggest we go up to my suite for a drink, the three of us. We've all had a tough day. Seriously. You guys deserve a little down time. We'll get them to send up a couple omelets or something. We'll call it morning."

"No thanks," Wilkins says. "Ronnie and I have a dead man's job to do back in Khartoum."

"Wait a minute," chirps Parakeet. "I have a say in this."

Wilkins glares at her. *Now* what's she doing?

"That's right," Marshall says. "What's the rush? You just earned enough brownie points to take it easy for a month."

"Why do you assume," Wilkins asks, "that we work for the same petty rewards you do?"

"I'll overlook that remark and offer you a lift back in my private jet. It's no trouble to touch down in Khartoum."

"What makes you think," Wilkins says, "that I couldn't arrange an airplane to take us back if I wanted to?"

"Stop it," orders Parakeet. "I am going upstairs. We've got a lot to talk about now, and I'm ordering some good, strong coffee since it looks like sleep is out of the question."

Wilkins shakes his head. *What is she trying to prove?*

"You know, there's more to this than you realize," Marshall tells him, as the three of them start up the stairs. "Even Johnny doesn't have the full story, not yet."

93

Marshall unlocks the door to his suite, throws it open, and waves Tory over the threshold. The odor of cologne permeating the air is no surprise, but the presence of Chen, enthroned in one of the rattan chairs by the window, is. At the very instant her eyes come to rest on him, arms circle her from behind.

With a surge of energy, her survival instinct compounded by rage, she jackknifes forward, frees herself with a twist, and lands a foot in the midsection of Umar. As he struggles to stay upright, she kicks him again, then pushes Wilkins backwards out into the hall. "Run," she shouts, as she clobbers Marshall with her backpack then throws it in his face. She tries to get past him through the doorway; she sees Marshall's fist coming at her face, then Wilkins has thrust his own arm in the way. "You're slowing down," Wilkins says as he twists the arm up behind Marshall's back and yanks the guy in front of himself like a shield. Too late. The mountain of Chen has lumbered over and plucked Tory away from the tangle of bodies as if she were a small, ornery child.

"Everyone will please be calm," Chen says. Almost hidden by the beefy hand he holds to her head is a sound-suppressed pistol.

"Don't worry about me," Tory tells Wilkins. "Get out!"

For a long moment no one moves.

Then Wilkins steps into the room, releasing Marshall. The next minute, Wilkins doubles over from a punch to the solar plexus.

"You still owe me," Marshall mutters, as he frisks the younger man, fishing the Norinco from under his tunic.

"My gun," says Umar, grabbing it. He points it at Wilkins' ankles. "This time I take that one too." He stoops to unholster the Beretta, and Wilkins jabs the side of his foot into his throat. Umar gags and drops to the floor. Chen aims his cocked pistol.

"Not yet, you idiot," Marshall screams. "He isn't going anywhere."

"Good. Chen prefer not clean up bloody mess," says the acupuncturist, shoving Tory and Wilkins into the bedroom. He pushes Tory onto one bed and Wilkins onto the other.

"Sorry," Tory whispers to Wilkins. "I figured this is the only way to find out the truth."

"What do you have against staying alive?"

"But we know now, right?"

"What exactly do we know that I didn't already—"

Coughing, Umar comes in and begins to wrap the Americans' ankles in duct tape.

"Now how about I order eggs all around?" Marshall calls from the living room. "Send up four omelets," he barks into the hotel phone.

Chen starts to salivate and smack his lips. A fake grin slits his eyes and puffs out his shiny jowls even more. *Angry man, with happy eyes, and bullet-proof vest.*

A buzzer in Wilkins' pocket vibrates.

"You better give me that phone of yours," Marshall says, striding into the room.

Wilkins digs into his pocket, pulls out his phone, and throws it on the floor.

Umar dives for it like a dog after a bone and hands it to Marshall. With a glance at the call coming in, Marshall announces, "Well, it's the Admiral himself. Want to take it?"

Wilkins reaches for the phone, but Marshall retracts it. "Wait a minute. Chen, a little insurance, please?"

Chen points his pistol at Tory.

"Perfect." Marshall turns on the speaker then flicks open the phone. "Admiral Johnny!" he says. "It's Adam. Adam Marshall."

"This is a surprise, Adam. Given that I just punched reply to a message from a Bart Wilkins."

"I wouldn't swear by that name, but he's here. Along with a lovely young lady also in the throes of an identity crisis. She doesn't want to admit she's Tyler Pierce's daughter."

Wilkins' head swings in her direction. Tory catches the aha! look on his face then looks down, aware of the weapon aimed at her left temple.

"She's doing what she's supposed to do, Adam, and I expect you to take good care of her."

"I have been. She was wondering whether the U.S. should lift sanctions against this god-forsaken place. I think we got her an answer."

"What's going on?"

"A couple canisters in that shipment from China that look suspiciously like nerve gas."

"What exactly did you see?"

"Not me. Pierce's girl and your guy are the ones who saw them. The girl has sent a full report."

"Are they the real reason you requested the Navy escort?"

"I wanted to make sure that rice got through, Johnny."

"How about putting Wilkins on?"

"Sure." Marshall holds the phone in front of Wilkins' mouth.

"Beat Army, Admiral. Sorry for the echo. We've got you on speaker mode. I'm a little tied up at the moment."

Chen gives Tory's head a jab with the barrel of his gun.

"Ah, I'm trying to get one of these cheap hotel things to make a pot of coffee," Wilkins explains.

"What are you guys doing sitting in a hotel room with canisters of WMD floating around?" asks the Admiral.

"Good question, sir," Wilkins says.

Marshall calls out, "The canisters aren't going anywhere, Johnny. I paid some guys to disable the trucks."

"Don't let them off the dock. I'm ordering that destroyer escort to reverse back and drop anchor outside Sudanese waters. Get me clear proof of WMD, and we can take action."

"I think the U.S. has worn out that pretext for invading a sovereign nation," Marshall says.

"What do *you* suggest?"

"I'm working on it," Marshall says. "Meanwhile read in the NCS at the Agency. It'd be easier to go the undercover route.

"Good idea," Johnny says.

"Beat Army!" Wilkins calls one last time, as Marshall snaps the phone shut.

94

19 September. McLean, Virginia. 1400 hours.

"Good news and bad news again," Johnny says, when Maud picks up Line Two to the Pentagon.

Maud's voice rises with apprehension. "What's happened?"

"I just spoke briefly with my CTG guy, and he's with Victoria in Port Sudan."

"Praise the Lord!"

"Yeah, but Adam Marshall's still with them."

"I don't like it."

"Me neither. I'm positive my man was trying to tell me something was wrong. He kept shouting, Beat Army!"

"I'm pulling Director Terrell in on this," says Maud.

"Wait a minute, Maud. You said yourself we don't want to move too soon."

"We've got two kids in harm's way."

"That rice shipment from China concealed a couple canisters of chemical agent."

"Good lord!"

"Yeah. Those two kids of ours discovered it. Which means we've caught a pretty big fish in your net, and we don't want it getting away. Tell me one thing. Is it possible Marshall's working undercover for us?"

"Never. Can't be trusted. He's an unscrupulous egomaniac."

"When has that disqualified anyone in the Agency's eyes?"

"Cut it out, Johnny. What your IT genius is doing for us over at ONI isn't exactly legal."

"OK, Marshall's floating the story that he facilitated the kids' discovery. He also said he's making sure the stuff will stay in Port Sudan. Apparently Victoria's filed a full report. He suggested I ask NCS to order back-up to handle the mess."

"Oh sure: Gordon Gray, who's been sweeping things under the rug for how long, I wonder?"

"No contact between him and Marshall yet?"

"Nada. I did note two contacts with Fred Scott a while back."

"Aha! Booth's Chief of Staff."

"That's right. A lot of 'how's the family?' garbage. I've forwarded it to your genius to check for code."

Johnny pauses. "The trouble is, it's not exactly a crime to expose illegal trafficking in chemical weapons. Hell, we report it, the U.S. imposes sanctions on China, and everybody but China's a hero."

"I know. The pieces don't fit. The alleged pieces. I'm not trusting Adam Marshall to keep the CW out of Sudanese hands. He's too close with their President. You know, I'd bet my VIP parking place, his Army has plans to hit the NIM with it, at that demonstration the rebels are staging, looks like the day after tomorrow. And Mukharabat is going to look the other way. If we don't go to Terrell yet, can you pry some Special Ops away from Iraq to reinforce security at the port?"

"Not overnight. I do have a Marine contingent on the destroyer sitting offshore."

Maud shakes her head. "This is really an op for the Agency's Special Activities Division, except that any request would have to go through Gordon. Or Director Terrell."

"I think we can give it twenty-four hours," Johnny says.

"That's cutting it close. If Gordon hasn't forwarded the report on Kimball's 'suicide' by 0600, how about we shift focus to getting the WMD out of the way?"

"I know this is hard for you, Maud," Johnny says. "But I don't think Adam Marshall would ever risk his own life. As long as Victoria is with him, she'll be safe."

95

20 September. Jebel Barkal, Sudan. 0100 hours.

"Do you recognize these people?" Lewis pulls a small leather folder from the pouch around his waist and flips it open to a photograph, which he shoves in front of each bound prisoner.

One by one, the three men sitting cross-legged on the floor hang their heads.

"Maybe you take a guess who they are," Lewis suggests, nodding to Francis. His Lieutenant squats in front of the man who rode shotgun in the truck, and puts his mouth against the man's ear. "Who is your commander. Where are you based?"

The man throws a panicky look in the direction of the older driver on his right, but Francis grabs his chin and wrenches it forward. "Where were you delivering the rice?"

"I am nobody soldier," the man stammers through Francis' grip.

Francis' other hand comes out of nowhere and slaps him hard. A volley of questions follows, and each time the man is slow to respond, Francis slaps him. "How many in your company? What are your orders after this?"

"What he knows is nothing." The voice of the driver, clearly the oldest of the captives, interrupts Francis' tirade.

Lewis shifts to stand over him. "And yourself?"

"I know we answer many questions, and you still have nothing."

Lewis pushes the folder with the photograph in front of the driver's face again. "This is my mother," he says in a menacingly calm voice. "These *children* are my sisters. Do you know what your Army did to them?"

The man averts his gaze.

"Aha! good guess. If such a thing happened to your mother and small sisters, how would you avenge their memory?"

Silence.

"So then you know what I want to do to you." Lewis pauses to let the idea sink in. "Only if you work with us, I will temper revenge with mercy."

"And if we do not temper revenge with mercy," declares a resonant voice, "we must all die." Kendacke ducks under the low lintel to enter the room then draws herself up to her full height. She is swathed in sacred garments, purple with golden fringes, ornaments around her neck and the pelt of a black leopard fastened around her shoulders with a gold double-cobra brooch.

The whites of the prisoners' eyes swell with awe. The driver addresses her: "You speak truth. It is what I try to tell these men."

Furious at the impertinence, Lewis shoves the driver off-balance with his boot. The bound man rolls helplessly to one side. Lewis places his boot on his ribs. "You are speaking to the woman who has dedicated her life to bringing peace to our country. There is no connection between her and scum like you, who—Kendacke!" Lewis throws up his arms, for she has stooped to pull the prisoner up to his seated position again.

She kneels beside the captive and peers into his eyes. "Your leaders have misled you. They care nothing for the people but only for themselves. They pay you today to murder your brothers and tomorrow will pay your brothers to murder you."

The driver lets out a sob. "We will all die."

"If you continue in this crazy way of believing your leaders, yes."

"No if. We will all die soon. A poison you cannot see will fill the air. It enters the body on the breath and then everything inside explodes, worse than a bomb."

"What are you talking about?" demands Lewis.

"Everyone whispers how it was hidden in the rice. And now airplanes will carry it to Jebel Barkal."

Lewis and Kendacke exchange horrified glances. "Which airplanes? Where do they take off? When?"

"I tell you all I know," the driver says.

"It's not enough," Lewis snarls, grabbing him by the collar.

"It's all he knows," Kendacke says. She shakes Lewis's arm and he lets go of the man.

As she pulls Lewis toward the low opening into the corridor to her apartment, the driver calls out, "Such a thing as happened to you happened to me also. At the hands of your rebel army, I lost *my* dear wife."

The Professor sits at Kendacke's table in one corner of her room, his forehead propped by his hands. When he looks up in the bluish light, he seems a hundred years old.

"Has there been any news about Mani?" Lewis asks.

"Apparently she is in the Capital, and ill," the Professor says in an exhausted voice.

"What? Where in the Capital? I'll go after her."

"She is hungry and will not eat."

"Who told you this, Professor?"

"It is what comes to me in my prayers," Kendacke says. "Hah! I see that expression on your face. My prayers are no proof for you."

"I cannot run all over the Capital on the basis of your prayers, Kendacke. We need concrete evidence. We need reason, not visions. Particularly now, with this new possibility of an airplane carrying poison. We must figure out a plan."

"What poison?" the old man asks, clutching his chest.

Kendacke shakes her lowered head. "When you kick the prisoners, Lewis, you kick me."

"That was nothing compared to what they do."

"If those men are ever to share *our* vision, we must demonstrate that we are different from *them*."

"He gave us information, didn't he?"

"He gave us information because he is about to become another victim of his own government."

"What poison are you talking about?" the Professor asks again.

Lewis ignores him. "You have asked me to command your troops, Kendacke. You must give me the freedom to do my work."

"We must end violence, not perpetuate—"

"You have three-hundred bags of rice, an Army truck, and one enemy corpse to dispose of outside," Lewis says. "I am taking the Hummingbird and six men to Port Sudan. There is a garrison outside the city, which merits investigation. If we can locate the poison and disable the airplane, I should say, *when* we do, we will fly to the Capital and find your daughter." He does an about-face and exits the room.

20 September. Port Sudan, Sudan. 0400 hours.

Umar shoves a tray of omelets close to Tory's face. "Be good, I feed you," he says. The aroma starts her stomach growling, but she pushes the tray away with her taped wrists. A still-groggy Wilkins does the same.

"They're laced with arsenic," Marshall says, relaxed in the room's easy chair. He lifts one plate off the tray. Above him, a single lit sconce casts an eerie glow. "I think your paranoia's working overtime." He takes a small, precise bite. "Not great, but adequate. Go ahead, Chen. One's for you."

Chen grabs a plate in one ham-like hand. He folds the omelet into quarters with the other, shoves it in his mouth, and swallows.

Marshall smiles at the performance, then after chewing a few more morsels, says, "Don't look so hostile. I'm only trying to keep you guys safe and out of trouble."

"Why?" Tory asks.

Marshall smirks and shakes his head. "You still won't trust me."

"It's no secret you've been feasting at the Generalissimo's table for years," Wilkins goes on. "And now you're shifting your loyalty to us? I don't think so. He's got plans for that stuff, and you don't want us interfering."

Marshall raises his eyebrows as he takes another bite. "Then why did I lead you right to the smoking gun?"

"That's what I'd like to know," Tory says.

"I wouldn't strain your brain too much. It's all completely out of your control." Marshall starts in on a second omelet. "Sorry. You had your chance."

"Thought you said food makes you lose concentration," Tory says.

"Got to fuel up for the long day ahead. A quick hop to Khartoum to pick up a friend, then home to the U.S. of A." He turns to Umar. "Better get back to the army base and check the progress." Umar draws himself up to his full five-and-a-half feet and swaggers from the room.

"You want it both ways, don't you?" Tory says.

Marshall throws her a suggestive look. "You aren't the first woman who's accused me of that."

"You score points with the Agency for alerting them to an imminent atrocity, and points with the Generalissimo for letting it happen."

"Try *making* it happen," Wilkins adds.

Marshall's smile stiffens. "An interesting theory."

"You're banking on my report taking forty-eight hours to get through the Agency pipeline," Tory says. "But by that time the chemical agent will have done its work."

Marshall dabs his mouth with his napkin. "Then why did I just tell Admiral Falco all about it?"

"You didn't," Wilkins says. "You assured him the agent wouldn't leave the Port. Plus you and he go back, and he's such a straight arrow, he'll believe you."

Marshall seems to be enjoying this game. "Then please explain why the Chinese government would risk their booming international trade in order to gas a few natives?"

Tory pounces. "So that *is* the plan."

"Though it's not entirely irrational," Marshall muses. "Considering that a certain religious rally is about to ratchet up the political chaos in this hellhole with a lot of voodoo mumbo jumbo for the masses, and the humanitarians and journalists have been pounding on the gates clamoring for visas, making it very hard for us self-respecting businessmen to conduct any business!"

Tory glares at him, appalled, as her mind's eye flashes to Kendacke and the thousands of makeshift tents around Jebel Barkal.

"But I would suspend this line of inquiry if I were you," Marshall says. "I'd hate to have to decide you know too much."

"How would you explain that decision to Admiral Falco?" Wilkins asks, looking almost prim, sitting with ankles taped together, on the opposite bed, wrists crossed in his lap.

Marshall looks at Chen, standing sentry at the bedroom door. They both shrug. "Accidents happen."

"You're a psychopath, you know that?" Tory blurts.

"Cool it, Ronnie," Wilkins says.

"You better start calling me Victoria Pierce."

---

98

20 September. Marafit Garrison, Sudan. 0400 hours.

The night sky has begun its inevitable lightening by the time Lewis Kvol, Francis Magok, and two brothers, Piol and Mayom Thon, land the Hummingbird beside a rocky butte, two kilometers east of the army base.

The four tall, dark men, their stride fast and fluid, make their way to the road and set out along it. Lewis takes the lead with night goggles, strafing flashlight, and compass. Francis' M-40 slaps against his shoulder; the brothers carry M-16's and ammunition draped across their chests. On their left the barbed wire barrier indicates the perimeter of military property.

They can hear their destination though they cannot see anything but a brightening in the distant sky. The sound increases as they approach: the echo of metal on metal, the loud stutter of riveting, the grinding of gears.

Beyond the fence about half a kilometer Lewis' night goggles discern a mud structure that appears from its dark windows to be unoccupied. He instructs his men to stay put and cover him. "I will find their weakness," he says, clipping an opening for himself in the barbed wire and easing through.

99

20 September. Port Sudan, Sudan. 0600 hours.

"Finally, you admit it," Marshall says, taking the final bite of the second omelet. "All that crap about Milwaukee—couldn't you guys do any better than that? Jesus, I was at your dad's funeral—you don't remember? I shook your goddamn—"

"He didn't have a funeral," Tory interrupts.

"Well, whatever you want to call it—the Agency's Bulova watch send-off for their fallen fuck-ups. Mr. Golden Boy. Personally I hate the type, always flaunting their integrity and good intentions, so sure that's what gets results."

"You sound jealous." Actually she has noted a shift in Marshall's voice. He sounds less clipped and definite. Maybe for once he's telling the truth, his truth. Maybe all that food *is* causing him to lose focus.

"That's a laugh. Me jealous of a dead guy? A guy who couldn't appreciate that it takes cold calculation to get to the top of the heap and ruthless vigilance to stay there?" He waves his fork around to make the point. A glob of egg falls onto his trousers, but he doesn't seem to notice.

"Let's see," Tory says. "Ruthless vigilance. Would that be arranging for thousands of innocent men, women and children to be gassed to death? Or kissing the ass of a self-serving dictator? Or both?"

Marshall staggers to his feet and the back of his hand across Tory's face cuts short her question. In a flash, Wilkins has heaved himself upright, ankles bound, and thrown himself at Marshall, knocking him onto the bed beside Tory. In the next minute Chen jabs two fat fingers into the side of the younger man's neck and sends him sprawling, lights out.

"Chen work magic wonders," Chen says, pulling a black leather bag from the armoire.

"Put that away," Marshall says, trying to gather his dignity as he stands and shifts his jacket straight. "I'm having too good a time." He turns to Tory, who is rubbing her cheek against her upper arm. "Though it looks like I'll have to teach you the same lesson I had to teach your old man."

Is it her imagination or do those putrid green eyes of his look a little dazed? "What lesson was that?"

Marshall lurches over to the door. "Don't make a deal with the wrong guy, for starters. When the Generalissimo lets a political enemy get out of jail free, don't jump at the bait." Marshall sounds like he's had too much to drink.

"Is that how you set up the ambush?" Tory asks.

"Maybe you should ask Chen. He is famous for his deft hand with needles."

Tory turns toward his bald bulk, and her stomach gives a heave. There is nothing in it to expel.

"Old Chinese practices, pass down centuries," Chen says.

"One of his ancestors who inclined more to fighting than healing perfected seventy-two variations of *dianxue*." Marshall hangs onto the doorframe, slurring his words. "Mr. Whatever-his-name-is over there is getting an extended lesson in one of them."

Wilkins groans as he regains consciousness.

"Your friend lucky," Chen tells Tory. "Strike on right vital point with right intention often fatal. With special, chemically enhanced needles, death certain, and nobody can explain." He pauses as if he deserves a pat on the back but Marshall is completely occupied with remaining upright.

"Kimball," Wilkins mumbles hoarsely.

"Kimball was a spineless guilt junkie," Marshall says, and slides to his knees in the doorway as if to demonstrate the adjective. "No amount of money gonna keep him quiet. 'Sides, he's begging to be offed, put out of his misery. Wanna know what was in my little note? *Come with us now. It's time.* Tell me that guy wasn't ready to check out." Tory and Wilkins watch amazed as Marshall collapses into a fetal heap on the rug.

100

20 September. Marafit Garrison, Sudan. 0700 hours.

In the dawning light, Lewis creeps back to the rocks and relays what he picked up with his binoculars: at least twenty men swarming around two white bi-planes parked outside a hangar. Six others with weapons standing guard.

"White airplanes!" Francis says with disgust. "They want to look like U.N. But you could see it, right, the poison?"

"I saw men wearing boots and masks and gloves. They have attached tanks to the undersides of the wings. A giant container on a flatbed sits at the edge of the tarmac and broken bags of rice all around. Nothing to contradict the information put out by our captives. Unfortunately the enemy has the numbers."

"It's only Sudanese Army," says Francis with contempt. "No discipline. They are whipped dogs, nothing to fight for."

"But it will be daylight soon," points out Piol.

"We have no choice," Lewis concludes. "We must plan an attack. Too many lives depend on us."

101

20 September. Port Sudan, Sudan. 0730 hours.

"Boss, Boss!" Chen's kneeling hulk checks Marshall's pulses. "Someone mess with Boss *chi*." He lumbers to his feet and heads for the armoire but realizes he's feeling a little sluggish himself, his head full of clouds. He drags out his black bag.

"We didn't do anything," the American lady says, shrinking back on the bed. She thinks the needles are for her. She don't know that needles do good too, and they are for Boss.

There's a tap-tap on the outside door. Chen freezes for a split second, then shoves his bag back in the armoire, pulls his gun, and releases the safety.

Another tap-tap, and then the click of a lock. "Housekeeping!" sings a soft voice from the front room, then a shocked, "*Ai ya, ai ya!*"

Chen jabs his gun into his belt under his jacket and steps over Marshall's body in the doorway. "No housekeeping," he says. He's taken aback at the sight of the maid, because she's a young Chinese woman with a long black braid and jeweled eye-glasses. So many Chinese workers in Africa now.

"*Kuài dá diàn huà jiào yī* shēng?" she asks, cradling sheets and towels in her arms, and nodding toward Boss's body with concern.

"Don't need doctor. I am doctor," Chen says. "You are Chinese?"

She nods, lowering her eyes shyly.

"Leave sheets and towels on sofa," he says. "Too early for housekeeping."

She turns obediently and carries the linens to the sofa, her hips swaying slightly. Chen can't help but appreciate the firm, curved flesh under the tight uniform.

"You have lady in bedroom?" the maid asks, turning and cocking her head like a flirt.

Chen laughs with embarrassment. "*Shi*, but not for what you think."

The maid sidles over to Chen. "I am from Huang Shan."

"Big mountains there," Chen says.

The maid laughs, throws back her shoulders, and rotates them a bit. "Very big mountains."

Chen can't drag his eyes from her breasts, and then suddenly there is a foot striking hard at his private parts.

"*Cào nǐ zǔzōng shíbā dài*: Fuck your ancestors to the eighteenth generation!" he manages to blurt as he doubles over in pain. He gropes under his jacket, seeking the handle of his pistol. The maid is all over his hunched body, chopping at his neck, kicking the small of his back, but her strikes only irritate. None finds weakness the way the first did.

As the throb in his crotch subsides, his hand grasps his weapon, his forefinger slides into the trigger, he starts to pull it out of his belt, when a sudden pain drills the back of one of his knees, jangling his *chi*. He turns his head looking for the source when something sharp probes his unprotected neck for more weak spots. He needs both hands for this and tries to free his thick finger from the trigger. Instead, an ear-shattering report. He staggers and slowly collapses on the marble tile. The agony in his mid-section this time is more than he can bear.

102

"Meiying!" Wilkins says. He is gripping two forks in each fist. Hunks of duct tape dangle from his ankles and wrists.

"Fancy meeting you here. When I tried to call you and you failed to answer, I concluded I better set out for Port Sudan. I've been on the road eighteen hours, no break."

"You're amazing," Wilkins says.

"It doesn't take rocket science to locate Caucasians in this haystack."

"You sound different."

"Ah, so you notice Chinese bimbo talk many different ways?"

"Hello?" Tory calls from the bedroom. "Remember me? I'm the one who helped you get *your* tape off."

Wilkins and Meiying climb over the fallen bodies. Meiying whips a penknife from under her apron, grins, and slices through the tape on Tory's ankles down to the last shred. Tory jumps up, and runs a few steps in place. "So what did you do to that food, anyway?" she asks Meiying.

"Turn about is fair play, right?" Meiying asks. "Also known as poetic justice."

"How did you know *we* wouldn't eat it?"

"I figure if you haven't learned your lesson with the bastard's brandy, you deserve to be dragged out of here by the feet." She reaches into the pile of linens on the couch and produces a Glock 21 for each of them.

"OK, you are amazing." Tory raises her right hand, and the two women exchange a high five. "And you come off a lot different without that wig and the fractured English."

"Bimbo always works against these bastards."

"We have to get out to those airplanes, asap," Wilkins reminds them, as he wraps Marshall's hands and feet with the roll of tape.

"I guess just leave these guys?" Tory asks, gazing down with revulsion at the dark stain on Chen's trousers. He looks finished.

"Not quite," Wilkins says. He drags a bloody pistol from Chen's pants. Meiying wipes it off with one of the towels while Wilkins yanks his sat phone out of Marshall's jacket pocket.

103

20 September. Jebel Barkal, Sudan. 0730 hours.

After a fitful night's sleep in the upper chamber, James Crawford shuffles down to knock on Kendacke's door. There's no response. He looks in to find the room empty.

His aging heart beats in alarm as he races up the stone stairs to the temple entrance. "Good morning, Professor," says the guard. "Do you feel ill?"

From outside drift the sounds of the camp awakening, as it has every morning for several weeks, oblivious to the looming horror. "Where is she?" Crawford asks, out of breath. "She isn't in her room?"

The guard takes the Professor's arm, guides him out into the light, and points a finger in the direction of the assembled tablets. There he sees a regal figure wrapped in brilliant blue, calling orders to several helpers, as if there were no threat on the horizon of a hideous, collective death.

The helpers are folding back the canvas that conceals his work of the last several years. The task is proceeding slowly because they keep stopping to admire the delicacy of the colors that have endured centuries, the mysterious beauty of the images. Sixty-four cream-yellow stars embedded in a blue-black sky on the left; on the right, a light blue sky holds the same number of black birds in flight.

These stones with their version of heaven undoubtedly decorated the ceiling of one of the ruined temples. But what they evoke in the Professor now is frustration, not admiration. For a gap separates the picture into two sections, and he has still not succeeded in unearthing the three missing tablets that connect the halves and depict the phase of transition from dark to light, star to bird.

He stands at the edge of the display, oppressed by a sense of all the devastation that preceded his existence on earth and the devastation about to come. "Kendacke!" he finally calls out. And when she glides over to him, he continues in a low voice. "We need to prepare for the poison gas."

"No, we must prepare for the celebration," she says.

"Kendacke, please. We have difficult decisions ahead. Who will take shelter in the mountain, and who will—"

She is gripping his arms. "But there is good news, dear James. Your stones have spoken to me this morning, and they tell me they are all present!"

He has come to recognize that certain blank brightness in her eye—it is focused on an inner vision. There is no point in trying to discuss anything.

"The break between the dark and the light is absolutely necessary," she goes on. "It signifies the break in the human soul."

"On another day, I suppose I might rejoice at this ingenious way of declaring my work complete," the Professor says with a sad smile. "But it is just those broken souls whose hatred will destroy us." The Professor shrugs off her grasp and steps into the space between the two sets of stones. He stoops to run a hand over the edges of those along the division. They *are* very smooth. Smoother than the interior edges.

Suddenly he stands upright, his hand over his mouth, his eyes taking in the ruins around him. "I can't believe I didn't see it," he says, a surge of energy returning to his voice. "There was an opening in the temple roof. Instead of a visual answer to the question of transformation, a view of the heavens themselves."

"Yes, James, yes. And without the break, there is no way for the divine spirit of unity to enter and perform its miracle."

James reins in his burst of excitement. "It's an interesting theory, Kendacke, but theories cannot neutralize hate."

104

20 September. Port Sudan, Sudan. 0830 hours.

Meiying is behind the wheel of a brand new white Land Rover LR3. As if to make up for no sleep, Wilkins and Tory are stuffing themselves from a box of bread and fruit on the rear seat.

"Nice vehicle," Tory observes from the back. "For an immigrant restaurant worker."

"I signed it out from the Embassy," Meiying says. "Practical for driving in anything from sand to mud."

"Meiying is with the Chinese Intelligence Service," Wilkins says.

"I'm just like you," Meiying says, meeting Tory's eyes in the rear view. "Except Chinese."

Tory stares out her window. Finally she says, "With all due gratitude for the rescue, China's the major provider of arms to the Sudanese government, arms they use to slaughter their own people."

"The U.S. has never furnished arms to a country to suppress insurgency?"

"This isn't insurgency. It's people fighting for their lives."

"And El Salvador? Nicaragua? Weren't they the same deal?" When no one answers, she adds, "Studying the history of the CIA is part of Chinese training."

"Look, what we're tracking at the moment are chemical weapons which your government has sold the Sudanese," says Tory. "Exporting chemical weapons is banned by international—"

"Bad rumor. False alarm. I am tracking illegal weapons also."

"What are you talking about?"

"Chemicals come from a private company, not the Chinese government. The Chinese Ministry of State Security has detained the company owner. An assistant Minister of Commerce hanged himself yesterday. In his farewell note, he said he thought chemicals were for spraying crops."

"What do you bet they're both business associates of Marshall's," Wilkins says.

"Adam Marshall is a very bad influence on China," Meiying says with a shudder. "It will cause a very big embarrassment to the government of my country if this chemical agent is deployed on Sudanese people."

"Embarrassment doesn't begin to describe it," Tory says.

"If I locate this chemical agent and stop it from deployment, I will be a national hero."

"We just better get to those planes," Tory says.

105

19 September. Fairfax, Virginia. 2300 hours.

"Go Navy!" Johnny shouts, when he hears the voice of his former midshipman.

Francesca and Maud sit forward on the leather sofa. Two open laptops hum on the oak coffee table in front of them. One screen displays the message Paul Livingston sent Gordon Gray the day before: *Suicide note found in David Kimball's pocket litter. Said he's distraught over NCS black Op against the First Vice President which resulted in VP's death. Blames self.* The other screen shows the same message Gordon finally forwarded to Genesis a k a Adam just two hours ago, with the added Intel: *Obtained autopsy results from Cairo. Cause of death inconclusive, does not invalidate above."*

"Admiral?" The young man's voice echoes now over the speaker phone.

"I thought you were going to keep me up to speed."

"Sorry, sir. We've been in survival mode."

Johnny plants himself in front of the brick fireplace. "You've succeeded, obviously."

"We're working on it."

"You still with Marshall?"

"He's temporarily disabled. The only reason I didn't put a bullet through his brain is I thought you'd want to interrogate him when the dust settles. Meanwhile his bodyguard's prognosis is unknown—looks like the guy shot his own balls off."

Francesca and Maud gag in unison.

Johnny begins pacing the plaid carpet. "You've got to be kidding."

"Well, there was a hell of a lot of blood. We didn't stick around to find out the exact source."

"How about Parakeet?"

"She'll have a hefty bruise on the side of her face, courtesy of your boyhood pal, but otherwise OK."

Maud's hand strokes her own cheek, as if that could comfort Victoria.

"We've been aided in our efforts by a Chinese operative stationed in Khartoum, Liu Meiying. In fact, we couldn't have escaped without her help. According to her, the WMD in the rice has nothing to do with her government. She's been assigned to track the stuff down herself."

"I'll notify my Chinese counterpart and let him know what's going on."

"Right, sir."

"We've downloaded Tory's report," Johnny goes on.

"Already?"

"Yeah, we got through to Cairo and expedited electronic delivery. Now, she said you saw two planes, right?"

"Yes sir".

"We're trying to figure that out. No need to send two planes to wipe out a religious rite. So what's the deal on the second?"

"I'll find out, sir."

"No, you won't," Johnny says as Maud shakes her head vigorously. "This op is getting bigger by the minute, and the wrong team's got some powerful players. You'll get yourself and Parakeet back to the Embassy in Khartoum."

"She's adamant about taking out those aircraft, sir."

"Then I'll have to order you off. Tell her this isn't her fight."

There is a muffled silence, and then a firm, female voice comes on the line. "With all due respect, sir, I'm afraid it is."

106

20 September. Marafit Garrison, Sudan. 1000 hours.

A rusted-out pick-up truck blocks one lane of the road. A man in baggy clothing leans against the cab, while the desert beyond is dotted with half-a-dozen kneeling women, their heads shielded from the sun by bright shawls. Their dark fingers comb the sand.

"Are they looking for something?" Tory asks.

"Gravel, I expect," Wilkins says.

"Get serious."

"Every day they scrape together two maybe three bucketfuls of stones—not too big, not too small—for the construction going on in the city. That's how they make a living, if you can call it that."

"Wait a minute," Tory shouts, a few minutes after they pass the truck. "How much money do we have?" She pulls out 10,000 dinars from a pouch in her backpack.

"I have plenty of that stuff," Meiying says.

"OK, go back. We're going to buy us some clothes," Tory explains, "and if we're lucky that guy'll trade his lovely vehicle for ours."

"No way," Meiying says. "This car is fully-loaded, hot off the assembly line."

"And it's obvious as hell," Tory says. "We're going to have to ditch it one way or the other, but I vote we make a deal with that guy, because I've got a plan."

Wilkins groans.

"Look, we've made it this far. And we found out what we needed, didn't we?"

"Does this plan of yours have an exit strategy this time?"

"I think it'll get us access to the planes," Tory says.

Meiying shifts into reverse.

Ten minutes later, the transaction is complete, and the Sudanese gravel pickers are happy. Tory takes the wheel of the pick-up, leaving Meiying and Wilkins to squeeze onto the hot plastic of the passenger side. In exchange for the maid's uniform and an extra shirt and pants Meiying brought along, Tory has obtained two of the women's wrapped dresses and several buckets.

Lewis and his men hear the falcon's *kee, kee* before they see her, circling overhead, growing from a speck in the blank blue sky. The journey that would take a car most of the night this bird can accomplish in one hour. Now she plunges downward on her wide, crescent wings, as Lewis scrambles to protect his wrist before she alights.

"What does this mean, Yar, this surprise visit?" Lewis asks nervously, regretting now the anger that soured his departure from Kendacke. When uncertainty threatens every future moment, explosions of rage are luxuries one cannot afford.

Lewis strokes the birds pale underbelly with his free hand while Francis detaches the message from her talon, unfolds it, and hands it to Lewis to read. After several seconds, the commander's jaw drops, and the note disappears in his fist. The bird gazes at his master with black, unblinking eyes.

108

20 September. Port Sudan, Sudan. 1300 hours.

Adam Marshall is not used to driving, even when he isn't groggy, and on roads this bad even a vehicle that handles like a bird in flight feels like it's getting nowhere fast.

"I can't believe you let them get away!" he yells, trying to dump some of his frustration on Chen. "Those bitches are half your size, and hell, that faggot of Johnny's, you could push him over with a feather."

Chen sits with his arms folded across his chest staring straight ahead. Under his trousers, a thick bandage winds from between his legs up around either side of his waist. His legs are spread to balance his weight and minimize the pain from the bumps.

Half-an-hour ago, while a nurse at a public clinic was dressing Chen's superficial wound, Marshall checked his Blackberry for messages he'd missed when he was out cold. He found one he didn't like: Gordon Gray granting validity to an absolutely bogus version of Kimball's death. Marshall emailed him back discrediting it unconditionally, and asking if he'd gotten a call for help from Johnny Falco. He has yet to receive a reply.

He also speed-dialed a number on his sat phone and reached Umar. "Everything ready?"

"No problem. All is according to plan."

"Not exactly," Marshall warned him. "Those goddamn kids have flown the coop. And I'm sure they're headed your way."

"When was that?"

"Two hours ago, three? I don't know."

"You don't know?"

"*I* ask the questions, Umar," he yelled. "Find them. And it goes without saying: keep them safe until I get there."

---

20 September. Marafit Garrison, Sudan. 1300 hours.

The pick-up's rattling vibrations stop. "This is far enough for now," Tory says. "We can use those rocks over there by that butte to change clothes."

Wilkins has slid out of the cab already. Meiying practically jumps on top of him in her eagerness. "Let's go get 'em," she cheers, jogging toward the formation twenty meters away.

That's right, be amazing, Tory is thinking when all at once Meiying isn't there.

"Wilkins, take cover!" Tory screams from the truck as she grabs her Glock and ducks below the dash. In the sliver of space between the cab and Meiying's open door, she sees him frozen halfway between the truck and the rocks, his head whipping around frantically. There is nowhere to go.

Two tall men, of identical face and build, step out from a crevice in the butte. One has wrapped both arms around a kicking, flailing Meiying. The other points an M-16 at Wilkins.

Tory props her weapon on the top hinge of the open door and takes careful aim at the gunman's head. Her finger is flexed to pull the trigger when a third and fourth man emerge from the rocks. The tallest lopes toward Wilkins. Instinctively, she shifts her target to this man, then realizes his hands are empty, and the right one is reaching for Wilkins'. "We are most happy to see you," he says. It's the one-eared man who tailed them from the airport.

Meiying gives her captor an elbow jab in the gut as a formality, before he can set her free.

Tory climbs out of the truck. "You knew this guy," she calls to Wilkins. "I almost took a shot at him the other day and you never told me."

"You weren't going to hit him."

"Condescension doesn't suit you," Tory says.

Wilkins gives her a look, then throws an arm across the taller man's shoulders. "We heard about your father," he says. "I'm very sorry. He was a brave man."

"Oh my god. Your father was First Vice President Kvol?" Tory asks.

"Lewis, this is Victoria Pierce and our friend, Liu Meiying. She brought us the sad news from Khartoum."

"I am truly sorry," Tory says. "It's a terrible shock."

"His death has not been the only shock, I'm afraid," Lewis says. But when Tory asks him to explain, he instead introduces his men—Frances, the brothers, Mayom, and Piol—as well as the helicopter at rest behind the butte. Then he recounts the capture of one truckload of rice, the information he extracted from his prisoners, and what he saw from the hut. "Two Antonov-3 biplanes with crop-dusting tanks riveted between their wings."

"And I don't guess they're taking any coffee breaks," Tory says.

"Unfortunately they will soon pump the deadly agent from the canisters into the tanks. We needed to act hours ago."

Everyone goes silent.

"One drop of that stuff is lethal," Wilkins says. "We're going to need protective gear. Let me touch base with the Admiral, and Meiying, do you have any back-up you can—"

"Forget all that, you guys," Tory says. "We have the plan, and it's a lot more viable now that there are seven of us instead of three. We've got to move on this right away."

110

20 September. Nubian Desert, Sudan. 1330 hours.

Punching in the secure number, Marshall gets Roger's flat voice telling him, "Speak at the beep."

"Fuck you!" Adam mutters and hits another number. Thousands of miles away a phone rings. And rings.

Finally a groggy voice asks, "Who is it?"

"What do you mean forwarding me this bullshit about Kimball?"

"Keeping you apprised of new developments, Adam. As we agreed."

"And where did that *development* come from?"

"It was only a direct communication obtained by Maud Olson, head of Intelligence, CIA," Gordon says sarcastically.

"And you fell for it. Have you heard anything from Johnny Falco?"

"Should I have?"

"Yes, you should have. Because I told him to contact you to obtain Special Activities back-up."

"Give me the details. We'll deploy asap."

"Don't be an *idiot*. The point was that you *wouldn't* deploy, and unfortunately Johnny seemed to realize that. This thing's going off the rails, Gordon."

"Relax. Remember, you're *working* for me: you're my most reliable source of level-5 intelligence on Sudan. You have exposed the government's importation of WMD. They're either going to succeed in deploying the stuff or they won't. We're blameless either way. We tried."

"Tell that to Roger Booth," Marshall says.

"Either way, Booth gets a boost for his China policy."

You don't know squat, Marshall wants to say, but clenches his teeth.

"We haven't done anything illegal, Adam. Or rather, we haven't done anything the Agency hasn't done countless times before. It's important to remain calm."

"I'll be calmer when you can assure me of a little damage control. The file you've got on Pierce's girl? Make sure it reads that she was inexperienced for her position and relied on me for my knowledge and expertise regarding Sudanese affairs."

"Why the past tense?"

"I managed to help her infiltrate a Sudanese garrison, then tried to talk her out of taking action against the government on her own."

There's a silence on the line.

"Got that, Gordon?"

"Consider it done," Gordon says.

III

20 September. Marafit Garrison, Sudan. 1400 hours

Under an incandescent sun, Francis and Lewis pull the pick-up within sight of the guard booth at the garrison entrance. Two figures wrapped from head to ankles in ragged but colorful clothing hop out of the truck bed carrying buckets and trudge out onto the barren expanse on the other side of the road. They drop to the sand and begin combing it with their fingers.

Inside the cab, the two men pretend to sleep.

It doesn't take long for the soldier in the guard booth, who has been smoking a cigarette and staring off into space, to come storming out to the road, hugging his Kalashnikov. A second soldier is right behind him.

The first punches Frances' shoulder through the open window. "You cannot stay here," he shouts in Arabic. "It's a restricted area."

"Tell that to our wives," Frances says, cocking his head in the direction of the figures sifting sand. "We tell them this was too close to army property. They say the stones are perfect here."

The lead sentry pushes his head into the cab and makes a show of checking the dashboard and the floor at Lewis' feet. It would be so easy, Lewis' thinks, to slide the dagger in his palm along the man's exposed neck. "Papers?" the sentry asks.

The First Vice President arranged work documents for Lewis so he can travel without incident throughout Sudan, and now he makes a big deal out of fishing them out of his pocket and handing them over.

The sentry grunts, stands upright, and turns them over to his mate. The second guy runs his eyes over them. Lewis doubts either man can read. Finally the second guy spits on the ground and says, "The stones are the same everywhere. Your wives better understand that."

Lewis crooks his head down so he can give the two men a knowing wink as he says, "They will listen to you. Go ahead. You have our permission to make them understand."

Both guards march across the sand. Each wife deposits a crop of pebbles into her bucket, but doesn't remove her hand.

"Attention," calls the lead sentry.

Both wives look up. Before their decidedly male faces can register on the guards, their silenced pistols have emerged from the buckets. The guards' own faces explode in pulp, and bloody tissue rains onto the sand.

The two "wives" rip the desert camouflage shirts off their victims as fast as they can to minimize stains. The berets, smeared with red gunk, are unusable. Then hitching their dresses above their knees, they help Lewis and Francis lug the bodies back to the guard booth.

In minutes Lewis and Piol, his former "wife," are transformed by the baggy Sudanese Army uniforms and possess the key to the Army jeep parked outside.

112

The workers pumping the CW from canister to tanks on the aircraft don't believe what they see, a figure swathed in glaring yellow, carrying the bucket of a gravel collector. The expanse of rock-strewn sand around her makes her look lost, vulnerable. One by one, they stop what they are doing and peer through their protective masks at this creature stumbling in their direction.

A clamor of shouted warnings and invitations rouses the armed guards from their doze in the shade of the hangar. "Halt," the commander bellows at the intruder, and she does. She stands there head bowed as if struck stupid by the blazing sun. Two of the guards jog over to her, their baggy camouflage shirts swinging. The workers have removed their hoods and goggles to stare and shake their heads.

"Restricted area," yells one of the guards. She nods then turns back toward the road and an empty, battered pick-up. They jog across the sand. The one who gets to her first reaches forward to grab her arm. In a flash, the bucket comes flying up and around, delivering a crack to the man's skull, as the woman's long, sinewy arm keeps him upright in a headlock, then tugs him in the direction of the parked truck.

His comrades straggling after him send up a shout and run faster, drawing weapons. They shoot into the air. "No, no. Hold fire," screams the stunned guard. "She is armed. No, *he* is armed." The sharp barrel of the intruder's pistol is digging into his back.

Workers leave their masks and gloves on the tarmac to swarm after the guards, who are following the strange pair, which is lurching away from the hangars toward the barbed wire perimeter.

Then a small, wiry man in a striped robe shoves through the crowd, a .44 Magnum Desert Eagle dangling so large from one hand it seems to drag the sand. The captured guard sees him coming and begs louder: "Wait. It's no problem. Don't shoot. I take care of this."

At the front of the crowd now the man in the tunic stops and raises the weapon. He spits a single word through his shaggy moustache: "Disgusting." An ear-splitting explosion blows open the guard's chest cavity in mid-scream.

The man in woman's clothes struggles to hold up the dead weight of his bloody shield. Another round of fire pulverizes his forearm, causing him to drop the body to the ground. He lets his own weapon fall and, raising his remaining arm in surrender, sinks to the sand. Blaming him for their comrade's murder, the surviving guards beg to be allowed to take him out, but Umar calls them off. He tears off a swath of the pervert's yellow dress and frantically wraps the pulpy stump of his arm. He has questions for him.

During the confusion, an odd quartet has crouched undetected from a hole cut in the fence that morning toward the crumbling bunker inside the base: a tall, white man, his head draped in a white scarf, his Muslim tunic cut off around the knees; a taller, ragged black man; a Chinese woman in a spandex jumpsuit; and a woman with lobster-pink skin in shapeless, rumpled shirt and pants. They are all armed, and the black man carries a bucket filled with ammunition and grenades.

They had managed to make it inside the abandoned structure when they heard the first shot.

113

Approaching the garrison, Marshall pulls his silver Mercedes onto the sandy shoulder and hits the brake hard enough to jam Chen up against the seatbelt.

"*Ay, Ni xin tai hei le!* Your heart is black," yells Chen grabbing his crotch.

Staring straight ahead, Marshall flips his phone open. "Any sign of the Americans yet?" he asks Umar.

"Nothing," Umar says, then tells him about the rebel they just picked up in women's dress.

"Idiot!" Marshall roars. "They must be right under your nose. Call Headquarters for reinforcements. Comb every inch of that base."

He snaps shut the phone and pulls a Blackberry from his inside breast pocket. He taps out a message to Booth.

Kimball story BS. Clamp down on Johnny however you can. ASAP.

114

Meiying has belly-crawled from the bunker to a row of empty army trucks parked fifty meters from the tarmac. She beckons to the others to join her.

"See you on the other side," Tory says, then lowers herself to her stomach and begins the maneuver she has practiced plenty of times in training—on soft, cool, Virginia grass. Now the sand rakes her sunburned skin and sneaks into her nostrils, her dry mouth, as she drags herself toward the trucks. As she focuses on keeping low but covering the distance fast, she hears the stutter of gunfire followed by shouts. Got to keep moving, even though from what she can tell, a bunch of soldiers is heading toward the same spot she is, weapons blazing.

She cranes her head up an inch to find Meiying has disappeared. *This is it.* She twists to extract her weapon from the back of her waistband, then hears the throaty sound of a diesel engine coming to life. The lead truck rolls away from the others and heads up the road. The soldiers swarm after it, firing, then fall back to the truck that is next in line and scramble in. It roars off after Meiying, who must be driving the first.

No time to worry about her because another detachment of soldiers is fanning out from the tarmac. If they haven't spotted Tory already, they will in seconds, sprawled in the open on her belly. She holds fire, waiting for them to come into better range. She prays that Wilkins and Frances can lay down a miracle of cover. Failing that, she will shoot until she can't shoot anymore.

A deafening thunder shakes the earth beneath her and turns the advancing soldiers into a giant cloud of body parts and sand.

She freezes, in shock, until the sand and hunks of bloody tissue start coming down on her. Adrenalin surging, she jumps to her feet, and races for the last parked truck. Wilkins and Francis bolt from the bunker in her direction, Wilkins picking off the stragglers spared by the grenade while Francis grabs a limp body by the armpits and hauls it over to where Tory squats behind the fat rear tire.

Then all is quiet. Nothing moves except Francis in back of her, furiously shedding his ragged blue jumpsuit in favor of the motley uniform on the corpse. "You cover the road," Wilkins tells Francis. "When reinforcements get here, hold them off as long as you can."

He motions to Tory to join him as he runs a hideous obstacle course of mutilated bodies toward the biplanes. The tarmac is totally and surprisingly deserted, but time-consuming caution isn't an option. Weapons drawn, they inspect the tanks attached between the biplanes' wings. An odor between cherries and camphor pervades the area.

"Don't touch anything you don't have to," Wilkins cautions.

Tory nods.

"Get in there and release the engine hoods," says Wilkins. "We're going to make sure these deadly birds never fly."

Tory has jumped into the open hatch and is about to ask where exactly the release is, when people start appearing one by one in the open hangar, like actors taking a curtain call. The guy in front, the star, is too familiar, in *jellabah* and skullcap, that out-sized .44 Magnum trained with both hands on Tory. Beyond his shoulder towers Mayom. At least she thinks the bloodied, swollen face belongs to Mayom. Then Meiying and Piol are thrust out of the crowd, their hands bound from behind.

20 September. Fairfax, Virginia. 0530 hours.

A haggard trio stares in silence at the laptop screen, too fatigued to cheer when one finally displays a message from Adam Marshall to Roger Booth, bearing the telltale reference to David Kimball. What pleasure can they take from inserting the final piece to the puzzle when the full picture—the danger to Victoria, the so-called Bart Wilkins, and thousands of Sudanese is so devastating? And they still don't know the destination of that second plane.

"If Roger's implicated, what about the President?" asks Francesca finally.

"Best guess is the President's in the dark," Maud says. "His wife dictates domestic policy while the VP controls foreign affairs. As long as the stock market does well, the President is content to chat up Heads of State and work on his golf game."

"What I want to know is what could Roger possibly have in mind?" Johnny says. "Adam, I understand. A rogue nation offers to pay enough money for nerve gas, and old Adam's going to show up with nerve gas for sale. But these guys have gone to a lot of trouble here—undermining our intelligence, violating international sanctions, murdering a diplomat. What's the pay-off?"

"Hey you guys, better forget about what you know or don't know and get moving." Francesca pushes Johnny's government phone into his hand.

"What do you think, Clevon Terrell?" Johnny asks. "Do we trust he's clean?"

Maud gives Johnny a resigned look. "If the Agency Director is in on this, we haven't a chance anyway," she says, then punches a number known only to the President, Vice President, Speaker of the House, Johnny, Gordon's boss, and herself.

"Code Red," answers the voice. "This better be good."

"Maud Olson, here. Leviticus 24:19-20."

"My office, an hour."

"What was that all about?" Francesca asks, as Maud and Johnny pack up computers and grab jackets.

"Code for *Time to get the bad guys*," Johnny says.

"*Anyone who maims another shall suffer the same injury in return*," Maud says. "What the Bible forgets to mention is if the victims happen to include Victoria Pierce, the stakes double."

---

20 September. Marafit Garrison, Sudan. 1600 hours.

This time Umar is more generous with the duct tape, calling for an extra layer on the hands and ankles. He jerks Tory's wrists tighter himself, smiling when she lets out a gasp at the pain. Someone gives her a shove, and she collapses onto the asphalt next to Meiying and Piol.

"I guess it's time for the same lesson I taught your father," says a voice above her.

She raises her eyes to meet Adam Marshall's yellowish stare. Like a traumatized duckling, Chen waddles over to back up his boss.

"I've got nothing to learn from you," Tory says.

"Here's how justice works in the real world. Someone tried to poison me. That's a crime. All of you must pay. That's called punishment."

Tory throws him a scornful look and shakes her head.

"I gave your father the same chance to convert that I gave you—and you both blew it. What do I have to do to convince you folks in white hats that the philosopher got it right? Life is nasty and brutish. Get it? Dog eat dog. That's the bad news. The good news for losers like you guys is that life can be pretty short too."

His words hum with subtext. She blocks it. She must save not just herself from Marshall's diabolic death-grip, but her father's memory too. "At least we tried to help humanity, not destroy it."

"You idealists are all alike. Oozing pipedreams. Like mutual trust. None of that crap is ever on the table. But control, political stability—now these are solid goals. Anything's justified to advance them."

"You know," Tory says. "No amount of philosophical BS can hide the fact that you've got the soul of a cockroach."

"Slap some tape on that mouth, Umar," Marshall says.

Umar slams her lower jaw into her upper while a guard secures the tape. Out of breath, she fights the panic of feeling her air intake cut in half.

"Believe me," Marshall says, "my argument with your father wasn't only philosophical."

Tory snorts indignant noises through the tape.

"Hey, take it easy," Wilkins tries to tell her. "You can't argue with a psychopath."

Umar slaps a strip of tape on Wilkins' mouth.

Marshall goes on: "I'm obviously wasting my breath here. Maybe a hands-on demonstration will convince you slow learners where words fail. Get me that idiot in the dress."

Two soldiers try to drag Mayom forward. When he plants his feet and resists, a third swings a wooden club to hit the small of his back.

"This would be a good time to run a little quality control check. You know, test the merchandise here. Umar! Got anything left in that pump? This guy wants to lick the bowl."

Tory's eyes widen in horror. Her grunts of protest have nowhere to go and remain stuck in her throat.

Mayom thrashes free of the hands gripping him and head-butts one captor before taking another bone-cracking smash with the club. His knees buckle and they push him to the asphalt. Four men in protective gear spread what remain of his limbs then kneel on them to hold him down. Mayom spits what sound like curses as Umar zips himself into a silver jumpsuit, puts on the mask, then a pair of the heavy gloves. He rolls a steel pump and hose out on the tarmac. Mayom clenches his mouth shut but doesn't stop the angry sounds. Umar calmly blocks Mayom's nose until his victim loosens his jaw and lets out a pitiful, screaming protest. Umar shoves in the end of the hose and depresses the pump.

Mayom gives a furious bellow. Twenty meters away, Tory tries in vain to writhe to her feet while Piol kicks the air frantically. The guys around them laugh at their efforts. Soon their laughter focuses on something else. Mayom has begun to twitch like someone receiving continuous shocks. The men holding him down jump away and back off. His protests are overcome by a gagging cough, a cough that fails to open the trachea, but continues, spasm after spasm, convulsing, along with Mayom's whole body.

The guffaws freeze on the faces of the soldiers witnessing this death. They don't want to watch anymore. They want to sneak away, as far away as they can go. Tory throws a look in Wilkins' direction but can't stand the despair she reads on his face. Tears stream down Piol's cheeks. She squeezes shut her burning eyes.

"Good," Marshall says through the mask he has put on to cover his nose and mouth. "The stuff works." Taking off the mask, he turns his attention to Tory and Wilkins. "You kids look a little morally outraged, but I want you to realize, you're in this up to your eyeballs. We couldn't have done it without you. You caught those nasty Chinese bringing in the agent, you filed your complete report, and now you get to continue your starring roles into the final act." He looks at Umar. "How close to being ready?"

"Pending final check. Then sundown."

"Good. I'll leave the GL for you and Chen to take back to Khartoum once the mission's finished. I need to relax after this. I'll hire a driver."

Umar nods.

"Let's get this mess cleaned up then, and these guys boarded. How about you go with cat-woman and Mr. Crybaby in one plane, Umar, and we let these two lovebirds go in the other. That way they can enter eternity hand-in-hand, almost. Chen, you're in charge of that."

"No," Chen says, in a voice that defies argument. "Chen have score to settle with her." He cocks head and torso in Meiying's direction.

Marshall gives him a long look. Although he lowers his voice and speaks in Chinese, Tory understands what he says. "Israel presents more risk to Chen. They have the big guns."

"Chen do *her*," the acupuncturist repeats.

"Not a problem, then." Marshall returns to English with a laugh. "Too bad you're in no shape to do her like a *man*."

"Chen get small scratch on leg," the bodyguard insists. "Manhood fine."

"Whatever you say, friend, but her high dive into the Red Sea ought to provide plenty of satisfaction. Then Umar, drop the love-birds over that mountain, OK, to die with their wacko friends. And better rip the tape off at the last minute, so when their corpses show up in the crowd, it'll look like they all just partied a little too hard."

117

The physical distress is nothing compared to Tory's sense of futility. She, Wilkins, Meiying and Piol have been tossed in the same corner of the hangar with Mayom's body. Sacks of worthless trash about to be permanently discarded. Mission failed. Mani lost. The NIM doomed. Israel targeted for a CW attack. And her father unavenged. If Marshall could inflict a hideous death on Mayom purely for shock value, god knows what his list of complaints against Tyler Pierce would have justified. *Highly functional psychopath*, that's what you'd call this guy. Supposedly there were a lot of them running around, running things. And if Tyler Pierce wound up succumbing to one, how could she expect to escape?

"Don't give up the fight," Meiying whispers, locking eyes with Tory.

Tory barely nods.

"There are still six of us," Meiying says. "We're in this together."

Outside the flood is lighting the darkening tarmac, and the activity around the planes subsides. Marshall is long gone—he's probably somewhere air-conditioned, guzzling delicious water. *Oh, for one sip of water*, Tory is dreaming, when strong hands grab her armpits and her ankles.

"Six of us," Meiying reminds her. "See you later."

Tory jerks her limbs stiffly in resistance, then figures, *why bother*, and goes limp. She is lugged over to the open hatch of one of the aircraft. Her feet are released and flung in, but whoever has her upper body hangs on. To her amazement, that person seems to be carefully settling her on the airplane floor. Then he jumps into the plane and drags her away from the opening.

Is it the darkness? Is she hallucinating? The soldier handling her is wearing tinted glasses and a beret, pulled down on one side, covering his ear. Or maybe the scarred remains of one. She widens her eyes to drink in every photon of available light. Is fear causing her to see things? She could swear she recognizes Lewis Kvol.

118

20 September. McLean, Virginia. 0800 hours.

The burly African-American in a rumpled brown suit shoves his wire-rims back on his nose and straightens his tie. He motions Maud and Johnny into two leather chairs facing his cluttered desk. "Hold my calls," he orders his assistant as she closes the door.

"It's been one of those nights," Maud says.

"Aren't they all?" Terrell's affable grin is missing its usual unlit cigar. Instead, he pops a mint, explaining that his wife has delivered an ultimatum against his tobacco habit.

Clevon Terrell joined the Directorate of Science and Technology out of college and moved up quickly, designing and operating satellite reconnaissance systems, until a defense contracting firm, Opportunix, made him an offer he couldn't refuse: Vice President of International Expansion. It took him three years to double the company's revenues and three more to get bored with the business mindset. When *the* vacancy occurred, he floated his name for Director. The rest, as they say, is truly history.

"Leviticus 24: that's serious stuff," he says now.

"Definitely," Maud says. "Unfortunately it's taken a while for the warning signs to gel in this brain of mine. I'm afraid my ability to think straight has been compromised by personal involvement in the case of Victoria Pierce, whom the Agency assigned to Sudan in spite of her lack of experience for a station like that. I seemed to be the only one disturbed by this, which led me to question—"

"Hold on a minute," Terrell says. "You're losing me fast."

"Sorry. The facts. First, intel from Sudan dries up. Who knows when that began, because the same old stuff my African desk was recycling was not inconsistent with general knowledge. Second, we send an inadequately briefed, novice junior officer to Khartoum. Third, she is taken captive by an American businessman—that's right, you heard me—and she's actually made to witness the unloading of chemical WMD imported from China."

"Jesus Christ. How long have you known this?"

"About twenty-four hours," Johnny says.

"And you sat on it?"

"To ensure we could nail all parties involved," Johnny says. "With due respect, Clevon, as Maud will explain, it has become increasingly unclear who can be trusted."

"Continue," Terrell says.

"Two aircraft are being equipped to deploy said WMD's as we speak. Thanks to Johnny, here, our junior officer's teamed up with a Navy Commander in-country with the CTG, and the two have escaped her captors and as far as we know, are currently attempting to disable the aircraft." Maud's composure wavers, and she chokes up, shaking her bowed head. Johnny rests a hand on her back.

"I presume you've ID'ed the American businessman," Terrell says.

"Adam Marshall," Johnny says as if turning in a family member.

"So there really is such a person," Terrell says sardonically.

"We've got an electronic trail that leads from Maud's top African analyst to Gordon Gray to Marshall—"

"Our Gordon Gray?"

Maud looks up. "He's a mole, Clevon. He's turned the Agency into an instrument for the private devices of Marshall and Roger Booth."

"Wait a minute!"

"Yup," Johnny replies to Terrell's surprise. "The VP looks like the last stop on the electronic trail."

Maud flips open her computer and turns it to face the Director. He studies the screen. "*Clamp down on Johnny however you can, ASAP?* I still don't get it."

"One of the loads of nerve gas is pretty clearly earmarked for a high-profile refugee camp maintained by a popular rebel group," Maud explains. "But the second must be destined for a target outside Sudan."

"A target in the Middle East," Terrell says. "Where our national interest would coincide with some brutal muscle-flexing by Sudan? I doubt there is such a place."

"Maybe Booth just wants more oil," Maud suggests. "He sets up Victoria to provide full documentation of the WMD *after* they're deployed. Then he's got world opinion with him when he goes after another oil-rich dictator."

"That's insane," Johnny declares. "We can't possibly take on another ill-defined invasion."

"Look," Terrell says, picking up one of his dozen phones. "Forget the unknowns. We've got plenty of knowns to tackle. We send the FBI Chief over for a little visit with Gray. And we get some Special Activities boots on the ground in Sudan to back up our guys."

"And pray it's not too late," adds Maud.

119

20 September. Marafit Garrison, Sudan. 2000 hours.

Wilkins has been slung into the aircraft against the cockpit bulkhead facing Tory. In the chaos of miserable sensations, somehow his knees are against hers, and that pressure of bone against bone helps her concentrate her forces—they have *got* to survive to abort this horrific mission. No excuses. No giving up.

"Take seats," the pilot calls in Arabic as the plane begins to roll.

Umar, standing over his captives, seems undecided.

"You go ahead," says his Sudanese Army partner, squatting beside them. His voice sounds familiar, but on his shoulders are glints of brass, the insignia of an officer. "I take care of these ones."

Umar buckles himself onto a low shelf against the side of the hold while the army officer wedges, knees bent, behind Wilkins on the floor. The minute the lights flicker out for take-off, Tory is aware of small movements in the dark beside her. Flexing every muscle in her neck, she lifts her head enough to make out the officer's hands at work. *Still six of us*, Meiying reminded her.

He extricates something from his right boot, something that looks like a knife. Wilkins' body jerks in pain, then jerks again. She makes herself swallow the sounds of protest in her throat, the sounds that would destroy her hope that this man is Lewis Kvol, that they are all working toward the same goal. The officer gives Wilkins a punch in the back. "Settle down," he says in English. "You don't go anywhere."

From where he sits, Umar seconds the warning with a hard kick to Wilkins' legs. "He's thinking about the impure woman by his side," Umar says. "Go ahead and indulge your immodest thoughts. This is as close to having her as you ever get."

The noise of the engines swells, as the bi-plane picks up speed down the runway and lifts off. Umar reaches into his tunic and pulls out some earplugs and Wilkins' Magnum, which he places across his knees.

"How long to the target?" the officer shouts in Arabic, before Umar inserts the second plug.

"One and one half hours approximately," Umar says, shifting in search of a more comfortable position.

In the dark, Tory barely breathes as the activity behind Wilkins resumes.

120

Umar is snoring, an elbow propped on each knee, his head in his hands. If he were to raise his head, he might notice Wilkins' left hand sneaking up to remove the tape over his mouth, or Wilkins' face craning closer to Tory's as if zeroing in for a kiss. In fact it's much better than a kiss: Wilkins positions his mouth on her ear and through the tape manages to get across, "It's Lewis Kvol. We're still in business."

Then a slow change takes place in the positions of the bodies. Lewis invisibly transfers his dagger to Wilkins while Tory rotates away from Wilkins, whose right arm remains in sight behind his back, while his left hand clasping the small knife goes to work on the tape around her wrists.

The double edge of the dagger makes it hard not to slice skin as Wilkins picks and saws, but her hands are numb, and her concentration elsewhere. She can hear the minutes ticking away in her ears. Her stomach feels like the plane's toxic cargo is burning a hole in it. They have got to bring this aircraft down safely, and soon.

Her wrists separate. She clenches and unclenches her fists. *Almost free. Freedom.* Something deep in her core responds to that thought with a surge of adrenalin: it's all she can do not to rip the tape off her mouth, and scream hallelujah! With a small nod, Wilkins offers her the knife and the opportunity to cut free her ankles although his are still secured. Instead she flexes forward and wills her dead and bleeding hands to work on the tape binding his.

That is enough motion to wake Umar. It's also enough to trigger Lewis, whose split-second advantage springing to his feet means that when Umar gropes for the Magnum, it is already in Lewis' grasp.

Umar yells, the co-pilot looms up out of his seat in the cabin doorway, uncertain where to point his gun. A simultaneous flash and horrendous *kaboom*, like thunder in the eye of a storm: Lewis at point blank range turns the co-pilot's lower torso inside out, spraying gore in all directions.

With her ears ringing, the pilot's shouts seem to come from miles away. Umar reaches under his tunic for another weapon. Tory, who opted to give up on Wilkins' duct tape to slash through hers, springs forward and drives the dagger through Umar's arm. A Norinco falls to the floor behind the still-bound Wilkins.

The radio erupts with unintelligible babble, as the plane's angle changes with a jolt, toppling Lewis onto the co-pilot's bloody corpse. Tory's insides sink. Her body gets heavy as the plane sharply climbs. Umar strains slowly forward to retrieve his gun. Wilkins slowly twists to beat him to it.

Tory lunges onto Umar's back, locking one arm around his neck, lodging the dagger against his carotid artery. "Cut it out," she yells at the pilot. "Level this thing off or I'll—"

"You will do nothing, stupid woman," Umar grunts, wrapping a hand around the knife. She tightens the headlock, but he throws himself back against the cabin wall, knocking the breath out of her and loosening her grasp. Smeared with blood, Lewis still strains to get to his feet against massive gravity, while Wilkins, Norinco in hand, can see Umar get control of the knife but has no safe shot at interfering. With his bloody arm, Umar drags Tory around into his lap. "Enough," he screams, pressing the dagger point into the cavity of her throat. "Or else I kill her."

121

The blood from Umar's arm is wet on her neck, and his pressure on the poised blade increases.

"Take him out, for god sake," she shouts to Wilkins, "don't worry about me." A whining alarm drowns her last words. Through the open cockpit door, a red light on the instrument panel pulses.

Umar removes the knifepoint from her neck and yells at the pilot. The plane slows palpably, and the frame begins to rattle. Umar lurches to his feet, dropping Tory and the dagger on the floor. He plunges past Wilkins and Lewis into the cockpit and grabs the co-pilot's control yoke, which flops around in his hands. The rattling climb stops but the whine continues. The floor of the plane shifts like a slow-motion see-saw: a few seconds of horizontal glide and then the heavier fore-section begins to prevail.

In those few seconds of stillness, Lewis is able to dive towards the cockpit Magnum in hand. "Get out," he orders Umar, as he grabs the man by the arm and flings him into the cabin. He hits the floor head first and doesn't move. Lewis slides into the empty seat and passes the over-sized pistol to Tory. Propped in the cockpit door on her knees, she keeps it trained two-handed on the pilot.

Lewis rolls the craft to the left and manipulates the yoke. The curses, the grunts, the thuds and scrapes of moving bodies—all that previous turmoil has gone still. Everything's weightless. The cockpit windows are dark all around, no sign of a starlit sky as the aircraft plummets down through the night. Lewis keeps fiddling with the control yoke as he pushes the throttle forward.

Finally something changes. Their plunge through the void meets resistance. There is air again under their wings. Angles flatten. Tory's insides reorient.

Suddenly the pilot yells, "No!" He grabs his own yoke, and begins countering Lewis' maneuvers. "If we don't complete mission," he pants, "it's better to die!"

Gritting her teeth, Tory grabs the Magnum by the barrel and cracks it against the man's skull. He releases his controls.

Umar stirs. He pushes himself to his knees and makes a desperate lunge at Wilkins, who bends his taped legs and delivers both heels to his attacker's nose. Umar crumples face down onto the floor.

She hangs on with both hands to the gun, but no one moves.

Lewis has increased the engine power and in a minute the plane achieves the correct angle with the ground. The radio squawks Arabic. Lewis slips on the co-pilot's headset, opens the channel, and says, "Some handling problems due to extra weight. Everything is taken care of. We are back on target."

122

20 September. En route to Khartoum. 2000 hours.

Puffing smoke rings from his cigar, Marshall muses on the idealistic fools who have met their deserved fate in Sudan: there was Golden Boy Pierce, who got sexual curiosity mixed up with politics, and there was that woman, mesmerized by her own self-serving delusions. They didn't stand a chance, not with him, Adam Marshall, manipulating the strings. And now the best part, the massive rebalancing of reality to fit his wishes: in one smart operation, he has taken out Pierce's wise-ass daughter and repossessed his own.

Sitting in the back seat of his hired Land Rover, he would have liked a built-in bar, a shot of brandy, but there will be plenty of time for celebrating in the luxury of his customized Gulfstream V back to JFK. *Gordon is right. I haven't done anything illegal. Just pulled off some god-damned Greek tragedy, that's all. The shrinks would go wild.*

He hits the direct dial on his phone, and gets Arthur's, "Yes, Boss?"

"I'm on my way. Mission accomplished. Snatched victory from the jaws of defeat. How's my girl?"

There's a moment's silence. "Groggy."

"You can hold off on the Valium. I want her alert and ready for our trip home."

"You're taking her with us?" Arthur asks.

"Of course, I'm taking her with us. What else would I do, now that she's in my hands?"

Arthur says, "I don't know, Boss."

"You're smarter than that, Arthur," Marshall says, and disconnects.

The desert is impenetrably dark, except for the litter of stars overhead and the headlights pointing out the straight, seemingly endless ribbon of tar. Marshall has saved a life, a rare experience for him. He is not only rescuing his daughter from a toxic cloudburst, but from this pathetic mess of a country altogether. He will introduce her into his world of wealth and luxury. She'll be sensational. And all his. *Who knows?* he thinks. *Maybe I'm really saving myself. Maybe it's time to grow up. Be the number one father.*

To the mute phone on the seat beside him, he says, "I've paid you back, Rodge. Big time. You can't hold that dead woman over my head anymore."

123

20 September. Khartoum, Sudan. 2300 hours.

A wave of emotion washes over Tory as she exits the bi-plane onto the solid ground of the disused runway beyond the Khartoum airport. There is Francis, alive and well, hopping out of the helicopter to shake her hand and embrace Lewis. She also recognizes the stout man standing beside a Honda as the asset of Wilkins' who drove her back to the Professor's after Kimball's death. Ahmed. He smiles warmly as he hands her a bottle of water. She still can't understand a word he says, but an important truth hits her: she is among friends.

Then Wilkins draws her aside. "Teamwork, A+," he says.

She stares at him. "Was this a test?"

"It has been my experience that you could use a little work in that department," he says, staring back.

She looks away. "You're right. But we did kick some butt, didn't we?"

"Yeah, thanks to my superhuman ability to flop around with my ankles taped."

What about my *abilities?* she's about to ask, then changes her mind. She gives him a wink. "I'm glad you guys were there to back me up."

"That's what it's all about," Wilkins says, beckoning to Ahmed. "Looks like we need to be driven to the residence of Adam Marshall."

"What in the world for?" Tory asks, while Ahmed's eyes get round, and he spits some more disjointed syllables.

Wilkins turns to Lewis. "You're sure about this?"

"Kendacke is," Lewis answers. He is busy trading his bloody shirt for Frances' clean one.

"Sure about what?" Tory asks.

"Lewis got a message from Kendacke: your girl is at Marshall's."

"Mani? I don't get it," Tory says. "How'd she find that out?"

"In her own way," Lewis says. "She knows."

"What would that asshole want with a teen-aged girl?" Wilkins asks.

"Maybe he's planning to turn her over to the government?" Tory suggests. "Don't know what use she'd be as a hostage, though, if they were going to wipe out all her people."

Lewis shakes his head sadly, as if there is more to the story than he's willing to say. Wilkins punches in a call. When the Admiral picks up, Wilkins clicks the speakerphone so Tory can hear.

"Good God. Tell me Navy won," a hearty voice says as soon as Wilkins identifies himself.

"Game's not over yet, sir," Wilkins says. "But I think we're definitely ahead."

"What about Parakeet?"

"Victoria Pierce is standing here next to me. A few more nicks and bruises, but otherwise OK. We just diverted the aircraft loaded with the chemical WMD."

"We were rooting for you," the Admiral says.

"I'm sure that's what did it, sir. We've set her down safely southeast of the international airport on the abandoned strip. Pilot alive but immobilized. Plus one rogue low-level Mukharabat. All set to hand everything over to Special Activities Division at this point, asap obviously."

"And we just happen to be in the Situation Room at the Agency with the Director himself," Johnny booms.

"Our friend Meiying was on a second plane to Israel, Admiral," Tory calls out, thinking, *Friend: someone you can count on.*

"And Piol also," adds Lewis, but Johnny's reaction squawks over him.

"*Israel!* Got that? Israel," he shouts to those around him, then turning back to Wilkins: "That's the first we've heard on the second target. The Director's on the phone to Tel Aviv. Jesus, there'll be hell to pay if that one gets through. OK. We've got three SAD guys on their way from Cairo and a destroyer off-shore if you need to call in the Marines. You're in charge."

"Actually, sir," Wilkins says, "I'm heading into Khartoum to pick up a young girl Marshall appears to have kidnapped."

"What are you talking about? You don't leave an aircraft outfitted with nerve gas sitting unattended."

"Right, sir. Two of our Sudanese teammates here are set to stand guard."

"You stay right where you are and guard those WMD's yourselves," Johnny orders, "until reinforcements arrive."

"Sir, the aircraft's almost out of fuel, and no one but the CTG knows about this airstrip."

"You've got your orders, Wilkins. For crying out loud, letting one life go to save thousands? That's a no-brainer."

"Yes sir."

"Now put Parakeet on. Maud Olson wants to tell her *Nice Job* and all that good stuff."

"I'm afraid she's not here, sir," Wilkins says, after the slightest pause.

"What are you frigging talking about? You just said—"

"You're on speakerphone, sir, and when you started reaming on me, she hopped into my asset's vehicle, and took off down the road."

"What the hell?"

"I told you, she's a pistol."

"You better be telling me the truth."

"It's important to her to get that girl."

A long silence. "Give me the make and color of her vehicle," Johnny says, sounding tired. "I'll pass it along."

After he disconnects, Wilkins turns to Lewis. "I better cover this front with Francis," Wilkins says. "You back up Pierce."

"We will return with Mani," Lewis says. "Then this Hummingbird will fly us all to Jebel Barkal."

Tory places her hand on Wilkins' arm. "I owe you big time."

"Break a leg," he says, bending to give her a quick hug. "This is your show."

124

Ahmed pulls up to the high, pink concrete wall topped with broken glass, and Tory and Lewis jump out. In a neighboring yard, a dog begins to howl. The streetlights are dark, but a flood mounted on one corner of the house illuminates the courtyard behind the wrought iron gate. Two meters high on either side, the black spikes shorten slightly toward the center to shape a curve.

"Give me a boost," Tory says. "When I'm in, I'll figure out how to get this thing to open."

Lewis laces his fingers into a stirrup. She tightens the cord of her waistband to secure Umar's pistol against her back, steps into his hands, and wraps her right hand around one of the shorter spikes. As he flings her foot upwards, she pulls herself up and over them, into a four-point landing on the concrete driveway on the other side.

She brushes off her hands, shakes out her stunned feet, grabs her gun, releases the safety, and hangs onto it with both hands. She moves around the side of the house, a stucco villa shaped almost like a pyramid: a sprawling base, a smaller second storey. Weird that the smallest, uppermost level has no windows. She tries the French door. To her surprise, it opens, and no alarm. *Where's the catch?* She doesn't have time to wonder.

Staring down at her are four mounted animal heads. A wild antelope, glassy eyes bulging as if he'd been caught in the headlights; two white tigers snuffed in mid-snarl; an elephant, tusks intact. *No human heads anyway,* Tory thinks. *The bastard.*

She takes the stairs curving up from the foyer. On the second floor two bedrooms in perfect order and a master bedroom suite. The last flight takes her to a narrower hallway and a room on the left that looks lived-in: bed unmade, a pair of shoes, a towel hanging on the open door. Ahead, a closed door.

She cracks it and peers into the windowless chamber at the profile of Arthur. He sits in a straight chair, eyes closed, earphones on, bobbing to a silent beat. She opens the door wider. He is facing a large bed. Mani's perfect head lies stark on the pillow, a white comforter pulled up to her chin.

Tory leaps into the room, gun braced in front of her. "Get up," she demands. "Get up and stick your arms in the air."

Arthur raises his face. It is haggard, the eyes mournful, like one of those tragic masks. "Thank the lord," he says.

She isn't falling for that one. She rips off his earphones. "I said get up! And put your hands on your head."

Arthur takes forever to comply.

"What the hell is going on?" she asks, as she rests her fingers on Mani's neck checking for a pulse. Her cheeks look shrunken. The girl's eyelids flutter, her lips make whimpering noises.

"She's only sleeping," says Arthur.

"You better be right," says Tory.

Photographs litter the floor. Mani with a bodyguard carrying her books. Mani with girl friends eating ice cream. Mani opening the door to her house. Tory looks at Arthur, her eyes hard.

"It's not me," Arthur says softly. "He wanted them. Mr. Marshall. But I'm going to protect her. I swore it to her, and myself. I'm not going to let him touch her. I owe him, but not this. I've had enough."

Tory moves over to a red curtain at the far end of the room. As her one hand yanks it back, Arthur flinches and looks away. On the stage behind it sits a wing chair upholstered in red fabric. Above the chair hangs a painting. "Oh shit," Tory mutters. It's a woman dressed like a dominatrix—black leather, thong, a lot of naked flesh. Her face sports a black devil's mask, complete with horns. She holds a whip in one hand, and has planted one boot on the naked man at her feet, who wears a matching mask. A brass plaque under the painting reads "Satan's Chamber."

"Please, shut the curtain," Arthur says. "In case she wakes up."

Tory lets the curtain drop. She'd assumed the machines lining the mirrored walls of the room were for working out. She doesn't assume that anymore.

"I know what you're thinking," Arthur says. "Because I've thought it enough times myself. What am I doing taking orders from a sicko like him? But it's a long story. And it's almost over. Because when Mr. Marshall shows up, I'm telling him—"

"He's a killer, Arthur. That awesome memory of yours hangs onto every other fact. Don't tell me you missed that one. You're his accomplice."

Arthur's protest is interrupted by the whine of a siren.

"What is that?" Tory asks.

"The police," he says. "Alarm based on motion sensors."

"I have got to get her out of here."

"I can help. Let me go down and talk to them."

Tory gives him a long look. So far, she can hardly boast an A+ where judging character's concerned. Can she trust her intuition now? "OK," she says, "but I'll be covering you from behind. And there's an officer in the Sudanese army in the car on the other side of the gate."

"Wait a minute! She's not going near anyone from the Sudan Army," Arthur says. "They want to tear her apart. She's connected to the rebels."

"OK, you passed that test. Now you can trust me," Tory says. "That guy is going to make sure Mani and I get back to her mother unharmed."

"Tie me up," Arthur says, after the puzzled police have driven off. Thanks to Arthur's assurances, what could the local cops conclude but false alarm? "When my boss shows—"

"When your boss shows, tell him we returned to the Hilton. With a little luck, we'll have someone there waiting for him."

"Don't worry about luck. I can take care of it."

"I trust you can," says Tory pulling two silk cords off one of the machines. She binds Arthur's hands behind his back then secures his legs to the chair. "Voila!" she says, as she repositions the headset around his neck.

Meanwhile Lewis has gathered up the drowsy girl, comforter and all. As he starts down the stairs, her eyes open. "Lewis!" she says, and starts to laugh and cry at once as she wraps her thin arms around his neck.

"We are going to take you to your mother," he promises, moving to the door.

She rouses herself further. "Why do you treat him that way?" Her long arm floats from the comforter in Arthur's direction. "He must come with us. He is not an evil man. Only sad. And very lonely."

"I'll catch up with you sometime," Arthur says, mustering a smile.

125

September 21. Jebel Barkal, Sudan. 0430 hours.

Beyond the glass, the night sky is beginning to fade. Tory is too wired to sleep. Too tired to sort out events. No choice but to be in the moment: Lewis in the seat beside her, holding a slumbering Mani; Wilkins in the cockpit with Francis, working the Hummingbird's controls. Tory almost smiles as her adrenaline subsides, then a flash-memory of the strangled face of Mayom startles her, and she lets out a scream. It's swallowed by the helicopter's drone. She makes herself stare out the blank, dark blue window.

The Hummingbird begins to drop like an elevator. Outside clouds of sand billow as five exhausted survivors close in on Jebel Barkal.

Some days this whole place feels like the edge of nowhere, and others it seems like the center of everything. She hears her father's voice, clear as the other end of a phone call. She tries to run the mental tape again, with no luck. But all at once, her fatigue melts, the muddle of the last nine days seems clear. She stepped onto Sudanese soil, feeling out of place, over-whelmed, determined to fight for her dad, for the truth about him. She real-izes now that she has been fighting for a lot more, and for herself, the person she could become.

A soft landing. Tory is last out, after Wilkins helps Lewis with Mani. The flying dust and bonfire smoke start her coughing. Eyes on the ground, she walks resolutely away from the aircraft and into her future.

She hears her name and looks up. Before her stands a different Kendacke, looking taller than ever in a blue helmet shaped like a hawk, wings spread to fly. Over her blue dress she wears a panther skin sashed at the waist by a golden belt and a single rope of gorgeous stones. Around her neck, hang many strands of the same stones—golden, deep blue, and black. They are all background for the rough gray one carved in the fertile curves of a woman.

Without thinking, Tory brings her hands together over her heart and bows her head.

"Your people are safe," Lewis says.

"They are your people also," Kendacke says, then repeats his words loudly, setting off a ripple of cheers, from the refugees pressing close and curious, outward to those in the hazy distance tending fires and moving between the tents and rows of plank tables at the perimeter of the site.

"Safe at least for today," Lewis goes on, speaking over the sound. "The poison threat to the celebration is being dismantled as we speak, thanks in great part to Mayom. He was destroyed in the effort."

"We have sacrificed three bulls for this occasion," Kendacke says. "They do not begin to measure our love for him, but at least his hero's spirit will have good company."

"I would rather *we* had the company of his living body," Lewis says.

Suddenly, Mani comes to life, struggles out of Lewis's grasp, and throws herself at the awesome figure, whose arms open to embrace her. For a split second, Tory has the impulse to do the same thing, then it comes to her: Kendacke is Mani's mother. Mani belongs to Kendacke. *That's what it's like, the mother-daughter thing.* She takes a step backward and wraps her arms around herself. The desert is chilly before sunrise.

A hand rests on her shoulder. She looks up at Wilkins, a tentative smile on his face.

"I suppose you knew this too," Tory says.

"Knew what, mademoiselle?"

Tory shakes her head and lets out a loud sigh. "Kendacke has a daughter. The Professor's ward."

"Actually, I did not know that, no. But it's pretty obvious when you get them side by side, isn't it? The thing is, I've never seen Kendacke in person before now," Wilkins says.

"So who's the father, I wonder?" She's not too tired to have quickly calculated that her own father cannot also be Mani's.

Behind them comes the Professor's voice. "Let's not further tarnish this happy moment. What matters is that the child is safe."

The eastern sky is streaked with dazzling shades of peach and rose. Black against it juts the pinnacle of Jebel Barkal, watching over the crowded, bustling site like a protective dragon. Kendacke shoos off the children who have gathered to gape at the helicopter, then draws the new arrivals away from the sounds of busyness and excitement, the cries of babies. "At the right moment, there will be formal introductions for you all," she says, as they move toward the temple entrance.

Lewis bends slightly to Kendacke. Tory overhears him whisper, "I am sorry I left in anger."

"And my heart weeps to lose Mayom," Kendacke whispers back. "Thank you for all you do."

Feeling raw and vulnerable, yet strangely energized, Tory breathes in the people around her. This feels like home.

126

On the threshold to the mountain temple, Kendacke turns and places her hands on Tory's shoulders. "There is a matter we must attend to alone before the celebration begins," she says. "Something I must explain to you, about your father."

Tory opens her mouth to respond with what she already knows, but closes it without saying anything.

"I'll take the others to see the *complete* tablets," the Professor offers, clasping Mani's hand. Lewis and Wilkins follow him away.

Kendacke leads Tory into the antechamber, behind the etched panel, down the flight of stairs, into the room where the two of them first met. She tugs open a wooden door and guides Tory into a space barely lit by a single candle, and smelling of burning wax. Kendacke bends to pick up a carbide lamp, which she turns on high. An alcove takes shape around them, at its center a flat stone slab balanced on two stone columns. On its horizontal surface sits an oblong box.

Kendacke strokes its lid. "I knew your father only a short time, but I loved him very much. When he first met with us, he was skeptical about our cause—not about its truth, but the possibility of ever attaining justice. Yet his was a courageous and compassionate spirit. Where others wear blindfolds, he was brave enough to witness our suffering. Immediately he embraced our people, our hope." Kendacke's eyes shine with tears. "Your father was punished for taking us on. He is a hero to our people. He died a noble death, despite the intentions of his killer."

"I think I can guess what happened."

"Adam Marshall is a ruthless man."

"So it *was* him?"

Kendacke nods. "He thinks he can own the world. Your father stood in his way. He refused to bow down before Marshall's power, so he was eliminated, most sadistically."

"I can vouch for the sadism," says Tory. "He gave the orders for Mayom's death. Horrible. Was it like that for my father?"

"I hope not," Kendacke says. "Inside this box are his remains."

Tory's hand flies up to her mouth. "Oh god." The finality of it.

"Yes, his bones."

"So you've had them all along?"

"No. They have come to us piece by piece. Shortly after your father died, I was attacked by the government here at the mountain. That was when they destroyed this eye. As a further gruesome warning to me not to pursue the NIM's cause, they left behind a part of your father's body: his arm with the attached wristwatch, which I have given you.

"At first, I too was traumatized, frightened, then I thought, you fools: thank you for returning this relic of Peter Thornton—because that is the name we called him. Through it we will consecrate his desecrated body and bring it to rest in our temple forever.

"As our work continued, other parts of his skeleton appeared at the sites of massacres, again to scare us into stopping our efforts."

Tory smiles. "But you didn't?"

"I began to look forward to finding his bones. They became a comfort, an incentive to continue defying the government's tyranny."

"Like Isis and her brother!" Tory says.

"Yes, very much."

Tory bends over the box and wraps her arms around it awkwardly. "I always wished that he could be more of a father to me," she confesses. "Now I understand his destiny was to care for those no one cares about, just as you do, Kendacke."

"Your father became light to Adam Marshall's dark," Kendacke says. "And you see, over time, which force prevails."

Tory presses her cheek against the wooden lid and the tears begin to flow.

"This is necessary and good," Kendacke says. "It is how we nourish a living heart." She withdraws and closes the door.

127

Tory's chest heaves with sobs. For five years she has kept her father alive in her wildest dreams. To keep herself going, she needed the future she'd constructed for them both: that joint assignment somewhere exotic where they would work together everyday, maybe share a house, maybe reclaim some of the girlhood she lost growing up such impossible distances from him.

She'd known he loved her. She'd known his job was too dangerous to include a place for a daughter. And his letters were wonderful, full of life, adventure, and guidance. She still has those, at least. And everything he stood for. And now friends. Wilkins spills into her thoughts, and she pushes him away.

At almost the same moment, she hears her name called twice.

"I don't believe it," she says aloud, wiping her eyes on her grubby shirttail. Wilkins calls her again.

She pulls herself to her feet and pushes open the door. "This is not a good time," she says.

"Kendacke asked me to help you with a box? Apparently it's going to be part of this major event that's in the works."

"Fine. But I need to be alone now."

"I think whatever it is is about to start."

"All right," Tory says. Wiping her face on her sleeve, she lets Wilkins enter the alcove.

"The Professor told me about your father, that his remains are here, in this box?"

"His bones. They make his death so real."

"Kendacke considers them sacred."

"They're still bones. He's dead, Wilkins."

"Look, I don't know what it's like to lose a parent, but I—"

"So maybe be quiet, OK?"

"Why do you have to act like that?"

"What do you mean *act*?"

"I'm sorry. I can see you're hurting," Wilkins says. "Would it be the end of the world to let someone in? After everything we've been through together, I might be a good shoulder to lean on."

"I don't lean on anyone."

"That's bullshit, and you know it by now. How do you think our *team* commandeered that plane, and saved this place from being gassed back to the stone age, and oh yes, rescued the young woman who may someday be the leader of the disenfranchised Sudanese tribes? It was a mess, and we were in it together, and one of us died."

She's surprised by his intensity. "So what's a shoulder going to solve now?"

"Nothing. Forget it. Stubborn is a much better choice. Now let's get this box up to whatever's going on outside."

Tory watches in silence as he lifts one end.

"Shit, it's not that heavy." He picks it up and grapples it to his chest vertically. Gravity sends the contents rumbling loudly to the lower end.

"Let me help, for god sake! That's my *father*."

As he turns it horizontal, it slips through his grasp. He raises one knee to stop its fall as Tory grabs for it so hard she bumps it with her chin. Then hysteria takes over and she dissolves into it. It infects Wilkins.

"Still clumsy, after all these years," Tory says, gasping for breath.

"That time it wasn't an act," says Wilkins.

"What are you talking about?"

"We better set this down."

As she bends to comply, she laughs harder, way out of control, then begins to sob again.

Wilkins puts one arm around her and with the other hand, presses her head against his rock-hard bicep. "You're too short for my shoulder anyway," he says.

The tears stop. "That was close," she says, picturing the box shattered, and her father's bones scattered everywhere.

"So is this," Wilkins says, turning her around into an embrace.

After a minute of warm contact, Tory pulls away. "You know, Wilkins, a few things about you don't add up."

He stands up and brushes off his pants. "I am Lt. Commander Bartholomew Wilkins, on a three year assignment as supply officer for the U.S. Embassy in Khartoum."

"Sounds like a cover to me."

Wilkins holds his hand out to help Tory up.

"We better get this box up there."

"No. Not until you come clean."

"The ceremony's about to begin—"

"Look, first, you were always a step ahead of me. Second, you are extremely well trained in combat maneuvers, not just securing toilet paper. And last but not least, Maud Olson told me a long time ago—you are CTG."

"So as I said, we're both on the same side. Let's go."

"Not until you tell me your name. You know who I am, it's only fair."

Silence. Tory's unblinking green eyes bore into the mystery man's baby blues.

"I'm not at liberty to say."

"I can find out. And after I do, I'll have to write to your mother and tell her you don't always behave like a gentleman."

"You wouldn't dare!"

"That's right. I wouldn't. So please."

He looks away then back, with a sly grin. "Two conditions."

Tory groans, then nods.

"First, obviously, this is need to know information, so you can *never* tell anyone else."

Her head bobs in agreement.

"Two, you can't laugh when you hear my name."

"Fine. Why would I laugh?"

"It's Thaddeus. Thaddeus Wharton."

Tory bursts out laughing, notices the indignation on his face, and covers her mouth with both hands.

"I knew you couldn't be trusted."

"Thaddeus! I just didn't expect it. I thought your name would be Matt, or Sam, or Joe. Thaddeus," she muses, "very aristocratic."

"Let's get this box outside," he says.

As they lift it, she grins and says, "Thaddeus is an awesome name. A whole lot better than Bartholomew, clumsy, know-it-all geek, who is now ancient history."

128

The horizon glows an iridescent peach as selected members of seven different tribes hoist the hollow horns of the sacrificed bulls and jointly sound the call for the ceremony to begin. Thousands of celebrants, scattered about the site, start moving toward the temple side of the mountain. Many have eaten their fill for the first time in years. Many are lame and must be helped or carried. They have all summoned the courage to hope. They have all risked placing this hope, for peace and well-being, in the woman who will climb the sacred peak and bless the Feast of the Double Cobra.

At the mouth of the temple, two guards watch over the long box. In the depths of the mountain, out of sight, Amanirenas is getting ready. The crowd around Tory hums like guests waiting for a wedding to begin.

A weird sensation envelops Tory, as if time were a permeable membrane and she could slip through this moment into the past. But does she really want that any more?

A tap on her back and she turns to find Thaddeus Wharton with a devastated look on his face.

"Just heard from the Admiral," he says, drawing her away from the crowd behind a natural buttress of stone.

"What's the matter?"

"Revise that to three of us died."

"Meiying?" She knows before she asks.

Thaddeus nods then shakes his head. "And Piol. It's never easy, this part."

"What happened?"

"Well, the two of them must have gone down fighting. The Admiral picked up their last moments on the radio: Chen screaming that he was taking care of business with the little whore, and . . . more stuff like that."

"Monster!"

"So he must have untied Meiying's legs. I bet she kicked him where it would have *really* hurt. There were screams, sounds of struggle, then the pilot yelling that Meiying had killed the co-pilot. Maybe she did it with her bare hands. There were no gun shots. A lot of shouting, a huge roar, then silence. A fisherman actually saw the aircraft plunge into the Red Sea."

"They saved the target in Israel. Meiying wanted to be a national hero, Thaddeus. She achieved her goal."

"But she's dead."

Tory hears the echo of her own comment less than an hour ago.

"I know. And she was a totally amazing agent and friend."

Thaddeus closes his eyes for a long moment then opens them. "I do have some good news, though. Adam Marshall finally *is* toast. Director Olson has turned the case over to the FBI. They're also arresting your boss."

"Not Gordon Gray."

"The same."

"God, I'm such an idiot."

Thaddeus opts for tactful silence.

"I owe Maud Olson about fifteen years worth of respect. That woman is a saint. And ever since grade school, I thought she was just a pain in the ass."

"While we're on the subject of your, shall we say, flawed judgment, maybe you'll join me in a prayer for Meiying and Piol today, when your father's bones are laid to rest."

"I didn't realize you believed in any of this."

"I don't. But I don't disbelieve either," Thaddeus says. "In the meantime, better hang onto this for safe keeping." He hands her Umar's Norinco.

"We are ready," Kendacke says, opening the door to her room to allow Lewis and James to behold the new Amanirenas, clothed in a simple blue wrapped gown and matching turban. Around her neck she is wearing a pendant, the figurine carved of stone.

Mother and daughter strike Lewis speechless, they radiate such inner beauty. *If only this spirit stuff could bestow political power*, he thinks, as he prepares to escort them up to their massed disciples.

Then Kendacke remembers something. She picks up a glass globe from her wooden table, causing a flurry of snow to bury the tiny alpine mountain inside. She extends it to Lewis. "We must take it with us," she says. "We have him to thank for today."

"I have no place to put that, Kendacke, really," Lewis says. "It's a cheap souvenir. It has nothing to do with our gratitude, which believe me, I—"

"I will carry it proudly," Amanirenas says. But as she reaches out to take the globe, it spurts from her hand like a wet cake of soap and shatters on the stone floor in a mess of oily liquid and flecks of white plastic.

Lewis grabs his head in exasperation.

"Souvenir means *to remember*," Kendacke says, her voice thin with irritation, "not *to destroy*."

Amanirenas remains serene. "I did not drop it. It freed itself from my hand," she says and bends to explore the debris. She picks up the base of the globe, and as if she has known all along what she would find, pulls off a strip of tape and unfolds the crumpled slip of paper it was protecting. She hands it to Lewis.

"*My dearest son*," Lewis reads aloud, "*when you find this letter I will have joined your sister and mother. Please know that no one but myself dictated the way I died.* I do know that, father," Lewis murmurs before he continues. "*Our resolve must remain steady. You and the beautiful one must not give up, but continue to provide hope and leadership to the suffering people of our land.*

"*Over the years I have saved a sum of money. 23 million U.S. dollars. It is deposited in The Nairobi branch of Habib Bank AG of Zurich. A Mr. Karl Acker, 011- 254-5541213, is expecting your call. Give him the following numbers 10-22-00432-0000 plus your numeric birth date and he will make the money available for your wise use. Live a long and prosperous life, my son. Your father.*"

September 21. Khartoum, Sudan. 0500 hours.

The Land Rover pulls into the courtyard under the floodlight, screeching to a stop.

"You're dismissed," Marshall tells the driver as he hops out. Before the wrought iron gate can swing shut behind the exiting vehicle, he jogs around to the side of the house and pushes open the French door.

"Arthur? Let's go!" he yells, though he knows his voice won't carry to the third floor. He bounds up the stairs, his heart pounding, sweat glands working overtime, mind racing. He is feeling very lucky. Number one, he has played Roger's game and won. Number two, he has beaten Tyler Pierce into oblivion. His two failures in life wiped out in a single offensive, clearing the way to the brand new territory lying open in front of him: his daughter. The girl belongs to him. This is what men brag about, and he feels it. For the first time.

"Call the airport and get the Gulfstream ready for take off," he shouts from the landing on the second floor. "We're leaving as soon as Chen arrives. No need to pack. We'll buy everything we need stateside."

At the top of the stairs, he strides down the corridor to the Gymnasium, throws open the door, and freezes in his tracks. Arthur is sitting next to the empty bed, his headset dangling around his neck. His hands are bound behind him, his feet tied to the legs of his chair.

"What the fuck?" Marshall yells. He shoves Arthur's chair over sideways, and as the younger man struggles against his bonds, starts tearing the sheets off the bed, as if a teen-aged girl could be hidden underneath them. When her absence is clear, he gives Arthur a kick in the head. "Where is she?"

Arthur grits his teeth.

"I don't see any signs of a struggle," Marshall says. "You were supposed to take care of her. I expected you to defend her with your life." He aims the toe of his shoe at Arthur's kidneys.

"They surprised me, Mr. Marshall," Arthur gasps through the pain. "Don't know how they got over the wall, hit me with something, out cold."

"Who? The NIM?"

"No." Arthur tucks his head and pulls his shoulders up, all he can do to defend against another kick. "That white lady. Young, red hair, from the U.S. Embassy?"

"What?" Marshall looks kicked himself. "No." His full weight plops on the torn-up bed. "No."

Arthur nods minutely.

"God damn it all!" He shoves himself back up again, fists clenched.

"There was an officer from the Sudanese army with her," Arthur says, sneaking an upward glance. The Boss looks like he's got some kind of major bomb going off inside him. "We can get her back," says Arthur softly.

"You don't know anything, you imbecile!" A vein at Marshall's temple throbs and his eyes bulge like they're going to pop out of their sockets. "It's that goddamn headset." The Boss yanks the headset off Arthur's neck, and hurls it at the armoire. "How do you expect to hear anything when you're listening to that garbage?"

He punches a number into his phone, then thinks better of it. "No, I'll deal with that later," he mutters as he heads over to the armoire and removes a .577 Manton box-lock double rifle. He breaks the gun and loads a shell in each barrel.

"I'll help you find her, Boss. Don't shoot me. Please."

"You think I'd waste a special weapon like this on you? I need to think." Marshall grabs a curved knife from the armoire and slices Arthur free.

"They said they were taking her back to the Hilton."

"And you believe them?"

Silence.

"Can't you see? It's a trap. No, they're taking the girl to that woo-woo mountain."

"Let's get out of this place, Boss. Back to the States. Home territory."

"Shut up." Adam kicks the head phones and they land near the curtain. "Goddamnit to hell! *They are not going to win!* Not this one. I may have lost the round with the planes, but those bastards don't know who they're fucking with. We're going to the mountain. Call the airport, alert the standby pilot, we'll take the Cessna."

"We better think this through, Boss. There's only two of us, and one hunting gun—"

"Have the pilot paint red crescents on both sides of the plane."

"That takes time, Boss."

"Don't contradict me, Arthur. They're going to think we're bringing medical supplies."

As he follows orders, Arthur's thoughts churn: the Boss has lost it, in more ways than one.

Then he's behind the wheel of the Mercedes. Mr. Marshall can't shut up. "You know, Arthur, my girl is going to be happy with us. We'll take her away from this god-forsaken country and give her a real life. Luxury, excitement, beyond her dreams. In time, she's going to love me. She won't be able to resist."

You worthless bag of garbage, thinks Arthur.

"She'll be a princess in the States. I'm going to give her everything I didn't have as a kid."

Wrong there. That girl is free from this bastard. And there aren't going to be any others. The safety of their innocent bodies rides on Arthur's own shoulders. *Accomplice.* Old guilt rises on a flood of adrenalin. He will resolve it for all time.

Ahead on the highway is the left exit he should take to the airport. He speeds past it. An instant later comes the cursing protest from the backseat. "What the hell are you doing, you fool?"

What am *I doing?* Arthur doesn't want to think about it. *Flooring the accelerator, whizzing past the few vehicles in the right lane, racing for the Kober Bridge.* "Missed the turn, Boss. Have to double back on the other side of the river," he says.

"Attaboy," Marshall says. "It'll be easy to grab her, like stealing an annuity from a widow. A mob of illiterate refugees doing their cult thing. And you're going to blend right in."

Arthur floors the accelerator. He flies onto the bridge. The curb along the side of it is minimal, the railings low. The first glimmers of dawn separate the sky from the water.

He swerves into the right lane and braces his arms to keep the steering wheel twisted right. The tires scrape the curb and bounce off.

"Christ, be careful!" Marshall yells.

Arthur swerves back into the left lane, then once more jerks the wheel sharply to the right. This time the tires jump the curb and the Mercedes crashes through the yellow railing and takes off into the air. In the same instant, the rosy eastern sky begins to release its beams of light.

"What the hell?" Marshall yells, shielding his eyes.

"I did it!" Arthur shouts back. "Zero to sixty in 7.4 seconds, just what the ad—"

The Mercedes completes its twenty-meter morning dive into the Nile.

131

September 21. Jebel Barkal, Sudan. 0545 hours.

Lewis waits just inside the temple with Mani, who continues to exude an inscrutable calm. While Kendacke wept then grew giddy at the thought of having sufficient funds to feed and school and rebuild, Amanirenas smiled slightly as if she had always expected twenty-three million dollars to be dropped in her lap.

Now at a signal from the Professor that the ceremony has begun, the sacred daughter steps out into the dawn.

From her mountain promontory, Kendacke's voice rings out across the site, "This is my precious child, Amanirenas, descendant of queens. She is young and strong, and the Great Spirit, Who empowers all gods, has blessed her with the ability to carry out our hopes. Together we can return the future to the people of Sudan." The crowd begins softly to chant *Amanirenas*.

Opposite the pinnacle, said to resemble the flared head of a cobra, Kendacke raises her arms, brandishing in her right hand the traditional black scepter with her ancient name inscribed on the stalk. She utters the forgotten language, then translates: "Power flows from Isis to Kendacke to all who are gathered here."

Her left hand waves a staff over the people who begin to sway in concert below. "This day we will bury the remains of a man who gave himself for our cause, Tyler Pierce, our brother. Like Osiris, he was killed by evil forces, and the parts of his body scattered across our land. We have found the parts and brought them here, where his daughter will help us lay them to rest."

The Professor steps forward and pulls Tory away from the mass of spectators to stand on his other side opposite the serene Mani. Tory's face turns a deeper pink.

"These martyr's bones will consecrate our efforts to unite in peace upon our land," Kendacke goes on from on high.

Beams of light stab the dawn sky, and an incandescent arc breaks the horizon.

"May Osiris guide us and protect us and provide us bounty," Kendacke sings as the arc grows larger. Soon the crowd is chanting with her.

Lewis is swaying also, in spite of himself. Around him smiles transform sadness; dead eyes come to life. Kendacke's power is hard to resist, he is thinking, no matter what you believe or don't believe. He thinks he may even be beginning to feel that power enter and strengthen him, when a shrill sound lends its overtone to the chanting. *Kee, kee*—it's coming from the crevice in the mountain, where twenty-four falcons leashed to their perches, are crying notes of alarm. His warrior-self wakes with a jolt, as the falcons' warning is answered by an all-too-familiar, thudding rumble.

Soon everyone has noticed, and faces, which a moment ago had softened with blessedness, tighten with fear. They turn toward the northern edge of the site, where the sound is coming from.

Dust first, then the camels with riders. So much for Kendacke's power, Lewis thinks. Overcome with exhaustion he wants to sink into the ground. The war never ends. In front of him, the sun's radiant disk is about to snap away from the land. On his right, a row of monstrous heads crests the horizon.

132

It happens so fast. Thundering hoofbeats, and as Tory turns to look along with everyone else, the horde of invaders emerges from a yellow cloud in the distance and bears down on them. They're encased in bulky suits that reflect the intensifying sunlight, their heads like magnified insects behind black gas masks.

The terrified crowd scatters. The Professor and Mani shrink back inside the temple. Thaddeus pushes his way toward open ground, yanks the Magnum he'd holstered under his shirt, and goes into a crouch. Lewis follows his lead while from her mountain heights Kendacke screams unintelligibly.

As Tory breaks away from the fleeing celebrants to follow Lewis, she draws the Norinco and, heart pounding, rushes toward the incursion along with Francis and a cohort of guards with M-16's.

They take up positions just inside the haphazard perimeter of razor wire, vehicles, scrap metal, and wait for the riders to come into range. Then beyond the barrier, the camels halt. They wrench their haughty heads from side to side; hoofs paw the sand. Tory can make out the tips of automatic rifles still strapped to their bearers' backs.

At that moment the sun hits the golden disk in the pinnacle. A broad stream of light bounces off the sacred ruins, seeming to ignite them.

Kendacke waves her staff shouting to the crowd to come back, put away fear, her voice reverberating from pinnacle to pyramids. From her higher vantage she is the first to understand.

The men on camels were expecting corpses. They were dispatched to confirm the devastation, perhaps to begin scavenging for spoils. The mass of living humanity has stunned them. Their leader removes his mask. "A miracle," he shouts, as he clumsily dismounts. He pulls the strap of his rifle over his bare head and throws the weapon to the ground. One by one his men do the same. Then awkward in their big shiny suits, they lift their hands in the air and approach the makeshift barrier.

"*As-salammu alaykum.* Peace be with you," shouts the leader. "Your power is great." Then facing in Kendacke's direction, they sink to their knees.

From on high, Kendacke shouts, "Forgive these men, for they are not our true enemies but our enemies' victims."

A moment of stillness ensues, broken only by the shrill sounds of impatient falcons. The crowd silently collects itself. To spare the invaders or set upon them and beat them to death? Here in the new morning light? In the shadow of the sacred mountain?

Suddenly cheers erupt and the celebrants stream toward the many gaps in the barrier, spilling out to grasp the newcomers' hands. From somewhere music begins to play, a bulls horn, beating drums and bodies break into spontaneous song and dancing, some whirling, some two-stepping, some stomping, depending on their tribe.

Tory lets the foreign pistol drop to the sand. She slips her hand into her pocket and clasps the stone figurine from her father. She ventures a glance at Thaddeus, who is moving closer. He tosses his pistol on top of hers then takes her free hand. "They're lousy weapons anyway," he says.

EPILOGUE

September 25. The Metropolitan Club, Washington, DC. Noon.

Gas flames dance behind glass in the ornate fireplace that dominates one end of the private smoking room. Facing it at angles, Johnny Falco and Roger Booth nurse their drinks in silence.

Roger chases each sip with a mouthful of ice. Finally he says, "Maybe we should get them to bring over another chair, to honor his memory. Remember? Blood brothers? Strength in numbers?"

"Cut the crap, Roger. You know why I'm here," Johnny says through clenched teeth.

"What are you talking about?"

"You behind bars."

"Jesus, anyone ever tell you you sound like a bad western?"

"Anyone ever tell you we don't want to start World War III?"

"It sounds like you've got things a little confused. With all due respect."

"You are so full of shit."

"Adam always thought he could live outside the law, you know that. He lured that poor slob in the NCS out there with him. Sad facts but true, and your friend in the DI, that aging Barbie doll, figured it out. May Adam rest in peace, and the other guy rot in jail."

"Un unh, no. What does Adam get out of gassing Israel?"

"Easy. He was trying to stay in the oil game with the Generalissimo over there. The guy kept raising the ante."

"Meanwhile you were going to get your excuse to pull out the tactical nukes against China. You've been itching to play *real* war, from the safety of the White House."

"Give me a little credit, Johnny. It doesn't take a foreign policy genius to see that Adam's Chinese connections were too close for comfort. The harder I looked, the clearer it got that he was running some kind of private operation with them, so I got myself judiciously involved. I pretended to go along, letting him think that a hundred million in a Swiss account could buy my support."

"What exactly did you go along with?"

Roger swirls the scotch in his tumbler. "The Chinese are after a lot more than Sudanese oil. From a Sudanese base of military operations, complete with WMD, they effectively control North Africa and the Middle East."

"Which one of your private intelligence sources invented that one?"

"What do you mean?"

"The Chinese government had nothing to do with this."

"Well, you don't think they would come clean about it, do you?"

Johnny doesn't answer.

"You believe them instead of me? Israel was going to be a preview of things to come."

"So you must be a rich man now. I assume you can produce some paperwork to confirm the Swiss account."

Roger downs the last half-inch of scotch then smacks the glass onto the table. "Don't go there, Johnny, understand?" His voice is tight, the bad cop. "It won't be productive. Maybe Adam never got around to setting it up."

"And maybe you wanted to get something big on China. Something to justify big retaliation."

"Maybe you should be able to understand that, if anyone can."

"No. I don't understand war for the sake of war. Only a guy who's never served in the military could be that stupid."

Roger doesn't blink.

Johnny shakes his head. "This is your work, Rodge. You nuke China and the American public is so patriotically scared shitless they have to vote you into the White House."

"Johnny, be reasonable. We both know this asymmetric terrorist shit has thrown everyone off stride. Half the time we don't know who we're fighting or why. I swear to you I am just trying to reframe the action, all right? Get us back on familiar ground."

"You probably had some dirt on Adam. That wouldn't be hard."

"Contrary to what you choose to think, Johnny, my ass is covered."

"We'll be asking for the numbers on that Swiss account."

"You and I are blood brothers."

Johnny tips his martini glass to his mouth even though it's empty, then replaces it on the table, heaves himself to his feet like a man overcome with fatigue, and trudges to the door. He doesn't look back.

Afterword

Stories unleash enormous power to move hearts and change minds. As a teacher, Molly found that the challenges of great literature enlivened the self-awareness of her students and broadened their view of the world. As a consultant to large and small companies teaching the value of diversity, Karetta found that the sharing of personal stories inspired quantum leaps toward harmony and mutual respect in the workplace.

Satan's Chamber springs from our desire to create a compelling, page-turner of a story that would, at the same time, help raise consciousness about important issues currently inflaming the world community. It is our belief that these desperate circumstances demand answers and solutions on a global scale.

Our story takes place in Washington, DC, center of geopolitical power, and Sudan, a nation on the edge, where an ancient civilization has fallen victim to modern economics. It portrays a struggle between what is unforgiving in human nature—greed that leads to violence—and what is best—altruistic courage, love, and forgiveness.

Acknowledgments

Satan's Chamber began as an idea for a story hatched by two friends. As its complicated plot developed over the next two and one half years, it became a passionately pursued education. We were extremely fortunate to have had many teachers along the way. To each, a heartfelt thank you.

For their specialized aeronautical expertise, we are indebted to CAPT Tom Myers, USN (Ret.), and CDR L. Mahoney, USN (Ret). Their invaluable suggestions enhanced the authenticity and suspense of many episodes. Thanks, too, to Eric Miller, Steven Browning, David H. Funderburk, and Edwin Miller for further technical advice. To Deborah Kahn for continuing encouragement and survey expertise.

Dr. Timothy Kendall, Senior Research Scientist, African Archaeology, Northeastern University, provided us with information about the amazing historical site, Jebel Barkal.

Our dear friends read early drafts of the book and offered their astute critiques: Charlie Zeitlin, Janet Greek, Alice Padwe, Alexis Miller, Lynne Revo-Cohen, and Sanjyot Dunung.

Our new friend, Jane Friedman, taught us how to navigate the world of book publishing, for which we are profoundly grateful.

What "the Team" from Georgetown University's McDonough School of Business taught us defies summary! Sung Jun Cho, Claire Yi Chun Lin, and Janny Frimpong: our success is your success. Without your talent, brains, and dedication, Satan's Chamber wouldn't exist.

As for our captive audience, family members who read and reread numerous early drafts and our husbands Jerry Klepner and Edwin Miller: your support and unflagging patience, generous insights, and wise counsel made this endeavor possible.